Third Act

Sydney Madison

ISBN: 9798989444236 (Paperback)

Printed in the United States of America

Published by PS Published

For the ones waiting to be found

Author's Note on Reading Order & Content

Reading Order

For the best reading experience, enjoy the series in the following order:

Astor Hill
Second Position
Third Act
Book 4

Content Warnings

Please visit www.sydneymadisonbooks.com for triggers. The Astor Hill series, while focusing on a group of rich kids, is at its heart an exploration of the human condition and our ability to find joy through hardship and pain. These characters are deeply flawed, but—just like us—are trying their best.

Prologue
Andy

March

We didn't have hurricanes in California. Our natural disasters came without much warning: a sudden fire, a surprising earthquake, a drought that would sneak up on you only to be followed by a flood you'd been sure wouldn't materialize, until it did. But a hurricane—you have fair warning, time to prepare. Time to decide if you want to ride it out or flee.

Luis hadn't entered our life yet and my sister hadn't been born when my mom decided to take six year old me on our first vacation. We flew down to Florida where we checked into a room with two double beds and navy blue carpet. The blinds were the stiff ones that run on a bent white rod. The towels in the bathroom were folded into ducks—I was ecstatic.

Cocoa Beach was a wonderland to me, despite the years I'd spent on the coastline collecting shells, learning to bend and glide with the water. For whatever reason, the weathered strip malls, character towels, plastic cups with little umbrellas stirred something in me. We rarely left our little town on the west coast; the trip was my first taste of possibility, even if it was worn and faded like the Ron Jon's sign still etched in my memory. Mom wouldn't tell me she was from there for years; that returning there felt like the opposite to her, but she couldn't pass it up, for me.

I looked forward to it for weeks, really not caring that I'd be missing the first week of school or the chance to claim a spot at a lunch table. Perfect weather all week; so much bright, white sunlight on that beach that I was sure I was going to peel in one gigantic layer; and then, all of a sudden, a storm was coming. Three days time, on the day we were supposed to go to the Magic Kingdom with the tickets I, later, learned were from the timeshare presentation I missed. She'd dropped me off at the arcade right next door with a bundle of other kids.

So instead of riding rollercoasters, we rode out the storm in a Hilton with hundreds of other tourists, watching the world outside twirl around itself. At some point we made our way down to the lobby, seeking company or maybe safety. I glued myself to the window, abandoning my mother at a table full of other parents and kids.

I couldn't stop watching that storm.

And I wasn't the only one—people lined the balconies, ran out from under the awning, cackling into the rough breeze, only to race back under cover. The calm came just as suddenly as the wind had picked up, and I kept hearing, "The eye, we're in the eye." People just stood there, in the middle of a *hurricane*, like they couldn't be blown away the moment the system changed its mind. They marveled at the sky, grey and pink and orange, in awe.

When Mom was distracted enough, I squeezed through the onlookers, and tried to relax into the calm. But I felt the chaos, like it was just skirting around us, teasing us. Asking us how long we could bear the uncertainty before we balked or ran straight into it. I stayed out there until my mom's shouts reeled me back in. Not two minutes later did the sky crack back open, did the hurricane churn the ocean into something horrifying.

It was the most surreal experience of my life; in hindsight, I think I loved being in that hurricane because I'd never felt so lost to something. It was just me and my mom for so long, and even once Luis found us and they had Carmen, we were so insulated. This happy, content, stable unit, despite the thin margins we lived on.

But that storm was dictating everything, putting on a show, inviting us in and showing us, for better or for worse, what was possible. It was a wave I would've willingly given myself to, would've willingly been swallowed whole by if Mom hadn't shouted my name.

Total chaos, destruction, a complete reorganization of the world around us. And after the storm: a rebirth, a reset, a silence that was slow to recede—that stays with you long after it's gone. You're not the same after a storm, and the feeling never really leaves you. You're sort of forever restless, waiting for the next storm to throw you off kilter.

Maybe that's why I'm here to begin with, watching Sloane attempt to destroy herself in this room of beautiful things, like she can't see she's the best of them. That she is everything, to me. Because she is a storm I was never going to stay away from, that I was always going to dive into head first.

1

Sloane

September, six months earlier

San Francisco had better bars. The shot glass loses itself in the beer I'm focusing on before bobbing to the surface, and all sound in this Boston pub dulls to a murmur, seems far away, until I pull my attention back to the man trying his hardest to pick me up and chug the drink.

"So an artist, huh?" he asks, finally done explaining how he's related to the Kennedys. His dark green button up, patterned with fine miniature crosses, is the ugliest thing I've ever seen, but his hair line might be the best I've seen tonight. His arms, beneath the hideous fabric, tell me he either was an athlete or still is in some capacity, and I watched him kindly hold the door open for more than a few patrons. Self absorbed, maybe, but he has manners.

"Yes," I say, leaning a little closer so I can pick out the shades of green in his eyes that, I realize, match his shirt. "I paint. Watercolors." My phone buzzes for the fifth time in my pocket, and I finally take a peek.

CLEMMIE

You get in ok?

Hiiiii let me know pls

Why don't I have your location by now?

Sloane, for the love of all things holy,
ANSWER ME

Final call. If you're dead in a ditch I'll pray
for your soul

I smirk down at the lit up rectangle and tap out a quick reply.

Safe and sound 🫶

I don't take her for granted—the girl who let me bully her into friendship as a precocious child—but her faith in me is virtually nonexistent.

"Landscapes? Fruit bowls?" the man laughs, his straight, white teeth on full display, and I'm sure he thinks they're dazzling. "People?" he smirks, and I slip my phone back in my bag, letting my mouth slide into a dimply smile and running my hand through my hair before glancing away. I track them back when I notice eyes so familiar, they could be my own. I squint, surprise zipping through me, my throat lodged with a nervous wedge making it hard to breathe. Because standing there clear across the bar, his own face a mixture of surprise and concern is my twin brother, Grant.

"Did you see a ghost?" the man chuckles, gently gliding his palm over my denim clad thigh as I slowly slide it away.

"A ghost would actually be better," I mumble. *Fuck.* "Thanks for the drink." I hope he sees the true apology in my eyes. He lifts a hand to halt me or use the force to pull me back, but I walk away, making my way to my twin brother, whose body has gone rigid with suspicion. I can already hear the barrage of questions. *Why are you here? What are you thinking? Why do you always fuck everything up?*

Running into him was *not* how I planned to let him know I entered his sacred little bubble. I need time to get my story straight, to figure out how I'm going to tell him that Connie, the birth mother he pretends doesn't exist, is sick. I needed more time to figure out what I'm doing after I get her and her treatment settled, to craft the perfect way to tell him and eventually our parents why I left San Francisco at all.

"Hi," I say to my brother, smaller than I intended. If he wasn't so busy scowling at me, I'd try to give him a hug.

"What are you doin' back here?" He's still predictable as ever as he crosses his arms and I grit my teeth. With everyone but me he's this easy going giant, understanding and patient. His capacity for grace is impressive; he's practically a saint. I take after our birth mother, though—deeply sensitive to the point of destruction or abandon. My nature is a lot easier to hide with people who haven't known me forever. But that's the trouble with twins—we've known each other from the start. That's why behind his judgmental gaze there's already a glimmer of concern. It's that sense we get about each other. He knows something is wrong.

"I—uh. I'm not technically back," I stutter over the words, attempting to gain some ground with a measured breath in.

"What do you mean 'technically'?" I didn't even notice Ben Cabot was standing there. Last time I checked he had disappeared into thin air, leaving Grant high and dry. When I visited at the beginning of the summer it was mainly to help my brother organize and declutter all the crap he'd collected while still living in the three bedroom apartment he shared with Ben. Ben's side of the apartment stayed vacant well into Grant's junior year, so he finally decided it was time to downsize.

"If he's coming back, I doubt it's to here," he'd told me, scoffing as he scribbled DONATE on the side of a box overflowing with old tupperware.

"I just think it's bizarre he never explained," I remember pondering, peering across the space into the empty bedroom Ben sent packers to clear out shortly after he left two years ago. "And his brother's never mentioned what happened? You don't find that odd?"

"They aren't close," my brother had said, suddenly defensive. "And I don't talk to Will if I don't have to," he added, lifting a few boxes before dropping them at his door.

I remember thinking it strange that you could avoid talking to your team captain, or that my brother seemed to be put off by this guy to begin with. My brother doesn't *overtly* dislike anyone.

Grant clears his throat and I'm back in the bar, my twin's eyes and Ben's staring daggers at me, like I've committed some secret crime.

"Meaning," I huff, annoyed, "I am 'technically' not supposed to be here, nor does anyone know I am." My eyes flare, a nonverbal attempt to get my brother to stop probing.

"What the fuck is that supposed to mean, Sloane?" he grills, and I step back. The small motion has his gaze softening, and I see a small opening.

"I had to get out of there, Grant," I admit, and even though it's all I say, he finally extends me some of that grace. Stepping forward, he wraps me in the kind of bear hug he'd give me after a bad night at our uncle's, or after we'd get returned to the state after not being a good fit in a foster home, and I let myself relax for a few seconds. I think I haven't really relaxed in weeks.

"Speaking of being back...I'm pretty sure the last time I was here, you were in some sort of witness protection program or somethin'?" I tilt my head toward Ben, hiding my real curiosity.

"Close—I was mostly just avoiding you," he jokes, verbally ducking behind that carefully crafted captain persona I clocked the second I met him all those years ago.

Grant loves Boston, has always felt like it was this place full of promise, but I know it just felt far enough from home. I understand that—wanting to be free of our adoptive parents' expectations—but Boston is so...cold. And Astor Hill College is *frigid*, devoid of life. Everything has a subtext, no one says what they mean, and it's just exhausting, being in this place. But it's where Connie's able to get treatment while trying to mend her relationship with Grant. And I can hide out until...I don't know when. When I know what to do next.

For once, I envy how easily he keeps everything bottled up. He functions—no, he *thrives* when things are kept under the surface. He can't stand a mess. Not in his house, and not in his life. I've always taken issue with this but, looking at him right now, I consider that his life is a lot more put together than mine.

Grant wouldn't be caught dead making the choices I've made.

I roll my eyes at Ben, playing along as I flick him off. "Asshole."

He shakes his head at me, knocking back his beer bottle to take a sip. A man I don't recognize slings his arm around Ben and looks me up and down, openly, unabashedly, and his lips curve into a too perfect smirk. He's cocky when he does it, like he's viscerally aware of the effect it *should* have on someone. I suck in my cheeks, tilting my head to the side as I study him, distantly aware of my brother and Ben bickering with him. They know each other—clearly.

My eyes catch on the subtle wave of his blonde hair, only long enough to barely fall in his face, and he pushes a few locks back because, I think, he sees me watching. His lips quirk, amused by my attention.

"That's my sister, you sick fuck," Grant tells him, shoving his lean frame that, upon closer inspection, totally gives away that he plays ball, and he pretends to stumble back, a hand flying to his heart. He's unbothered by my brother's aversion, but I am on high alert, desperate to avoid getting on Grant's bad side already.

"Forgive me." He takes my hand, slowly lifts it before stopping, and looks up at me, rolling his lips like he knows I'm waiting for them on the back of my hand. "You look nothing like your brother," he finally says with a wink, and I drag my hand away, sensing my brother's ire. Somehow, his friend hitting on me would be *my* fault.

"I need a drink," I scoff, turning away and rolling my eyes.

The bar's packed now, and my shoulders brush with strangers, one after another, as we inch our way towards the bar. Ben lingers at the high top while Grant and his friend follow close behind me, but once we approach a slate of empty bar stools, I notice it's only my brother.

"Where did...what's–his–face go?"

"Andy? Probably off to find a new victim," he laughs, and I don't have to wonder what he means because I can see him, only fifteen or so feet away with a tiny brunette flanking him, her hair cropped close to her ears. I sigh, equal parts relieved that he found a warm body to fixate on and jealous of his freedom, of the weightlessness of it. I glance at my brother, feeling the pressure he puts on everyone around him to be perfect all the time. "God, Sloane—please. Don't even think about it."

I hate it here already, I think, scowling at the bar top, missing the life I had before everything happened.

Grant checks his phone, brows furrowing before clicking it off with rapt speed and I brush off his comment. "Wanna tell me what's going on?"

I trace the lines of the cartoonishly illustrated bar top with my index finger, trying to follow it to a conclusion. I consider spilling everything right now: telling him about Elliot, about Mom contacting me and telling me she's sick but sober, about the twelve sticks I peed on before calling Clemmie, about leaving my art program without notice, about how if our parents find out any of this they'll probably, finally, cut off my allowance and then I'll be directionless *and* poor.

Instead, I say: "Nope. Bartender?" The wide, bulky man who crafted my drink earlier flicks his brows up at us. "Can we get—"

"She'll have water," my brother interrupts. "Thanks." He checks his phone again, and I decide not to get into it with him so he doesn't keep prying.

I squint my eyes, studying him for a long moment. His gaze flits around the bar, like he's fighting the urge to check his phone again, and it's so unlike him. The only other time I've ever seen him this distracted was in the tenth grade, with that one girl...

"This is crazy," I finally say, my smile bleeding true contentment.

"What?" he asks, oblivious.

"You have a crush," I tell him softly. "Is she supposed to be meetin' you?" I imagine my brother, open-hearted in a way he rarely is and smile a little deeper.

He shakes his head, scoffing. "I don't have a crush. And no one—she's not meetin' me."

"So there is a she?" I challenge him. "And if you don't have a crush, why are you checkin' your phone?" I pause when I notice how unsettled he looks. "Oh my god...does she have a boyfriend?" I gasp, pretending to be scandalized.

The look he gives me is full of disgust, and I have the urge to preach at him about judgement. He's so full of it that I sometimes wonder how we're *this* related.

"No, Sloane. She's just...unavailable." He glances away, clearly irritated by my probing. He's so occupied by thoughts of her, so lost in thought about this mystery woman, that he doesn't notice when I slide his phone off the counter and unlock it.

The only girl name in his entire text log is a "Gen," and it feels right. I tap a message into his phone, hiding it under the table when his seat swivels toward me, but it swivels back.

"What's her name, at least?" I ask innocently.

"Gen," he admits gruffly, and I hum like it's the most interesting thing I've ever heard. Unfortunately, my brother hears his phone buzz beneath the bar, and I'm found out. "Sloane," he groans, swiping his hand down his face.

"You needed a push! You were being kind of pathetic. Look." I pull his phone out and show him the "I need to see you" message I sent. "She answered! See?" I show him her *where are you?* response, but he's not nearly as pleased as I thought he would be.

"Did you consider that maybe I *don't* need to see her?" he says, annoyance lacing the anticipation I'm tracking in his posture.

"Trouble in paradise?" I reply cheekily, typing out *Pub 24* before hitting send.

"You're here for thirty minutes..." Grant muses, and I feel

his disappointment in me drop like a rock in my gut. The quick reply from Gen does little to make me feel better.

"Well...you're welcome. I'm gonna go to the restroom," I lie, desperate for the kind of disillusionment I usually find in places like this.

I spot the billiards table behind the thick haze of cigarette smoke and feel oddly at home when a buzzy Budweiser sign comes into focus, the blue glow like a homing beacon. I run my hand along the smooth velvet that runs parallel to the wood of the table, shutting my eyes for the briefest second. I think about my flight earlier, and the stale pretzels they offered; I think about the last night in my apartment, already emptied into a storage unit; I think about breathing Elliot in, curled up against his side on the oversized bean bag chair in the loft over the top of the studio.

I let the smoke curling through the air from the couple in the corner cleanse me, and I open my eyes to find Andy, a curious smirk tugging on his lips, approaching me.

"Sloane, was it?" He says my name slowly, like he's memorizing the feel of it and for a second I'm surprised he knows it until I remember where I am and how quickly news spreads here.

"I see you've been asking around about me, Andrew?" I mock, walking past him to grab a pool stick from the rack, fighting the way my lips want to pull upward.

"I could say the same to you," he nods, a cocky grin on his face as he rests against the wall near the rack so that he's facing me. "Everyone calls me Andy, by the way."

He's distracting to look at, with this sadness in his heavy-lidded gaze, a sea of story raging behind them, the messy tousle of his hair, the ease with which he carries himself, all broad shoulders and leaned out strength, and it's *hot*. Unfortunately.

I assemble the balls in the triangle, rolling it back and forth until it's right. Out of the corner of my eye, Andrew preps a pool stick with a blue cube of chalk.

"How do you know my brother?" I ask, hoping I'm setting an obvious boundary.

The last thing I want is Grant's disapproval or irritation, when what I desperately need is his support—for Connie's sake. All she wants is to make amends with her son, to heal all the hurt she caused for however long she has left, and I told her I could do it. I would get him to talk to her...eventually.

His eyes, an amber brown, narrow at me. "I'm on the team," he says, his smirk softening into an assessing smile as he takes me in shamelessly. I can tell by the heated glint in his eyes that he appreciates my red cowboy boots, the black miniskirt wrapped tightly around my hips, the sliver of skin left exposed by my crop top despite the oversized bomber jacket I have on.

There's this unspoken dialogue that happens in the space after this question. It happens when he lets my gaze rest on him, when he doesn't look away, and it's full of recognition. Like, this could easily happen and, under other circumstances, it would.

I pull my bottom lip through my teeth, letting my head roll before leveling him with a knowing look. "So you play ball." I glance at him sideways, through my lashes, and lean across the edge of the pool table, lining up my first shot. "Point guard?"

"Yeah," he says, surprised. "You play?" I'm tall, and Grant's my twin, so it's not a crazy assumption, but there was only one athletic gene to spare when we were in the womb. It went solely to him.

"*No*," I laugh, wiggling my fingers as I hold up my hand. "I paint."

"She paints," he murmurs, his gaze casting downward like he's mulling something over. "Why haven't I seen you before?"

When his gaze pulls back up, his eyes are filled with subtle intensity, like we're the only people in the room.

"I only visit when I have to."

"So you're visiting?" he pries, and I hate the blush that gives me away.

"Visiting...for the foreseeable future," I laugh, and the white ball violently shatters the careful pyramid. "I was in San Francisco."

"And you left?" he asks, watching the balls scatter. "I grew up in Huntington Beach, but we made our way up north at least once a year."

Warmth emerges in his tone when he talks about it, and I immediately know he loved it there. That he, like me, wouldn't be here if he didn't have to be.

"You miss it?" The balls roll to a slow stop.

"Everyday," he says, like it's the only right answer. "Why'd you leave?" he asks, the sound softly brushing against my skin, and my stomach dips. Somewhere in this bar is that handsome stranger who wouldn't have asked any questions, but I ended up here. He takes his shot, sinking a solid ball in with ease.

"Are you always this nosy when you meet someone new?" I plant a hand on my hip, cognizant of the way Andrew watches the lazy swing of my long hair.

His throat bobs as he steps forward, shaking his head. "No. But it isn't everyday that a woman like you walks into a bar." Thinly veiled lust burns in the back of his gaze, and I laugh.

I roll my eyes, wondering how often that line gets used. He starts to say something, but I cut him off, deciding to save him the effort. "Andy—" my head dips "—this isn't gonna happen."

His eyes narrow in amusement, his lips tugging up as he huffs a laugh. "Because...of your brother?"

"That's honestly insultin'," I say instead of *yes*, because I hate that I'm having to tip toe around his irrationality. "And makes this even more of no." Another lie, because I've always loved an arrogant man.

See: Elliot.

Stop thinking about Elliot.

He steps toward me, a smile playing at the corners of his eyes. "Can I at least plead my case?" he asks in a low murmur that feels like he's wrapping his arms around my waist. He's not touching me, though. He's good at this.

"For what? I know who you are, Andrew," I say on a breathy laugh, fidgeting with the blue chalk.

"And who am I, exactly?" he says, and when I look up I really notice the gorgeously hard lines and muscle subtly rippling beneath his calm exterior. I notice the perceptiveness that probably makes him a superior point guard, because underneath all of that cool exterior, beneath the cocky confidence and charm, he's calculating, reading the room, reading *me*. I hate that he's trying to see anything at all, when I just want to disappear.

Hands firmly planted on the velvet edge of the table, I lean forward, pinning him with my gaze, and try to rattle him.

"A fuck boy, for one." That barely amuses him, so I try harder. "Deceptively laidback. No strings attached, a *good time*." I cock my head to the side, smirking as his jaw twitches. "I bet you make girls feel *real* special." He winces and I catch it before I take my shot. "And when you let them down, no one can really blame you, because you're just not *that* serious. Except you are." I see his throat bob. "You're way too determined to be that superficial. I know your playbook," I tell him, flicking my gaze down. "Your turn."

Andrew sidles up beside me, closer than he needs to, and

sinks one of his solids with barely any force, watching as the other balls ricochet across the table, unbothered. *Fucker.*

"Then you know." Any trace of that over confident smile is gone. In its place is a quiet one—overwhelming and intoxicating. It pins me in place.

"Know what?" I turn my head to face him, only to find we're closer than I expected. He's surveying every inch of my face, until his gaze lands on my lips.

"Exactly what you'd get," he tells me, wetting his lips as the hint of a smirk travels from the corners of his mouth to his eyes and it's like I can see it in the dark pools of his irises—the tension. It's palpable—feels easily combustible—and I could lean just an inch forward and take it, no questions asked.

I know it, and he knows that I know it, and that is exactly the kind of power I refuse to hand a man ever again, even for just one night. This already feels lopsided, like the beginnings of a power struggle.

Where the hell is ugly shirt man?

"It's not happenin'," I whisper, stepping back, pulling the usual nonchalance back into my features. "Clearly, you haven't seen my brother when he's angry," I add with a wink, registering my brother zeroing in on us.

"Or I have, and I just don't care," he says. My eyes dip to his mouth without my permission. He sees it, that cockiness broadening his shoulders in real time, and I briskly turn away.

"Well maybe I'm just not into you," I tell him, leaning across the table as I try to sink a solid green. A curse flies out of my mouth when I fail.

"Sure," he says, dipping his head low to whisper right in my fucking ear. To my dismay, I *shiver* just before he rights himself, busying himself with lining up his next shot.

"Thought you got lost in the toilet," Grant huffs as he

swipes at the profuse amount of smoke in the back corner of the bar. "Can you smoke indoors?"

"Don't be such a Debbie Downer. Live a little," I tell him as I shove the stick into his chest, sneaking off toward the dance floor before Andrew says another infuriating thing.

2

Sloane

"Sloane, shut that damn thing off!" Grant bellows from somewhere in the apartment and I blindly feel around the coffee table from where I lay on the couch, trying to find my phone without fully committing to opening my eyes.

The irritation in his voice, that he doesn't bother to hide, is confusing because were it not for *me*, Genevieve Dupont wouldn't have graced our presence at that dingy bar the other night. More gratitude—that's what I'd like for shoving him toward the woman of his dreams. She walked into the room and he calmed down entirely. Returned to who I know he really can be, just by being near her. It shocked me, and, well I wouldn't say this to Grant because he's far too practical and not nearly whimsical enough to really get it, but I feel like I've known her forever. Felt it when we spun each other around the dance floor until we were dizzy, that there'd always been a part of my heart waiting for her to get here.

But maybe my brother does feel that way. I wouldn't know because getting him to open up about anything feels like all the times I siphoned gasoline from Clemmie's neighbor's car. Slow and painful, with the intermittent taste of poison. I'll think I'm getting somewhere with him but make the wrong move and he'll seize up. Try to distract from the point at hand.

Like Connie. Or Genevieve.

Somehow, we've managed to focus far more on my life in San Francisco than anything else, which is extremely inconvenient because I'm actively trying to forget so much of it. Gen's managed to get me a job at the Boston Conservatory where she dances. It should help; I'm hoping it helps. Not painting has, I'm sure, *not* been helping me move on from Elliot and all my mess.

Connie's treatment plan will be finalized today, so I imagine most of my weeks will be spent with her if she'll allow it, but even my early attempts to just catch up were met with push back. And I get it: she's sick. But I want to be there for her, came all this way to do just that.

My alarm goes off again.

"Sloane!" Grant's voice comes again. Really, he needs a muzzle. "I'm grabbin' breakfast at Vida's with Ben if you can get it together in the next—" he pauses. "—ten minutes."

I'd rather poke pins in my eyes than watch the rich kids of Astor Hill kiki at their glorified dining hall. It's not that I'm a stranger to grotesque levels of wealth. Growing up with Evie and Beau, it was almost unavoidable. But the art scene in San Francisco had been such a breath of fresh air after all that, and to come back here to more of it? My nausea pitches just at the thought.

A bunch of nepo babies, walkin' around with Daddy's credit card.

"Aren't you just describin' yourself?" my brother mumbles from the kitchen, I think.

I didn't realize I'd said that out loud. The curtains

protecting me from the blistering sun are wrenched open, and I fling my arm across my face in a panic.

"Grant!" I try to chuck a pillow toward him, but it just rattles the wall art instead. "If that's what I am, what does that make you?" I stick my tongue out, forcing myself into a more upright position only to find that my head is throbbing.

A pair of painkillers and a glass of water are shoved in my direction across the coffee table, and I look up to find my brother sternly glaring at me, arms crossed like he's looking at a fugitive. Like somehow, he knows my one chief aim in life right now is convincing him to repair his relationship with Connie. I already know what's coming, and I'm by no means prepared to navigate the mine field that is Grant Fielder. My brother, with the cross he bears and his holier than thou attitude, is the *worst* person to peer pressure into anything.

Grant, come try this cigarette. Glare.

Come on, Beau and Evie left the liquor cabinet open. Eyebrow raise.

Xavier has the keys to the rec center. Either come or keep your mouth shut. He stayed home.

For all his perfectionism, he's also the only person I'd actually trust with my life; I know that at the end of the day, he would risk life and limb for me. Would wreak havoc on anyone who messed with me.

And this is how I know he'll fight this hard, how I know he'll either shut down or blow up on me rather than have a normal conversation if I even mention Connie wanting to see him. He closed that door a long time ago and I know, by the death stare he's serving me, that he's going to do anything to keep it that way. Not just because he stopped trusting our birth mother years ago, but because he'll think he's protecting me. He'll be right, I'll be wrong, and that'll be the whole story.

God, he has a savior complex.

But if there's one thing I *do* know, it's that slow and steady really does win the race. I'll wear him down with my good graces and more good behavior than he can ever imagine. He'll trust me, and once he does, he'll see her. I know it.

"Is there a reason you're interruptin' my beauty sleep?" I ask him with just the right amount of cheer and cluelessness. If he even senses he's being manipulated, it'll be game over for me. And Connie.

He cocks his head to the side, lifting one brow with expert precision. "Well you can't sleep on the couch forever," he says, annoyed. My eyes shift in confusion until he shoves his phone at me, gently kicking one of my trash bags of belongings. "There. Pick one. And buy more luggage while you're at. Since we're *nepo* babies."

"Adoptive nepo babies," I grumble, staring into the screen at a series of same day delivery mattresses before handing his phone back. "Not necessary. I don't even know how long I'm gonna be here." I don't say it's because I'm still hoping Connie will change her mind about me staying with her. He'd blow a gasket.

He heaves a sigh before plopping down next to me, bracing his elbows against his knees as he lets his head hang. "Sloane. What the hell happened out there?"

Pursing my lips, I avoid his gaze, jutting up from the sofa to busy myself with his coffee maker.

"*Sloane.*"

I rifle through this fridge, desperate for some heavy cream. All he has is two percent.

"Sloane, if you don't tell me why you left your program, why you're hiding it from Mom and Dad, and why you're acting *weird as fuck,* I swear to god—I will call them." His tone is the one that says *I'm older than you by a minute,* and I know he's serious.

I spin around, holding the watery milk and a mug in my hand, the cold plaster chilling my fingers. The same ones that haven't been able to paint anything in over a month. Not since the piece I was working on with Elliot, that now sits somewhere in his iconic warehouse, unfinished. Not since before.

Sloane, you idiot.

Telling my brother, with his brow all hard set, that I not only got involved with my professor, but that I let myself get so lost in him that it sucked all the artistic passion out of me, feels like I'd be telling a brick wall. He wouldn't get it. He'd blame me; he wouldn't say it, but in the undercurrent of his awkward soothings there would be the truth: that it is so like me to be so careless and chaotic with my feelings. And it still wouldn't be the whole truth. The whole truth would gut him.

Not to mention, Connie's cancer. Jesus, I'm just the bearer of all things bad.

I hesitate, wanting so badly for him to be open to some of my burden. "I was stupid. I got involved with this guy and—" He's already rolling his eyes at me, and I feel my spine stiffen before I will myself to continue. "—it just kind of ruined the vibe," I finish, shrugging, but I can tell he doesn't buy it. Eyes narrowed at me he gets up and strides over to the counter.

"The vibe?" His condescension is thick in the air, and if it wasn't for Connie I would just leave.

"The conditions were not," I wiggle my head around, trying to find the word, "conducive for me to create anything." Sort of the truth. "I would've been wastin' my time. Listen, if you could please save whatever demoralizin' thing you have sittin' on the tip of your tongue, that'd be great."

I turn abruptly and spoon coffee grounds into the filter, hoping he'll disappear into his cave at the back of the apartment. Instead, I can feel him lingering by the counter.

"What?" I spit, spinning on him. He doesn't even flinch.

Just gives me this pathetic smile that spells out how predictable I am.

"Remember when you almost got expelled?" A smile tugs at the corner of his mouth, just as a frown tugs at mine. This is at once nothing like that time and *just* like that time.

"Suspended," I correct him. "Because the dean refused to listen to my side of the story."

"Whatever," he shrugs, and I can't help but scoff. "You packed that rollie luggage Evie'd gotten you for Christmas and walked to the end of the road."

"Yeah, because I felt like no one was lis—" I stop, shaking my head. "What's your point?" I feel myself shrink in real time as nostalgia pools in his gaze, this unsettling memory of mine somehow funny and sweet to him.

"You just do this. You run whenever you make a mistake or—"

"Who says I made a mistake?" I hate how shrill it comes out, hate how I'm sure he can see my molars grinding.

Grant's mouth opens and shuts, his thoughts coalescing around an exaggerated inhale. "No one. But tell me that's not what you're doin'? Runnin' away from somethin' and toward..." His jaw twitches.

"Go on," I say, seething. Small. Embarrassed. "Spit it out."

"Oh come on, Sloane. It's Connie. It's *always* about Connie with you. Your life goes to shit and you think it's Connie who's gonna make everythin' better, like she isn't the reason you're messed up to begin with."

I press my lips hard into each other, lifting my hair as a small reprieve from the hot anger radiating off my neck. "So it's just me who's messed up. *Got it.*" I turn back to the bag of coffee, inhaling deep enough for the fumes to distract me from his insult. Grinds dirty the counter top, and I mindlessly swipe them onto the floor.

"Sloane." I spoon more coffee into the filter. "I just know she's gonna hurt you. That's all."

Taking a deep breath, I face him. "If you cared about that, you wouldn't say such *hurtful* things to me." I squint, staunching the tears that so badly want to bleed across my waterline.

Grant's throat bobs, and I witness the apology take hold in his gaze. "I'm sorry. I could've said all of that differently."

Relief washes over me, and I can almost see my point of entry. "Thank—"

"But I'm serious about Connie. Leave me out of it."

And just like that, it closes. *He* closes up, just like I knew he would. Shoulders squared he shakes his head, frowning. He can't even begin to see how much his grudge is eating at him. Some selfish part of me wants to just tell him about her cancer. Let his stubborn rationality try to metabolize that.

"One day she won't be here. And that guilt will keep eatin' you alive," I tell him, instead, biting the inside of my cheek until that familiar metallic taste clouds my senses.

"I don't feel guilty. That is just...not my life anymore, Sloane." He plants his hands on the counter, glancing down distractedly. "If you're gonna stay here, it's on my terms."

"And they are?" I cross my arms, trying to school my breath.

"One—you'll drop the Connie shit." It's a non-starter, but this is going nowhere. I need to wear him down slowly, over time.

So I shrug one shoulder, rolling my eyes. "Sure," I lie. "Two?"

"No parties in my house."

I scoff. "Who do you think I *am*?"

"My sister. Which is why I hate that this even has to be a

rule, but three," he pauses, raising his brows, "no sleeping with my teammates."

My jaw drops from the sheer audacity. "How we're related is sometimes beyond me. Who cares who I sleep with?"

"Me. I do. The team's already been thrown through a loop with Ben comin' back. The last thing they need is any of your chaos."

I still, blinking furiously to staunch the tears that press behind my eyes.

"That's it. I won't tip off Beau or Evie, will let you crash in my spare room—just follow my rules. Please."

I inhale deeply, exhaling as I let my eyes shut, knowing I don't have any choice in the matter. "Your turf, your rules, I guess."

"Great." A genuine smile spreads across his face, and I wonder just how good the dopamine rush of control feels for him, and just how painful it feels when he loses it. How painful it will be, eventually. The thought twists like a dagger in my own heart because I love my brother, and I hate that he's like this. I hate that I couldn't just run here and share everything with him, that he's so in denial about his own fragility that he's created a bubble that he thinks will shield him forever.

But then I remember Gen, and the pain subsides.

"Is a certain ballerina off limits, though? Because I have a million ideas about—"

His hand flies up, eyes shutting hard as a blush overcomes the face that so reminds me of my own. "I will let you know. If I need...advice. Or whatever."

My own smile is sheepish as I try to catch his gaze. "Sure. Just know, I like her. A lot. She'll be good for you." His eyes tip back as he shakes his head, walking out the door. "I have a sense about these things!" I call after him with forced playfulness, tipping the pot into the reservoir and flicking the machine to life.

Coffee slowly drips into the pot, unhurried by my migraine or fatigue, and I wish I had all the time in the world, because then I'd do everything I needed and wanted to do. And everything I'd ever done wrong, I'd do right.

3

Andy

The palms of my hands burn as I grip the bar, pulling my chin just over it.

"Twenty," I say, not letting my voice waver. I let myself drop to the floor, pulling down the towel hanging on one of the lower pull up bars, roughly using it to wipe the sweat off my face. My eyes catch on the glow of my phone screen, where **DAD** has apparently texted me. I know what he wants to know: how Will's handling Ben's reappearance. He hasn't explicitly told me Ben's a problem, but it's clear. And of course, he'll use me to manage it. I ignore it, sniffing as I roll my neck, deciding he can wait.

The weight room is empty today, just Will, Josiah and Scott. Josiah's over near the mirrors, taking more photos of himself lifting free weights than actually working out. Will and Scott, on the other hand, are by the bench press, where Will's spotting him.

"Jesus, Scott. You really are just a bitch boy, huh?" Will grins as Scott struggles to lift the bar back on to the rack, his face red as his arms shake. I sigh, walking over for an assist, pulling the bar onto the rack for him, and Will rolls his eyes. "He had that man."

Scott doesn't look too pleased either. "Yeah, what the fuck? I had it," he pants, wiping his own towel across the back of his neck.

"Right…is that why you looked like you were about to pop an artery?" I chuckle, snapping my towel at Scott's arm. Will swats the back of his head.

"He has a point, man. You really need to be training more. You're barely at one sixty."

Ever since Ben, Will's older brother and our old captain returned to campus, Will's had all of us in the gym for extra weight time and speed training. Not that he needs it; the only guy on the team who can lift heavier is Grant and that's because the dude's basically a brick wall. Will's easily the fastest —other than me. I've learned in my years of friendship with Will Chapman that staying in second is usually in your best interest.

We move to the free weights, cracking up at the sight of Josiah mid pose.

"Fuck you guys. The ladies love this," he says, using the weight to gesture toward himself.

Scott joins us as we roll our eyes and grab some weight for bicep curls, and I consider how much I dislike the guy. Will's always keeping him around, likely because Scott is the epitome of a yes man. Literally—Will asked him to jump off a bridge when we were all tubing over spring break. Scott did it. Gladly.

"Speaking of ladies…what are we getting into tonight?" Scott's voice is overly goofy and anytime we bring him anywhere he completely fucks up my game. I glare at Will in the mirror, a subtle warning to shut the fuck up, but I see that mischievous glint in his eye.

"Why don't you hit up your boy Ian, Scotty? I could be up

for a party tonight." Scott's cheeks flame at the mention of *your boy*. Honestly, he'd be far less insufferable if he gave up being a misogynist and embraced whoever he actually is, but that's none of my business.

"We aren't really boys...but yeah, sure. I can hit him up." He clears his throat, grabbing lighter weights than the ones he originally attempted, the same dumbbells both Will and I are using. I wince, because I can't help it. I'm an empath, for fuck's sake.

"You gonna invite Olivia?" I ask, sort of a punch back at Will on Scott's behalf because I know the pure tenacity with which Will avoids his girlfriend. I don't really get the fascination. Olivia's cool? Fine? I don't know. She's clearly a beautiful woman but a little too tightly wound for my taste. She keeps to herself, is the picture of control. When she does socialize, she talks down to whoever she's speaking to. Actually, *that* might be the hottest thing about her.

Still, she's a prop, as if Will keeps her around to show he's *not* completely out of control. I'd argue he's been spiraling the entire time I've known him. And I don't dislike the guy; disliking him would've made all of this a lot easier. Unfortunately, I'd probably call him my best friend. He has a heart in there. Buried deep in shit, sure, but it's there. He's never blown my flimsy old money cover, even though he's been to my mom's tiny two bedroom in the city. Even though he's helped me out with Carmen on more than one occasion.

No one at Astor knows I'm not a legacy or new money, except for him. He's held that fact close to his chest. Hasn't used it as a bargaining chip like I've seen him do with so many of the other guys' on the team, using their deepest scars against them. I've learned that's just the cost of being part of this world. Every piece of you is up for scrutiny—is fair game. I sure as hell don't need these rich assholes knowing that I'm broke as fuck and I *definitely* don't need them digging into who I am or how I'm here, both things Will's never bothered asking.

Yeah—behind the douchery, he's a good person. And when he isn't, I know we have his father to thank for that.

Will's jaw hardens at the mention of Liv and I can tell I pressed too far. But Scott's soft, and I worry about going too hard on him, even as he and Josiah file out toward the locker room.

"Let *me* worry about *my* girlfriend." Will's arms flex as he continues his bicep curls and I watch his technique for a second.

"Elbow." I point out the error in his form and his eyes meet mine for a second, violence there at the forefront of his gaze before it dissipates and he chuckles.

"Fuck you, man." He drops the dumbbells into the rack. "I'm gonna shower. Want me to DD tonight?"

I contemplate it for a second. "Yeah that works. I'm not planning on leaving alone, so you *should* probably have your car," I grin and he shakes his head laughing.

"You're the biggest slut I know." He grabs his towel from the bars heading toward the lockers.

"You still got time man!" Another reminder that he still has a whole year to end things with his girlfriend. Be each other's wingman. He waves me off not turning back.

I watch my own form in the mirror, picking up the heavier weights now that Will's gone, finally feeling my muscles strain, and hyper focus on my reps before seeing my phone remind me of my dad's text message. I drop the weight, unbothered by the way it bounces across the floor and into a bench.

When he first contacted me in my senior year of high school, it felt kismet. My mom spent so much of my life warning me off the idea of him that I formed this unrealistic attachment to his ghost. Luis was everything I could've needed in a father, but that's the kind of thing you only ever realize in hindsight. I loved him as much as humanly possible, but that small bubble of paternal insecurity convinced me, for a long time, that maybe I'd love my real father even more. Which is fucked, I know, but seeing him there, outside my high school gym, so soon after Luis had died, made so much sense to me.

Here was the man I'd never so much as seen a photo of but who looked so much like me, who I'd tried filling in the gaps for my entire life. The supposed villain in my mom's story—the older man with a secret family—rolling into my life late one afternoon, offering me the world on a silver fucking platter. Felt a lot like a love I maybe just didn't have any experience with.

Admission to Astor: paid. A spot on the team, even though they'd passed me up initially: done. Access to all the things I didn't have. What he didn't mention were all the god damned "simple" favors he'd be asking. Like keeping my eye on Will Chapman.

Refusing him didn't even cross my mind because he was my father. I think he knew that; think that's why he chose me to begin with. His other son knew him too well to fall for it.

It's really done a number on how I see myself. It's just updates that I give, answers to innocuous questions, and for a while it didn't bother me. But I'm not an idiot; I pieced together that he's a fixer, a corporate attorney who can covertly make your problems disappear should you have enough money. That world was so intangible to me, even through that first year, but now? Now the men who hire my father are the parents of my peers. Peers I know and like, who I drink with on the weekends, who I study with in those too small cubicles that line the library.

If my father's morality is in question, his clients' are already damned. And Dan Chapman? Damned more than any of them. Will looms larger than him now, so he can't beat him anymore, but I've seen him flinch. A grown man, flinching when his father's voice dips in disappointment. A man past his prime, *spying* on his son instead of just talking to him.

But for whatever reason that I'm not privy to, Dan needed Will watched, and my dad decided he'd manipulate me into doing it for him. He holds the keys to the kingdom, so I don't really have a choice, and I've resigned myself to that.

But quietly, in my mind, I can hate it.

I switch to single arm overhead presses, moving up more than I should, hoping it'll quiet my mind. The phone practically glows at me instead, until I finally check the message.

DAD

Call me when you have a minute.

Great.
The ringing sounds colder when it's his number I'm dialing, and I swear the AC goes down a notch.

"Yes?" I'm more curt than I should be, and I brace myself for the blow back.

"Is that anyway to greet your father?" he asks, his voice thick with mockery. "You'd think you'd be more grateful."

I want to say *for what*—after all, it's not like I'm getting his financial support for free. Just selling my soul one secret at a time.

"I'm just in the gym," I say, walking back my obvious irritation. "What's up?"

"I need you to keep an eye on someone." Papers shuffling against a desk sound in the background. "Sloane Fielder."

Grant's sister, bent across that pool table, hair spilling down her back, plays vividly in my mind.

What the hell could he want with her?

"Uh…" I hesitate, already imagining the inconvenience. "Why?"

"Because I said so, Andrew," he says, like the question is outlandish.

"No, no I know. It's just…" I glance around the gym before knocking my head back. "It's harder with people I'm not already around, you know?"

"She's your teammate's sister. If that's too hard for you to figure out—"

"It's not," I cut him off, avoiding the latent threat he's always ready to throw in my face—that he can make this all go away in an instant. That he can rip the rug out from my family's life with a simple phone call. "Can I at least know what I'm supposed to be looking out for?"

"Not important. I just need to know where she goes, who she's with. That kind of thing."

"So you want me to stalk her?" I scoff, gathering my bag from the bench I left it on.

"Of course not," he laughs, and I hear the papers again. "She's your type. I was told she's staying with her brother, so whenever she's around just…do whatever it is you do. Get her to open up."

The insinuation that I could and should use sex to manipulate someone has me grinding my teeth, but I know I wouldn't be so bothered if he was wrong. The trouble is, he isn't. That woman is *exactly* my type. If she wasn't, maybe my gut wouldn't be churning with premature guilt.

It's for that reason that I *know* I can't do this. It's a line I'm realizing I can't cross, but telling my father that is not an option. His lines are nonexistent, and he expects me to follow suit if I want him to keep paying me the stipend that barely helps my mom make ends meet.

A flimsy plan formulates in the silence on the end of the

phone: if I barely see Sloane, I'll have nothing to tell, and I'll chalk my failure up to chance. Easy.

"Andrew?" my father cuts through my thoughts with a decisive edge that confirms what I already know—refusing him will never be an option.

I run a hand through my hair, relishing the cool air that hits my face as I walk to my car.

"Yeah. Got it," I lie, praying he doesn't hear the slippery deception in my voice.

"Great. Talk soon, kiddo."

Fucking kiddo, I think to myself, as walk back to the fraternity housing he cuts the check for.

4

Sloane

Fourteen years ago

Gloria, our social worker, is a round woman, her cheeks red in that splotchy way that people who sweat a lot tend to have, and she smells like maple syrup, which only makes me want to throw up more on the bumpy ride through northern Georgia. Grant squeezes my hand in the back seat as the beefy woman turns, a hollow smile on her face like she isn't *really* happy about this outcome, but professionally can't say otherwise.

"We're almost there!"

I swallow the throw up forming at the bottom of my throat and suck in a deep breath.

Almost there, almost home, almost to mom.

We pass a sign graffiti'd with something I don't understand. I barely make out *Pineridge Community* in the faded letters. We pass trailer after trailer, some better kept than others, until finally we reach one painted light yellow, the color singing to me that this one has to be Mom's. We get out of the boxy car and Grant pulls our trash bags from the trunk.

This will be our first time home in over six months and while I'm nauseous, I also feel like I could float. I've thought about my mom everyday, waiting to see her again, waiting until she'd be able to tuck me in at night—just waiting. Grant tried to pull me out of it, tried to distract me with new art pencils or the sketch book he swiped from one of the other kids. It never worked. Most nights, I just sat at the big bay window in the group home, the only beautiful spot in the whole place, and I'd wait.

Gloria uses her clipboard which she holds like a weapon to knock on Mom's door and the shuffling behind it fills me with excitement.

"Shit, shit, shit," we hear muffled behind it as more shuffling ensues. I notice Grant shifting on his feet, the way he does when he knows something is off. I just focus on the door, knowing his feeling is wrong.

When it opens, a skunky smell is everywhere and I know. I can't quite see Mom; she's crouched behind the worn doorway, her blue eyes all that's visible in the sliver she's opened.

"I'm sorry, um—" Gloria flips through the papers on her clipboard, confused. "I'm looking for the residence of Constance Tucker?" She clears her throat awkwardly, confirming the addresses match.

"I didn't realize—I didn't realize it was today." Every word sounds like it barely made its way out, and the thick sound of tears in it has me digging my nails into the palm of my hand. I try to focus on them, how I painted them this soft blue because it's Mom's favorite color, how I was so upset when they chipped on the way here because I was scared she wouldn't like them.

Gloria pushes the door open so she can see in and Mom stumbles back. Grant knew something was wrong and, of course, he was right. He's always right. An unfamiliar man is shirtless, his head lolled back on the couch, ashes accumulated on the coffee table along with several small pieces of tinfoil. A bunch of tools, cans and bottles are scattered all over the place.

"Please. Just—just give me a week." Mom reaches for Gloria like she's desperate, but the woman's already on the radio she wears on her belt buckle, calling for additional help. "I can fix this. I'm—I'm better. I'm better. I swear. This isn't what it looks like."

Tears well at the bottom of my eyes because *I know*. I know they aren't going to let us stay. I see Grant turn in my periphery, wordlessly walk back toward the car we just got out of. My bottom lip starts to tremble.

"Mama..." Sobs choke my throat as my mom sees me, her face the same it's always been to me and for a second I forget—forget I have to leave again just as I got back to her. She moves toward me and Gloria tries to block her but I shove her to the side, falling into my mom's embrace. "Mama, I wanna stay. Please Mama, I wanna stay." I breathe it into her like a wish I know won't come true.

"I'm so sorry, bug. I'm so, so sorry." I feel Gloria's grasp, gently trying to pull me back. "No." Mom's voice is harsh. "No, you can't do this. Not again." Her voice is stumbling over itself, sharp with pain. "She's mine! Stop, she's mine!" I barely hear the sirens wailing behind us now, hardly hear the police officer's voice, telling me it's time to let go.

"Ma'am, we are going to take her now." His voice is so soft as he tugs me back but even so, I scream. I scream and wail and kick as hard as I can, trying to free myself. My mom's a crumpled pile on the porch.

"Mama! Please! Don't make me leave. Don't make me leave." She doesn't look up. Just lays there wilted, lifeless. Grant tries to hold my hand, but he's not even crying. Just sitting there, waiting to leave. I stare out the rear window at that yellow trailer until it's engrained in my mind, tears clouding my vision, until that exact shade of yellow is all I see.

* * *

September

"So what do you think?" My mother, with her long flaxen hair and laughter softened eyes, spreads her arms, gesturing toward the space and I finally look away from the pale yellow curtains, lightly blowing in the breeze of the open window.

There was a point where I assumed I'd never get this. I was always hopeful, but there was a time when that hope dimmed. We hadn't heard from her in so long, and asking about her felt worse than just imagining her happy and alive somewhere. I was a junior in high school when she called my phone from an unknown number, of course. And then that's the way it was for a time. Two Christmases ago, she finally gave me an address and I sent her a painting I'd done of the redwoods. It's here, on the wall leading to the bedroom, and I can't help but feel right for once.

I train my gaze back on her; she's so much smaller than she was even a few months ago, when she first was diagnosed. Her hair has lost its shine, her skin is more sallow, even her eyes seem weary which may be the most jarring. Even at her worst, her eyes always told me she was alive.

She smiles patiently, awaiting my answer. In reality, the apartment is not great. Sure, she's put her little Constance spin on it the way she always did when we were kids, when she was sober. She'd paint some walls, hang up pictures, but even so, the smell of mildew was always unflappable. The floors never stopped feeling rough and sticky under your feet even with shoes and the dingy kitchen could never be completely cleaned, no matter how much bleach you used. This place reminds me a little of that, and I wish she'd let me lease the apartment I'd picked out for her.

Getting her moved and set up in Boston was the first time she really allowed me to do anything for her and that was only because she had no choice. Well, I left her no choice after she called me to tell me she had cancer. It was a few days after Elliot had all but kicked me to the curb, and it felt like some sick twist of fate. Like the universe had ejected me from one world so I'd be ready to navigate another.

Terminal, she'd said on the phone, but she'd only gotten *one* opinion. Thank god she'd given us up for adoption, I'd joked, because I'd figure everything out with my gold-plated trust fund. She didn't laugh; just sighed into the telephone and told me she wasn't worried about all that, but that she needed to talk to Grant. And, in another sinister move by the universe, Grant happens to live near the Dana–Farber Cancer Institute, one of the best in the country. Much better than any care she'd be getting in the middle of nowhere Georgia.

If I'd left it up to Connie, she'd be doing all of this alone, waiting on a call from Grant that would never come. No—this is as good as it can be. *This* is fate.

"It's great, Momma," I finally say and her face perks up. "We should probably get goin'. The hospital's across town and we really can't miss this first appointment." I check my phone, feeling a little too much like Grant, watching the time on the Uber tick up. He's usually the one ushering me along.

"Sloane." I glance up and can tell my mom is uncomfortable, can tell this whole arrangement is antithetical to her entire ethos as a person and for a second I feel bad for trapping her here. But she's sick and as much as she fought me on getting treatment here, I know her time on Earth is a long way from being done. "Thank you, for doin' all this…" She teeters off nervously, her voice a little shaky, reminding me just how old she's gotten. "I know things haven't always been what they should be with me...but I do love you and your brother and—"

I walk toward her and wrap my arms around her slender frame that used to be so similar to my own. I feel her body melt into mine, a small surrender that says she'll let me steer this ship for now.

"It's going to be okay. I promise." I squeeze her hard once and she nods absentmindedly just as the ding of my phone alerts us that our Uber is here.

"You ready?"

"As I'll ever be." She smiles a sad roaming smile that takes over her entire face, and quietly watches out the car window the entire ride.

The hospital has that familiar fluorescent hue, the one that seems to be consistent no matter what medical building you go in. My mom lays casually on the bed in the center of the room, flipping through the same ten or so cable TV channels the hospital offers. So far things have gone as expected. Words like terminal, and inoperable are thrown around and I squeeze my mom's hand after each one. Finally, we get to discussing her treatment plan which the doctor *insists* on reiterating only has a twelve percent chance of working, and I want to ask him if he's ever heard of the law of attraction but think better of it. Mom's eyes turn steely, her emotions inaccessible to me.

"You're sure you want to move forward with this? It won't be easy and it definitely won't be fun," he says to my mom, turning so there's only room for her to answer. Staring him down with as much irritation in my gaze as I can muster, I feel my mom's gaze on me.

"That's uh, why we're here," she says, smirking at me like the doctor didn't just suggest this is all pointless. "Don't think this one would have it any other way."

Dr. Whitman chuckles, nodding, and I bite the inside of my cheek.

"Alright, well, I'm going to keep you overnight to run the remaining tests, so go ahead and get comfortable." He gestures to the bed. "We'll start our first round of treatment in the morning. I assume you'll be back for that." I nod. "Great. I'll be in touch later this evening and we can discuss the plan a little more in detail." Dr. Whitman leaves, and I watch my mother tip her head up toward the ceiling, like the fluorescent lights have something to offer her.

More than a few people in the hallway asked if we were sisters because we look so alike, and because she's a little too young to be the mom of a twenty-two year old. Same long blonde unruly hair, same deep tan from being in the sun, and same deep blue eyes—although Grant has those too.

Mom shifts in her bed, eyeing me, eyeing her. "Will you stop starin' at me like that? It's unsettlin'." She rolls her eyes, and I do it back. "You should go. What—you're just gonna stay here all night? Don't you have stuff to do?"

"Such as?"

A thoughtfulness I don't remember seeing as a child crosses her gaze. "Anything, Sloane. You could do anything other than sit by a dyin' woman all day."

"Well, good thing I don't wanna do anything else, and *good thing* you're not dyin'," I retort, sliding into the narrow cot alongside her. "No place I'd rather be, Connie bee." I boop her nose and admire the way her laughter rolls out of her as I lean into the feeling.

5

Sloane

"Can we light stage left with the spot instead?" I yell to Bill, the lighting designer who is currently situated in the small booth at the top of the theatre. I stick the end of a paint brush in my mouth, considering the lighting on the colors I chose for the backdrop. If you told me a few months ago I'd be living in the northeast, designing sets, I'd have laughed in your face.

"Serious artists don't settle into predictable fields," Elliot's voice practically screams at me anytime I find myself enjoying the work I'm doing here. But it's temporary. That's the mantra I've stuck, with at least. I'm here for mom's treatment and then I'm gone.

But in the meantime, the Boston Conservatory for the Arts seems like the perfect little side quest. Gen floated the idea to me a few weeks ago when I met her at the bar and honestly I thought maybe it was a drunken promise made in the line to the bathroom, but when she texted a few days later giving me the details and stating the job was mine if I wanted it it was an easy decision. I'm hoping it'll quiet my mind. Give me something to do between hospital visits with Mom. Spark inspiration in my finger tips that haven't seemed to work since I left California. I thought whatever was blocking me from creating would dissipate, the way it's come and gone so many times over the course of my life. This time it feels like I'm stuck in cement, even the paint brush feels wrong in my hands.

That's why this is good for me: a prompt, the setting of the nutcracker, a ballet I've seen countless times with millions of references. It's mindless but just involved enough to make me feel like I'm still pursuing whatever it is I once wished to pursue.

"Her hair is like Rapunzel," I hear one of the little voices behind me squeak. A small redhead with curls pulled up into a ridiculously tight top knot. I smile to myself, letting the child's comment momentarily stroke my ego before an even tinier raven haired girl chimes in.

"Sure, if Rapunzel was like seven feet tall." I glance over and watch the red head and another little girl frantically *shhh* her but she doesn't shy away. Instead she meets my gaze, raises an eyebrow like someone twice her age as if to say *your move*.

"I'm five ten. Not seven feet." I cross my arms, raising my eyebrows back.

"Cool?" Her voice is bored and her friends are looking at her in sheer horror, but the audacity of this child has me laughing.

"You're pretty vicious for a toddler," I note and her eyes narrow.

"I'm eleven."

"Cool?" I smile because I know I've won and sure, I shouldn't find pleasure in arguing with a child but I'll take a win where I can get it. I turn back, fixating on the wood grain in front of me, letting myself get lost in the gliding movement of the brush.

Rehearsal has been brutal today for the dancers. Gen very briefly introduced me to the stage manager before running off and has barely stopped to hydrate. I'm playing around with the half painted backdrop left behind by the artist I'm apparently replacing, making sure each snow flake has a glazed sheen so it glimmers against the warm hues the backlights are creating when the choreographer whose name I can't pronounce claps her hands, signaling the end of rehearsal for the day. The dancers scatter like flies, and Gen nods at me to follow her, the art director in tow as we trek toward backstage.

She's a goddess, and watching her lithe arms waft around as she tries to translate the art director's vision for the set piece is mesmerizing. I think this girl's incapable of moving without grace; every move she makes is loaded with a soft sensuality that I'm convinced she doesn't even recognize. I saw it the moment she walked into that bar, and I see it now.

"And I know you said you paint watercolors, but he really —" the art director interrupts Gen, a flurry of French flying out of his pursed lips, "—oui. Je suis sûr qu'elle peut," she tells him, brows furrowed. "Can you do oil? He's insisting," she addresses me, rolling her eyes.

"Of course!" I lie, a fist sized knot forming in my throat. I've avoided painting with oils since I fled the art studio my adoptive mother, Evie, designed for the both of us. "I'm a little out of practice, but yes."

The gallery wall in the west wing library of my childhood home explodes in my mind's eye, and all I can see are Evie's bright, effusive oil paintings, blindingly contrasting my numerous attempts at capturing dawn and dusk. I wonder if it looks the same now, or if Evie boxed up that part of me like she stowed away all the others that didn't fit into her conception of the perfect daughter.

"Do you believe in fate?" Gen's question comes out of left

field as we march up the stairs to the cat walk, a supposed short cut to the workshop I'll be spending most of my time in.

"One thousand percent," I tell her, peeking over the railing into the darkened audience seating below. "Do you?"

"Sometimes," she says, faintly. "I think it's fate that I met you, since we desperately needed a set painter. But then, other things..."

"Like meetin' my brother?" I quip, and I can feel the heat of her embarrassment. I stay quiet though, letting her sift through the feeling.

"Well, we didn't *just* meet," she starts to say.

"But somehow the stars have aligned, and the timin' is just right?" I grin through the dimness, knowing she can hear it.

"That's just the thing. I don't really know if the timing's right. It sort of feels like it's never been on my side." There's a quiet defeat in her voice, so at odds with the way she was moving just minutes before.

"It's not just fate, though," I tell her as we hop off the platform, confronted with one too many corridors to choose from. I follow her to the right, immediately at home when I see a feral looking woman in a tattered, paint smeared smock, her mass of mahogany hair piled high on her head. She gives us a small smile, briefly nodding as she hurries past us. "There's fate, and then there's waitin' around for something to happen to you. Sometimes, the universe needs a little nudge."

Gen wrenches open a pine door and it gives way to a beautifully bright studio. Canvas and massive wooden cutouts lean against the walls, a shelf of color coordinated paints separated by medium on the wall nearest the door. The light, I realize when I gaze up, comes from the multiple skylights above, like the sky is bleeding its way into the room.

"So I think these have shades..." Gen fumbles with some buttons and the room plummets into darkness as electric shades shield the daylight from entering. She flicks on the softest, haziest lights I've ever seen in my life. "Obviously, you can mess with the lighting."

"I'm obsessed," I laugh, turning toward her. "*Thank you.* You have no idea how much I needed something like this."

"Glad to be the nudge in your universe," she grins, offering me her hand, but I take it and yank her into me. She's quiet strength wrapped in a strawberry and vanilla scented package of beauty, and I know it's premature, but I love her already.

"Gen," a voice calls from the hallway, and suddenly our little cavern is being invaded by the smell of expensive soap and sage. "What the fuck are you doing in here with the lights off?"

The shades above zip away, and the heavens shine down on a dark-haired angel, the tattoos that pepper his forearms only a slight distraction from his angular face, his pouty mouth, the creamy skin that is the most perfect canvas I've seen in my life.

"Oh," he says, blinking at me. "Jean." He offers me his hand and I grasp it, shocked by its roughness.

"Sloane," I grin, finding something kindred in his smokey, gray blue eyes.

"She's painting sets for us. She's, uh, Grant's sister." Out of the corner of my eye, I see Gen shifting her weight.

"I knew you looked familiar. You're like, glamazon him," he says, cocking his head as he whips it toward Gen, his eyes flying wide as his lips curl into a gleeful smile.

"Yeah, well, we're twins," I chuckle. "Oh my god, wait. *Jean*, as in, Gen's friend Jean at the bonfire..." I squint, looking between the two as my new friend hides her beautiful face in her hands, but Jean just steps forward.

"So you're familiar with my work?" he quips, looking at me through his inky black lashes with a furious little flutter that pulls an obnoxious laugh out of me.

Grant filled me in on the night he saw Jean and Gen

giggling by a tree just moments before he called my brother over. Before that bonfire, she and my brother pretty much steered clear of each other. One thing led to another, including me inviting her to the bar, and now we're here, watching Gen blush at his mention.

Jean stands a few feet back, arms crossed as he leans against a wall, openly perceiving me in his baggy black cargo pants and intentionally tattered, olive sweater with a mischievous glint in his stare.

"Okay..." she laughs, turning to leave. "If you're riding with me, I gotta go," she says pointedly at Jean. "I'll see you later?"

I nod, grinning as she disappears.

"I see you, new girl," he says, lifting his chin. "Little match maker, are we?"

"I prefer *the Lord's work*."

"Religious?" His brows furrow.

I shrug. "Spiritual. And southern."

His eyes shine with mirth, and a throaty rumble filters out of him as he pushes off the wall.

"Jean!" Gen yells, and he winces.

"Get my number from Gen," he throws back, following Gen's trail, and I make my way back into the main atrium to keep picking away at the unfinished piece, heart burning with the prospect of new friendship.

I lose track of time in the large theatre, the lack of windows making it seem like time ceases to exist. I'm just finishing adding a deeper green hue to some trees when I hear a small sneeze toward the back of the auditorium. I look out but the lights are blinding making it impossible to see. Bill agreed to leave the stage lights on for me as long as I promised to turn them off before I head out.

"Hello?" I ask, the silence eerie as I continue to squint out into the pool of seats. I move to the edge of the stage using my hands to frame my face and see the small dark haired girl from before, her hair down now, ebony waves shadowing her small face, she has on a pair of cat ear headphones that are a glittery pink color as she stares at her phone. I jump down, walking toward the back of the theater and watch as her eyes flicker up to me.

"You're still here?" I ask, but she just holds up a finger, signaling for me to hold on before taking off her head phones.

"What?" she asks, her voice short and to the point.

"You're still here?" I look at her amused. As a former child who also took themselves a little too seriously, I can appreciate the way she doesn't take shit from anyone, even and *especially* adults.

"It appears so." She pushes back on her headphones.

"Isn't it gettin' late? Do you need me to call your mom?" I force myself to be friendly, to not come off creepy but the look of disgust she gives me shows I'm failing. She slides back off her headphones, annoyed.

"My mom isn't coming. She's at work. I'm waiting for my brother."

"Ah, I see." I slide down into the chair beside her and she shuffles her body slightly away. I pull out my phone, checking the time. 8:15 PM. Rehearsal ended about an hour and a half ago. "This brother of yours...he got a watch?" I smile to show I'm kidding but she rolls her eyes.

"He's at practice. He'll come after. Don't worry, I'm used to it." Her face is completely closed off. Devoid of emotion, so similar to how I was as a kid and I feel this pull toward her.

"Hungry?" I ask, nodding toward the back stage. "I know where they keep all the good snacks."

She eyes me suspiciously but then stands, heaving a worn out Jan sport over her shoulder.

"Lead the way, Rapunzel."

I roll my eyes but offer her a friendly smile to signal a truce. She doesn't return it but I know we're getting somewhere.

* * *

We've made it halfway through a giant bag of hot Cheetos and are both snorting laughing at almost getting caught by a rogue front of house employee.

"Shhh, we can't get you kicked out of the program," I say as we tuck ourselves behind an old box of stage props.

"Program? I'm *not* in this *program*." She giggles more, elongating the word program like someone imitating Scrooge McDuck.

My brows dip, confused as to how she's in the show when all the other dancers, with their designer travel bags and dance company logo plastered to the sides of them, are in this elite and very expensive ballet. My eyes land on her Jan sport again, worn and gray, black sharpie crosses out the initials A.S., new initials replacing them. I know a hand me down when I see one, spent years living off them, and my heart instantly flares for the little girl beside me. Not with pity like I'm sure she gets from the rest of Boston's elite, but with respect, with familiarity. She sees it, the realization surely written all over my face.

"I'm not really into ballet, anyway. I usually only do the spring musical and summer show but they're doing Mom a favor, I guess."

I nod, catching her eye for a second but she cringes away.

"Don't feel bad for me," she says accusatorially.

"I don't," I laugh and I can tell she knows I mean it. "We aren't so different." I nudge her with my elbow but she rolls her eyes.

"Please. I heard the others talking. Don't your parents own

50

like that big grocery store or whatever?" Her eyes hold so much accusation and I get it because I'm sure mine did too when I was her age. The endless blame I put on those who had more than me. Those who could help the people who really needed it but only helped in ways that were beneficial to them.

"Nope, the people who adopted me do," I wink, pushing to stand now that the footsteps of whoever was back here have long since disappeared. I dust myself off, extending her a hand. She's wary but curious and takes it looking at me with a bit more recognition as if she's starting to see some of herself in me too.

"Fine," she says, shaking my hand in a truce that's slightly undermined by her sly grin. "So tell me, is it really true that you got banned from that sleep away camp in Sweden?" An image of that gossip article from *years* ago is pulled from the recesses of my memory, and I cringe.

"Rule number one, little bird—*do not* Google me," I say, chuckling as I poke at her nose.

"Carmen!" A strong, masculine voice interrupts us and the footsteps reappear.

"I swear she was in the auditorium thirty minutes ago, working on her homework just like always." The employee who was back here earlier sounds closer now and I widen my eyes at the girl who I now realize is the Carmen they're looking for. She sighs, pulling back on the backpack.

"Back here," her little voice rings out and for a second I wonder if I could actually get in trouble for this.

"Thank god. Where the hell were you?"

I spot him before he spots me, his eyes hard as he takes in the girl who skipped out from behind the large box before I could register what was going on.

"I was hanging out with—" Carmen flicks her eyes around the room before pointing right at me, "—her."

I take a step out of the deep shadow of the prop closet and smile innocently.

"*Sloane*?" Andy's voice is as surprised as I feel.

"Andrew," I blush, nodding as I remember our flirtation at the bar..

"What are you doing here?" I watch as Andy's thoughts go every which way, his brow scrunches in suspicion as if this is some sort of prank and Carmen looks at him like he's grown two heads.

"Wait, do you...know her?" She stares at her brother.

"You could say that," I offer my own confusion must be visible because Andy's face softens. "And you know him?" I direct it at Carmen.

"My brother? Yeah, I know him."

Realization dawns on me, my mind circling back to the initials on the backpack.

"Right...sorry to scare you guys." I nod politely toward the Boston Conservatory employee who is clearly pissed.

"Thanks, Meryl. I'll take it from here." Andy nods to her, too and she glances down at Carmen.

"Next time, let me know if you're going to galavant backstage," she says to the wisp of a girl, and Carmen mocks a salute. I crack a smile before quickly burying it at the glare Meryl shoots at me. *Sorry*, I mouth before she turns and leaves.

"She was getting me a snack. You guys need to chill. I was gone for like fifteen minutes." Carmen seems bored by this entire situation.

"More like half an hour. I called and texted you," Andy says, his tone almost identical to the one Grant sometimes takes with me.

She holds up her phone smiling. "Dead." She shrugs and then smiles at me in victory. I shake my head slightly, silently begging to not be brought into this but Andy catches it.

"And why are you here?" He looks at me expectantly, only a hint of that unbridled interest from the other night on display behind this bizarrely authoritative version of him. I fight the heat that threatens to warm my cheeks.

"I work here?" I say my voice is more defensive than I want it to be.

"She's doing our sets for the Nutcracker," Carmen chimes in.

"And apparently stealing small children in her spare time. Didn't really think of you as much of a kidnapper," he says, that boyish charm filtering back in.

"Well, you shouldn't really be thinkin' of me at all." I give him a tight smile. Andy's eyes flash with the memory of the bar as he smirks.

Carmen's face wrinkles in disgust. "Please tell me you guys don't know each other...like that?" I match it, even though, I'm not sure she's *completely* wrong.

"Definitely not," I mimic Carmen's stance, hands on my hips, eyes directed at her brother. He looks between us and I see stress wrinkle between his brows—guilt, which is not really what I expected if I'm being honest.

"Were you mean to my friend, Andy?" Carmen asks, and I bite my lip to hide my smile. Andy's face is incredulous.

"Turning my own sister against me?" he asks, and I roll my eyes to distract from my amusement. I shouldn't be enjoying this as much as I am.

"Pretty sure you're doin' that all by yourself."

A growl sounds from Carmen's stomach, and we both turn our heads at her as she flashes an irritated smile. "Okay, can we go to Taco Bell, *please*?"

"Maybe." Andy shuts his eyes, dragging a hand down his face before dipping his head toward her bag and nudging her out the door before turning around toward me.

"Good to see you, Sloane," he says, differently now that his sister is down the hallway. There's sincerity behind his tired shrug of a smile. "Almost like it was fate."

"Definitely *not* fate," I say in a flurry, wincing internally.

"Serendipity, then."

"Did you just learn that one?" I run a hand through my hair, trying to disguise the way I watch him more closely. His exhaustion is apparent and I remember what Carmen had said —that her brother was at practice. There's a slight sheen on his tanned skin, a hint of tautness in his neck and arms, like he's still recovering from the exertion, and I can't help but wonder how often he does this: speeding over from Astor to Boston's city center, picking up his sister who's clearly on a scholarship with a hand me down back pack.

He laughs. "There's a movie—"

"Yeah, I've seen it." I cut him off, wincing at the way my attention snaps to him, at his ability to draw me in even when I don't want to be drawn. I need to be a good sister, because once Grant finds out about Connie—finds out about Elliot— hooking up with his teammate will seem like child's play. The least I can do is not break the only two rules he's given me.

"Thanks. For staying with Carm," he says, just as I'm about to exit. Genuine gratitude in his amber speckled eyes. "I owe you one."

"It was nothin'." I let a genuine smile slip out, frustrated by my inability to fully reject this boy, because I know myself and he *will* wear me down. Get me to do something that might wreck all my plans. Like staying in Grant's good graces so he'll finally see our mom. I turn toward the parking lot, each stomp an attempt at extinguishing the small flame that lights inside me whenever that boy gives me that toothy grin of his.

I take the long way, trying to avoid Carmen where she's waiting in the lobby, only to see them pulling out of the conservatory just as I reach the street corner. She waves—way more kindly than I would've suspected for a child who taunted me with the nickname Rapunzel all afternoon—and I feel my heart swell.

And then Andrew locks eyes with me and *fucking winks*.

6

Andy

The chipped black door handle of the club is sticky as I pull it open to reveal the dark, smoky, black box theatre. I've worked at Johnny's for a while now, since before I started at Astor. Johnny, Luis' best friend, moved to Boston alongside mom, he made it seem like it was to open a second location for his infamous comedy club but I knew the truth, it was to keep an eye on mom, on Carmen. Like he promised anytime Luis got into a perilous situation, which wasn't uncommon for a firefighter in California.

I still remember, though, the first time Luis had a close call. He'd been gone all night and Johnny came over before my mom even picked up the phone and held my mom, held Carm and promised he'd have their back if it ever happened. And it did.

So, here he is, all the way on the east coast, keeping that promise.

"Look who decided to join us..." Johnny's gruff Italian accent fills the small club, his button down stressed at the seams as he wipes the bar counter. I lift the latch to let myself behind the bar, picking up a crate of freshly washed glassware to begin polishing.

"Sorry, Johnny." I slap his shoulder reaching over him to grab an extra towel. "Ran a little behind taking Carm to rehearsal." He sighs, nodding his head because as long as Carmen's involved I can be excused from almost anything.

"How's Mom?" he asks sympathetically as I start working the towel against the mass of water stains covering tonight's drink ware.

"Tired," I grumble, reaching under the bar to grab the cleaning solution we keep down there for the times we need to clean a glass on the fly.

"She works too hard." He shakes his head then claps my back and I know what it is—pity. I don't blame him for it. I feel it, too, with every small new crease that forms along my mom's eyes when she smiles, feel it when she texts to see if I can stay an extra hour and make Carmen something to eat, when she asks if she can pay me back next month. Pity and guilt have worked their way in and out of me more times than I care to count. The feeling's so intertwined with my family I wonder if things always felt this hard. That's part of why I begged Johnny not to tell mom I started working here a few nights a week and also likely why he obliged.

He perches his large body on a small black stool, peeking over the society pages of the Boston Globe.

I chuckle, snatching the pages from him. "You really need to stop reading all this garbage."

"What—scared I'll see you in there one day at your big fancy school?"

I roll my eyes as he grabs the paper back from me. "I doubt they'd find anyone at my *big fancy school* that interesting," I say, moving back to the glasses.

"Ah. So I guess you don't know—" he pulls the small spectacles off his head and onto his eyes as he squints at the tiny serif font, "—the Fielder twins?" I narrow my eyes and he raises his brows in amusement. "You do know them, then!" He chuckles that loud boisterous laugh of his, slapping his hand on the counter with glee. "They say the girl one—" he squints back down, "Sloane. They say she's a *real* train wreck."

I feel my eyebrows furrow before I can stop them, feel the way my arm instinctively rips the paper off the counter quickly scanning it before chucking it in the trash can. She's there, right smack dab in the center of a huge spread dedicated primarily to the 'Grocery Store Heiress ready to take New England by Storm.' I stare at the photo longer than I should. I can tell it's an older photo, probably from California, definitely before she came to Boston. She's dancing on a bar, a mini dress so small that a slight bend would expose her ass to the mass of men staring at her and sure. That pisses me off but what I can't look away from is how her eyes are shut, arms in the air, looking...free. I shake my head, tearing the paper before tossing it in the trash.

"Like I said, garbage." My jaw's set and I look at Johnny who looks both outraged and amused.

"Alright, alright. Testy today, huh?" He laughs again before nodding to my knuckles, now red from the way I'm gripping the silver tumbler I'm not polishing. "What's eating you, kid?"

I let out the breath I'm holding because there's no way in hell I'm going to talk to Johnny about Sloane, least of all because he wouldn't understand why I need to keep my distance. It shouldn't be bothering me at all, actually, and the fact that she's been occupying any space in my mind at all is probably what's irritating me the most.

My phone moves in my pocket and I pull it out, hiding my screen as I read the text.

DAD
Updates on the girl??

Read the paper.

Don't test me. I know she works at the
theater. Do your job.

My molars grind as I sigh, cracking my neck before throwing a towel over my shoulder. Of course, he knows that. He sees everything, and I'd be willing to bet he saw how I can barely control myself when she's in my line of sight. It's tunnel vision, apparently. All I can see is her, and all I can think about is how I'm going to make her laugh, blush, or say something mean to me.

Fuck.

"It's just been a long week." I focus on the job at hand, steadily polishing each glass before moving to the next one. I can feel Johnny's concerned gaze on my back.

"Let me give you some extra cash this week. Maybe you can refill Carm's bus pass, get her those dance shoes your mom's been saving for." He squeezes my shoulder.

"You don't have to do that, seriously. I'm handling it," I say, a little gruffer than I mean to, but it's true. I am handling it and I know Johnny just wants to help but that's my job. They're my family and he's already helping more than he needs to. My mom would hate it if she found out he was offering me pity money. Know she'd hate that I accepted a job here, like a handout. Johnny eyes me before slapping me upside the head.

"Jesus," I moan, rubbing the spot he just walloped.

"Grow up, Andy. If someone wants to give you some cash don't make it a bigger deal than it is. You and Becs are the exact same, I swear." He moves to the small safe under the bar and pulls out a few twenties. "Get yourself a burger and get Carm a bus pass, and please, help me sleep at night." I sigh but ultimately accept the money, shoving it in the pocket of my apron. "Jessica's been asking about you. Something about you not calling her back? You know what I said about the girls at the club." I'd been pretty intent on taking Jessica out but her name hasn't crossed my mind all week.

I wonder why.

I need to get distracted, need to remind myself that Grant's sister *is* just some girl by throwing myself into a sea of new ones.

Genius.

"That's why I didn't call her back." I quirk a smile and then duck when he goes to slap me upside the head again.

"You're a pain in my ass, you know that?" He chuckles, grabbing an envelope of cash out of the safe to take to the back office. "Once you're done with your side work, go ahead and set up the servers' stations. I think the girls are gonna be late tonight." The girls he's referring to are our two front of house servers, Vanessa and Tammy, both in their mid forties with smoker's voices that would put the Marlboro man to shame. "You're a good boy, Andrew." He nods, before going to the back, and I slip my phone out to text Will about our plans tonight.

* * *

"*Fuck*," Will groans he's stuffing an oversized piece of banana bread in his mouth as we careen down a narrow side street in my car. It's an upgrade from the one I came to Astor with, courtesy of my father. Told my mom it was a perk from being on a team like the Lions. If she wasn't so stretched, she would've caught the lie. "What is in this?"

I chuckle. "Pretty sure it's just a box mix."

"No way. No," he shakes his head. "I've made boxed banana bread with Gen. This is not from a box. Your mom should open a bakery. Wait—" he turns sharply toward me, his eyes flying wide. "That's it. Bec's Bakery? Are you fucking kidding me?"

"You should tell her," I smirk, keeping my eyes on the road. "How's Gen, anyway?"

That night at the bar, when Gen showed up and practically melted into Grant, is something I've kept carefully hidden from Will, mostly because Grant asked me not to mention it, but also because it's none of Will's business. What *is* my business is how my friend is doing, and whatever messed up childhood he had, that is somewhat correlated to the hold he has on every person in his circle.

The car slices through a puddle as I turn on a road lit by a neon sign, a long line that descends downward wrapping around the block.

"She's busy with dance, so I've barely seen her," he says, but I can tell something's eating at him. "Pretty sure Grant's fucking with her."

I cut him a skeptical glance. "You don't think he might like her?"

Will stares at me for a long second before scoffing. "He probably does. But he's wasting his time and hers." Out of the corner of my eye, I can see his jaw grinding before he takes a deep breath. "Let's not talk about her. Or Liv—*please*. Let's just go to this weird art party—"

"Performance art is not weird, Will. Don't be dick. A friend invited me, so you're gonna be nice," I tell him pointedly as I slide out of the car, slamming the door shut.

Will grins, hands shoved into his pockets as he eyes the growing line of people who look nothing like the ones that pepper our campus. The show is a mashup of performance and visual artists, but that's all Autumn, my friend, said. She's been begging me to come into the city for one of these for months, and I can tell by the eager smile spread across her face as she waits by the door that finally agreeing to it is a big deal to her. We're friends—*actually* friends. Her girlfriend looms behind, dark hair falling around her shoulders as she scans the street for us.

"Andrew," she says, her British accent swallowed whole the minute we enter the underground warehouse. Slate, concrete walls run seamlessly into an identical floor, but you can barely even make it out because of the strobe lights that flicker across the sea of bodies. "You've met Frida?" I glance over, nodding my head at her before she pulls me in for a hug.

"Refreshing, seeing you away from those pretentious douches," she yells over the thumping bass before she notices Will. "Oh. Hello."

"Will Chapman," he says on a laugh, the corner of his mouth tugging up in a smirk that visibly softens Autumn's usually unaffected girlfriend. "Some people call me a pretentious douche."

"I didn't mean—" she starts to explain, but I cut her off while Autumn fights her own amusement.

"No, no. He actually is a douche, so. No harm done."

We're all awash in a red glow, the music in sync with the way the lights flash as we slip through the room. The yeasty scent of beer and acrid notes of liquor fills my senses as the bass rumbles against my skin, and I relax back into myself after the longest shift of my life. The club was mostly dead, so everyone else got cut early. Just me and my thoughts, all night. That Will answered and agreed to come into the city for a last minute art exhibition is a testament to how good of a friend he can be.

"Where's the art?" Will asks as I snag a beer off the platter of someone dressed like an overly rotted zombie.

"Look up," Autumn tells us and when I do, I almost laugh. The ceiling is an intricate web of plastics, soda cans, netting and water bottles, but some has been melted down and reshaped to mimic sea life. It's kind of violent with the red lights, all the little pieces together.

"Is this PETA?" I turn to Frida. "Is this you converting me?"

"No." Frida's eyes roll dramatically. "The theme tonight is decay. Environmental decay, social decay, moral decay. You know." She shrugs, inching past someone until we meet the bar.

"Okay, I have to check on my actors and Frida's not allowed to leave my side," Autumn says cheekily, tugging on her arm. "But I'll be back at some point. Wait—are either of you squeamish?" Will and I shake our heads, but skepticism crosses between us. "Okay. Just checking." The girls dart away, and when I turn around toward the bar, I notice Will's already grabbed a seat and ordered a drink, is already staring at the wall deep in thought.

"You good?" My brows pull together and I watch him all but slam his fresh beer onto the bar top.

"Yeah. I'll catch up with you," he tells me, breezily, like I imagined the lost expression I just clocked in his gaze, and I squint. "I *have* a girlfriend, Andy. Remember?" The bitterness shocks me.

My cheeks puff full of air before I let it out. "Right. Of course. I'll...be back?"

"Dude, chill. I'm just gonna look at the..." he glances up. "The decay," he huffs, a small smile pulling toward his eyes as his gaze locks on someone behind me. "Fucking Ian."

"Huh?" My neck pricks as I turn and see him immediately, his attention already trained on me. "Oh. Weird," I say as nonchalantly as possible, knowing that look. He needs to talk to me.

"*Will Chapman seen at a PETA art party. Will he turn vegan?*" he laughs, mimicking Ian's snide tone as he knocks his beer back. Someone's hand lands on Will's shoulder with a thud, and congratulations on his last season win start pouring out the stranger's mouth as I pull away, discreetly trying to find Ian.

His blue buzzcut bobs behind a different head every few seconds as I nudge my way through the crowd of sweaty people swishing every which way to the music. As carefully as I can, I step my way between people, keeping my eye on Ian's hair, my hands softly brushing against the backs of strangers, until one with a too familiar mass of blonde waves spins into me, her own hands pressing against me as her chest glitters and heaves.

"Andrew?" Sloane says, breathless and flushed, her cheeks crimson with exertion, her lashes fluttering beneath the red glow.

I descend into someone different, entirely, when she says my name like that—the only way she's said it. It's becoming harder to ignore that she's distinct from everyone and everything else as she stands here with her brows pulled tight, surprised wonder in her dark eyes.

"We've got to stop running into each other like this," I manage to say as her palms glide up my shoulders until she's looped her arms around my neck.

Head cocked to the side, her grin deepens until her dimples are obvious, and she rolls those eyes. "If you asked me, I'd say you were followin' me. Are you followin' me, Spellman?" she slurs, just slightly, but the heat of her hands on my neck and the languid ways she's moving tell me she's been here longer than me.

I let my eyes quickly scan the room as I scoff. "Definitely

not." No sight of Ian, and at the realization that he might've left, I relax, chuckling. "Maybe you're following me."

"Like I've got nothin' better to do?" she asks, swaying to the beat. Gaze dipping, I catch the short hem of her dress, and those red cowboy boots, and smile to myself.

"I don't know. What do you do? Other than paint." I tell myself this is a useful question, not a selfish one. That knowing this could satisfy my dad or his client, not my own desire to sketch a picture of her in my mind that I could reference later.

She wets her lips before tugging the corner of her bottom one between her teeth, glancing away thoughtfully. "I used to like goin' to the beach with Delilah. Drivin' around anywhere in her, really."

"And Delilah is a...?"

"A car," she laughs, and she might as well run her fingers across my skin before sinking them into me because I can't imagine it would invade me any less.

"When she gets here, I can take you for a spin." She grins up at me like nothing else matters, and I wish I was even a little bit drunk so I could delude myself with her. "She's vintage. You'd like her."

"So you're moving here? For good?" Worry pools low in my stomach.

Her head falls back on a groan, the sound electric against my skin. "Andy," she moans, and I have to glance away. "Don't be a joy kill," she whispers when her head falls forward, leveling her gaze with mine as she closes the distance between us. "I don't wanna think about all that."

I just want to kiss her. I want to cradle her face in one hand and pull her flush against me with the other. Tangle that hand in her golden waves, brush my lips across hers and taste her— kiss her senseless and not think about anything at all.

"Why'd you come to Boston?" I ask abruptly, unwinding

her arms from around my neck, unsurprised by the scowl that blooms on her face.

"What are *you* doin' at an art exhibition?" *Trying not to think about you.* "There wasn't a house party you could loiter at?" Her hand rests in the dip of her waist as she kicks out the opposite leg, but her own amusement threatens to flood the scowl away.

"Oh, I forgot. You know me." I stifle my grin, rolling my lips together where the ghost of a kiss that'll never happen burns me. "Didn't answer my question, though."

"I assumed you were smart enough to know my non answer *was* an answer."

I feign feeling wounded, my hand pressing against my chest as I watch for her own smile to break free. Which it does. Her head shakes on the sound of her laughter and holy fuck I wish this was different. I'd spend the rest of the night listening to her laugh like this.

I dip my head, flicking my gaze up at her, knowing I need to cut this off. "Goodnight, Sloane."

"You're lettin' me go?" Genuine shock laces her tone, her lashes blinking one too many times before she recovers, but the damage is done. Now I know there's something there; that she wasn't posturing. That she felt it, too. "You're just usually a dog with a bone."

"Thought you said this was never gonna happen?" I tease, watching her blush travel across her cheekbones, taking in everything. The freckles on her cheeks, the fullness of her lips, the honeyed sound of that voice, the stubborn cut of her jaw—all of it, because I hope to God I'm never this close again. I don't know what I'll do the next time she's in my arms, so there can't *be* a next time. "Something about your brother...?"

She clears her throat, sobering up at his mention like I threw a bucket of ice on her. "I was flirtin' with you, Spellman.

If I wanted to fuck you, you would know," she says, eyes narrowed as I flick my gaze to the floor so she won't see my amusement.

"Jesus Christ, Sloane, I thought I lost you," a familiar voice croons over the music, and I turn to see Jean wedging his way between a cluster of people. "Andy? What are you doing here?"

I open my mouth to answer, but my half brother—Ian Rivers—steps around his boyfriend and slyly grins at me. "He has theater connections. Autumn from his theater survey section sophomore year probably invited him, didn't she?" he says, perky and unbothered, as my blood runs cold.

"Okay, it's creepy that you just know things about everyone," Jean says, rolling his eyes. "You know Andy?" he asks Sloane, confused.

I watch as Ian glances between Sloane and I, a wealth of knowledge lodged in the look.

"Barely," she says at the same time I say, "Hardly," and Jean's brow draws tight.

"Okay..." he chuckles nervously. "You ready to go?" He turns toward Sloane, who's already looped her arm through his and began dragging him to the entrance, but not before he presses a quick kiss on Ian's cheek. "Bye. Text you after I drop her off!"

Jean's voice slips away as he disappears into the crowd, and suddenly, she's not here anymore. It should be a relief but it's not—it's just more want for something I can't have.

"What's troubling you, brother?" Ian's voice is glib and way too fucking chummy for one o'clock in the morning, and I narrow my gaze at my half-brother: the prodigal son who's only marginally less shady than our father. But give him time. He'll get there.

"What is it?" I sigh, shooting a quick glance toward the bar. Will is nowhere in sight. "I've gotta find—"

"Will? In the bathroom. Doing something illicit. I didn't ask."

"What do you need, Ian?" I say behind gritted teeth.

"Will's not doing well," he says like it's this grave, objective thing.

"Okay? His brother just came back and ripped captain out from under him. He's coping."

"He hasn't mentioned anything else?"

"No," I say emphatically, feeling my voice turn hoarse from talking over the metal now clanging through the speakers. "And I'm not your source, Ian. So fuck off."

I storm away, reaching the smokey bathroom within seconds where I find Will with eyes red rimmed as he grins over at me.

"Come on. Time to go," I tell him, nodding toward the door.

"Five more minutes?" he pleads, a smile cracked wide across his face as he stands up straight and sighs. "Yeah, okay. Not really my scene. A fucking *zombie* gave me this." He holds up a small joint, and I snatch it away, tossing it in the trash can.

"Probably shouldn't take weed from a zombie," I laugh, smacking his back as we make our way through the warehouse.

Will glances back at me, squinting. "I could really go for more of that banana bread."

"I'm sure you could."

7

Sloane

New England moves past me in a blur when I look out the car window, trying to find the sea that lies somewhere beyond all this concrete. With this little daylight left hanging in the sky, I can almost imagine we're on our way to Jekyll Island. Crack the window and it's almost like the top of my car is down, like I'm eighteen again—impossibly naive.

The Jekyll house is where we celebrated our impending adulthood: me, Clemmie, Grant, all our friends. The freedom was so close, tasted prematurely sweet; I didn't know what I was going to do yet, but I knew with everyone else starting college I'd have the time to figure it out. It's how I ended up in California, how I ended up at Francis College; it's how I wound up in Elliot's seminar just a few years later.

Impulsively, I open my school inbox like I'll find evidence of him. An old syllabus, maybe one of the dry emails he sent me before things changed between us. Clementine deleted all of it, so all I find are the unread messages that remind me I haven't logged any activity and am at risk of expulsion. I scroll through them, annoyed at their incessance, before stopping at an out of place subject line.

LET'S TALK

I've never seen the e-mail address—*h.cooper@thejournal.com*—but the tone feels overtly familiar. My finger hovers over the message for a second before I realize "the journal" is *The Journal*, a national news publication, and swipe to delete it. The press can kiss my ass; talking to them is the last thing I would ever gift those nosy idiots.

"Can you?" Grant asks, nodding to the window noisily leaking salty air into his pristine car. One hand on the stereo dial, he turns the music to a dull murmur as the street lights glitter against the otherwise dark road. "Promise me—" he starts to say, but I already know.

"I *won't* flirt with any of your little boyfriends—"

"Teammates," Grant corrects, his voice stern as he stares at the long winding path that takes us to whatever restaurant this 'team dinner' is at. I was surprised when he invited me. Typically, Grant is what some may describe as private. Because I call it like I see it, I know he's just got a stick up his ass.

I assess his profile, studying him like the angle of his brow might tell me if he knows that I saw Andy the other night. Not that it should matter, because nothing happened.

"Already had this conversation, remember?" I clear my throat.. "So...what am I walkin' into? Are the Lions a house divided?" I jeer, only for his jaw to twitch. He *hates* conflict.

The car jolts against the onset of cobblestone as he pulls in a heavy sigh, rotating his head like he needs to crack his neck. "You could say that."

I can just see it: the loyalists standing by Will versus the traitors who hopped at the chance to be on Ben's good side.

"But they're brothers? Maybe your coach should make them do therapy. Actually—" I turn in my seat. "—you guys should go on a retreat! Wait, I could plan it. I've got nothin' better to do. There's this—"

"Sloane. Please." My brother shakes his head, a tired chuckle escaping him as he drags a hand down his face. "Look, when we get to this dinner please just...be cool. Don't be...you know." He raises his eyebrows sarcastically.

"No. I don't know. Please, enlighten me." I cross my arms over my seatbelt in defiance even though I do know. I have a way of stirring shit up, and while Grant sees it as one of my more unfortunate qualities, I have found that meddling is usually pretty helpful. If I hadn't texted Gen, *for example*, Grant would've still been secretly pining over her.

"Just don't talk to anyone." He nods to himself as if this will solve his problem and I gasp a laugh.

"You want me to sit at a table, with your entire team, and not say a word?"

"If only..." he says wistfully, giving me a smile, and I punch him in the arm. "For real, though. Don't leave with any of them—we had a deal."

I scoff, rolling my eyes.

"Your bar for me is really that low?"

I know I shouldn't be offended because technically I've done it before. Slept with his teammates. *Thought* about sleeping with his current teammate—but I didn't.

"The bar's in hell, Sloane." With that he turns into a busy parking lot, many a sports car parked precariously in spaces that verge on too small. It could be a luxury dealership.

"Don't forget your jacket." His voice is firm as we step into the cool October air.

"Jacket?" I wince, because no, I did not bring a jacket to

cover up the short red dress I have on. It honestly didn't even occur to me.

"Christ," he grumbles, and I roll my eyes, linking my arm with his.

"I promise to be good." I nod, smiling politely as if the option to be anything but is completely out of the question.

* * *

"No, Grant is actually the best roommate. It's like living with a house keeper. I swear, I didn't have to touch a dish the entire time we lived together." Ben's smile is wide as we both take turns making jabs at my brother.

"I promise you he was secretly resentin' you the entire time. Just wouldn't say anything because he's a big ol' baby." I poke Grant's forearm and he makes a dramatic *ha ha* sound, but I can tell he doesn't mind our teasing.

"Okay fair, fair. But he didn't think I was that bad, did he?" Ben's hands are up in surrender.

"Sure, if you don't count the time you vanished out of thin air only to come back years later, like nothin' happened," I say, scooping artichoke dip onto a chip with precision.

Grant stills, his drink mid air, and I feel him side eye me for saying too much. Ben pauses for a second too, the air heavy, almost suffocating, before he finally barrels over with laughter. Grant snorts a laugh, whiskey coming out of his nose. I shriek as the liquid drips all over our bread plates and all three of us, plus a few of the other team's members, die of laughter, the sound wrapping around me like a hug. For the life of me, I don't know what he was so worried about, and I make a mental note to thank him for including me in this later.

We are all so preoccupied, we seem to miss the couple who just made their way into the private dining room. It isn't until an expertly coiffed brunette clears her throat across from Grant that I look over. Ben's still saying something to Grant across me, his arm slung around the back of my chair. The familiarity seems to be jarring to the girl openly gaping at us. My stomach sinks, like maybe I did something wrong, although I can't fathom what.

But then I see the man beside her. I notice his eyes first, green, like money. So green, I want to paint them. His jaw is hard, but it's not flexed; it's like someone hammered it right out of stone. Broad shoulders, his physique sitting somewhere between Ben and Grant's and I instantly know who it is. Gen's beautiful face flashes in my mind as I clock the similarities between the man before me and his brother. Ben's mouth, Ben's height, Ben's eyebrows, but somehow more bold, more severe.

Ben's arm slides off my chair, so naturally that from a distance, you'd never guess at the tension in the air. I don't miss the way his eyes lock with the woman standing next to his brother.

"Hey, Will." Ben's smile is tight as he adds: "Olivia." He nods and I can tell there's something happening here. Something I can't put my finger on but nevertheless feel the need to extinguish.

"Hi," I say, letting my southern twang move to the forefront of my mouth, knowing it usually makes people feel a bit more at ease.

Olivia's face remains stoic, her eyes sliding to me as if just noticing I exist. She looks like a young Brooke Shields, her dark brows framing her eyes in a way that takes her from pretty to stunning. It's not hard to tell what kind of girl she is, or is *trying* to be, I should say. The straight line of her mouth makes her weariness obvious to me, and the harsh indifference of her gaze makes it clear she wants to stay at arms length.

"I'm Sloane." I reach out my hand, but she doesn't take it; to recover, I act like I'm going for her sweater, feeling the soft fabric as I run it between my fingertips. Her eyes widen at the contact. "Where did you get that sweater? I absolutely *love*!"

She pulls back a little and I fall back into my chair, trying not to laugh at the sheer terror flashing through Olivia's eyes.

"Uh...Veronica Beard, over on Newbury."

I watch as her eyes glance over at Ben, just for a second, but I see it. There *is* something there.

Interesting.

I nudge Grant with my elbow, grabbing his arm as it falls off the table.

"Remind me to stop at Veronica Beard when we go to Newbury tomorrow. I have to have that sweater. Do they have it in anything less...dreary?" I watch the girl stiffen and Grant rolls his eyes, clearly seeing that I'm fucking with her a little bit, but I can't help it. Her discomfort is palpable and I'm drinking it up.

"I see you've met my sister..." Grant chimes in and I watch the girl put two and two together, realizing who I am and why I'm here. Her shoulders unhinge slightly as she relaxes in her chair. Curiosity claws its way up my spine.

"Sorry, I was just so distracted by how soft your sweater looks!" I try to genuinely smile at the girl but her gaze has changed from guarded to sad.

"I'm glad someone likes it. This one thought it was just fine." Her head tilts toward Will who barely looks her way at the mention. All her previous hardness softens slightly and it's clear that all of that was an act, a way to protect herself. Again, tension fills the air, Ben's stillness a signal that he's somehow involved in whatever is going on. I glance at Grant, his head down as he spreads butter onto his bread. Pussy.

I mock a gasp, looking between Will and his exceptionally

gorgeous girlfriend and I catch a quick spark of amusement in her gaze. Like she's letting me in on something and she doesn't do that often. Right then, I decide I like her.

Will can't even spare a glance. He's slouched back in his chair, his menu leaning on his lap against the table as his long arm dangles on the back of Olivia's chair. A cocktail waitress wearing a skirt almost as short as mine saunters over, holding what appears to be a whiskey on the rocks. She leans beside him, her cleavage on full display as she sets down his glass.

"Your usual," she says, giving him a coy smile which he returns, overtly flirtatious for someone seated directly beside his girlfriend. He turns his snaky, green eyes toward me, and any trace of attractiveness I once saw is washed away by the red now painting Olivia's cheeks.

"I said you look totally fine—to be clear." He shrugs at me disinterested before returning to his menu. "And yeah, I mean it's nothing to write home about. Not worth being late over." His tone is bored and makes me want to grab my fork, reach over, and stab him with it as his eyes flick over the menu. Ben seems to match the violence that has entered my mood, his whole arm flexed near his stake knife.

"You look great Olivia." Ben's deep voice has gravity to it and I watch Olivia's blush deepen. "You were right when you saw it on the rack—that color suits you."

Both Grant and I freeze, Ben's words hanging heavy over the table. Any suspicion that something was going on with the three of them was confirmed with the petty way the words left Ben's mouth. They catch Will's attention, his eyes flicking up venomously.

"What does he mean *you were right*?" The words come out like a hiss fully directed at Olivia. I watch her lock up, her posture prim, her expression restrained. The hypocrisy is clear to everyone at the table, as just seconds ago he was fully checking out our waitress. Still, I find it hard to believe that something *is* going on with Ben and Olivia. Even if Will is the absolute worst, which I suspect he is, that's still his brother. Olivia seems far too high strung to be a cheater. Surely, Ben wouldn't come back to campus after years away only to steal his captain spot *and* his girlfriend?

She mumbles some response quietly, so myself and the others can't hear. I'm trying my best to appear like I'm not eavesdropping when my attention pulls to further down the room.

"Finally!" One of the guys shouts from the other side of the dining room. The guys jeer and shout as a red head in sky high heels that she definitely hasn't practiced walking in traipses into the room. She smiles sheepishly, like she wasn't expecting this reaction, as she glances back, tugging on her date's hand.

"Alright man, get your ass in here," Josiah calls. My curiosity is piqued and I finally realize exactly who's been missing this evening just as he walks through the doorway, slipping his phone in his pocket on a sigh, before a cocky smile blooms across his beautiful face.

Of course.

Andrew's hand casually wraps around the red head's waist and my mind drifts back to our brief dance at the warehouse party, remembering the feel of his hands on me. Seeing his hand on someone else is a blowback it shouldn't be. He's exactly who he's been since day one, but my body can't seem to get in line. I itch with irritation as my heart rate increases.

The girl actually preens, like she's just caught the biggest fish in the pond. And unfortunately, standing there in his blue knit sweater, his hair expertly tucked under a backwards baseball hat, I find that I wouldn't mind going fishing myself.

Nope. Nope, nope, nope, I tell myself, mindlessly clutching a roll to slather butter on.

"Yo, Andrew." Will raises his hand, signaling him over with the curl of his fingers like a dog and I look up as Andy jogs over. I sip the red wine Ben just refilled for me, distracting myself by looking at the menu, but I can feel his eyes on me like a million camera flashes in a dark room. They burn into me, pleading for me to look back.

"Don't bother man. Fielder's sister." Will's tone is suggestive, as if they know something about me that I don't. I drop my menu, finally meeting Andy's gaze and watch as his hesitant smile slowly unfolds.

It shouldn't be this disarming, this genuine, like early morning sunshine peaking through curtains. I feel the corners of my own mouth start to tug, this animalistic need to return what he's giving me pushing against my sensibility, but I stamp out any trace of authenticity, replacing it with sarcasm. I make a show of peeking around Andy to glance at his date.

"So is it like Tuesday's for brunettes and Friday's for red heads? Just tryin' to understand your schedulin' strategy..." I have no clue how he actually spends his free time, but I have my guesses.

Andy's eyes shift, heat and amusement flashing in them as he and his date walk past me, but not before dipping his head just enough to mutter in my ear.

"Jealousy looks good on you." He straightens, cocking his head to the side, signaling Scott, who I've learned is second string and bottom of the social food chain, to move down a few seats. He abides, moving over so there's two seats open. I narrow my eyes as Andy's date stalks away, the clack of her heels unfortunate as she finds her seat, a lobster-hued blush swallowing her face whole.

"In your dreams, Spellman," I tell him, rolling my eyes as

he winks, taking his seat next to his date. For what it's worth, he says some placating thing about her heels not being that loud in her ear, because she relaxes in her chair and reaches under the table so that, I'm assuming she's touching his thigh. She finds her earlier confidence, unbothered that her date was just flirting with another woman.

But then I guess, the expectations are clear.

My teeth grind.

"*Sloane*," Grant's irritating voice cuts in, low and foreboding. I force myself to glance back down at my menu, frustrated by Andy's insinuation and my brother's attention to me at all, and fight the way my gaze wants to pull up and toward the annoying charming man across the table.

Still, I feel his eyes on me. Feel the way they trace my face, and I want to ask if he'd like a photograph so he can study it later, but that'd be more flirting. I need to stop speaking to him, need to stop caring whether he's looking or not. I shift in my chair to face Olivia who gladly accepts the distraction, but only for so long: we're thirty minutes into a conversation about the democratization of art when her eyes look like they're starting to glaze over.

"Sorry—this is so *so* interesting," she says, covering her yawn and I appreciate her attempt at a lie. "I just need to use the restroom." She slides out of her seat, and heads toward the open dining room housing the other patrons, leaving me alone with my thoughts.

The guys are all engrossed in a conversation about playoffs and I can see Andy's date, who I've since learned is named Bridget, sucking down her fourth glass of champagne. She attempts to flirt with Scott, whose vulgar questions about the carpets matching the drapes are met with more and more giggles.

Andy doesn't notice; he doesn't care, which makes me feel better than it should. He nods at something Ben's saying and I let myself watch him for a minute. The way his brow furrows when he considers whatever's being said is adorable and at odds with the cocky, fuck boy attitude he's so committed to. I track the small quirk of his lips and the effortless confidence evident in the way he's casually leaning back in his chair, arms crossed so I can see the curved shape of his biceps. He shrugs in response to something, and it exaggerates the powerful outline of his shoulders. Like he could feel me watching, he suddenly shifts his gaze to my side of the table. My face flushes when he catches my stare.

He looks as thrown off as I feel, his face heating as his eyes pin me, but I don't look away. It feels like a year in the span of a second. And when Bridget notices and grasps his arm, giggling in his ear, his eyes still don't leave mine. A familiar, sweeping feeling passes over me. Like a song you felt deep in your soul as a child, memorized every word to, even though you didn't know what they meant.

I hate that I think of Elliot now, and all the pain that made me come here; it forces me to break eye contact, and I shift my attention to Olivia who's just making her way back.

"Have you gone to Little Boo's yet? Their ice cream is quite literally a spiritual awakening." Her smile is friendly as she pulls out her chair. It would take an idiot not to notice that in the hour her boyfriend has ignored her she's seemed much more herself. I force my expression to match hers, still feeling the warmth of Andy's attention.

"Darlin', a spiritual awakening sounds exactly like what I need right now."

8

Andy

My phone feels like dynamite in my hand as I fidget with it, waiting for my father to demand an update. I release it to the counter and only feel marginally better.

Yeah, I've seen Sloane a few times actually, and now I can't stop thinking about her, would be the truth, but instead I'll have to just tell him no. Whenever he finally asks.

The rich aroma of coffee spirals out of the moka pot through the air of my mom's apartment, and if I didn't know better, I'd think Luis was at the stove doing it himself. Instead, I see Carmen standing on a stool, pouring milk into the bottom of a Peanuts mug.

"Carm—no stoves! What the hell?"

"I'm making her coffee," she shoots back, eyes wide with disgust at my bad attempt at anything close to parenting. "Mom let's me. Take a breath," she laughs, modeling an obnoxiously deep breath as she tips the moka pot into the mug.

Jesus.

In my mind, my sister's still the same kid who'd need her chicken cut into tiny bites, or would only drink water if it was in a Minnie Mouse cup. Watching her pull four waffles out of the double toaster and finishing plating lunch that looks a lot like breakfast for her and our mother has me realizing she hasn't been that girl in a long time. She's self sufficient in ways she shouldn't be, and I make a mental note to try harder.

"What a nice surprise!" my mom sings, rounding the corner of the only hallway in the cramped apartment in her diner uniform. She presses a warm kiss on my cheek and ruffles my hair with an endearing grin on her face. Her hair, a longer, lusher version of mine, is braided to the side this morning, so I can see the exhaustion that's been painted on her face for the past four years. "Don't you have the gala tonight?"

Astor Hill Athletic's annual charity gala is a hot bed for Boston high society, and Coach knows it. Our attendance is mandatory, and our play time in the upcoming season is suspiciously linked to how many donors we pull in.

"Yeah, *tonight*. Just wanted to bring these," I tell her, resting the Rodgers and Hammerstein DVD collection I snagged at the thrift store just outside of campus.

Carmen rushes over at the sight of Julie Andrews on the cover of the boxset. "*South Pacific*? This is like, vintage." She holds the set up, inspecting it like it came from an archaeological dig.

"DVDs aren't that old," Mom says between bites of Eggos, drenched in too much syrup. "I never threw away your old player," she says to me, a nostalgic look flitting across her face. I know she's imagining a very different life, the one we had in San Diego with Luis, Carmen's dad. The life we had before fire stole it from us.

"I figured you could watch these today, since I can't be around," I tell my sister, her eyes glued to the single sleeve of *State Fair* as she kneels precariously on a chair, elbows on mom's old wooden table. Carmen peeks up, brows furrowing.

"Why?" she asks, and guilt coils around my gut the way it always does when I have to disappoint her. She's had so much of that already.

"I've got this thing tonight, and I gotta get ready. I just wanted to bring you this." I hop up from the table, helping myself to coffee in order to avoid having to see her be let down. I catch the nod of her head and watch as her inky black waves shift. "But...I did get tickets for the show."

She squints before her eyes light up with recognition. "Wait —really?"

The community theater on the south side is putting on Matilda in a few months, but they're notoriously hard to get tickets for. Lucky for me, it's only a few buildings down from the club, and one of our door girls is in it.

My phone lights up with a text from Josiah, and I regret the moment I look at it.

Sloane, on some god damned bar top, in a black, velvet dress with fringe that cuts off just beneath the swell of her ass, with this caption:

Atlanta socialite Sloane Fielder seems to have joined ranks with her twin for the fall season, wasting no time learning the lay of the land. Will Boston have a new princess ruling our concrete jungle, or will she follow the suite of her notoriously private grocery heir brother?

JOSIAH

No way she's related to Grant

Irritation strains at my temples. The papers in this town love to run old photos and pass them off like they were from the night before. It happens to Will constantly, the only difference is when it happens to him it doesn't piss me off. I rub the bridge of my nose, reminding myself to get a grip. She's not mine and I'm supposed to be *spying* on her. *For fuck's sake.* I momentarily contemplate passing the article along to my father. Maybe if the majority of Bostonians believe this crock of shit to be true, so will he.

"Earth to Andy? Earth to *loser*?" Carmen playfully shouts, jumping off her seat. "Can Will come?"

I shake my head, trying to forget how we danced at the party last night. "I only got two tickets, kiddo. But maybe we can all hit the diner this week," I tell her, giving her a smile that's only half the consolation she's looking for.

"Good. He owes me a Labubu," she says low, squinting her eyes suspiciously.

"A what?" I laugh, rifling through the bills piled on the kitchen counter. Water, electric, the phone bill—her car note. Past due. I stuff it into my back pocket and make another mental note to call the lender later.

Carmen runs off without answering, her door slamming shut a few minutes later. My mom's lost in thought, gazing down into her coffee.

"Did she fuck it up?" I joke, quirking a smile.

"Language," my mom says, flicking a gaze up toward me that's only a fraction as lethal as the sentiment. She was never strict; she left the discipline up to Luis, but even he was as soft as they come. "No, she actually makes a really good cup." She shrugs this tired smile, one laced with memories she'd rather let torture her than forget.

"I can give you a little more this month," I tell her, hoping that'll bring a smile to her face. Instead she scowls, her deep brown eyes sparking with frustration.

"We're fine."

I pull in a deep breath, deciding not to push back. It's a dignity thing—I know that. But they're not fine. If she knew how I afford giving her five hundred, six hundred, sometimes a thousand a month, she'd be even worse. She needs the help; she's barely making ends meet, forgoing paying the car note to pay for Carmen's activities. And that girl deserves the world, not a small life in the confines of a tiny apartment. She deserves the life she had before her dad passed. Hell, she deserves the kind of life *my* dad black mails me with every day—and that is why I do it. That is why I take his money, even as the strings attached to them grow tighter and tighter.

"I wish you'd stop worrying about us. You should be... studying abroad. Taking trips with those fancy friends of yours," she chuckles, the corners of her eyes creasing in a way that feels distinctly hers. The warmth in that gaze, and the way her eyes wrinkle when she's happy, are tattooed on every good memory I have.

"Away games—" I start to argue, but she tilts her head.

"*Don't* count. I'm serious, Andy. Carm's fine. You can relax," she gives me a look that says she knows better. "Stop holding on to us so tight."

I want to tell her that *this* is what you do when loss is etched in your cards; you hold on to the things you have and you stay grateful for the good. You don't hope for more. She thinks hope is this universally good thing, that it makes everything better. She doesn't know the sacrifices I've had to make, that every shred of my own hope is now permanently entangled in the lies I told to make it possible. Not just for me but for them. I'd never tell her that though, never let that crease of worry between her brows deepen even further because I know that whatever I think I've sacrificed, whatever hard decisions I think I've made, it was harder for her tenfold. *She's* the one who was left alone with an infant, a single mother at nineteen. *She's* the one who was widowed at thirty-six. Despite it all, *she* lets hope live behind all that heaviness; she looks at me like the world is mine for the taking.

So I don't say this to my mom. I bite my tongue and keep it in, like I always do.

Instead I say: "It's two forty-five."

She juts up from her seat, mumbling a poorly hidden *shit* as she wraps her apron around her waist, hastily tying a knot as she slips on her diner shoes. "Carm," she shouts, and my sister lazily rolls out of her room. Her brows flick up, a half eaten candy bar in her hand.

"Where the hell did you get that?" I ask her, imagining a secret stash piled high under a laundry basket.

"People," she says at the exact moment my mom rolls her eyes and says, "Will."

Third mental note of the day: remind Will *not* to bring chocolates from the front desk of the athletic's center. He doesn't realize she's already had two cavities this year, but he means well. Picks up my mom's grocery order if I can't and she's still at work. Has shown up with me to support Carm at the theater. Discreetly, of course. Somewhere along the way we've decided that the people we are out here—in the city, with my family—are only for out here. Within the confines of Astor society, there are different roles we need to play, neither of which reveal who we truly are.

As much as I'd like to believe my friends wouldn't think less of me for being the kind of guy without access to a black card, I know they would. They'd stop inviting me out; they'd have different kinds of conversations. They'd pity me. Going to Astor is a leg up in the world *because* of these friends. Without them, I could've just gone to state school, pocketed the excess scholarship funds they would've handed me and given them to Mom—cut ties with my real father years ago.

Will's different, though. The first time he came home with

me was after our gala freshman year. He'd only been dating Liv for a few months, and she was a fucking storm cloud. Her best friend had just passed so it was understandable, but Will would have these moments where he'd need to step away.

Booze flowed that night; everyone had a fake but it didn't matter, the bartenders weren't ID-ing. At some point, Liv was bawling on Ian's shoulder on the balcony, and Will was in a quiet conversation with Gen, which didn't end well. I could see them arguing from inside the ballroom and knew this was my shot. The opportune moment to deliver on what I thought would be my father's only request in exchange for my full ride at Astor, this was a moment I could use to get close to him. It was opportunistic and...slimy, but once I got to him, I wanted to help. He looked tortured; he was tortured.

I offered to take him home with me and when he looked up from the concrete floor, there was barely controlled agony warring in his gaze. Once we stepped off campus though, you could physically see the change, levity breathing life back into his shoulders as we both wolfed down an egregious amount of McDonald's. We pulled up to my mom's and I had that nervous swirl in my stomach, my body trying to make out what the lie was.

Was I just pretending to take this guy in, be his friend and if so why bring him to my moms that first night? Why pull him in closer than anyone else?

"Lock up when you leave please," my mom says, interrupting my thoughts as she slides her purse over her arm and rifles around for her keys. "See you this week? Maybe we can do dinner one night if you don't have practice." She pulls my sister to her, squeezing her tight as she plops a kiss on her raven hair.

"For sure," I tell her, smiling tightly as she shuts the door.

"What's up with you?" Carmen says from beside me and I

quickly turn my head because even at eleven Carmen can read me like a book.

"Uh...nothing," I huff a laugh. I steal away the half eaten Cadbury bar and break off a piece for myself. "Tax." I chew the bar hard, a physical reminder that Will's friendship is real, that even if my dad didn't instigate our first interactions we would've found each other.

She yanks it back. "Rude. And not *nothing*." She walks a half circle around me, eyes narrowing like she's a human x-ray machine. "You're like...busy. In your brain." A pause, then a rueful smile. "You know, I like Sloane."

I glare back, ignoring her and gathering the bills on the counter because for the first time in the past few days I wasn't thinking about her but now that Carm's brought her up she's back at the forefront of my brain, taking up all the space as if her limbs have physically wrapped themselves around it.

"Don't open the door for strangers. Don't use the st—"

"*Okay, okay*," she moans, rolling her eyes. "You know I can fend for myself. I have pepper spray."

"Pepper spray?" Alarm shoots through me and I shut my eyes. *Let go*, I tell myself. "You know what? That's probably really smart."

"Thank you. Mommy thought so, too," she beams up at me, like my approval is a lunar eclipse. "Now go, so I can lock up," she grins, and I do as I'm told, jogging down the stairs when I realize how little time I have to get ready for this damn gala.

9

Sloane

I took my time stretching the thick muslin over the frame, the alabaster fabric rough in my palms as I stapled it taught to the wooden structure I built with the tiniest nails to ever grace planet earth, courtesy of Grant's 'tool box'. For a man who comes off rough and tumble, his tool collection is quite the shame. I can picture the way Beau's brows would pinch at the sight.

"Ya ain't even got an Allen wrench in here, son."

I miss him—Beau. The way he always smelled like cheap Folgers coffee, his hands permanently calloused. When I first moved in it was unsettling, a multimillionaire with working hands. The hands of my uncle, or the kind man in the trailer beside moms who had kids of his own but always found a way to scrape together a few extra meals for me and Grant when things got really bad, weathered canvas work gloves tucked in his pocket. Eventually those hands, Beau's hands, felt like home.

I don't know why it was so much easier to let him in than it was with Evie. I never knew my birth dad so I assume that helped, a big gaping wound begging to be filled by Beau's quiet strong stature. He was the first and only father figure in my life. When I walked into his garage on my thirteenth birthday— *a big one*, he'd say—and saw Delilah, her red paint chipped missing both headlights, it was just her and Beau's timid smile, his big hands tucked carefully into his pocket. That moment opened me right up. He was my dad right then and always after, because he knew me. We never talked about anything really because we never had to; he knew me and never asked for anything else. I wish I could tell him how that meant more to me than the car.

I begin mixing the greens trying to get something close to how I remember Beau's work shirt that day, the Fielder Foods logo on the right pocket. I smear in too much brown, the small pot turning a sickly sticky brown and my eyes sting.

I miss him. I know though if I see him he'll know. Just like Grant but maybe more, like his life experience will allow him to piece together what happened in California, what happened with Elliott. I can feel the end of the well, his kindness and grace running out, like if I tilt my toes just slightly I might touch the bottom. Everyone has their limit.

I feel hot salty liquid on my face now, the perfectly stretched canvas barren in front of me. I swallow and it feels like glass in my throat, glancing at my phone I see another missed call from Clem. Another person I let in only to become a burden to later. Her need to protect me, like a splinter in my thumb. I set my brushes down, taking the scissors from the small bedside table beside me, one of the few pieces of furniture in Grant's guest room. I let them tear into the grain of the canvas, the rip satisfying in a way that it shouldn't be, like I'm cutting out parts of myself instead of a perfectly blank canvas. Maybe because the canvas isn't blank, just empty.

My phone buzzes beside me, Clem's name appearing yet

again and for a second panic zigs it's way through me because what if she needs *me*. What if in my avoidance I miss the chance at being there.

"Hello." I tried to hide my sniff from the phone's receiver, using the back of my hand to wipe my face, still holding the scissors.

"Jesus Sloane. I literally thought you died." Her worried voice pulls something liquid out of me and I immediately feel like I might vomit.

"Nope—still here." I slip into that tired quiet tone I only ever use with her because I know she won't leave. There was a time I tried to make her. In our early teens, I'd push her so hard, with my words, with my actions, I'd swear she'd never come back. Yet there she was. *Here* she was. Clementine always came back because she'd never leave in the first place.

"Have you called any of those counselors I sent over?" Her voice is careful, like she's talking to one of her horses who needs breaking in.

"I don't need a shrink, Clem," I sigh into the phone, flopping down on Grant's guest bed, the milky white duvet almost creamy.

"Sloane, you went through—"

"I'm fine." I cut her off, brushing my hand over the marshmallowy texture of the blanket. "Look, can I call you back? I'm actually painting right now." For a second I think she can hear the lie because if anyone could it's her and maybe she can but wants so badly to think that I'm better that she lets herself believe it because I can hear the smile in her voice, the way it hitches slightly with relief.

"Painting? That's great! That's really good, Sloane."

"Yup," I mumble, letting my face fall to the shredded canvas annoyed at my impulsivity and the realization that I'll have to stretch another.

"Okay. I'll stop mama birding you but answer your damn phone. I'm not Evie, you can't just ghost me." I roll my eyes but feel a familiar smirk tug at my lips. "I love you, I'll call you tomorrow," she says definitively and I can almost see the tiny nod she makes when she's making a silent promise to herself.

"Love you, too, Clemmie." I click the call button and rest my hand on my stomach. A new habit that's been hard to break.

* * *

This past summer

"I can't believe that asshole isn't taking you." Clementine's fingers wrap around the wheel, her dark waves cascading across her long tanned arms as she merges onto the highway.

"He's going to pick me up," I say out the car window and I can hear the thrum of my own voice, the sensation like speaking underwater. I pull the sleeves of my navy blue UCLA sweatshirt over my fingertips, letting my forehead press against the passenger side window. I feel Clem's hand on my arm, rubbing it a little too harshly, like someone who learned empathy from watching others. I can tell she doesn't know how to act in this situation, which goes against every fiber of her being as someone who knows how to act in every situation.

"You sure about this?" she asks, her voice a ghost in the space between us. I can feel her dark assessing eyes on me, calculating, thinking through every version of what happens next, like if she can sift through her thoughts fast enough, look close enough, she'll find a jagged edge to grab, to catch me. This isn't that, though. This isn't some crisis to solve or a story we can laugh about later. This, right now—it's just this. My head against a cold window pane watching the blur of the interstate, ordinary, unremarkable, mundane and yet, there's an unmovable weight to it. Like the snapping of blinds in a too bright room, sunshine in an attic filled with dust you can suddenly see, a microwave you watch until the seconds run out because you need something to end. That's what this is, just an ordinary moment stretched thin around something I can't take back. I finally nod, shutting my eyes, letting the steady hum of the car absorb me, letting it bring me back to him.

"I don't want this with you." His voice is like wet paint, familiar and slippery. His gaze narrows, zeroing in on the hand on my belly, the one I've been unable to keep away since looking down at that stupid stick. I wonder if this is just an instinct, something ancient and hardwired in our anatomy. Or maybe it's a way for me to remember that I'm real, this is real. My face feels prickly and hot and I get that sensation you get right before you cry, like water up your nose or thickness in your throat. I let my eyes fixate on something on the floor, an Orange peel, just barely in view, brown with rot and curling inward.

"Sloane, we're here."

I look up, the Hospital sign glows through the windshield, not like a beacon, not a symbol or warning, just what it is. Words on a building.

"Are you sure you don't need me to come in there? I can cancel my interview. Seriously, it's just graduate school," Clem smiles, a joke that doesn't meet her eyes, that familiar sad smile, the one begging to carry the weight of this. She'd clean up every messy part of me if it meant she could make sure I'm okay. She loves me. She may be the only one who ever really has. The thought has me biting the inside of my cheek, trying to hold the feeling in its place, keep it from rising. Because I want to be alone. Maybe it's guilt, the craving to feel all of this. Every slow second.

"He'll be here Clem, I'm fine." I nod and I see the worry

flash in her eyes, the recognition that the typical Sloane performance has slipped, that she's leaving me at intermission.

"I love you, Sloane." She squeezes my arm again, but this time it isn't rehearsed.

The automatic doors open immediately after I get out of the car and I want to run to catch them, the space between me and them long and awkward and wrong. A few men and a woman are holding large picket signs to the left. They're graphic but also not displaying any sort of realistic imagery, just mutilated fully developed fetuses and murder written in bold red letters. I try to force myself to care about their message. Try to make myself see their point of view. As I approach, a woman in scrubs comes out to greet me, wrapping a long warm arm around my shoulders.

"Ignore them," she grits out, her jaw furiously clenched as she grimaces at the small crowd.

Normally I'd laugh, try to deflate the situation but that feels wrong, too—everything feels wrong. I think of Evie, how badly she wanted us. Imagine how she must have whispered that hope into the dark like a spell that might finally take, baby names etched in her heart that never reached her lips and for a second, I do feel bad. Not about the decision I'm making but for all of the women who break themselves trying to be what the world wants and never quite fitting. Who ache for something that never takes. Sometimes I wonder if being a woman is just grief in a million directions, longing for something that never comes, mourning what you choose to lose. Evie prayed for a child for years while I walk into this building to let one go and somehow we both feel like we failed.

"What's your name, sweetie?" The nurse asks, leading me to reception where she goes behind one of the gleaming computers, bathed in the blue light. I see the way her eyes crinkle at the edges, her lips slightly chapped. I wish I had the energy to make her life easier.

"Sloane." She nods at my response typing something into her keyboard.

"Okay, honey. I got you all checked in and you'll be called back in just a bit to run some tests before the procedure. Do you have someone who can drive you home today?" Her eyes meet mine and she must read something because she continues. "You'll need to have someone driving you due to the sedation. It's very mild, but still—you'll be groggy."

I roll my lips together.

"Yeah, sorry. I have someone coming, they're just a little late."

She gives me a tight lipped smile that registers something I don't before nodding to the chairs behind me. I take a seat, the blue plastic cold and hard as I flip through an STD pamphlet, carefully reading about each disease like I'm here for a quiz and not an abortion.

"Sloane Fielder," a kind voice comes through the door to my left, and I grab my bag, following a young brunette woman in light purple scrubs to one of the many patient rooms. She shuts the door, staring down at my chart. "How many pregnancies have you had?"

"One," I say, forcing myself to meet her eyes as I settle on the crinkly paper. They're brown, just brown and heavy. I wonder the toll it takes on her, having to deal with women at peak emotional exhaustion.

"Sorry...how many to completion?"

"Oh um..." She sits on a stool so she's level with my knees. Her smile is kinder than it should be. This is her job. She doesn't owe me this.

"Is this your first?"

I just nod because that lump is back in my throat and I

don't want to cry, don't want to burden her with that. She smiles and it's like a small pocket of air in the otherwise suffocating room.

"It's going to be okay. Everything feels hard now but if you're doing what's in your heart...it'll be okay." She tips her head back at her clipboard. "How many sexual partners do you have?"

"Just one."

She continues asking questions and then draws three vials of my blood before flicking off the lights.

"Okay honey. Lay back for me." I do what she says as she wheels over an ultrasound machine.

"Oh. I don't—" Panic flares in my chest.

"It's protocol. I'm sorry, but you don't have to look. Let me just—" Her voice is gentle,

practiced, as she tilts the monitor away so I can't see and tears flood my eyes because I should see, shouldn't I? Isn't that what my instincts should be telling me? To protect, to cling, to see? But my instincts are tangled, at war with my body which feels at war with my mind.

She spreads a warm gooey substance across the base of my stomach and for a moment the room is silent save for the quick clack of the keyboard. Seconds feel like minutes as I stare at the tiled ceiling, anchoring myself in the lines of grout. I feel a towel wipe away the goo and then feel a tissue on my arm. "Here," she says. "For your eyes."

"Thanks," I whisper, my voice hoarse.

"You opted for the D&C so we are going to send you back in just a few minutes once the room is prepped." Her voice falls into the steady rhythm of reciting information. "The procedure only takes about ten minutes but we'll monitor you for at least thirty while the sedation wears off. You'll have some bleeding, similar to a standard period that will last anywhere from two to three weeks. You have someone in the waiting room to drive you home?"

"He's on his way," I say, my voice flat and she gives me that same tight lipped smile I saw on the receptionist earlier. Like someone who wants to be kind but isn't sure how. It says, I see you but only as far as I'm allowed.

Minutes go by until she finally leads me back to the procedure room.

She was right: ten minutes. That was all that separated me from holding life and letting it go, the drugs making it feel even shorter, like seconds, the time it takes to light a candle and blow it out.

The brunette wheels me into the recovery room and says something that the sedative doesn't allow me to register. I watch her gesture toward the juice box and saltines on a table to my left. I take a small sip which earns me an appreciative smile.

"What name should we call in the waiting room? We want to inform them that you'll be leaving in the next thirty minutes. Give them a chance to pull their car around."

"Oh um, Elliot."

She nods, patting my shoulder gingerly before leaving. I lay back in the hospital recliner, closing my eyes and letting my hand find that spot on my belly, the one strange comfort in this entire ordeal and it feels the same, flat, soft, empty. I watch the sun shift in the blinds, letting my eyes close and reopen as I fight the endless sleep the painkillers brought on.

I'm awoken by the receptionist, her crinkled eyes worried as she gently rubs my arm.

"Sloane, we thought maybe he ran to grab a snack or something but it's been about thirty minutes and we still haven't seen him in the waiting area. Do you have a good number we can call for him?"

I blink the sleep away, letting what she's saying filter into my cloudy mind.

"Oh, I might have given him the wrong time. Could I use my phone to—" The nurse interrupts, rushing to grab my bag from the table on the farther end of the room.

"Yes of course." She hands me the bag and I find my phone flicking through it until I get to Elliot's name. It goes straight to voicemail. I smile to ease the worry in the woman's eyes and call again. Voicemail.

"He's probably on his way. Let me just text." I type out a quick message and stare at the blue screen, waiting.

"We'll give him a little more time, sweetie." The nurse looks uncomfortable, like maybe this isn't protocol but her pity outweighs the rules. Still she leaves me, staring at my phone. More time passes and finally my phone chimes.

ELLIOT

Sorry, running late. Be there soon. Xx

The brunette pops her head in. "Anything?"

I know she must need the room.

"He's almost here," I lie. A full hour passes before the receptionist comes in with a wheel chair to bring me out, which feels a bit ridiculous now that the sedation has completely worn off. Still, I abide by her rules, settling in the chair. I see him, in the reception area, hands in his pockets, a grin that feels out of place plastered on his face and I sense the nurse's displeasure. Normally, I would assume it was because of the age gap, but it's likely due to him being two hours late to his girlfriend's abortion.

"Sloane, if you need anything or have any questions at all, please give us a call." The nurse eyes me and it's obvious she wants to say more, wants to warn me of something I'm already aware of.

Elliot grabs the chair, not bothering to make eye contact with the woman and something about the slight makes me hate him. Not all of him—not yet. Just enough to fold into that little pocket of my heart that I refuse to fully open up and examine. We reach Delilah, her red paint glistening in the California sun and I wish I didn't let him drive her as I watch his fingers curl around her large steering wheel, sitting in the passenger seat of my own car.

"Well, you look fine." His voice is chipper and so at odds with the tone of my day. "I'm surprised they made you get a ride home," he chuckles at the hospital's ridiculous rules, unlatching the roof of the car. I don't have the fight in me to tell him I want the roof up as he pulls onto I-80.

I reach over, grasping his hand, letting myself feel a shred of comfort from the one person I think can understand. He glances over at me, his jaw hardening. "Why are you doing that?"

"What?" I blink, confusion rattling my mind.

"Holding my hand." He glances down where my hand covers his on the stick. I blink, nausea rising in the back of my throat before releasing him. "We're not doing that anymore, Sloane." His words tangle in the wind that blows from the car's open roof and I feel stunned and then mortified and I wish there was a button I could press to eject myself from this situation, let the passenger seat hurtle me into the ocean.

He pulls off the exit leading back to the student housing. I thought we were going to his place. His apartment that has all my stuff, my paints, my clothes. He silently pulls into a space just outside the duplex I share with a few girls in the program. Girls I barely have taken the time to know, so consumed by every moment with him.

"Look, Sloane..." His voice is imbued with the inevitable fade of an ending, the final notes of a song I'm not ready to be over. I search his eyes but there's nothing. No recognition of what I was to him and I wonder if I was ever anything at all, or just a means to an end, a muse to stroke his ego. Disposable, not serious.

"I think we should take some time. I need to focus right now with the new series I'm doing and with the whole—" He gestures at me, his hand smearing the air before me like a mess he wants to brush away. I sniff a breath and before I can open my mouth he opens the driver door, pulling my bags out of Delilah's trunk. The life I had with him in two duffles. "There may be some paint left behind. If I find them I'll bring them to class." He nods, wrapping my hand around the cold car keys.

I reach in every direction trying to grasp anything, a word, a plea, even an accusation but my thoughts crash in on themselves and I can't decide if I want to scream or cry, to push him away or pull him back.

"This isn't goodbye, Sloane. It's a see you later." He cocks his head at the Uber that seems to have materialized out of thin air before squeezing my shoulder and just like that, he's gone, so quick that I wonder if he ever existed.

Ten minutes, that's what the nurse said. Ten minutes. That's all that separates us from holding life and letting it go.

10

Andy

October

A harpist plucks a soft melody up on the balcony, warring for airtime while the DJ on the floor level spins a bass heavy mix for the sponsors getting wasted on Astor Hill Athletic's dime. A waiter offers me a glass of champagne and I throw it back far too fast, still tense from the car. I spot Grant in the distance, grinning at Ben, unshaken by the way he and Will almost brawled on the way here.

Logic didn't play a role in offering Grant a ride, nor did it make an appearance when Gen called me an hour ago, exasperated and needing me to pick Will up. He struggled to form a complete thought when I picked him up off the curb. He should be tucked into bed, not ordering more to drink.

I imagine the bar failing to keep him upright, hallucinate him tumbling to the ground, feel the ghost of a tremor in my hand like it could almost happen. He's so near falling apart, and I know I shouldn't have brought him. When he saunters back over to me, I notice his hollow gaze, the distractedness that has him blinking more than he should, and I prepare myself for a one sided conversation.

"Is that smart?" I ask him, nodding at his cocktail.

He crooks his finger at me, dipping his head as he smirks. "If I was sober, I wouldn't be here. And that's not an option," he slurs, his laugh bubbling over as he sips the drink.

I sigh, glancing around to make sure no one's listening. "Does this have to do with Gen, or Liv?" Asking him in the car was less than ideal.

He purses his lips, seriously considering which is gutting him more: that Gen reamed him out before kicking him out of his own car, or that Liv broke up with him last night—didn't come with him at all. In the distance, her dress flashes a metallic brown at the same moment I clock the back of Ben's head.

Jesus.

"Liv. Gen didn't help, though. She was so *mean*," he says thoughtfully, looking down at the marble tile. "Like, what the fuck did I do?"

"Well—" I start to say, desperate to remind him that Gen's loved him for years and he did fuck all about it until she moved on with Grant, but his face just falls. Like the sinew can't keep it together anymore, and I save it for some other time. "Don't think about them tonight. Worry about all of it tomorrow."

The rest of his drink goes down in one swift motion before he pats my shoulder and pushes past me and toward the coat check. The tug that tells me to follow him, to protect him from his own recklessness, is hard to push against, but I do. I pull in a deep breath, clearing my throat, and try to take my own advice for once.

I will worry about him tomorrow because tonight, I have a job to do. Basketball, this once sacred thing that was just for me, is something I'm now desperate for. I want play time; I want to be good; I want my team to need me for something real. This is a part I play willingly, and I won't fuck it up.

Wealth litters the parquet, packs the bar, and clings to each other's elbows. I scan the room, trying to decide who won't mind having their pockets wrung dry tonight. They've all given to the department; tonight is about giving more. Cutting bigger checks, pouring more of their cash into our athletics' department because you can never have enough, right?

That's the thought, anyway. Some of it goes to scholarships, the kind I would've been on if Glenn hadn't pulled his strings and paid my way. It isn't lost on me that I could've said no to all this and that my life would've been okay. That proximity to this is a luxury, not a hard won necessity. I chose this and, once upon a time, I wanted it all. So I take a step.

"Andy Spellman," someone says, her vocal fry dipping into something seductive. "You've proven to be quite the underdog."

I sigh and turn to face her, unsurprised by the interest pooling in her gaze. Pleased by the money dripping off of her.

For my first catch of the night, I guess she'll do.

"The season makes it tough," I explain, smiling tightly as the dean for the School of Fine Arts rolls his eyes, mouth twitching at the chief financial officer for some company based out of the Finger Lakes, of all places. "I'd love to spend more time on the stage but—"

"But we're not as prestigious as these guys, right?" Dean Withers winks at his wife, who grins over the lip of her champagne glass.

"Make me a better offer, Withers," I joke, letting my mouth slide into the kind of cocksure smirk that wins me some throaty laughs. "Promise me a lead." I lean in, feigning a whisper. "We won't tell anyone." More laughs, belly ones, so I throw up a hand and excuse myself, desperate for a minute alone.

The deserted foyer is good enough, so I lean against the cool wall and check my watch. Only an hour to go before Coach won't rip our heads off for heading home. I knock my head back and shut my eyes, letting the stillness of the hall float me anywhere but here.

In the quiet, in the dark, I let myself feel the disappointment. This is growing up, I think. Hard choices, realistic ones, laughing at the things you want because you can't actually have them. It's all funnier when you're the one making the joke. Hurts less when you buff out the edges of the otherwise sharp loss with your own amusement at what you once thought your life could be.

And it's not that I wanted to be an actor, but maybe just the time to do it at all. God, I never think of this and this is why—it fucking hurts to remember I'm not who I wanted to be.

The sharp clack of someone's heels jolts me out of my dark thoughts, and I straighten when Sloane Fielder's long legs rush past the massive olive tree jutting out of the floor before coming to a halt. Head cocked to the side she purses her lips, the ghost of a smile there.

"Ma'am, are you—" the door man, a nervous eyed student volunteer, stutters as he scrolls through what must be an invite list on a tablet.

"She's with me," I tell him, pushing off the wall.

Sloane's scoff skits across the polished floor. "I'm not," she clarifies.

I give the man a grim, apologetic smile as he wearily glances between us. Sloane's eyes dare him to kick her out and, of course, he doesn't. He walks backward and crouches behind his station, all but disappearing.

"You are everywhere you shouldn't be, aren't you?" I lean against a Roman column and she mirrors me, doing the same with a poorly concealed scowl.

"It's a *charity* gala—you're tellin' me it's actually 'invite only'?" Her arms cross over the baby pink fabric wrapped across her torso, and my gaze can't help but dip to the dark pants slung low across her hips.

"Kind of," I smirk, trailing my attention up her body until I'm met with dusky cheeks and twinkly eyes that catch the light from a distant disco ball. "So. Why *are* you here?" I eye her suspiciously, noting that the sliver of skin between her shirt and pants, and the floor length coat, don't meet the dress code.

"My brother invited me." Her shoulder hitches, her brow arching sky high, and she says *brother* like he's the king of fucking Egypt. I shouldn't find it funny, shouldn't be smiling within three feet of her, but I can't help it. "Oh, fuck off, Spellman. I've been to a million of these. I'm a Fielder. Why would I ever need to crash a charity gala?"

"Because you're a hellion." Shock has her eyes pulling wide, her mouth spreading into a toothy grin, a dimple deepening in her cheek, and it's electric, watching her anticipate my words. "Because you have a heart of gold," I say, emphatically, my brows pulling together in earnest as she tips her head back and laughs. "Or maybe you are stalking me," I add, shrugging.

Mouth popped open, Sloane looks at me. I look back, my sarcastic smirk melting into something I can't really control as my heart thrums. Her lips come together and curve just enough, and if I could look away I would but she's drawn me in and tied me there, right to her.

"I'm secretly rescuing a drunken Genevieve from a janitor's

closet," she finally says, her voice only softly carrying to right where I'm across from her.

"Oh." My throat bobs; my hands find my pockets. "So, heart of gold then."

She chuckles softly to herself, wetting her lips as she considers me. My skin warms, and I hope to god I'm not blushing.

"Who are you hidin' from?" she asks, not a hint of sarcasm in her southern lilt.

"Who says I'm hiding?" She flicks her brows, calling me on my bullshit. "Everyone," I admit with a small shake of my head, trying to cut the sincerity in half.

"Thought this was your scene, frat boy." A guarded smile pulls at the corner of glossed lips as she toes the marble with her shoe.

"Yeah...I did, too," I say, absentmindedly, wishing I could swallow the words as soon as they're out.

Like she can sense the embarrassment, she sighs, raking her finger through her hair. "You know, there's a song about that. About changin'."

I huff a laugh. "Lots of songs, actually."

She inhales sharply, anticipation lighting her gaze. "I'll burn you some."

"In the age of handheld devices?" I joke, heat pricking the back of my neck because anything from her is a bad idea. "I'll be fine, Sloane."

She rakes me over with her gaze, gnawing on her bottom lip. "You sure?" It's another genuine question, free of social conventions or politeness or what you should say. She looks at me, and I know she means it: *am I sure I'll be fine?*

"Course," I smirk, pushing back the unruly waves that've freed themselves from their pomade hold.

"Hmph," she hums, those dimples deepening again before

she finally lets her gaze fall away from me. She crosses the hall without a goodbye, just puts a finger to those lips in a silent shush before whispering: "You never saw me."

"Scouts honor," I tell her, even though I was never a scout, we were always too poor for that, and I was never interested in wearing a vest with patches my mom would have to iron on. Her eyes tip backwards and, somehow, I think she knows that.

It's always like this with her—separate, apart from everything else, even though I know it isn't. That isolated connection is an illusion, a trick of my over active imagination. The mind can't actually distinguish between reality and fiction, is the thing. So I feel the warmth of her attention long after she walks away, feel it in spite of the cool air that brushes past me as I walk out the building, just to take a lap. Get my thoughts together.

The fiction that is Sloane as an option, Sloane as a woman I could pursue without the devil on my shoulder, assaults me within seconds of stepping onto the sidewalk because a fire red Mustang convertible, oversized dice hanging from the mirror, is sloppily parked under the valet tent.

I walk past it, even though it looks so much like the one Luis sold when I was sixteen.

I keep walking, even though it reminds me of driving through the old orange groves with him.

I make it down the block and decide it wasn't even real, because what are the odds?

I get back to the revolving door and then, when I see that it's still standing there, I let myself get a glimpse of the license plate.

DELILAH

But of course I knew it was hers. God, I wish it wasn't hers. I love that it's hers when I shouldn't love anything about her at all. I cut back through the front door, pretending not to hear

Gen cooing on Sloane's shoulder at the end of the long hallway, shaking the smirks and the dimples and teasing and the look out of my mind, and head to the bar.

"Just a Jack and Coke." I pluck the crumpled ten dollar bill from my wallet and slide it across the counter, only for a crisp one to lay itself right on top.

"Make it a Manhattan," my father says, and I sniff, glancing in the opposite direction before looking at him. The gray at his temples would look distinguished if I didn't know it was more likely stress induced from being a career liar than from genetics. His watch swallows his wrist, and his suit, a crass sort of maroon with black lapels, looks too new and is ugly.

"Didn't know you were coming to this." The bartender nudges my drink toward me, but I don't take it.

"You'll find, Andrew, that there's a time to be hands off and a time to get those hands dirty. It's that way with basketball, right?"

"No, actually. It's not." My mouth feels dry, and I almost take the glass and satisfy that urge.

"Well, you wouldn't know, would you?" He knocks my shoulder, chuckling. "Not really a leader." He gazes straight ahead, mouth twisting before he sips the drink he ordered for me.

I eye him from the side, nodding to myself before turning to him, standing a little taller. "You come here to insult me, or?"

"No," he sighs, like he got away from himself for a second. "I came here to give to my favorite cause."

Back tense, I fist my hand at my side, flexing it like it'll calm the anxiety beginning to roil just beneath my skin. There's this look my father gets right before he pulls the rug out from someone. I've only seen it a few times, when he's been with a client and I've arrived at the townhouse early. Right now, he's giving it to me.

"The Lions?" I ask, stupidly. My molars grind.

My father's mouth pulls into a tight grimace as he looks straight ahead. "*You*. But I just saw you making heart eyes at the Fielder girl. And I sure as hell don't think you have a clue where William is. Do you?" His voice is a low murmur, the words carefully enunciated so that there's no confusion, but soft enough that only I can hear him. It's practiced. He's practiced.

I swallow, cracking my neck. "He's an adult. He can handle himself."

"Then why the fuck do I pay you to do it?" He turns sharply, blinking at me furious. "You know, I haven't had to worry about you. You do what you're told. Not like Ian—never listened, not a day in his life. Not to me anyway. But when I found you, Andrew, I knew you'd be good. What happened?" Glenn's eyes sadden, and I wonder, for a split second, if he might actually care. They slide into disgust not even a moment later. "Eye on the ball, son. You're gonna let some girl distract you? Mess up all your hard work, and for what?" He cranes his head so he can look me right in the eye. "For what?"

My jaw flexes. "I'm not distracted."

He studies me, some of his anger boiling off after a short inhale. "Good. Tell me about her." Another drink makes its way across the bar, and this time, he makes sure I take it.

The drink makes this easier; everything tastes bitter, including the words clawing their way up my throat. "She's, uh...a painter." He nods, like he knows this, because he does. "And she's...running. I think. I don't know. She hasn't told me. Really, she hasn't told me anything important." Shame drops heavy in my stomach, drapes itself across my shoulders like it belongs there and I think it does. Any attempt to forget the shame is naive; when you hide the things I've hid and lie the lies I've lied, shame is part of the bargain.

He nods to himself, appeased by still musing over something. "What I need is to know if she's talked to a reporter," he says, tipping the rest of his drink back, craning his head more than he needs, all while guilt sluices down my spine. "And if she hasn't—make sure she doesn't."

"Got it," I murmur, trying to let the task rest lightly within me as I take in a measured breath. My father, for his part, just walks straight out the door without confirmation that my agreement is good enough for him, and without a glance at Ian, who lingers by the spiral staircase.

Something needs to be said, but what—I don't know. 'I'm sorry' seems insufficient and out of place, because what am I even sorry for? That he threatened me but didn't give him a hug? I start to move toward my brother, like his grace will do what I can't do for myself, but the air in the room shifts.

From across the ball room, I hear Will's voice crack as he says, "And *you*." There's a pause, and I don't even have to turn my head to know who he's talking to. "If you want to fuck her so bad, do it."

My eyes go wide the moment Ian's do, and I rush toward the sound of fist against bone, of Olivia's hoarse shouts, of the unrestrained whispers that are just rehashed tidbit's from Ian's fucking column.

I whirl on him, knowing he can't be far behind. "You," I sneer. "You need to go. This is not fodder for your piece of shit gossip blog." Liv's screams fade, and when I glance down the room, I can just make out Ben's pallid face. It's the face I imagine someone makes when they've been gutted. When their intestines are being laid out in front of them. He's making this face, and it's Olivia he can't take his eyes from.

"I didn't make them do anything. If Olivia was doing her

job, this wouldn't even be happening." His face looks hot to the touch, like he could burst, but not from glee. From anticipation, maybe.

"What are you talking about?" I wince as Liv pulls past me, dabbing Will's face with a towel as they shuffle out the front doors. The room that had just fallen to a murmur now balloons with sick excitement. It'll be everywhere tomorrow—I know it.

Ian's gaze locks on mine, buffering on a thought I can tell he's desperate to share, but he decides against it. Shakes his head, scoffs, rolls his eyes like he can't be bothered with me.

Out the glass doorway, I can see Will, in his blood stained three piece tux, and Olivia, in her floor length chocolate gown, the tips of her hair wet with blood, too, quietly arguing as they wait for a car. It pulls up, and she carefully folds him into the passenger seat, her face drawn tight with anguish.

"Unbelievable," Ian huffs out, watching with silent fury in his gaze as they drive away.

It's all a mess—a horrible mountain of the worst things we can do to each other—all of it. Painful and twisted, and he is standing here, stringing together a headline. And for who? For what?

"When you write about this tomorrow, I hope you know that you're scum." I push past him, my shoulder roughly knocking him. Standing on the pavement, waiting for my car, I stare into the endless night sky and wonder if somewhere, on a star I can't see, is a different version of all this. If somewhere, it's all unfolding, but everything is good.

11

Sloane

"This one is my favorite," Elliot says, brushing his hand across the muddled colors on my canvas.

"Oh," I huff, part laugh, part sarcasm. "Thanks."

"Don't you want to know why?" He turns toward me, the smile on his lips meeting his eyes.

I pull in a breath. "Sure," I tell him, smiling tight. He does this: pretends he's into something when he isn't. He enjoys bringing students to the edge of glory, only to take it away. At first, we all thought he was just an asshole, but he has imparted some artistic wisdom to us. I'm bracing myself because I'm ninety percent sure he's going to say the dark image before us, a stark deviation from what I've been doing all summer, is convoluted trash. But he said "paint what we feel" rather than giving us a prompt. So I painted the complicated feelings around my mother.

"I'm drawn to this," he says, lowering his voice so only I can hear as he faces the piece, "because it's like a wound. See the way you're not afraid to let the colors blend? There's no definition." He traces a barely there line on the canvas. "You almost try to control it, try to box it in, but then it just...falls apart."

My breath feels shallow, and each one feels like a feeble attempt at trying to catch oxygen.

"You don't see it?" he asks, tilting his head as he searches my eyes. I purse my lips and cross my arms like it'll ward against whatever vulnerability rays he's shooting me with.

"I'm just surprised you did," I say, and he narrows his eyes in confusion. "I was expecting somethin' flippant. Not profound."

"Well. You surprised me, Sloane," he smirks, and it's this dazzling smile that erases the lines between professor and student. Novice and legend. "Take the compliment."

My alarm shatters the vignette. I was sleeping restlessly anyway after the art show and then from picking up Gen, who was a mess, from the janitor's closet she'd been hiding in with my brother at the charity gala last night. Worse than a mess if her multiple attempts to empty her guts over the side of Delilah were any indication. In my sleepless delirium, I keep having these vivid dreams that are just memories of Elliot.

I sit up, sipping from the glass of now lukewarm water beside me, the condensation from the melted ice now a puddle on the dresser. Water colors are everywhere, their slim palettes littering every table top available to me and I know if Grant came in he'd have a cow. I sigh, beginning to put them in small stacks the way I stored them back at school. My thumb brushes a thick tube of blue oil paint, one I brought home from the theatre to experiment with technique. Now seems as good a time as any considering any actual inspiration feels like a distant memory.

I sit cross legged at a large canvas propped against the far wall of the bedroom and squeeze the tub out on one of the paper plates I ate pizza off of a few nights ago. I bite the inside of my cheek trying to remember everything Evie told me about oils, how finicky they are, how permanent. *You can always make it into something new, texture is your friend, it tells the story of what you were and how you became what you are.* I sigh, letting the small scalpel like tool I also swiped from backstage at the ballet and slathering thick layers of the blue onto the canvas. I'm doing this wrong. Why the fuck did I tell them I could do oil. I grab for my phone on the mattress, hoping to find a good youtube on oil technique. I could call Evie but I've learned the hard way that if you crack the door even slightly she'll try to kick it wide open.

I unlock the screen just as a text appears.

JEAN

Open up whore.

I smile, trotting into the living room, I couldn't have asked for a more perfect time for a distraction. I swing open the door and there's Jean, arms wrapped around breakfast sandwiches and iced coffees, a cropped band tee that just barely hits the waist band of his wide leg slouchy jeans. His wavy hair is perfectly messy, and a cigarette dangles from his lips. I snag it taking a puff before flicking it out the door and letting him in. He immediately drops the goods on the counter, looking around my brother's place.

"Where is he?" he says in a hushed tone.

"The gym probably," I tell him, rolling my eyes at the satisfied huff that leaves his throat. "Alright—do *not* make a sound like that about my brother ever again."

He sighs, feigning defeat. "I guess that's fair," he smirks, snagging the iced drink that seems more milk than coffee from the counter as he eyes me. "You look tired, babe."

"Hmph," is all I say, grabbing what I assume is mine and taking a long sip.

"What's going on?" His voice turns solemn, more solemn than I've heard it in the short history of our friendship, and it's a comfort I didn't realize I even wanted.

I purse my lips, taking a deep breath. "I didn't sleep."

"*Obviously*," he smiles gently, tilting his head. "Who is he, and how do I find him?"

I scoff, turning my head and he narrows his eyes.

"Somethings bothering you, you're usually much more... spritely?"

"Spritely?" I chuckle and roll my eyes. I know he's right, there is something, a slow pull at the base of my stomach that never really goes away but seems a little stronger lately. I could pretend I don't know why, usually I do. But why not tell Jean? Maybe it'll help unwind whatever's furled up inside me, to let one person in. I let out a long breath, perching myself on the bar stool at the counter. His eyes shine with mirth and expectation but something in my face changes him because all of a sudden he's serious. A look I haven't really seen on him before but somehow makes him even more handsome. "My internship at that gallery, that I was tellin' you about?" He nods. "My...professor got me that."

He says nothing, just barely narrows his eyes in concentration.

"But at that point, he wasn't *just* my professor," I admit, and just the telling of it makes me feel a little lighter. I realize I haven't said this to anyone.

Jean tries to fight the surprise on his face, but fails. "Okay. That's...problematic?" He studies me and I feel my walls start to rise, defensive of a choice I know was the wrong one. His face starts to fall, "Fuck, Sloane. Did he—"

"No! *No,*" I reiterate, desperate not to make this something it wasn't. To minimize. It was two consenting adults falling in love, or maybe one- for the falling in love part. "He just," I start to say, my voice small, "he'd done the same kind of thing before. I was dumb and took it more seriously than him."

His shoulders fall and he put his coffee on the counter

before taking my hands. "I need you to hear me, Sloane. You *are not* dumb. Some asshole exploiting your naiveté doesn't say anything about you."

Tears press at the backs of my eyes, and I blink hard against them. "No I know," I say, not believing it. I let myself trust the things Elliot said to me; I let myself believe he would be there for me no matter what.

"But...?" Jean presses, and I purse my lips. "I know there's something else. Usually, you can't shut up."

I swat at his arm, missing him when he leans back, laughing.

"Do you...miss him?"

"A lot." I train my gaze just past him, the admission feels like I crashed head on into something I've been avoiding. "When we were together, I felt all this passion. Like I couldn't stop creating. I was his muse but he was also mine. We were lost in each other's artistry. It was *intense* and... I was so lost in it that when it ended, I think something broke in me." I almost want to tell him the rest, but I can't.

"Sloane you're not broken, you're perfect." he says, his voice small and gentle like he's afraid to contribute to the fracture.

"No I'm broken Jean, I can't paint. Like for myself—I can't do it. I had never needed anyone to help me paint. It feels like all that passion, that sureness was wrung out of me and I don't know how to get it back and now with this reporter..."

"Reporter?" Jean's voice moves to curiosity as he examines me, his eyes softer than I've ever seen them.

"I'm being harassed by a reporter doing a story about all his *victims*." I shake my head, quoting the word hollowly because maybe that is what I am, it's certainly how people have painted me.

"Maybe you should talk to her—"

"No!" I cut him off, a sharp silence wedging between us and I use my fingers crusted with blue paint to squeeze the bridge of my nose. "I'm sorry I just—I can't, not with everything going on. My parents don't even know I left California, if they found this out..." I shake my head and Jean appears beside me squeezing my shoulder.

"You don't ever have to explain yourself to me." He rubs my back and my heart warms with the realization of how lucky I am to have found this boy in the mess of my life. "What was his name again?" Jean says, some levity enters his voice as his voice shudders with mock violence, shoulders squared, he pulls his phone out. "Maybe torching his shit will bring your inspiration back."

"Stop," I chuckle, sniffing back the little bit of emotion that bled over. "It's not his fault."

"I'm sorry," he says, brows furrowing. "Sloane Fielder? Are you in there?"

A laugh pulls from deep within me. "Entirely. It's not his fault *entirely*. I should've known better than to let a man be anythin' at all."

"Well, he's officially on my shit list. Where do these old ass men get off abusing their power like that? Trying, but *failing*, to derail a woman like you?" He rolls his eyes, taking another sip of coffee.

I snap my head towards him. "I'm not derailed."

"*Failing*," he says pointedly and his lips quirk in a knowing grin.

"Speaking of men—" I sigh, tilting my head. A natural point to resteer the conversation away from myself.

"*What?*" he moans, knowing what's coming as he sets his iced coffee back on the counter.

"Do you want to tell me about Ian bein' at your house this mornin'?" I raise my eyebrows pressing my lips together.

He pulls in a deep breath. "You know, it's not even that I don't love him. Cause I do."

"Sure," I tell him, tilting my head. "But?"

"He's my person, like, ninety percent of the time. But what he does with the paper is just...we always fight about it. And then that turns into fights about other things but its values, right? That's what any fight's about?" He flicks his gaze up from where it's been resting on the counter, and I wish I could tell him that wasn't true. That some confrontations were superficial, could easily be solved by a quick concession. But I knew, more than most, that fault lines run deep.

"Yeah," I concede, my lips shrugging, and I grab his hands. "But I also think sometimes we're arguin' the same thing. That our principles are really the same, but principles in practice can be more complicated." I say it for myself as much as him, because it reminds me that Grant's the same, that his heart is in the right place when it comes to the whole Connie thing, just in a different place than mine.

Every time I've brought it up, he balks, and I just shelve it for later. If he can love our adoptive parents enough to join the family company, to give up his basketball dreams, then he can muster the strength to go see his birth mother. I know he can; know that in principle making amends with Connie would be important to him. But he's scared. And instead of saying that, he's just an asshole but maybe I am too.

Jean nods, checking the time on his phone. "So—what are we doing about our third troubled soul?"

"Well," I start, thankful for the pivot. "First, I need to call in a favor. You have Andrew's number?" I fan out my palm, only for him to contort his face in disbelief.

"Why does *Spellman* owe you a favor?"

"That's between him and I," I say, keeping my expression steady, implicitly knowing that his sister and her worn backpack are not common knowledge. "But I need him to bring Grant out tonight."

"Cause they're thick as thieves," he shakes his head, huffing a laugh.

"Well Will's out of commission and apparently, so is Ben. And I don't know anyone else on that team."

"You just keep bringing him up. You *danced* with him at that art show." I roll my eyes, but I know my cheeks are a powdery pink giveaway. "Sloane," he chides, like we're kids on the playground spying my crush on the monkey bars. "He's gorgeous. You could do worse. And maybe...you need to get under someone new." His eyes twinkle, his trademark mischievousness on full display.

Rolling my eyes, I turn my back toward him, eager not to have to strain myself into a mask of ambivalence. "The last thing either of us needs is another man to tangle our lives," I say, but he's not wrong. I could do *much* worse. Grant's well on his way to a quiet happiness with Gen, courtesy of *me*, and I think that, maybe, someone new and unserious is exactly what the doctor ordered.

12

Andy

The restaurant door bell chimes for the tenth time since I got here and, I swear, my head might crack open, right on this table. I squint past the rows of cookie cutter booths, their sleek sage green benches the opposite vibe of Vida's, whose weekend endless mimosas would probably cure my hangover.

Clutching the ice water I'm committed to finishing I finally spot Will saunter in. Even behind his shades, I can see where Ben attempted to obliterate his eye socket. The closer he gets, the more I can see the intensity of the bruising. I'm confident it's throbbing with pain, if the harsh set of his already strong jaw is any indication. He slides into the bench across from me, wincing, and I remember that Ben got way more than one shot in.

There was only one person *truly* to blame for what went down last night, but at this point it doesn't matter that Ben should've stayed away from Liv. That he shouldn't have poured salt into whatever wounds were already festering between them. Because he did...and Will took the fucking bait.

Before I get a chance at a good look, he props the menu up

—an additional layer of armor beyond the sunglasses and the hoodie pulled up around his head. I gently pull it down, grimacing.

"You...look like shit." I watch carefully for a sign of life. I know that Will really only has two roads he tends to go down: the dark, emotionally volatile one from last night or the shallow one buffered by his humor and feigned ignorance.

When he lets the menu fall, I'm shocked to find he's not half way down either road. There's a stoicism in his gaze that freaks me out. He swallows hard, shooting his gaze down at the table.

"Yeah," he says on an exhale that feels years in the making.

"He's right you know—" Mom takes a steaming cup of coffee off her tray, sliding it over to Will's side of the booth and he gives her a rare, genuine smile. What started as Mom temporarily working at the diner until she got her sea legs in Boston turned into a full time management role, but she always finds an apron to tie on when Will and I come in.

"*I've got to serve my boys!*" she'll mutter, fussing over menus and burying us in stacks of free pancakes.

"Hi, Ms. Spellman." His grin turns to the one he uses on the women he's trying to pick up and Mom swats him over the head with a menu.

"Don't try that move with me. What's with the eye?" She crosses her arms and I chuckle. Will slumps in his seat.

"I fell off a bike." "He fell down some steps," we say in unison.

"Uh huh..." Mom nods. "You know what—it's probably better if I don't know. The usual?" Will nods and she rolls her eyes, a small motherly scowl deepening the lines around her mouth.

"Oh wait!" He digs into the back pack he had over his shoulder when he walked in digging out a little egg that contains some weird slime thing both he and Carmen have been obsessed with the past couple months. "For Carm." A smile leaks through my mother's previously frustrated face.

"You make it hard to stay mad." She shakes her head. "I'll be back with ice," she says, almost like a threat, her finger jutting toward him. He laughs as she turns and walks back to the clash and clang of the kitchen.

I sit back, taking him in and shit is an understatement. He looks like he has yet to sleep and I can still smell the alcohol on him. "How are you?" I dare to ask, even though I know it's a stupid question.

"I messed up...everything." He slouches back into the booth, pressing his hand into his unbruised eye socket. When he finally lets up, his eyes are bloodshot to hell.

"But Liv took you home?"

"She went home with me because she's actually a good person."

"Well, that's up for debate," I say, risking a slight chuckle. He smiles, just barely. "I mean, they're in the wrong, Will. You're not perfect, but you didn't deserve that." Finding your girlfriend—technically *ex*, but whatever—in your brother's arm on the dance floor must've been a gut punch. I can't blame him for being angry, even if he doesn't have the most tactful approach to confrontation.

As if he reads my mind, he shakes his head. "I shouldn't have said all that shit to her. I've hurt her enough," he adds, but it's mumbled and I know it wasn't for me. It was some small admission to himself that sits awkwardly in my chest because I don't know what he means. And I thought he told me everything.

"Have you, uh, talked to Gen?" I side step the comment, knowing he'll tell me when he's ready.

"Nope. Blew that up, too," he says, looking up with a

disbelieving glint in his eyes. Like he's in awe of what a shit show his life is. His laughter is soft rumble as Mom comes back with an orange juice, setting it down only to get flagged by another table in the corner. As soon as she's out of sight he pulls out a tiny bottle of vodka, dumping it into his cup.

"Sure that's a good idea?" I wince.

"Hair of the dog," he shrugs, taking a sip and closing his eyes as he does it, as if this is his first drink in years, not in the span of an hour. I sigh, wrinkling my nose and he raises an eyebrow. "A bit judgmental for a guy I've seen hammered more times than I can count."

He's right, but this feels different somehow. Back then we were drinking for fun. Right now it feels like he's punishing himself, but for what, I'm unsure. Maybe I get it, though. Olivia and Will were a weird sort of promise that we all bore witness to and without them, it feels like everything else is free game. Like anything can be brought into question.

He blinks into the blank space before pulling in a deep breath. "Do you think I'm codependent?"

Yes.

"No," I laugh, shaking my head, but he just dips his brow at me. "Who cares if you are?"

"Liv said I...possessed her." He breathes a sigh of relief as his spiked orange juice appears in front of him. "And losing her feels like that. Like I lost *something*. Like I could lose every-thing." He stares into his drink before tipping it back, his throat bobbing with each impressive gulp. I reach out and pull his arm down, forcing him to pace himself.

"Okay, let's not jump off a cliff," I chuckle, trying to bring him back to reality. "You got broken up with. Your childhood best friend called you out on your shit." He winces at the mention of Gen, but he has to know I'm right. Showing up to her place before the gala shit faced was a terrible *and* irresponsible move. "And you're on your own, really...for the first time in your adult life."

He looks at me, startled. "Shit. You're right."

I sit back, feeling smug and relieved. "Just...take it one day at a time, man. Eat your body weight in pancakes," I say as I watch mom tray up entirely too much food across the restaurant, "go slow on the liquor, and give yourself some grace."

"Grace," he repeats like it's a foreign word, and he retreats back into the dark abyss of his inner turmoil for a moment.

"Hey," I bark, getting his attention. "I'm serious. I'm here for you. I care about you. There *is* another side, and you will get there." It comes out like a reminder, not just to him but to myself and guilt flows through me like poison in a wound, stinging until the words feel sour in my mouth. I wish I could be the man I say I am, wish I wasn't the real snake in the grass, the one that makes his brother's misgivings look pitiful in comparison.

He exhales, leaning back into a stretch that has him expanding into the bench before he right himself. A genuine smile, the first all morning, finally graces his face and it's another punch to the gut. I wonder if he can see the guilt the way I can feel it pulse in my temples.

"Thanks," he says right, as Mom sets down a plate with what appears to be a half pound of bacon on it. Will snags a slice before it can hit the table.

"I have to go to the back and do the schedules for next week so I might not see you boys before you leave. William, you're coming for dinner soon, right?" she asks, hands on her hips, but it's not really a question.

"Yes ma'am."

"Good." She pats his head before turning to me. "Love you." She squeezes my shoulder before disappearing into the hustle and bustle of the restaurant.

Will cuts out a large bite of syrupy pancake pausing before it disappears into his mouth. "Wait—why are *you* here and not in some girl's bed?"

I breathe out, letting myself melt back into who I let Will know me to be. I start to make up some excuse, saying I was doing damage control with him for Coach, but my phone dings.

256-400-5143

Hi! calling in that favor if ur free tonight?

I stare at my phone a second too long which has Will snagging it from me without giving me a second to blink.

"A favor?" He wiggles his eyebrows and I'm glad for the momentary respite into normalcy. I watch him type in a reply, crossing my arms over my chest.

"Dude what the fuck? *Sloane Fielder* is hitting you up?" Amusement laces his tone, and he almost looks sober as he wrinkles his face at my phone.

"Stop—" I blurt, attempting to snatch it back but he fakes left, shouldering me before I can grab it. "Will, please. It's really not like that with—"

"Just trust me." I can hear the grin in his voice as he thumbs out a response to whatever Sloane sent him. I tilt my head backward, looking up at the fluorescently lit linoleum ceiling.

I shouldn't even care. I don't know what it is about her; normally, I'd be fine digging up some dirt on a one night stand. But Sloane isn't even that. We're not sleeping together. It'd be better if we had because then I could've put her in the back mirror.

Instead, I'm forced to admit that I'm letting my father slowly melt away any ounce of humanity I have left in exchange for the chance to what? Attend a school of fractured rich kids with big wallets but broken souls? At least I know after all is said and done we'll have that in common. I came here naive, wanting to be one of them and I'm sure as hell leaving that way. Dad made sure of that, forcing me to choke her with the same web that Will's currently strangled in.

"Done." He slides my phone back across the booth, amusement lighting his eyes, almost distracting from his battered face.

"What's done?" I groan, flicking my phone open only to find out Will agreed to taking Grant—not even Sloane, but her brother—to a party tonight. Relief ebbs my mounting anxiety as I slip my cell into my pocket, and my mind quiets slightly at the knowledge that I won't have to spill the secrets of both Will and Sloane in a single day.

"A date with her brother is your version of *done*? I thought you said to trust you. " I take a sip of my coffee, letting mock frustration ring in my tone.

"Cheers," he starts, raising his mug of vodka and orange juice jovially, "to the last person in Boston to trust me." His smile is hollow as he swallows his screwdriver in one go.

I wish I could help him, I mean really help him. Introduce him to the life I had before coming here, something quieter, easier, another option.

My phone buzzes again, Sloane's now saved contact, courtesy of Will, flashing before me.

SLOANE

don't worry i'll be there too!

* * *

The address Sloane sent me leads deep into the woods. I've

been to a few keggers out here but typically try to stay a little closer to campus.

"You bringin' me out here to murder me, Spellman?" Grant asks, his gaze remains hard on the road.

"Ah, you caught me. Guess we have to turn around," I joke but he, of course, doesn't laugh. Doesn't even crack a smile. "Tough crowd," I mumble under my breath.

It's pitch black out here, the presence of street lights a distant memory as we make the trek to what Sloane called the party of the year. I make a sharp turn, and my headlights finally land on a string of cars parked off the road that lead to the long rolling driveway of someone's vacation home, I assume. I parallel park, thankful to get out of the silent car. The door swings open to unveil the steady bumping of speakers, letting me know we are in the right place.

"You ready?"

Grant just nods, tight lipped and I sigh. I know the guy hates Will and I probably didn't earn any points when I agreed to give him a ride to the gala last night and showed up with Will in the passenger seat. I should've seen their tense car conversation, in such close quarters, from a *mile* away. But I didn't, because when any of the guys need a favor, I don't even blink. Still—not one smile, laugh or conversation the entire drive to this damn party. It was brutal.

Inside it's like the entire campus has shifted into this singular house. I look around the sea of familiar faces, most of which are already trashed. Grant's arms are crossed and his mouth's set in a line. I can't help but feel bad for the guy. I got the idea that maybe this was about Gen when Sloane texted me right before I left double checking that Will was out of commission for the evening. Seeing Grant now though, it's obvious: the only person who can make a man down and out like this, is a woman.

"Look, I'm trying to make last night up to you. I should've told you he was in the car." I watch Grant's eyes go from murderous to only a slight promise of violence as he gives me a stiff nod.

"You should've."

"I didn't realize it was going to be like...that. The bar with Gen? I thought that was a fluke." He stares at the endless sea of our peers filling every crevice of the house and I can tell he's looking for her. "Look, this will be a good time. Sloane said you need to get out of your head, anyway. So just try to ha—"

"Why are you talking to Sloane?" Any simmering rage has now been fully brought to a boil at the mere mention of his sister's name.

Don't tell him I sent you. That and don't invite Will were her only instructions.

"We're...friends." The word feels hollow and wrong in my mouth. "She said you seemed in your head and she said she'd... owe me a favor if I could get you here."

Grant chuckles beside me and I know how fucking pathetic it sounds the moment I say it.

"You have an interesting definition of friends." He claps me on the shoulder and for a second it destabilizes me, because he's right, a friend probably wouldn't siphon information to their father in exchange for tuition and they sure as hell wouldn't agree to keep tabs on your every move. I sigh and as if he can sense my discomfort he finally throws me a bone. "The least you can do is show me a good time." He nudges me forward into the pool of bodies and the night ahead.

13

Andy

"So my roommate isn't going to be home tonight...I mean, if you don't have plans." The girl—Meg—has blue strands that fall around her face and I should want to brush them back, trail my lips across it and take her up on her offer. Going through the motions has been easy—it's muscle memory for me. But it's half-assed. A sad attempt at interest that Meg is not committed to noticing. Scott slaps me on the back before I have time to answer her.

"Ay, you up for some beer pong?" Scott is clearly intoxicated as he usually is at these sorts of things.

"I'm good, man. I just played with Grant."

He looks at me, his face morphing into something comical, his bewilderment clear.

"Grant? What the fuck? Didn't you hear about Ben and Will?" I roll my eyes and sigh, lifting my hand off the wall where it was resting right above Meg's head. I tilt my head in the opposite direction, insinuating I'll catch up with her later, and she goes, eyes heavy with lust. I straighten, crossing my arms.

"Yes Scott. I was there."

Scout's mouth is set in a pout, and I know he can hear my annoyance. "We aren't friends with Grant. Will would flip the fuck out if he—"

"Have you tried growing up, Scott?" I shake my head at him like he's an idiot because he is, and shove my hands in my pockets, scanning the crowd. He mutters something under his breath, but I ignore him, waiting for him to walk away as I scan the room for Meg, finding her at the bar. But in the center of the room is a tall mess of blonde hair that wasn't here twenty minutes ago, swaying to a song I've never heard. Scott, still within two feet of me, follows my gaze.

"So you do have an ulterior motive...shouldn't be hard. I heard she gets around," he snickers, nudging me with his elbow and I can't stop my scowl. I wonder if he can see the guilt binding itself around my ribs, because I do have an ulterior motive with Sloane, whether I like it or not.

"Scott. Shut the fuck up."

I push past him and decide to walk towards Meg—the woman waiting for me, who's a chess champion, who's laugh is soft and forgiving, who's uncomplicated and who's touch doesn't do a thing to me except what it scientifically should. No magic. Just a reaction, untethered from anything that lasts.

I pivot toward the kitchen bar, really meaning to meet her, not ready to do the fucked up thing I'm supposed to be doing to Sloane. But somewhere along the way, I decide to wander through the crowd, not around it, because the need to get just a little closer is all consuming, even as it's tinged with hot dread. Keeping a few people between us as I move, I just let myself look.

Eyes closed. Long tanned limbs moving fluidly to the pop song blaring from the speakers. Cowboy boots on her feet and an oversized, distressed t-shirt that hides the shorts that may or may not be there hung over her deceptively athletic frame. Glitter on those eye lids. Unbothered and innocent, and it feels unfair that she's ended up in my father's crosshairs.

"Spellman!" Josiah throws an arm around me and I watch Sloane's eyes snap open, catching me looking. A small, mischievous grin lights up her face and I quickly turn to Josiah, trying to seem busy, *trying* to look like I wasn't fixated on her.

"Yo, bro—you in love?" Josiah smiles and I wonder how long I was looking.

"Just taking in the sights." I give him a douchey grin to cover it all up.

"Yeah, man. You and every other guy here." He nods to the guys I clocked looking at Sloane and I feel rage heat the pit of my stomach. "Shit, looks like someone beat you to it."

I turn and spot Ryan McMahon, one of the hockey guys, with his hands firmly planted on Sloane's waist. The hem of her shirt dress leaving little to the imagination as she sways, her ass way too close to the guy for it to be a first encounter. My jaw clenches and my whole body feels on fire, even though I'm the *last* person who gets to feel possessive over her.

"Damn Andy, don't kill the guy. Besides, weren't you talking to that blue haired chick? Where'd she go?" I glance over at the bar where Meg is sipping a drink and staring at her phone, oblivious. I look back over at Sloane who seems to have forgotten my existence entirely, her attention fully on Ryan.

The sight burns, has that jealousy warming my chest, but I know it's not really jealousy. It's self-pity that I can't do what I usually do, can't just talk her up all night, and fall into her like I swear she'd want to fall into me if it weren't for her brother.

It's self-hatred, the kind that's never stayed around this long.

And isn't it the path of least resistance that solves most problems? If this is the source of my angst, then through it, not around it, is the only way to the other side. There, in a post-Sloane world, things won't be complicated and I won't be putting everything at risk.

"I'm not sure," I mumble to Josiah, taking the path that brings me closest to the woman who, unintentionally, has become the most beautiful bane of my existence, only halfway committed to snuffing out this feeling between us. Suddenly, I'm close enough that her citrus and sugar and woodsmoke lap against me, a taunt only I can feel.

"Hey, man," Ryan chuckles, offering me a fist to bump while his other hand still clings to her waist.

Adrenaline rushes through my veins like waves pummeling the sea shore when I give him a quick hey in return, when Sloane hears me, spins in Ryan's hold, and gazes up at me as her hips grind into him.

"Hey, you," she shouts above the music, still moving. I grind my teeth, willing myself not to care.

"You know Grant's sister?" Ryan says, his grin toothy and dumb while he shakes his head in disbelief.

Envy sticks to every inch of my skin and this close to her, it threatens to pull me under. My pulse taps erratically as I shift my gaze downward, locking with those deep sea eyes. And I can't do it, can't utter a single thing that would make sense because all I *need* to know is if she's talked to some fucking reporter, but all I *want* to ask is if she'd go out with me sometime. If she'd look past all the assumptions she, rightly, made about me and take a chance because I can't shake her out of my damn mind.

Instead, I muster a crooked smile and brush past the two of them, like the coward I am.

"Andy," she calls after me, her finger tips brushing my wrist and I pause in the empty space of a doorway, cracked open to let the cool October breeze filter into the foggy house. "I didn't get to say thank you."

The bridge of her nose, her cheekbones—they glisten with sweat. Her chest rises and falls and my heart pulses loudly in my ear drums, every other sound in the room warping until it's really just us and the night air that softly whispers.

"It's fine," I manage to mutter. "I owed you."

She narrows her eyes. "Did I do somethin'?"

I can see the way her cheeks pulls inward, get clamped between her teeth. Her usual breeziness recedes, and I can see the thin resolve in her gaze. Like me, of all people, could break the invisible dam I'm just now realizing is probably always there.

She asked if I would be fine and now I, in the midst of this damp room, need to know if she is. Her eyes silently beg me to explain my sudden indifference but I can't without telling it all. So I just recoil at myself, internally, far beneath the surface, and keep my real questions there.

"Why would I be mad at you?" I feel my eyes crinkle at the corners when I force a subtle smile. It disarms her like I hoped it would and she sucks her teeth, purses her lips the way she does before she toys with you, and I wait for it. Hungry for it.

"Oh, I have no idea." She pushes her hip out, letting her head fall the opposite way as she studies me, the confident steel in eyes reassembling itself. "I've really been sweet as pie. Offered to make you a sad boy mix CD..." She shakes her head.

"That I would have no way of playing..." I muse, dipping my head against my better judgment. A blush wisps across her cheeks.

"My car's got a real fancy receiver. Installed it myself."

"Look at you. Generous *and* handy...sweet as pie," I joke, counting off, ignoring the easy feeling. "Heart of gold."

"Exactly. Which is why for the life of me, I can't figure out why you're actin' like you didn't try to jump my bones the moment you met me." The dimples in both cheeks deepen, her blush turning rosy, like the mention of that night embarrasses her too.

I bite back a smile. A real one. "Is that what you want, Sloane? For me to make a fool of myself for you?" *Because I would.*

She rolls those lips together, the corners tugging upward. "Maybe I do."

Her gaze dips to my lips as hers part, and the pull is heavy. It's a hot, suffocating press; it's gravity, the laws of physics, and ignoring it feels wrong in a way nothing ever has. It's bone deep and painful...that ache again, but worse. When she lifts her gaze to mine, she doesn't know she's twisting the knife intended for her, deep between my ribs. I'd rather it this way—where she never knows who I am and it's just me bleeding out the lie in silence.

A wide backed man—football, most likely—wedges himself between us because we're blocking the door to the patio, and the spell shatters. Sloane looks away, clearing her throat as his jersey chafes against her shirt when he passes.

"I found the roof," she finally says, looking up at me with all this good will and friendship, and I want to tell her to give it to someone else but, selfishly, I want it. "Should we?" she asks, brows raised as she tips her head toward the staircase. She looks like she's invested in my answer. The *no* is right there, on the tip of my tongue, but doesn't make it out.

Even though I know this is how I sully our waters enough that there's no return to innocence—by saying yes instead of no.

"Yeah. Sure." I watch the easy swish of her hips as we ascend the stairs, tracking the silence of her authority, the one that forces my walls to retreat. I wonder if she knows she does that, or if it's a force of nature thing. A consequence of who she is, such an integral part of her makeup and how she moves in the world that it doesn't mean anything that it affects me, specifically.

We escape into a room peppered with Polaroids fastened to the wall with thumbtacks, before Sloane pushes up on a wide but narrow window frame.

"I used to do this all the time when I was younger, in Atlanta," she says, glancing back at me like a kid in a candy store. I step through the window, shocked by the intensity of the slope, looking at her with brief alarm. "Come on, Spellman. Don't be a pussy."

I drop down onto the roof and lay back, sensing my hand just a few inches away from hers. She doesn't move it, just turns her head to the side so she's facing me, an unrushed smile settling on her lips when I do the same. From her other side, she pulls out a joint.

"Got a light?" she asks, quiet excitement creasing at the corners of her eyes as she lifts it to her lips. My eyes are on the spliff as I focus on catching the flame, but her eyes are on me, searing into me with single minded determination. When it's done I back away, watching as her eyes flutter shut and take a hit, holding it for a long moment before blowing it over her shoulder. She passes it to me and I take a long drag, feeling the laces of my guilt loosen.

Sloane subtly grins, watching. "For the life of me, I can't get a read on you. Thought you were gonna try to convince us to get off this thing. "

"No way," I huff out, coughing. "Would you even have listened?" I ask, watching in awe as she bursts out in laughter.

"Of course not." She lolls her head away from me so she's staring back at the sky, the stars beginning to shine as the clouds drift away. "Maybe out of pity. Seems Carmen gives you a hard time," she adds, but I know there's a question hidden there.

I help myself to another hit before passing the joint back.

"She does. But she's also having a hard time," I admit, losing a breath.

"She appreciates you. That's why she does it," she says to the stars instead of me. "I gave my family a hard time."

"Yeah?" I trace the outline of her against the roof, barely lit by the moon.

"I was adopted," she says, like it's as much a revelation to her as it is to me. "Grant doesn't really tell people. The Fielder's adopted us when we were barely teenagers."

"Shit. How was that?" I'd be lying if I didn't worry about Carmen, about what would happen to her if something happened to Mom. It's unlikely, but so was Luis dying after that fire.

"Crazy," she laughs, but it's sad, a tragic weight to her usually feather light voice. "I was horrible. Probably still am, dependin' on who you ask," she says, the subtle lilt of her voice skating across me like the breeze.

"I find that hard to believe." That telltale weightlessness comes over me, and I let the roof hold me as any tension finally melts away. I only really smoke with Will, and even then it's when he thinks he can keep it from Liv.

Sloane hums, and it buzzes just beneath my skin, warms me despite the chill in the air.

"You don't really know me," she muses, her soft giggles vibrating into the roof tiles, and I know she feels it, too.

"And you don't know me. But I have a feeling," I say to the sky, and I hear her roll over until she's on her stomach, head propped in her hands.

It's gone in this moment—the perimeters that dictate my life. I try to grab for the thread that binds this all together, that casts me as a villain in disguise, but it's been blown away. Right now, I'm just a guy looking at a girl, wanting to kiss her, and anything else that I could be feels like pure fiction. The task echoes in the back of my mind and, were it not for the pot, it'd probably be crisper, but it isn't. It's as hazy as the smoke we're blowing between us.

"What does this *feeling* tell you?" she asks, peering at me through her lashes. Her deep sea eyes almost glitter.

"That it's all a front." She reels back just slightly, like I just peeled a layer she wasn't ready to shed.

"You're a front, too," she challenges, her tone dipping into defensiveness, and I still, my skin buzzing at her perception.

"And what is it? My front?" I counter, knowing I should leave it alone, but I'm mesmerized by the way she talks. By the way her lips move when she's talking about me.

"Carelessness. The whole douchey shtick you do when everyone's watching. The...playin' dumb. Kind of an asshole." She rolls those lips of hers, narrowing her eyes at me. "You weren't like that in the prop closet. You're not like that when it's just me."

It's too raw, that perception, and I bristle.

"I say thank you for watching my sister and, all of a sudden, I have a sensitive side I don't show?" I try to joke in an attempt to reel this conversation back into safe territory, but she doesn't budge.

"You're doin' it again."

Head tilted to the side and framed by the golden spillage of her hair, she looks like an angel, and I wonder: what does that make me?

"I'm not pretending, Sloane. Sometimes I just am an asshole." I work my jaw as I trace the almost black outline at the edges of indigo in her eyes.

"Bullshit," she says, sitting up so that we're face to face.

We're *too* close, but I can't seem to make myself move. "I saw you with Carmen. You care about things."

"Why do you care so much?" I ask, irritation attempting to claw its way through the hazy cloud we're slowly falling from. "I don't know if you remember, but all those nights ago, you wanted nothing to do with me."

Her scoff is hard, grates across my skin like a rug burn. "Because I was trying *not* to do somethin' stupid with my brother's teammate." Her scoff is bitter, laced with hurt pride and tired amusement as she shakes her head at me.

"So you admit it. You did want me." I let my gaze play across her lean lines and she smacks my arm, biting back a smirk as she scowls at me.

"Can you be serious?"

I breathe in the cool night air, embracing the way it burns. "Hand me that." I reach toward the joint, taking a brief hit. "Fine," I confirm, blowing the smoke out in a long stream.

"Okay," she says, sighing. "Tell me something real."

"Too vague." Parameters. I need parameters so I know how to avoid tripping a wire.

I hear her shift on the roof. "Fine. Why were you talking to Ian at the warehouse?"

Well shit.

"Watching me, Fielder?" I ask, hiding my dread.

"*Serious*, Andrew."

"He was just trying to get a quote." I can sense Sloane deciding if she believes me, so I move on. "My turn."

She hums, and I can see the moment she decides to move on. "Fine. Go ahead."

I look into the night, my nerves newly rattled by the line it feels we've crossed, the curtain we've started to lift.

I should ask. Just ask, without committing to telling anyone what I know.

"Why'd you really leave California?" Gravity presses into my chest, shoves any sense of calm away as I watch her mull over the question.

"Sloane!" Jean's voice comes from below, and I can imagine him roaming the dark tree line, thinking to look anywhere but up.

Neither of us move, like we know leaving the roof will shatter the moment—our first real one, I think. Sloane's teeth rake her bottom lip as a smile teases at the corners of her mouth, and the moonlight cuts across her cheekbones, highlighting the freckles that fall across the bridge of her nose—the ones I suddenly want to count. Trace.

A breath whooshes out of her and her smile falters, turns serious. "I left my art program and am hiding out here while I take care of my birth mom who's sick and probably dying."

"Jesus, Sloane." I sit up and face her, shaking my head, feeling like shit for dragging that out of her. "Are you...okay?" Real concern courses through me because I get the sense she hasn't shared this. That for whatever reason, she's leaving this with me.

"Oh my god, yeah," she forces a laugh. "Just high. Sorry I told you that."

"No, don't be. You can..." I wet my lips, rolling them together as I dread the words begging to leave my mouth. "You can tell me anything."

"Are we secretly friends, Andrew?" she smirks, tilting her head at me.

I swallow hard. "Don't tell Carmen. She'll never let me hear the end of it."

"See, now I have to tell her. She was my friend first," she whispers playfully, leaning into me with all the subtlety of a rock. She rolls her lips, drops her gaze before flicking it back up, and suddenly, we're closer than we should be.

"Sloane," I mutter, hating myself.

"Andrew," she mocks, the corner of her mouth tugging into a smile I want nothing more than to kiss off her. She looks at me, her confidence down-sliding into uncertainty, and I immediately reach for her.

"I just," I start, throat bobbing. "I just think we should be friends." The words might as well be acetone in my mouth, that's how badly I want to wash them away, say something entirely new. Instead, I level my gaze at her, bringing all the surety I can find to the fore.

Her brows lift in surprise, amusement playing at her lips. "I agree," she says, a dimple popping, a shoulder shrugging, a strand of her golden hair gently blown by the wind.

"Okay, so…" I chuckle, furrowing my brows. "What's happening here, Sloane?"

"I just…felt like kissin' you. But if that's confusing—"

"I mean, your brother—"

"Right." She looks down, pressing her lips into a tight line. "Forget it, Spellman. I'm like…very high."

The window we came through slides up, the sudden air pressure shattering the bubble.

"Why can I *never* find you?" Jean complains, popping his head through. "Oh. Andy."

"See you later, *friend*," Sloane says, her voice soft with smoke, as she pushes up off the roof before disappearing through the window, already regretting the kiss I didn't take.

14

Sloane

I hold the sweater near my neck, admiring the subtlety in the golden fibers woven throughout the brown wool. It's earthen and rich and soft, and it pulls my own blonde hair warmer, less severe than it is when I stick to cool tones. Olivia dangled it before me, her eye for refinement much better than mine. It could do with a fringe, or a frayed edge. Maybe a cold shoulder.

I quickly put it back when I realize it reminds me of Andrew's eyes, suddenly thinking about the way he didn't want to kiss me. About the way I offered the easy kind of intimacy he wanted to begin with, and he rebuffed it. It'd be a lie to say my pride wasn't somewhat sore; that I haven't thought about what it would've been like even more often than I did before. It's a hazard of knowing someone like him—tall, imposing, charming, like a nineties movie star. Just a hazard, one I'm managing fairly well when I don't see sweaters that remind me of his gaze.

"That sweater would've looked fabulous on you." Olivia slides on her black Prada sunglasses, designer shopping bags slung across her arm as she sips from the to-go coffee we snagged from the Nordstrom cafe. I'm struck once again by how different she is from the way I saw her at the team dinner.

Wallflower, she is not.

I discerned that just from our visit at Veronica Beard. She commanded the space, gave every employee a task and yet they seemed to be eating out of the palm of her hand. Her entire presence opens up without Will around. Her posture straight, her shoulders back, her head arched up ever so slightly, her eyes intense when she's pinning you with a question. I admire it but can also see how some may find it a little intimidating. And maybe I would too if I didn't watch this magnificent force dim the moment her shitty boyfriend made a backhanded compliment. I tighten my hold on my own shopping bags at the memory. At how one mediocre man could have such a hold on not just her, but Gen, too.

I put my aviators on and watch Olivia inspect me from my periphery. I've noticed her doing this a few times, cataloging in the same way I've catalogued her. Appreciating, envying, judging every little detail.

We constantly compare ourselves to women who aren't even our mirror but a framework for a different life we could've led.

I feel that sickening sense of being perceived, of someone etching a story in their brain that isn't quite right but is, nevertheless, the one I've thrown into the world. The story I've decided people will remember me by, even if it is a fiction so carefully laid over the facts that it's hard to distinguish what's real.

I shake the thoughts away and turn my face to the sun on a sigh.

"I'm starvin'," I say, looping my arm through hers and can feel her tense at the unexpected physical touch, before quickly relaxing.

"There's a cute little brunch spot up the street. They have incredible french toast," she smiles, warmer than what you might expect from her, and it's an honest detail that means something.

"Sounds perfect," I nod and we begin our trek down the cobblestone street. I breathe in the freshly cool air, the muggy greenness of the summer giving way to a canvas of yellow, orange and red.

I'll give Boston one thing: it's beautiful in the fall.

We pass an art gallery and I linger on a window placed portrait of a mother and son. It's a mixed media piece, done using a photo transfer technique that leaves them looking almost haunted.

"Do you want to go in?" Olivia asks, noticing. She nods her head at the door, her eyes curious.

"You don't mind?" I ask but my foot's already halfway through the door. She laughs, untangling herself so I can explore freely. The gallery assistant is clad in all black, in a way I've noticed they always are. An attempt to look like they are from New York, especially when they aren't. I gaze at the different collages, sculptures, and everyday items altered to have a whole new meaning when my eyes land on a large, familiar white canvas littered with dried citrus.

The sticky sweet juice from slicing and squeezing haunts my finger tips now. The death it's had since I breathed life into it is startling, and I still, studying it as my gut churns.

On first glance the canvas radiates warmth, an endless summer that I can almost smell, can almost remember, but the longer I stare the more the illusion fades. And that was the point—to cover the fruit in a thin layer of resin, preserve its texture but not its vitality. Highlight the edges of the oranges that curl in on themselves, the dark moldy spots of the lemons that even I, the artist, somehow missed at first glance, the pulp now brittle from time. Some of the fruit has become translucent, so the audience can see the love notes underneath, promises written in my hand that send a familiar wave of nausea through me.

I have the urge to tear them from the canvas and burn them.

"Oh, we just got this one in—it's an Elliot Walker original." The curate rounds her desk and grins, waiting for me to be impressed.

My eyes fixate on the small white card near the canvas.

Sun Dried, love exposed to life.

My gaze settles on the love note under an almost rotted blood red orange, the familiar slope in the *E* matching the one permanently etched to my inner arm and it's like I feel him, his breath, his touch, the way his stubble would brush my neck. It's suffocating and terrifying, the way I miss it. The way I can't seem to unframe the version of me he painted, his damage radiating through every stroke. I fear that, regardless of how much time has passed, regardless of how well my mind releases all claim to him, that piece of him that no doctor could ever purge will haunt my bones. Will ring through me and make me remember who I almost was with him.

I turn my back to the woman whose slightly pretentious smile senses none of the torrent of emotion roiling within me and I head straight back through the gallery door, the brisk Massachusetts air a reminder of all that I've lost as I rush down the long street. I finally stop, shutting my eyes and leaning against the cold brick of a store I don't recognize.

"What the hell just happened?" Olivia's breathy voice interrupts my thoughts as I watch her swat away the stray hairs that sprang from her long ponytail in her jog to catch up, her shopping bags spun so messily in her arms that she gives up on them, dropping them on the brick street. "You ran out of there...?" Her eyes are asking a million different questions but she must catch something in my expression because she nods to the building across the street. "French toast?"

I suck in a breath, silently nodding, attempting to shake off the memory of him and reminding myself that I came here to find the girl I was before his brush touched me.

I slice into the thick piece of french toast, the crispy outer edges perfectly complimenting the fluffy interior and I'll give it to Olivia, I do feel a hell of a lot better. Elliot's been pushed away, even though fragments of him still swirl in the base of my stomach. But I can feel them settling.

"Sugar fixes all," she says with a mouth full of brunch and I laugh because I'm seeing yet another side of her.

I find myself wanting to paint this version. Powdered sugar is sprinkled against her black turtleneck and her previously coiffed ponytail is now haphazardly pushed up into a messy bun, the perspiration of the day melting away her foundation to reveal a smattering of freckles I didn't notice before. The harsh discerning glint in her eye gives way to pure amber flecked warmth, and I can already see the pigments on my shelf.

"You ever modeled?" I ask, stacking pieces of cut toast on my fork. When I flick my gaze up to her, her brows are drawn tight, a disbelieving smirk on her face.

"Not my thing."

"I'm serious. You're stunning, Liv. No one's ever approached you?" The comment takes her aback. She stops mid-bite like she didn't expect it, her corners of her mouth turning downwards. Caution pools in her eyes like I'm tricking her or trying to hurt her in some way. I shrug, not wanting to force her to sit in this discomfort and suck down the final dregs of the house iced coffee they poured us when we walked in.

"I was a late bloomer," she finally says, clearing her throat. "Unibrow and all."

"Stop it. You'd kill a unibrow." The ferocity of her brow should've made it more obvious that she's plucking a barrier between the two sides of her face, and I nod vigorously so she knows I'm being serious. "Your body your choice and all that, but you're fucking gorgeous, Olivia. Free the brow," I shrug, shoving the sugary bread into my mouth.

Her hesitance shrinks a little, her lips melting into the softest smile. "Well, you are, too. Obviously."

I roll my eyes, smirking. "God, you really don't have girlfriends, do you?" I signal the waiter for a refill and glance back at Olivia who's more closed off, her cheeks a rosy hue signaling her unease. "What I mean is...we could just exist. There's no measuring stick. If I tell you you're pretty, you can trust I told you because you deserved to know...not because I want something from you. You know?" I dip my head, taking a long sip from my newly refilled iced coffee, keeping my eyes tipped up to her.

She hums to herself, her gaze going far off before blinking back to the present. "That is new for me. But I'll try it. For *you*, 'midnight princess'." Her mouth twists into a playful smile as she recalls just one of the many names the gossip columns call me.

"You looked me up?"

She shrugs, easing into us. "Course I did. You can't just pop up out of thin air and expect people *not* to ask questions." She eyes me, tilting her head. "Call me crazy but...could it have something to do with the way you bolted out of that gallery?"

Pulling in a breath that reaches my diaphragm, I nod, slowly. "Have you ever been involved with someone you knew you shouldn't be?" I use my fork to move the final pieces of egg still lingering on my plate.

Liv shifts in her seat, discomfort now stifling the air around us and my mind flicks back to the team dinner, to the heat between Ben, Will, and Olivia, and I realize that may have been the wrong question to lead with.

"That...piece of art..." I trail off trying to find the words.

"With the oranges?" she asks, interest overtaking her former embarrassment now that she realizes the question was rhetorical.

"Right. I, um—" I take a sip of my coffee, nodding at the waiter in thanks. "I collaborated on that piece." Olivia's eyebrows shoot up in excitement and I realize yet again I am not framing this well.

"No way! Sloane—that's amazing. Oh my god, we can go back? I can get a picture of you with it and—"

"It's not really known. That I collaborated, I mean." Her eyebrows bunch in confusion before her mouth forms an oh shape, clearly realizing there's more to the story.

"With the person you shouldn't have..."

I nod, trying to reel in this story that I've hidden so deep within myself until I can almost feel the pulp of the oranges that I so carefully sliced: not too jagged, not too perfect but somewhere in between.

"Like us."

Elliot's voice rings in my head like dust traveling through air, the clarity transporting me to the floor of his loft. Every note we'd pass before and after his lectures sprawled between us like stolen scripture, sacred and trembling with the things we couldn't say out loud.

At the time he'd convinced me that the installation was about the ripeness of new love. How alive one person could feel when they met another. I feel stupid, seeing that fruit in the gallery, how it's been preserved. Every bruise lacquered into permanence, nothing softened with time, the rot just settling deeper. I swallow, the hatred now souring in my mouth with the realization that he had me help him immortalize our decay, and with the understanding that all the evidence of what I was to him is just framed and hung on a wall.

I can still see his genius. Still want it all to mean more than it does.

Olivia sighs, reaching over to squeeze my hand, a gesture I can sense is foreign to her which makes it all the more meaningful. "Do you want to talk about it?" Her eyes are sincere. Tender.

Still, I shake my head. "Honestly, I just need to get my mind off it." I begin to push around the eggs again.

"Well…if it's any consolation, I do have a taser. So, if we ever see him." A warm laugh miraculously finds its way through me and I smile at my new friend. "Seriously though, I know what it's like to have to deal with a man who doesn't want all of you." She's nodding into her food, the mousiness from the other night making an appearance and I pinch my eyes trying to see what she's not saying.

"Anyway…" she interrupts my scrutinizing. "Should we go get a manicure?" She eyes my chipped nails that have been bitten down to the stub and I mock a gasp.

"Don't judge me! I haven't had time—"

She holds her hands up in innocence but rolls her eyes. "Would I be a good friend if I didn't tell you when you were in need of a french tip?"

I shake my head, allowing myself to push Elliot back down just underneath my surface, and feel all the better for it. Olivia grins, pleased, and for a moment we sit in the charged space of the restaurant, dish ware clinking somewhere in the background, in what is no longer the silence of strangers but two women slowly unlearning the need to perform for each other. I signal for the check and when I look back she's still watching me, not cataloging this time, just...noticing. I wonder if she notices that I feel lighter, like I notice she does.

"Thanks." It comes out like a whisper but I hear the genuineness of my own voice.

"Anytime." Her smile is soft, like she knows exactly what I mean. I pull some cash out, leaving a generous tip, and loop my arm through hers again as we rise and this time, she doesn't tense at all.

15

Sloane

It's interesting—getting better at something. It starts slowly and then all of a sudden you can feel the confidence in your hand. It's the way the brush feels when you're painting a certain line, when what's in your head somehow appears in front of you just like you planned it.

"*Fuck*," I moan, and I wish I could say that is how oils have been. I use a spatula to scrape the thick backdrop structure, carving off the clumped paint that's collected in the area I've been working on. I swipe the sweat from my neck, schlepping my hair into a french twist with a stray pencil I found on the floor, one of the few things I willingly let Evie show me how to do, if only for the sake of convenience.

Jean stalks in, pushing Gen by the shoulders and she melts down onto the floor. They both look spent, exhaustion covering their faces in small dewy droplets. "She's dancing like shit today and needs a pep talk."

I frown, slightly unsure if I'm the right person to give it as I stare at the now scraped clean board in front of me. I scooch away until I'm cross legged right in front of Gen who's fresh off rolling her eyes and now chugging from a giant lavender water bottle.

"Now I highly doubt you're dancin' like shit. You're probably just a sliver away from incredible, if I know anything about this one's dramatics." I nod toward Jean, setting my hands on Gen's knees. "You good?"

She squeezes her eyes shut and sucks in a huge breath. "I want to tell you but I'm going to look horrible," she says quickly, like she's been waiting to let whatever is eating her up out.

"Impossible—you could never look *horrible*," I say, squeezing her knee for encouragement.

"*Ehhhh...*" Jean winces and I shoot him a look. Gen pulls her knees to her chest before burying her head in her sweatshirt clad arms. "What? I mean...it *is* pretty bad." He shrugs, sliding down beside us.

"Lucky for you," I say, shooting him a glare that I hope will shut him up, "I have a knack for loving horrible people." She glances up and I smile encouragingly.

"Grant found out I've been keeping a secret for Will and... now we are in a huge fight because apparently if I don't tell the person who the secret involves I'm a terrible person." Her voice trembles slightly at the end, exhaustion prevalent in her tone as her eyes carry a watery sheen.

"Oh Gen..." I wrap my arm around her, pulling her into my side. "If there's one thing about my brother it's that his moral superiority knows no bounds." She chuckles slightly, quickly wiping her cheek to hide her emotion. "Can I ask who the secret involves?"

"Well Will..."

"Obviously," Jean chimes in and I reach my arm out to pinch him.

"*Ow,*" he hisses.

"And...Olivia."

My eyebrows shoot up as I look at Jean and he gestures as if to say it gets worse. "Okay...do you want to share the—"

"He was dating her dead best friend Lily the summer before she died and never told her or anyone else. I only know because I was there. He's basically hidden it from her and everyone else at Astor and—"

"Wait, Olivia has a dead best friend?" Confusion wrinkles my forehead and Jean rolls his eyes.

"Keep up!" Jean chides. I move to pinch him again but he flinches away.

"Yes. It was the whole terrible tragedy our freshman year, and she was Will's first love I guess because since her death he's been just *different*. I just..." she trails off rubbing her temples. "Telling Olivia would really blow up his life and you didn't see him after Lily passed. It was bad." Tears well fully in Gen's eyes now and my heart aches for the girl. "He's my best friend Sloane, but your brother...he doesn't see it that way. He thinks I'm protecting him because I love him and maybe I am. I don't know. I just—I don't know what he'll do if Liv finds out." She lays her head back until she's staring at the ceiling and I join her, grabbing her hand and squeezing it.

"Gen—you're needed stage right for Act II!" a too young voice interrupts us, her shy freckled face peeking through the cracked door. Gen squeezes her eyes shut, inhaling a long deep breath.

"You're going to that Halloween party right? At the frat?" she asks, her eyes hopeful, and it's clear she doesn't want to be in this alone, that she's drowning in secrets, a feeling I know all too well. Hell, if it was someone I loved I'd probably be keeping them, too. My mind shoots to Connie and how Grant still doesn't know the real reason she's here, and I quickly compartmentalize the thought.

"Of course. I promised I'd help with your costume, remember?"

She nods, sliding her hands on her pants before climbing to her feet.

"I'm here for you, whether you tell her or not. Unfortunately for Grant and the Fielder's, I'm not as put off by gray areas. In fact, I prefer them." I bump her shoulder with mine.

"Uh...Gen?" the shy voice interrupts again.

"Coming!" she calls, her voice so polite I can hardly believe anyone has ever called her an ice queen. She gives me an appreciative glance before following the girl out the door.

"Oof," I groan, approaching Jean as he stretches on an art cart a few feet away. I begin to organize the paint brushes, a nervous habit that Beau would joke I get from Evie, the accusation always met with an icy roll of my eyes. The memory makes me feel squirmy and tired.

"You can say that again..." Jean picks up a few brushes and sets them in what he thinks are the right cups, laughing at the winces I make when he sorts one wrong. "You have the worst poker face," he chides and I wish he knew how good my poker face actually was, how I can so easily store away my own thoughts and feelings to make room for others.

"So, how's Ian?" I decide to change the subject instead.

"I've been avoiding him like the plague since Gen told me about this Lily thing. If he ever found out..." He shakes his head and I nod. We both know he'd have to be crazy not to run a story like this.

"Are *you* goin' to the party?"

Jean sighs, pushing his pale hand through his jet black waves. "Probably not. Will, Grant, Gen and Ian in one room?" He looks at me knowingly.

"Cmon. She needs us."

He raises an eyebrow smirking. "Sure," he shrugs, forcing me to wrinkle my brows.

"What?" I cross my arms.

"I can think of another reason why you may want to attend that party." He clucks his tongue, turning toward the sink to wash his now paint smattered hands.

"Enlighten me, because none seem to come to mind." I know my scowl proves the opposite and this only amuses Jean more.

"A certain Andrew Spellman?" His voice is like a parent's chastising a child and I feel my defenses rolling up.

"You're ridiculous, you know that?" I nudge him at the sink, reaching over to pump some soap into my own palm.

"Ridiculous is you pretending you haven't been ogling that boy for like a month." He rips a paper towel from the machine.

"I—"

"Stop. Terrible poker face, remember?" He cuts me off. "What is stopping you from ripping his clothes off?"

"I just don't feel like it, okay?" My tone comes out sharp and Jean softens a bit.

"Is it because of the whole...professor thing?" Anger flares in my nostrils and he must notice the tone shift because he holds his hands up as if to pause the reaction. "Look, it's clear you're figuring some shit out, but just like you told Gen, I am here for *you,* too. We don't have to talk about it," he nods his head as if to gesture to the subject that is sleeping with my professor, "but if you ever do want to...we can." I release the breath I'm holding and it feels like something is stuck in my lungs.

"Thanks," I say weakly and he gives my arm a squeeze.

"Jean. You're needed stage left," the same meek voice interrupts.

"Gotta jet!" He jogs toward the door.

"Come to the party—please, *I* need *you*!" I yell after him.

"I'll check my schedule." He winks before exiting and I'm left with nothing but scraped wood boards and dirty brushes.

16

Sloane

I'm so late. I check my phone, taking another huge bite of my bagel and choking it down with the lukewarm coffee I poured when I rolled out of bed twenty minutes ago.

"Have I ever told you that you remind me of the Grinch?" Grant's rubbing his face as he enters the kitchen, a surprising glint of humor in his eye after his past few days of moping around the house.

"Everyday." I make a show of grinning through the stale chewed up bagel in my mouth and he sneers.

"Gross, Sloane." He moves toward the coffee pot and I watch his shoulders sink, whatever levity was there instantly dissipating as he takes in the open bag of bagels and cream cheese. I knew I should have used a cutting board. He starts putting things away in jabby sharp movements intended to show me how pissed off he is.

"*Stop*. I was going to clean that up!" He can be such an asshole when his equilibrium is fucked up. One thing gone wrong in life? Let's take it out on every human being on planet earth.

"Sure you were," he responds sharply.

I use my arm to divert him from the few objects on the counter, quickly putting them away. I wish I could replicate his movements, be as passive aggressive as he is and maybe it translates because he says, "What?" his arms crossed as he watches me swallow the rest of my bagel.

"*What* Sloane? Just say what you want to say."

I subtly check my phone because I really don't have time for this but he is being a dick and it's fine if he wants to self sabotage his own life but he doesn't get to take it on the rest of us in the aftermath.

"You're being cranky to me because of your fight with Gen," I shrug matter of factly, hoping he'll sigh and go stew in his room—his typical mode of handling conflict.

"Is there more?" he asks and I raise my eyebrows, surprised but also expect the question to be a trap. He wants me to explode, gives him a reason to put me out on my ass.

"You should apologize to her," I say calmly, getting up to stick my plate in the dishwasher.

"Apologize for what? Asking her to tell the truth?"

So this is a trap.

"It's not her truth to tell," I say the words to myself, an internal thought whispered out loud. But based on the way Grant's looking at me I know this is about to be a big one. Betrayal and frustration are so poignant in his gaze and it's not that I don't care about his problems, but if I don't leave now I'll probably miss Mom's appointment.

I don't have time to theorize morality with Grant, a discussion we have had so many times in the past. It never goes well. I live in the gray but he only sees black and white.

"What do you mean? You're telling me she should just keep this huge secret, one that would shake up Olivia's life completely, for *Will*? The same Will who's been shitty to basically every person I've cared about since I've known him?"

"Sort of!" I snap. This is so like Grant, blaming his life's problems on one person.

If only so and so didn't do this, then my life would be great.

I don't like Will, but this isn't about Will. It's about Gen— about her making the choice to protect someone she cares about, and about Grant seeing that as a flaw instead of a positive.

I look at the time on the stove. *Fuck.* "Look, I have to go. I'm going to be late." I grab my keys, and tug on my boots, sitting haphazardly by the bar stool.

"Late for what?" His voice is full of accusation, suspicion, and I hear it now. How he groups me in with all these things he considers bad.

"Late for *what*, Sloane?" he spits, and something about the hatred, the rage in his voice has tension pulling at my head like if I don't explode I'll cry. Exploding feels easier. Cleaner.

"I have a thing...with Mom."

I watch that betrayal amplify and morph into something more. A break in whatever cosmic bond twins have. The feeling that the one person who should understand you doesn't understand you at all.

"Why?"

It's the way he says it that makes me erupt, like I have something to apologize for, like I proved him right about some unsaid thing between us. Like me seeing our mother hurts him as much as our mother did.

"You know what Grant, not all of us are constantly holding people to an entirely impossible standard. Normal people can't just decide if someone is good or bad like *that*. People change Grant, people have reasons they do things. Maybe they don't want to share those things with the *gate-*

keeper of morality." Blood courses through my ears and I feel sweat begin to tickle the back of my neck, my heart beating hard in my chest.

"People like Will, people like Connie..." His voice is restrained, like I won't be able to handle whatever truth he thinks he's expounding on me. "They don't just *change* Sloane. They don't get to use their issues as an excuse for fucking up someone's life." I wonder if that's what he thinks I'm doing. Coming in here with all my issues and fucking up his life. This wounds me somewhere, a cut I don't feel right now but deep enough that I know it"ll come back later when I think I've forgiven him.

"Sometimes things are morally grey, Grant. Do I think Gen should be protecting Will? No. Absolutely not. But Will was Gen's person for a really, *really* long time. That was her best friend, so maybe she thinks protecting him is more important than the truth. *Maybe* there's a whole lot of pain under that secret that she knows he's not ready to face." I swallow hard. "What makes Will less worthy of empathy, Grant? Just because he's fucked up? What about Mom? Why is she okay to abandon and we weren't?" I feel the tears before I can process them, and I don't know when this argument became less about Gen and more about us.

"She was our *mom*, Sloane." He says it like this should mean something, like his pain should trump everyone else's but all I can think is how this proves my point.

"She *is* our mom." My voice has a hard edge as I use my hand to brush away the tears.

"This is a mistake. Don't let her in." For a second he's fifteen, eighteen, twenty year old Grant again, giving me a warning he knows I won't take. Because for him it's so easy to turn away someone you love when they don't meet your expectations.

Is there a world in which I could fuck up so bad that he turns me away too? Is it this one?

"Don't let her in."

I shake my head, a cruel laugh snaking its way up my rib cage.

"That's your advice? To just keep pushing her away? Grant, you can't just keep everyone at arm's length and expect things to get better for you."

"I let people in. I let you in—I let my friends in. For fuck's sake this entire argument is because I *let* Gen in."

I let you in, I know he wants to say.

The unspoken words ring between us, like it was a favor, like if he could do away with me he would. Because he's never *really* let me in. He's sat a pillar above me, high up on his moral high horse. A smaller version of Mom who he wishes would abandon him, too just so he could point his finger and say: *see —I told you so.*

"This entire argument is because you *refuse* to let anyone in." I feel the knot in my throat, like at any moment I'll completely fall apart. I grab my keys and my bag, the need to escape, to get far away from this conversation, from the truth of what he thinks of me, because it's suffocating. "Apologize to Gen, Grant," I say, my tone void of emotion as I throw his front door closed behind me, covering my face with my hands to stifle my sob.

* * *

Nine years ago

From where I stand at the entrance of Evie Fielder's bedroom, I can smell it. I don't need to see the purple bottle to know it's super hold—that it's Aqua-net. A memory of that can on a counter I can't quite reach swims in my vision before it disappears.

I inch forward across the waxy hardwood, as much as I can without her seeing me, inhaling the powdery scent and mentally marking each step of her routine. There's a round brush in her hand; a blow dryer in the other. The little machine roars to life as she lifts her arms like she's done in silent rhythm for the past thirty minutes. Tugging like it takes effort, she pulls it through a chunk of hair while her blow dryer gushes hot air from the other direction.

Then, it's silent, except for the pointed *shhh* of the hairspray can. It invades my nostrils and now, I notice she's done. Her glossy blonde hair sits perfectly on her shoulders with a gentle wave, and it doesn't move. A life sized doll—not even the wind could toss it out of place.

My adoptive mother is so beautiful, it hurts to look. I shut my eyes and strain to see my actual mother, try to let the familiar fumes build an image of her in the likeness of Evie. Youthful. Radiant. Healthy.

Nothing happens. I can't see anything but stringy strands and smudged mascara but I *know* she must've been like this before. Otherwise, why would she have needed Aqua-net, too?

"Sloane, sweetie?" Evie's hands are gentle, but they're on me for only a second before I shrug them away, my eyes flying back open.

She looks into my eyes with way too much concern, and I roll them like it'll stop her from knowing all my thoughts. Grant loves that about her. He's always saying how nurturing she is, how understanding.

And I get it; becoming a mother to a pair of eleven year olds is probably an uphill climb, and it must suck not knowing us the way a mother does.

But no one asked her to.

And I have a mother.

When she tilts her head to the side, I know she doesn't care. She's going to try to understand me anyway.

"You know, I've been meanin' to give you somethin'," she says, walking across the hallway towards the art studio, expecting me to follow.

"I'm meetin' Clementine. Remember?" I cross my arms and push my hip out, a fight I don't remember the start of pulsing through my bones. She ignores it, patiently waving me toward her.

The room used to be her painting studio but now she says it's mine. Before it was just a desk, some bookcases, and an easel; all signs of her have been erased now, other than the few pieces she's deemed too abstract for the rest of the house. I almost like her best in this room, with her canvases streaked in a mess of oily hues. The rest of this house is like an assault on my senses: everything matches. There isn't a hint of contradiction, other than me.

My skin doesn't feel as tight in this room, though. When I'm not at Clemmie's, this is where they can find me, a brush in hand, trying but failing to paint the night sky with my watercolors. Every attempt leads to a purplish looking ocean more than anything, but I'm not bothered.

When I paint, it's like I'm blissfully lost in the sea. Like I'm drowning but without the lack of oxygen. It's a relief. Everything and everyone is muffled, blurry; they're just a dream I once had—not really real. I feel weightless and free. I had a teacher once say art is about process, that the final piece is not as important as what you had to do to get there. And I get that now, especially with this night sky. I kind of dread the day I figure it out. What'll happen then?

I stare down my latest starry night, nowhere near perfect, and sigh, feeling calmer already.

"It might be easier if you could layer," Evie tells me, washing that calm away.

"Thanks," I try to be polite. "I'll figure it out."

She sucks in a small breath, like she's gonna say something, but then just disappears into the closet. When she remerges, she's holding a set of small silver tubes that reflect off the light that slices through the curtains.

"I saw these colors at the supply store and thought of what you're workin' on." She moves forward, setting them on one of the built in ledges behind my easel. "Take it or leave it," she shrugs with a small smile that scrapes. She doesn't mean for it to. It just does.

Her too soft hand brushes my shoulder as she leaves, but not before she tells me to be careful. To only take the side streets to Clem's. To not talk to strangers. To take the phone she's got a GPS app downloaded onto.

I bolt out the door to Clementine's as soon as her footsteps fade to nothing.

"Clemmie. I think I might be broken."

Mathletes, or Mathgeeks, or...something—that's why I've been lounging in the Rivera's stables all alone for the past hour. But I couldn't very well stay in that room, with those tubes gawking at me.

I turn my head, and all I can see is the shiny embroidery on her new riding boots. Pale yellow light floods the stable entrance, and she stands in front of it, all dark and imposing. Serious and totally sure of who she is with her hands on her hips, her raven hair falling around her in glossy waves.

"Why?" she asks, gathering Beulah's saddle as she tries to look at me where I lay. On the ground. Possibly in animal feces. "There's a perfectly good bench, Sloane."

I sit up, shaking hay and feed out of hair before I blindly braid the length of it. "I think better lookin' up."

She hands me the set of reigns I usually take as I roll my neck, waking my body up from the almost slumber I fell into.

"You taking Thea?" Clemmie asks me, gesturing at "my" horse before smiling at her stubborn little filly. Beulah will only let Clemmie ride her; I've tried. Thea's not a baby, though. She's a wise old mare who now whinnies at me, gently tossing her mane, like she knows the first time I walked in here I walked right past her.

"Oh hush," I croon, taking a brush to her long neck. "You know I'm not strayin'."

Her golden coat shines brighter with each stroke and I find myself thinking about Evie's hair again.

"So you're broken." Clemmie is a no bull kind of girl, but she isn't loud about it. All her thoughts are tightly wound up in her pretty little head, and she always doles them out at the perfect moment. I've never seen her have an outburst, not like me. "What happened?"

I sigh, my arms going limp as I rest my face against Thea. "Evie tried bein' nice to me and, I don't know why, but I can't stand it when she does that. Like what are you tryin' to do?"

"Context clues would say she was trying to be...nice...?" Her brows quirk. "What'd she *actually* do?"

"She got me oil paints."

"Don't you do watercolor?"

"Yes!" I shout, and Thea startles. "Sorry. Yes, thank you. *Everyone* knows that."

"I mean..." she rounds her horse carefully, gnawing in her bottom lip. "It's kind of thoughtful of her to expose you to new things. Don't you think?"

Suddenly, my chest feels like it could cave in on itself. I abandon Thea, needing the sky as I rush out of the stables and turn left. The sunflower fields I helped them till last year hold me close enough, but the sky above gives me that air I need.

"Sloane!" I hear Clemmie shouting. "Stop walkin'! You know you can't find your way out!"

She's right. I'm already mindlessly lost in the field with no sense of north or south. I sit, crushing a few stalks, chest heaving as I drop my head onto my knees.

"Wanna tell me why that triggered you?" Clemmie says quietly, taking the spot next to me.

I know better than to avoid her question.

"Because it *was* thoughtful," I tell her, water welling in my eyes as I grind my jaw. "And I know she's tryin' to love me, but it feels like she just wants me different. Like the watercolors. She could've gotten more of those, better brushes, but instead she got me oil paints."

Clemmie barely dips her head. "Okay?"

"*She* oil paints. I don't wanna be like her—what doesn't she get?"

Clemmie hums as the sunshine bathes her in golden light, and I'm jealous. Jealous of her little life in their little cottage on all this land, just her and her mom, who understands her more than anyone in this world. She's always reminding me that she doesn't have a dad, like she doesn't understand how lucky she is to have a *mother*. And even though she and Lucía are so different, they only really exist because of each other. I see it every time I'm sitting in the corner of their couch, watching them.

Clemmie gets to know who she is every time her mother sees her.

I won't say it out loud, cause she won't understand, but sometimes I worry I'll never know myself like that. And every time Evie starts to see me, it's like I get a little hopeful that maybe I will. That she'll see me and like it.

She's never once liked it, not really. She tries to smooth out the edges of her discomfort, but I know I'm not really what she wanted. I was just part of the package deal.

"Come on." Clemmie leaps up and gives me her hand, yanking me toward her even as I sit here like dead weight. "Mamí made you picadillo," she tells me, her nose wrinkling in disgust, rolling her eyes at me.

I let her pull me to standing, a smile blooming on my face as we trek back toward their cottage. The savory aroma, with its undercurrent of sweetness, spills out into the estate the closer we get, and I let my head fall back as I breathe it in.

"You're so easy," Clem laughs, swinging the front door open. "It's just stew."

That she made for me. I don't say it, just hum nonchalantly as I skip toward where Lucía stands, gathering bowls and singing softly, out into the garden beyond their kitchen window.

17

Andy

There's a blanket draped across Sloane's legs that's also strewn across mine, only because the fire blazing in the pit is insufficient and there weren't enough to go around. No other reason, because we—Sloane and I—are friends.

"And you're supposed to be...?" a newly joined Princess Peach in an iridescent mask asks. My fraternity's annual halloween party usually has stricter guidelines, but a lapse in leadership meant that *masquerade* was all that made it onto the invitation.

"A barber," I tell her, not bothering to clarify that I'm specifically a demon barber from Fleet Street, even when she squints at the streak of gray I impulsively added before walking over here with Ben. He's since disappeared to God knows where, but he is not my problem.

They are not my problem tonight.

Sloane grins over at the girl, wistfully shaking her head. "A beautiful fool." And I smile—can't help it, but I do. She's nothing like Daisy Buchanan and yet, I can see the ways she wishes she was.

If Sloane is careless, if she's carefree and flighty and strong-willed, it's because everyone's asked her to be. That's what I've seen, and I think if anyone bothered to look they'd see it, too. That Sloane's care runs deep and wide, runs far and away, maybe. I bet it feels easier to ignore it, to act like she couldn't care less.

Flames play in her midnight eyes as she fishes for her phone in her bag, her shoulders stilling when she reads whatever she finds there.

"Shit. I need to go," she murmurs, flinging the blanket off, standing. "You should probably come, too." Her gaze catches mine, all that featherlight levity dissipating, replaced by the concern I know lingers just out of sight.

My stomach sinks, like it already knows, and I follow, the two of us shoulder to shoulder even though walking one behind the other would be faster. And it shouldn't matter that even in this—a disaster waiting a few miles down the road—she wants me by her side.

"Gen needs me. She's at Will's." Her jaw twitches as she heads toward the front.

The cavernous house is hard to peer through, what with the smoke and smog machines, and I wave a hand as we make the trek to the front yard. That car—Delilah—is parked worse than I've ever seen on a cluster of driveway stones.

"If this is your car," Sloane shouts to no one in particular, arms shoving air at the Corolla parked behind Delilah, "move it!" Her hands find her hips, frustration creasing adorably between her brows. "Jesus Christ," she mutters, walking around the vehicle like she'll find a magical key to move it herself.

"Come on. Let's just go."

"I literally can't—"

Offering her my palm, I get her to give me the keys, telling her to trust me. Where I expect more of a fight, I find nothing but surrender. She drops into the passenger seat of her car, teeth pulling at her pink bottom lip as she pulls her bare legs up. She lets me maneuver her car over the easement, between the Corolla and a truck, without so much as a scratch.

Her eyes are closed as we veer onto the little campus streets that connect every Astor landmark. Fraternity Row. The practice gym. Churchill Hall. The Mark Maxwell Arena. The Arboretum. The Athletics Center, connected to the Newhouse Health and Wellness Center. Kellman Hall, where someone probably found the cure for polio. Black metal poles shoot toward the sky, washing the road with golden light as we race toward Will's apartment on the opposite side of campus.

"How'd you know how to do that?"

She pulls her champagne mask up and tosses it to the floor, shaking her hair out as it whips through the wind. Nose tipped a rosy hue, she sniffs, and her hands wrap tighter around her folded up frame. I hike my knee up, keeping the wheel steady, and shrug out of my letterman, tossing it in her lap.

She inhales, looking smug. "I'm honored."

"You were freezing."

"Don't be embarrassed. I like you, too," she says, reaching over to ruffle my hair before falling back into her seat. "So what, are you secretly into street racin'? How'd you get us out of there?"

I wet my lips, dragging the bottom through my teeth as the memories start to resonate. "I learned how to drive on this." It's like a low, warm hum, remembering life with my step dad, and it pulls a smile from deep inside me.

Her face falls. "You're jokin'?"

"I would not joke about this," I laugh, chancing another glance her way. She's shaking her head in disbelief, and I can tell something is churning inside her. "I mean, it's just a coincidence, Sloane."

"I don't believe in those," she says, slight alarm etched in a crease above her brow.

"Oh, right. You believe in God," I tell her, flicking my gaze to the cross charm on her bracelet.

"I'm spiritual—there's a difference," she rebuffs, like the notion is an insult.

"Nothing wrong with it. Pretty sure Will went through a church phase…" I peter off just as she playfully knocks my arm. We take a left, getting closer.

"I just believe there's a right way this is all supposed to go. And if that's the case, nothin's a coincidence." She nibbles on her lip. "When you're out of tune with yourself, with God or the universe, you get lost."

"So if this isn't a coincidence, what is it?" I don't look at her when I ask it, just swallow against the wind the whips around us.

"A sign, I guess," she says, helplessly. I flick my gaze over, watching as she traces her lips with one manicured finger. "That I'm headin' in the right direction."

"Towards me?" I joke, secretly self-deprecating, because if anything the universe should be steering her well clear of me.

"Maybe," she admits, and my jaw twitches. "Maybe we were meant to be friends."

I hum, nodding my head to myself as guilt churns deep in my gut. I wonder if she can feel it, the way we're actually pulled together by a thread that isn't cosmic, but entirely fucking manmade; if she can feel the times I tried to snip it, only for her to tie it back together. A thread, knotted in places that make all of this stronger than it needed to be.

"What happened to '*it's-definitely-not-fate*' Sloane?"

We pull to a light, the only car there, and wait.

"She realized you're not a total ass-hat."

"So it's fate when you like me, a coincidence when you don't?" I chuckle, wrapping my hand tighter around the steering wheel. I lean against the inside of the car door, knowing I could just blow this light. There's no cameras, but I like the way her stare's trying to dig into my soul, like there's something worth inspecting there.

"I never *didn't* like you," she mutters, mostly to herself, the light shifting to green.

We coast toward Will's building, me unwilling to throttle the engine and her unwilling to ask me too. Like we both know this peace is about to be shattered.

"So you really think there's a right way in all of this?"

"Of course. Don't you?"

Her certainty sends a flash of regret through me, and wonder what it's like to still believe that everyone, *everything*, is good.

"I think what's right for one person is wrong for another. And that feels pretty hellish to me. Doesn't feel divine at all." On some level, she has to know this. She can't have existed in this world and skated past the realization that there's a cost to everything.

She considers it, purses her lips before nodding.

"I think in the end, it all works out," she says, her voice tinged with brittle hope as we park in front of Will's building. I can see Gen, head in her hands, on a bench, and that hope does fuck all to prepare me for whatever I'll find upstairs.

"Well...this is you," I joke, and Sloane huffs on a thin smile, making no move to leave.

"And that's you." She tips her head toward the top of the building, rolling her lips together. "I had fun tonight. Makes me wonder why I didn't give in to fate sooner."

Because I don't want to be just friends. Because I don't want to be more but betray you. Because I don't know how to do anything real anymore.

"I should get up there," I say instead, watching her lashes flutter one too many times when I change the subject. Her recovery is impressive, her eyes rolling at Will's mention.

"Everyone needs a cheerleader," she laments as she steps out of the car. "Night, Spellman."

"Night," I tell her, shutting off the ignition but leaving the keys.

* * *

"Come on, man. Don't do this, tonight." I jiggle the handle, desperation finally taking over once I cross the fifteen minute mark. I turn in a circle, wondering which of these neighbors would have a key, when the overnight attendant walks out of the elevator, confused. "I'm uh...his brother. If I could just—"

The man doesn't flinch, just flashes a key card over the door handle and walks away. When I step into the space, the dull yeast of weeks old beer creeps up my nostrils while the shower loudly sprays in the distance.

So he's alive.

I grab a trash bag, tossing everything more than half empty in the flimsy plastic before moving to his bedroom. There's a Will sized dent in the sheets, and a Gen sized one, too. Hot steam pours through the crack beneath the bathroom door, and I bang on it loudly.

"Will. Will, it's me. Andy."

Nothing.

"I'm coming in," I warn him before turning the knob.

And it isn't so much that Will's standing there in the shower naked, because I've seen every man on the team in various states of undress; it's that Will's skin is raw. His face, his arms, his chest—they're all as red as the tired veins traversing his bloodshot eyes, as the blood running from his hands down his legs, circling the drain.

I have to turn the water handle completely around, that's how high he's turned it up. When the fiery assault to his body stops, he blinks back into himself and sees me for the first time.

"You should go."

"No fucking way, Will." I disappear into his bedroom, pulling a fresh pair of sweatpants, shirt and underwear out of a drawer, and throw them on the bathroom counter. When he emerges, I consider at what point I should call someone. If telling someone to leave is grounds for a wellness check, or if the threat needs to be more substantial.

I decide that if he says the words, I won't hesitate.

But he barely says any words at all. He collapses on my shoulder and cries, and I let him, until he falls asleep, his face twisting with the kind of guilt and self-hatred I only ever see when I'm alone.

18

Andy

November

"Sloane, huh?"

I shoot my attention back over my shoulder and find Ian leaning against a mostly bare maple tree, its red and golden leaves littering the ground. The smirk permanently etched on his face is a distraction, so similar to the one our father wears, and I wonder if he knows he does it. Kind of wonder if I do it, too, when I'm not paying attention to whatever I've schooled my expression into.

I turn back around to the coffee counter, nodding a quick thanks to the underclassman manning the chilly campus beverage cart.

"What about her?" I ask, walking away, knowing he'll follow if his curious gaze is any indication.

"What, no funny dumbed down joke? You're off your game, Spellman."

I roll my neck, really not in the mood for whatever he's trying to get at. He has to know I'd never let him quote me for his idiotic paper. When I don't say anything, he clears his throat, increasing his speed so that we're in lock step, crunching the fall foliage at the same time.

"That's four times now you've been seen with her. Five times, if you count Pub 24." I cut him a glare, clenching my jaw. "I have eyes everywhere, Andy."

He's just like him.

I inhale icy November air, forcing myself to calm down. "And why," I begin to ask, shakily exhaling, "are you watching me to begin with?"

Something in his carefully crafted facade shudders, his gladiator shield falling as he glances around, tugging me by the arm until we're in a gazebo. Nervous energy slithers out of him, so at odds with his usual confidence, and I can't help but remember we're technically brothers. That maybe he's coming to me because he's in trouble and has no one else to turn to. Knocking my head back, I let the possibility wash over me and decide to be a decent human, whatever comes next, even if he doesn't deserve it.

"Listen—"

"I know he's watching Sloane," he says in one barely coherent ramble, and I freeze. "I know he told you to watch her."

I contemplate lying to him, feigning ignorance, but he'd see through it. You can't bullshit a bullshitter and he learned from the best.

Wind rattles the shutters of the gazebo as I sit on the bench—the white paint peeling, the wood ice cold—and draw my letterman tighter. Ian follows suit, eyeing me carefully as he takes the spot opposite me. He's waiting to see if I'll lie. He's estimating something, in real time, by the way I react. I'm fucking freezing, though, the hot coffee clasped between my hands barely enough to warm me as stick season threatens to wipe out any semblance of cheer. And I'm tired —of lying, of pretending. Ironically enough, this secret brother of mine is the only person who knows most of my truth.

"Yeah," I say softly. "Yeah, he did."

Ian's eyes narrow, understanding somehow softening the usually predatory gleam they hold. "And you don't want to?"

"Of course not." It's harsher than I mean it to be, the implication more grating than it should be. I've been informing on my friends for years.

"Sorry, it's just...shocking." A slight smile playing at the corners of his mouth.

"Shocking? You don't know me." I let out a bitter laugh. "Spying on people isn't the same as knowing them, Ian." His scoff sears against my pride, its target glaringly obvious, and it spurs me further. "I don't have a *choice*, asshole. You choose to spend your time writing hit pieces on kids you're what— jealous of?" His eyes flare, and I know I've hit something. "It's actually fucking pathetic."

He rises, eerily calm as he squares his shoulder, shoving his hands in his pockets. "Not as pathetic as selling your friends out for connections. What would they say if they knew?"

I swallow hard, heart racing. "They'd understand."

"Would they? You think they care about you that much?" He shakes his head, his jaw grinding. "Olivia all but stomped on me when I tried to tell her the truth, despite years of friendship. They seem to have a lot of trouble with nuance. With notions of morality or suffering."

"And you do?" I laugh, watching my breath puff out before me. "You're just like them. We're all screwing each other over, but at least some of us have a reason." I step forward, anger roiling in my bones. "You think I want connections? I want my mom to have food on her fucking table. I want my sister to have hot water. I want them to live a normal fucking life. What could *you* possibly want?"

He balks, looks like he's on the verge of saying something, before his face pulls tight.

"Forget it," he says, storming out of the gazebo as I sit there, wondering what the hell just happened.

* * *

Will's building glows with lit windows, students beginning to pack bags for the impending fall break. I stopped in with a container of food Mom made him, the closest I could get to offering him care. He promised me he wouldn't do anything stupid, but I've been checking on him everyday regardless, pulling his curtains back, throwing away the liquor bottles he's managing to keep full stock of.

I told Coach and I told Ben. They said they were handling it, but the details of that handling feel hollow and dangerous because they include his parents and—maybe I'm cynical, but Will didn't become a shell of himself in a loving, balanced home. I shrug it off, sending him an aspirational quote about climbing mountains as I brace the cold, and head home.

The long walk to frat housing, with the wind rasping against my cheeks and nose, leads me right by the row of new builds that try their best to mimic the historic homes that've rested here for over a century—the ones where Ian lives. The bricks are too red, the grout too stark in contrast, especially when you consider the way the stones on the old buildings have been weathered by sun and rain. The lamp lights on this part of campus are crisp and dark, the black paint not having had enough time to chip. Even my frat house, built sometime between the beginning and now, has this inherent charm that seems to be missing from the row of buildings here. They feel overeager, like they desperately want to prove they're just like the rest despite all the evidence.

Guilt trickles down my awareness when I think about what I said to Ian.

I told him that he's just like them, but I know he's not. He's an outsider with money. I'm an outsider without. I should've listened, instead of acting on impulse. More importantly, I should've wondered why he was coming to me about Sloane to begin with.

He answers the knocking sequence almost immediately. Ian doesn't seem surprised to be seeing me; he just ushers me in, popping his head out the door like he's checking for someone.

His laptop sits on a stack of books in his living room, the glow of the screen illuminating the wall to wall bookcase behind it. Papers are strewn across the coffee table, and a fresh cup of black brew rests there, the family crest on the side of it sending a jolt of resentment down my chest.

"Want it?" Ian says flatly, and I glance away, ignoring him.

"I wanted to apologize for being shitty earlier."

One of his brows arches, his eyes lazily assessing me. "So do it?"

Thank god I wasn't actually raised with him. "Sorry," I tell him, almost swallowing the word. "I've had a lot on my mind but I shouldn't have spoken to you like that.

He adjusts the collar on his maroon cable knit sweater, clearing his throat. "I could've approached things differently." His version of an apology, I guess. "But you're here because, unlike what you'd like the masses to believe, you're *not* an idiot."

Teeth grating against each other, I try to control the slight twitch happening in my jaw. "It was pretty fucking dumb to take his deal."

Ian nods to the couch he's refused to claim, opting for the

floor where he can access his laptop, and I sink into the expensive cushions and wait. His attention cuts, and I realize it's this attention that's made him the nationally recognized student journalist he is today. Without his relentless observation, the gossip column, the sports column, the politics column, would be carbon copies of what every other collegiate press is doing.

"What if I told you," he suddenly says, my gaze snapping to his, "I could help you get out."

"Why would you do that?" Hope takes root, and I willfully keep it in the shadows where it can't bloom.

"Because our father is a piece of shit dirtbag who helps other pieces of shit dirtbags hide from the consequences of their actions." The air in the room shifts and my heart beats loudly in my ears as a light automatically warms from a harsh white to a warm yellow.

"I agree. This isn't news to me," I scoff, shaking my head as I release a heavy breath.

"No. But what if I told you that he's hiding something. That he *did* something big. That he's desperate because things are falling apart." He eyes me, like I'm supposed to be reading something into the vague shit he just told me. He tilts his head, exasperated. "Are things *not* falling apart right now?"

"Yeah, no thanks to you." I shrug, then pause, understanding dawning on me. "*Because* of you. It's for a reason," I say, more of a question than anything.

"Of course I have a reason," he spits, and I recall our conversation in the gazebo. "He's only as safe as the number of secrets we keep. It's his entire business model: secrets."

I glance down at my shoes, trying to unravel the threads wound tightly around all of us, unable to neatly follow it to Will even though I *know* he's at the center of it.

"Andy, think."

"Shit. Lily?" I suddenly realize, the enormity of that secret

—that Will dated her, Olivia's best friend, before her death—slams into me.

Ian just stares at me, his gaze begging me to go on, like I'm missing something.

"Okay, so...Will dated Lily. Olivia and Lily were best friends. She...died," I say, my voice dipping. "Clearly, Liv didn't know, but that's just a moral failing on Will's part. What else is there?"

"I need to know if you want to be involved. I'm not telling you anything until I know you're in."

"How does this solve my problem, though? I mean, I'm...I'm all for taking him down. But I have bills to pay, Ian. People who depend on me. He owns me." The words are lead—are poison in my mouth.

"I know," he says, his voice soft as his gaze dips to the ground. "My trust is substantial. I'll cover whatever he was covering."

My hand rakes through my hair all on its own, and I realize I'm standing. "No way," I tell him, my brows drawing tight as I try to understand this man who's usually so cold. So calculated. "Just so you can own me instead? No thanks." I head toward the door, sadness skating between the vertebrae in my spine—in and out, like it knows it has no right to be here. I never assumed I would get out of this early. This shouldn't feel so gutting.

"Tell me, Andrew," he says, voice raised as he follows me. "What would it be like to stop lying? Do you even remember the truth anymore?"

"Do you?" It comes out more desperate than I thought possible, and I feel over exposed.

"I *wish* I didn't remember the truth. But once you do, turning away from it will eat at you. Necrotize *everything* you touch. Everything you think about touching." He pauses; I think about Sloane, the way I've wanted her and the way I shouldn't. "I said I had a way out. Yes, it involves helping me. But once he's been exposed, we're both free. We are all free."

The thudding is so loud, in my ears, in my chest, in my throat. Breathing is hard, like I'm on the peak looking down, hard for oxygen and terrified to fall.

"I need to think about it."

"Of course. You know where to find me.

19

Sloane

The linoleum in the room is mocking me. It's too pallid, too yellow, too clean, and it smells sour, like the disinfectant was so pure they couldn't bear to throw some lemon in there. I run the rubber toe of my converse against it until a dark line appears and smile, satisfied.

"Ms. Tucker?" a woman we aren't familiar with says, her head popping between the door and the frame.

"Hi." Mom sits straighter in her chair, and I wince because it takes effort. She's all brittle bones and thinly disguised apathy, but that is why today I brought a puzzle. These rooms are so dreary, and the treatment bays are worse when the dogs aren't there. Things were so busy this week, what with the Gen and Grant of it all, that I forgot to check what programming is happening today.

Problem-solving, though: it's really what I do best, maybe other than painting, and so I brought this puzzle. It's kittens, something Connie really loves, on a beach of all things. Not entirely sure if cats can, in fact, swim, but they looked so precious on the box, and my mom's not a stickler about realism —neither am I, and—

"—is not working as well as we'd hoped."

"I figured," my mom says, her smile more of a shrug, and I look between the doctor and my mother.

"Okay," I say, my third cup of coffee skipping through my veins. "What's next? There was a list—"

"Sloane." My mom's frail hand finds mine, squeezes it, and the doctor slips out of the room.

"Did you already talk about the next option? Sorry I was lost in my thoughts," I huff, nervously, dread pricking my cold skin. I reach for my sweater, hastily pulling it over myself before pumping the hand sanitizer, suddenly conscious of all the germs.

"Honey…" Connie's eyes, the sockets hollow from the way she's been wasting away, are tired, and I know what she'll say if I let her.

"*Why* don't you want to try?" I snap. "What is so wrong with just trying?"

Her throat bobs, the fine ligaments there, accentuated by the thinness of her skin, shifting as she breathes. "I did try. But there's somethin' to knowin' when to call it."

"Well I don't know!" Pressure builds behind my eyes. "How about we both know? How about you ask me if I think it's time to call it?" Gripping the edges of my long sleeves, and I wrap my arms tightly around me. She takes a steadying breath instead, blinking over at me, and I can see the steel collecting in her gaze.

"Alright," she says softly, her smile sun-dried and creaky, revealing that one tooth that chipped sometime after she lost us the second time. "A little more, Sloane." I feel my chest, which had constricted, let out the smallest bit. "But promise me that when it's time, you'll let it be."

Behind my closed mouth smile, my teeth chatter. Adrenaline runs cold through me, and it's only my oversized sweatshirt that can stop the shivers. I have the thought that a hug, that being held, would help me keep it all in, but it's not something I want to ask for. Not right now.

A ring sounds through the room, and I reach for my phone before it clatters off the chair and onto the sickly floor. "Hello," I answer, unsure of who I picked up. I just did, accepted their intrusion like the life line Connie is too broken to throw me.

"Hey," the voice says, and it's Andrew, his voice wary and tinged with vocal fry—like he just woke up or like he's been talking all afternoon. Contentment cracks against the cold shell I'm rattling against, makes its way in the more I hear him through the phone. "Are you at the conservatory today?"

"I'm near there." Connie squints, like it'll help her hear. I hold up a finger, still feeling the cold sting of anxiety when I do.

"Carm usually takes the city bus on Wednesdays but rehearsal ran late..." he drifts off for a second. "I'm not gonna be able to get over there for an hour." The noise of wherever he is falls to a murmur, and a door shuts.

"*Go,*" she mouths, the squinting having worked. I tilt my head as she picks up her phone, showing a screen with a car lift app, and I scowl.

"I get it if you can't, or—" Connie rolls her eyes, and I whisper shout that the doctor still needs to come back in. "Sorry, what?" Andy asks, uncertainty lacing his tone.

"Sloane, I can handle it. Now get out of this god forsaken place, or else—" she lifts her brows, the skin pulling taut, and I finally relent.

"Sorry—yes, of course I can pick up Carmen. Give me like, twenty minutes."

"Thank you, Sloane," he says quietly, but it's incomplete,

something else hanging on the other side. He hangs up anyway, and I stare into my phone.

"You wanna tell me who that was?" Amused curiosity sits in her gaze, that tooth poking out again, but all I can think about when I look back up at her is the defeat I caught in it just ten minutes earlier. And maybe I shouldn't be mad at my sick mother, but I am.

"Not really," I admit, crossing my arms. "But it's time to go." I gather my bag, hold my palm out for her to clasp it.

"Darlin', you are wound up like a—"

"Connie," I cut her off, making a concerted effort not to lose it. "I'm takin' you home, and before that, we're stoppin' at the nurses' station."

Huffing out a breath, my mother grabs her oversized bag, resigning herself to my will, and I can't help but wonder why it isn't easier to convince her to stay.

* * *

Getting Carmen to put her seatbelt on was a battle in and of itself, so when she tells me I don't need to walk her up, I just follow her up the stairs anyway, unsurprised by the way she greets every single person we pass.

She slots the key in the door, glancing over her shoulder to shoot me a tight smile. "Thanks for the ride, Rapunzel." She slides inside so quickly, my fingers almost get crushed by the paint chipped door.

"Wait," I say, forcing the door back open, ignoring her eye roll. "Are you gonna be fine alone?" A door slams shut at the end of the hallway and Carmen flinches. A less than put together man drunkenly holding himself up against the wall. It's four in the afternoon, for God's sake.

It isn't a rough area—I remember living in worse at her age

184

—but she's not fighting size, not like I was when I'd walk the dirt path to my uncle's trailer with only the moon as my guide. And while her personality is ferocious, I'm not entirely sure she can even reach a cabinet without stacking something on a chair.

"Yeah," she shrugs, but I can feel the hint of wariness in her voice, and I know my question's not even one she should have to answer. I push my way in, my earlier bullishness finding a new target. "Suit yourself," she says, but whatever burden was in her voice is lighter now.

The apartment, with its inelegant assembly of vinyl and carpet, is charming. Knick-knacks pepper the kitchen counter, the built in shelves that frame the television, the modest coffee table. Everything feels loved—the couch, whose worn appearance is evidence of how often this family's curled up on it; the table in the nook off the kitchen, where more than one pen mark mar the deep wooden grain; the kitchen towels hanging off the oven door, faded and stitched—one with ghosts and one with turkeys.

"If you're hungry—" I start to say, but she's already illuminated by the fridge's glow. Two cheese sticks in hand, she waltzes past me and flops down onto the sofa. The carpet, while faded, looks clean, so I kick off my shoes before padding across it to join her on the couch. She flings one of the sticks at me before grabbing the remote.

"Do you...have homework?" I dare to ask, and she scrunches her entire face at me. The smile I crack restores a small part of the goodwill I lost back at the hospital. Connie and I barely spoke on the short drive to her apartment, hardly acknowledged that we were parting ways until after I get back from Atlanta for Thanksgiving, in part because she was visibly agitated when I let the nurses know that she would be continuing treatment.

Like my vested interest in her was inconvenient, rather than a god damn blessing.

"No," Carmen says flatly. I study the slump of her shoulders; something about her feels deflated. Fresh off a conversation with her friends, she'd been lively. *Snarky*, sure, but in better form than she is now. Since we pulled up to her house, it's like all the air has slowly leaked out of her.

"You know," I start to tell her, glancing up at the popcorn ceiling. "I had a pretty shit day."

She smirks. "I had a shit day, too."

I flare my eyes at her. "Okay, don't do as I *do*, little bird."

Eyes rolling, she lets her head fall to the side and continues her scroll on the glowing TV.

"Do you want to talk about it?"

"Nope." Still, the click of a television show carousel, the beat steady. I can tell she's not even really looking for anything.

I nod, lips pursed as I scramble for something to do or say, thinking back to the shenanigans Clemmie and I would get into on the hard days. We were only a little older than Carmen is now, I realize, and the thought of us painting ceramics at her mom's kitchen table pulls a smile to my face. I leap up and she startles, watching me as I rifle through her cabinets until I find some plain mugs.

"These special?" I ask, holding them up for her to see. She squints, studying them for a long moment.

"No. Dollar tree," is all she gives me. "We don't have a normal coffee maker, so—"

"Come here," I call to her, layering paper towels on the table before setting them down. The random set of acrylics I found in the donate box yesterday just so happen to be the perfect palette for some fall themed mugs, so they join the impromptu craft station I'm designing, filling a few glasses with an inch of water. I feel deep into the recesses of my bag, hoping I accidentally left some cheap brushes in there and find nothing but my reliable, expensive Windsor & Newtons.

"These," I start, leveling my most serious gaze at Carmen as she sits back on her heels in the chair next to me, "are usually for watercolors, but they're all I have right now. If you can promise to rinse your brush well between colors, we can use them."

"Oh," she says, her voice smaller than it usually is. "Yeah. I can do that." Her eyes sparkle as she looks between the hues, opting for a soft, sage like blue for her base. "Can I play music?"

"Girl, your house, your rules," I tell her, pulling out my phone. "Here. Go crazy."

She quirks a brow and leaves the phone on the table. "Hey Google? Play my Broadway hits." She grins back at me just as a song I've never heard starts playing.

Mumbling some sad song about no one being alone, she continues layering on the misty blue color and I challenge myself to make something interesting. Maybe this could be the spark that leads to a fire, could be the thing that reignites the artist side of my brain.

Like I thought, I can't even choose which orange to go with. I lay my brushes down and listen closely to the song now playing, the melody vaguely familiar.

"What's this one?" I ask the wispy girl leaning forward in her chair, brows drawn close together in concentration.

"...Defying Gravity?" she says, like I'm an idiot, and I guess I am.

"It's been a while," I try to excuse, laughing through my embarrassment. "What's your favorite show?"

She thinks for a long moment, pulling her gaze away from the mug.

"Tick, Tick, Boom." She dips her head back down, diving

back into her work with shocking dedication. I can't help but smile at the little artist.

"Like the movie?" I ask, warily.

"Close enough. But there's this really good boot leg on Youtube I used to watch with my dad and Andy."

I saw the film. Concern lances through me at the idea that *this*—a story about living a life not wasted that ultimately ends in tragedy—is her favorite show. Like she senses my worry, she continues.

"It's just, like, nostalgic, I guess. We still watch it, just me and Andy. Mom can't. She doesn't watch anything with death." She says it so bluntly, I almost laugh and she *actually* does.

"That was morbid, little bird," I tell her, falling into a muscle cramping bout of laughter.

"*Little bird*," she mocks me, shimmying her shoulders. "My second favorite show is Beetlejuice." Her brows flare and I gasp for air at her delivery.

I can just imagine her on the stage.

"Stop. Who is lettin' you see these?" I take a deep breath, calming myself.

She shrugs. "My brother."

"I think I need to have a word."

"Have a *word, little bird*," she giggles, dipping her brush into a burnished gold. "What, are you from Kentucky?"

"Atlanta," I declare, a little offended. "That's in Georgia," I clarify, and she whips her head toward me.

"I know." She lets her brush drop and pivots so we're face to face. "Go ahead. Quiz me."

I narrow my eyes, letting the bubbly feeling wash over me as I think of a city. "Philade—"

"Pennsylvania."

"Orlan–"

"Florida! Come on, don't go easy on me," she says, wiggling in her seat.

My lips press into a firm line as I dig for another city. "Carmel."

She goes bug eyed as she leans forward, like she'll find the answer somewhere in the ether, before she suddenly springs back. "California!"

The door creaks open, swallowing my attempt at another question, and her brother walks in, and the air shifts, my skin pricking with awareness as I watch him take me in, watch his gaze sweep over me in one long brush.

"Nice jacket," he says, fighting a grin.

I touch the leather I'm wrapped in, the coolness reminding me of Halloween in my car, and I fail to fight the blush before shrugging his jacket off, handing it his way. When he makes no attempt at taking it back, I hang it over a chair, clearing my throat.

"The windows were down and it was still in my car." I glance around at the table, littered with paints as it is, and lock eyes with Carmen. The expectant heaviness I find there tugs on my heart strings. I can tell she doesn't want me to leave yet. "We were just painting, but if you guys had plans—"

"Spaghetti." He lifts to two grocery bags, and another hangs in the crook of his jacketed elbow. My brows dip in question. "Those are the plans. As long as Carmen doesn't have a problem with it..." Andrew grins, all coy and practiced, like he's teased his sister a million times, and my heart warms when she glues her eyes to mine, pleading.

"Please stay," she tells me, the smallest hint of a smile playing at the corner of her lips, and I nod.

"I do love spaghetti."

"Be worried if you didn't," he says to just me as he walks past, disappearing down the hall.

"He likes you a whole lot," Carmen mutters while fixated on the white outline of a clover, her physical attention never leaving the mug.

The roof comes into focus, and I remember the way he didn't want to kiss me, fresh embarrassment burning the bridge of my nose. *Doesn't matter anymore. We're friends.*

"I can promise you he doesn't," I chuckle, dipping my brush into a maroon tinged clay color. "But if he did...it wouldn't be none—" I boop her nose with the color "—of your business." Carmen squeals, her brush quickly finding my face, and I let her swipe me with one too many colors, only pretending to protect myself from her, before we quietly settle back into our pieces, paint drying on our skin.

When Andy finally emerges, hair wet and tousled, messily falling across his brow, in a gray Astor Hill crewneck and jeans, I pull my legs up to my chest and grin over at him.

"That's all ya'll wear, isn't it? *Astor Hill* this, *Astor Hill* that."

"I'm sorry is that—is that jealousy, I hear?" His crooked smirk threatens to undo me, has something burning in the center of my chest as he crosses behind me, close enough to touch.

"Sloane doesn't *need* your pretentious college merch. She's an artist—a student of the world," Carmen says, echoing something I said as a joke to her and her little friends behind the set design wing. I'm reminded that sarcasm, and the ability to discern it, is in fact honed over time.

Andy's back shifts, his laughter floating across the cozy apartment as the first notes of garlic, blooming in olive oil, burst through the air, and I shut my eyes for a second, letting the ease of being here wash over me.

The evening descends into a comfortable calm, like deep pressure, smothering the worries that have bled into my awareness the past few weeks. Here, now, I can hardly recreate the dread I felt earlier at the hospital; it's abstract and out of reach, blown away by the hazy bliss of this little home.

Carmen and I paint, moving onto the few white plates they own, while her brother cooks. The apartment turns fragrant the longer he stands there, sautéing onions, dicing and crushing tomatoes. I watch as he drains the pasta, singular focus etched into his features, and mindlessly admire the strain of his forearms.

The dinner is unearthly perfection, and I'm reminded of the way Clemmie's mom would cook for me, of the few times Evie made something she didn't find in a cookbook. When I'd be sick with a cold, she'd make me chicken soup, "the way her grammy made it."

"You start with the whole chicken, and there's no other way about it," she'd said as I lay curled up on the formal sofa, made more comfortable by every pillow in the house and a quilted blanket, as she salted an oversized pot. She'd stir and I'd hear the soft thud of chicken bones on the pot's walls, hear her curse under her breath when something would start to boil over. I'd close my eyes and breathe in, convinced the smell alone was making me better.

I think about this, about how different things taste when someone makes them with you in mind, as I twirl my fork and slide in a mouthful of pasta. Eyes fluttering shut, I sigh, warmth oozing over me as I let the bright notes only fresh tomatoes can bring spread across my taste buds.

"No one feeding you?" Andy peers up over his loaded fork, a smirk tugging at the corners of his mouth, as Carmen regales us of tales from today's rehearsal. It's a fleeting look but one that sears, and I flick my gaze down to my plate, feeling flustered.

I try to leave after dinner, but Carmen's hand is practically super glued to mine as she drags me back to the sofa and finds a movie for all three of us to enjoy. It's horrible—something about zombies and werewolves, but lazily coded as a tale of prejudice for children. She holds my hand the entire time, and maybe I hold hers.

Andrew's on one side; I'm on the other. We've only made it forty-five minutes in before her soft snores vibrate between us and he carefully lifts her up, seamlessly transferring her to her bed. I stay on the couch, watching from a distance as he lingers in her doorway before softly shutting the door.

When he collapses back on the couch, head falling back, I feel my pulse across my skin. Like before it was thumping in the background, muffled, but now that we're alone it knows it can beat recklessly.

"That was impressive," I admit, giving him a sidelong glance as I unwind my bun, enjoying the freedom.

He tracks the movement. "She's famous for falling asleep mid movie."

"She's lucky," I tell him, meaning it. Andy's brows furrow at my random show of sincerity, so I add: "Pretty sure Grant's never even considered bringin' me a pillow."

His huffed laughter is muted as he looks at the ground. "She loved having you here."

"But did *you* love havin' me here?" I joke, my silent insecurity weaving through my ordinary defenses, just as I guess he has, and I wonder when I started to care about what he thought at all.

Andy just blinks over at me, swallows, strong throat bobbing as something pained flits across his expression.

"Right," I say, feeling flayed raw for no good reason. "Well, I really should be goin'."

I push up from the edge of the sofa and throw my bag over my shoulder, evading his gaze, my pulse erratic in my throat. I replay the moment he came home, try to dissect the moment I should've left; I scour dinner at the table and wonder if I shouldn't have pried Carmen's hand from mine and let them be. It's no use though, because I'm not good at telling about anything anymore. That sense has been frayed, completely.

I reach the door and he reaches me, and it's his lips against my hair that I swear I feel, the closest we've ever been. Teeth sinking into my cheek, I blink into the beveled wood, fighting the way every inch of my skin is like a live wire, my heart a loud, rapturous thud, high in my chest, almost to my throat.

"Of course, I did," he finally says, softly, his hands bracing themselves above my head, against the door frame, like he couldn't stand otherwise, and I spin around.

"But?" I ask, lifting my face to him. The roguish charm that drew me to him months ago isn't roguish at all; directed at me, it's an intensity that burns just beneath my skin, that says he's mine for the taking if I want it. His eyes pin me, swim with lust, and I feel *vindicated*. Feel less crazy but still endlessly vulnerable as I give up pretending I'm not dying for him to kiss me senseless. That I don't want him to drown me the way I haven't drowned since my fingers gave out and my creativity washed away.

My lips part, my gaze drops to his full mouth, and I wait for him to crash into me. I expect it to be a rush, for him to scorch me, overwhelm me like I'd hoped—but he doesn't. One hand finds my waist, grips me with throat clawing tenderness, and he presses me into the door. His other hand lands just beneath my collar bone and travels up my neck, his thumb skating over the edge of my jaw slowly. So slowly that I tremble.

He just shakes his head, watching me, touching me. My breaths are a small series of heaves that I can't seem to keep under control; I earnestly try, sinking my teeth into my lip like the pain will bring a sense of calm, but it doesn't.

I want him to shut his eyes, eat me alive, and move on. I want to move on.

Instead, his thumb frees my lip from my hold, before heavily, greedily, kissing me. He isn't interested in eating me alive; he's savoring me. It isn't something anyone does—savor me—and the realization has me falling into his touch. His grip on me deepens, holding me close to him as his weight presses us both into the door. His lips are feather soft on mine, every brush of them like oxygen on a fire. I want to feel them down my neck, across my skin, under my skin.

And it dawns on me that I've craved this. Being touched in a way that isn't a claiming. The glide of his tongue against mine is so unrushed, goosebumps erupt across my skin as desire pulls tears into my waterline. I gasp against his parted lips, breathe into the feel of his fingers gently tracing the outline of my bra, of their sudden heat against the skin beneath my sweater. He presses warm, open mouthed kisses along my neck, and I shudder, pressing the length of my body against him like all of him at once might blunt this feeling.

Andy's fingers rake through my nape, tangle in my hair. His teeth scrape down the length of my neck before his lips find mine again so he can taste me—so I can really taste him. I groan, pushing my chest against his as I deepen the angle, wrapping my hand around his neck while the other rushes up the hard terrain beneath his sweater.

"Sloane," he murmurs, against my mouth, the sound of him wanting me so plainly cracking something in my chest and I yank myself away, shocked. Sore between the ribs.

I reach behind me and turn the knob, relieved at the cool rush of air. He doesn't get a word out before I turn and run away.

20

Sloane

Pots of apple and cinnamon, clove and star anise, still simmer in the kitchen under Anders's watchful eye, and the house is full of people—so full that no one's noticed the way I keep siphoning Beau's best whiskey from the ledge in his office. Except maybe Grant, whose watchful gaze keeps finding me.

We haven't talked since our blow up, other than exchanging a few words when completely necessary, mostly to fool our parents, trick them into thinking we're good. It's not working.

I watch Grant shake his head, his eyes narrow with disapproval while he moves his attention back to the conversation he's in with the suits who work for Beau.

"Sloane?" Brennan, whose eyes are still a muddy grey color, just like they were in high school, says beneath me, and I remember I'm still collapsed in his lap. "You were saying?"

"Daydreamin'," I giggle. His brows furrow at me in conspiracy, and I know he's already jumped to the conclusion I'm still trying to conclude. I sneak another sip of whiskey from the crystal Evie puts out for use on special occasions like this, and sink a little deeper in him. He's not nearly as solid as I imagine someone like Andy is. He's sort of a shell of a solid person, I notice as I let him hold the brunt of me. It doesn't even feel particularly nice, but I do it anyway, hoping it's all just muscle memory and that I'm out of practice.

Grant's eyes flit toward me again, and the slight tilt of his head tells me he's trying to eavesdrop. *Bastard.* Instead of just talking to me, he'll try to spy on every little thing I say to everyone else.

"Connie—"

"Your birth mom?" Brennan clarifies, and I let my head loll back an annoyed guttural sound.

"My *mom.* Anyway she called, and the number wouldn't show anything but *unknown,* so I knew it was her. Turns out she wanted to see us! Me and Grant that is." My hand slaps my knee with so much gusto, we both jolt a little in the chair he's braced in, and I huff a tired laugh. "So *then* I dropped everythin' and went to Boston, because she was tryin' to contact Grant, which—"

Like clockwork, he takes up the whole goddamn frame and looms over us, like he likes to lord over everything. The morality police. The conversation police. The when and where police. My eyes roll nearly to the back of my head as Brennan shifts, trying to distract from the very sensual hold he has on me. I don't help him, because I don't really care what my brother—or anyone here—thinks about me.

I slice my gaze up to Grant. "Oh goodie! We were *just* talkin' about you," I taunt, baring my teeth for a smile that I hope translates to 'fuck off.' Brennan fucks off instead, muttering something about getting another drink, but I know Grant's hawkish attention has shattered the little bubble I've been drinking myself into and sent my entertainment along with it.

The lack of sadness I feel at his loss only adds insult to injury; I should at least feel disappointed. Lots of fish in the sea, Clem always says, but I'm only irritated—not gutted—that someone let one off the hook.

"You ruin *everything*," I spit. "Have you ever just *not cared*, for like, a minute of your life? Oh wait—you tried that. Didn't work out for you," I say, sweetly, cocking my head to the side, hoping the reference to Gen hurts.

"Do you want me to get you some water?" is all he says, and I feel a flush rise up my neck, the overwhelm of being talked down to only driving me to drink more.

"Stop actin' like I'm unhinged, Grant." I push off the chair and make my way to Beau's study with the intermittent hand on the wall, trying to look less drunk than I am. I clasp the cool bottle of whiskey only for him to snatch it out of my hands.

"Well, you're spillin' your guts about Connie to anyone who will listen, so."

So like him to exaggerate when it suits him, to blow something entirely normal and rational out of proportion, simply because it triggers something in him. He can't bear to hear our mother's name, so it's my job to shield him from it?

"Some of us talk about things. I know that's a foreign concept to you."

"I talk to y—"

A loud bout of laughter leaps out of my throat, the notion that he *communicates* with me, of all people, comical, and I snatch my whiskey back. "Not me, Grant—her. Talk to mom. Hell, talk to *Gen.* You just shut down the moment things get hard, or real. You're never goin' to feel anything worth feelin' if you keep livin' like this."

Brushing a tear from the corner of my eyes, I realize my cheeks are wet entirely, that tears aren't just leaking, but flowing down my face, and I feel my chest start to heave. We're so messed up. The wires in our brains crossed somewhere along the way, and neither of us know how to hold anything good. At least Grant can pretend to have it together; I just fall apart, revealing all the ways I'm fractured and broken for anyone to see. I feel my lip start to tremble, frustration welling in me at his refusal to walk through any of this.

Throwing Connie and her illness on him might not be fair, but what is fair to me? Not once since we were adopted has my brother sat down and heard me. Listened to my feelings without immediately negating them with a heavy handed corrective to just be grateful instead.

"Let's not talk about this here, Sloane," he tells me, voice low and assertive, like I'm a thing to be handled, and it's the exact wrong thing to say to me when a near half bottle of whiskey courses through my veins.

"Why not?" I feel the way my voice shoots out of me as I let my glass hit our dad's desk, my anger red hot and searing, cutting away at the cool I try so hard to keep together.

"Because it's Thanksgiving," he seethes, and I step back, shocked. "And Mom is having a great time, if you haven't noticed, and no one wants to hear about the deadbeat who abandoned us." The word choice is intended to slice me, to wound me, and I stare at him in true wonder, because our scars *are* the same.

How he could disregard that pain, rub salt right into the gashes still so clearly there, is a mystery that belies more than he probably knows.

There's a distance he places between himself and those memories, like he's somehow a different person from the one Connie gave up all those years ago. But he isn't. It's that boy, the one who waited for her to come back and shut his heart down when she didn't, who also told Gen to leave him.

"How long are you goin' to pretend that *this*," I ask him,

waving at the heavy built-ins packed with special edition texts and knick knacks that could afford a family groceries for a year, "is the entirety of your life? Have you even told Dad about the draft?"

The thing you've wanted to do since you were a boy? Where is that Grant?

"I don't need to tell him yet, there's time—"

"No, Grant!" I scream, earning me some stares around the room, my voice turning hoarse, feeling desperate. "There isn't time. Eventually the words are due. The feelings come. Life happens," I gasp, my breath stuttering. "And the longer you keep pushing off anything that leaves you feeling even a little vulnerable, the longer you're going to spend that life alone. Unhappy. A sad excuse of the person you could be."

His eyes descend into something dark and guarded, like the words landed only to be locked up with all the other truths he'd rather not look at, and fresh tears supersede my old ones.

"So what do you prescribe, Sloane? Since you're so fucking wise? Am I supposed to live like you? Don't look any happier than me, from where I stand. You say I don't face my problems —you literally *run* from yours. What even happened in California?"

"Fuck you," I seethe before I feel my chest cave in, my face turning hot and damp with sweat, the tears making it hard to see anything but blurry figures. I burst through the study door, brushing my hand along the jacquard wallpaper in the hallway that leads to the back stairwell, and sprint up the steps, desperate for solitude.

Shoving up the window in my childhood bedroom, I crouch through it, and curl up on my side, letting a weathered slate shingle dig into my cheek. Sobs rack my body, vibrate through me as I ricochet against the roof in small, uncontrolled bursts. The fear wells in me, over and over, before spilling, releasing, leading me to relief, only to well all over again.

To realize you'll never evolve past who you hate, become more than your worst self, is devastating, because sometimes you can forget. You can live life in these broad, beautiful strokes that feel infinite, can pour yourself into those moments and let the paint bleed, feeling certain you're not ruining anything, because you've become good. You've become who you always wanted to be, a woman capable. You can live that life, only for it to be a myth —you were a myth. It wasn't you, it was a projection of who you wished you could be. The girl you've always been will always claw her way out, regardless of how many layers you add, how many broad strokes you manage, no matter how much time has passed.

Is there a universe where Connie keeps me? Where I don't get adopted? Where I don't take my professor up on his drink invitation because I'm so eager for approval? Where I don't have an abortion? Where I actually regret it? Where Connie isn't sick? Where I'm worthy of being kept, by anyone?

The stars twinkle down at me, laughing, because they know and I never will. All I know is this, and it's hell.

The kitchen island is blessedly cool, and I lay my face against it in hopes it'll staunch the nausea that won't subside. Small bites of bacon, courtesy of Anders, are all I can manage between sips of water, which I can only handle between bouts of cold stone pressed against my cheek.

The house is quiet, save for the birds that chirp through the perpetually open kitchen windows, and I let the silence numb me since there isn't anything socially acceptable at this hour that will. I know that once the hangover wears off, once

I've kept a good meal down and I've showered, changed, I'll be well on my way to normalcy.

Normalcy.

I huff an exhausted laugh against the counter before slowly pulling my head up, jolting when I find Evie waiting by the tea kettle, watching me.

"Good mornin' my little wild cat," she says, her smile a small warm thing that I don't want. I glance down at the counter, blinking at my bacon. "How are you feelin'?"

"Like shit. Obviously." I swallow, pulling in a breath as I shut my eyes against the brightness.

"Beau told me about your fight with Grant." Those eyes of hers crinkle in curiosity as her head tilts, the freshly washed waves, not yet blown and sprayed into place, falling to the side. She's older, and the realization has something sinking in my stomach.

"Don't worry about it," I mutter, spinning off the kitchen stool to grab a mug for some coffee.

"Sloane," she orders, shockingly stern. "I need to talk to you."

Sighing, I turn to face her, a blue striped mug cradled in my hand.

"Your father doesn't know you aren't attending your program yet."

My heart trips over itself, my shoulders freezing in place. "But you do."

"You know he doesn't read those tabloids. How can you be so careless, Sloane?" Evie eyes me like this is some grave thing I've done, and I know it isn't ideal. I know.

But given the context—the context being the woman who gave me life is nearly on her deathbed—I could actually give two fucks about getting a piece of paper from a ritzy art program who hires professors that regularly engage in sexual relationships with their students.

"I'm sorry?" she asks on a small gasp, and I'm not even sure which part of that I mumbled out loud. "Sloane—" she reaches out, her fingers only brushing my wrist as I wrench myself away and flee up the stairs.

It's unsurprising that she follows because she's never known when to give me an inch or give me a mile; she always seems to choose the wrong one. Not bothering to knock on my door, she bursts in, her eyes glassy as her lips purse the way they do when she's furious.

"I do not," she starts, taking a calming breath, "I do not pretend to know what it is like to be you. And I don't deny that you had a hard life. But Sloane, you have people. You have *us*. I—" she falters, pressing her lips together. "I *am* your mother in the ways that count, and it kills me that you don't think I can carry any of that with you." A streak glistens down the side of her face, and she knocks it away with the back of her hand.

"I have," I say, voice hushed, "a mother."

"How is she?" she asks, the sincerity in her gaze lancing across my skin, because how can it be sincere when she took us from her. When she laid claim to me when I'd already laid claim to Connie.

"Sick," I whisper, the world unfurling that deep seated dread inside me.

"Does Grant know?"

"He doesn't want to talk to her. She wants to tell him herself." Evie nods, understanding.

"And this prof—"

"Don't do this," I cut her off, my lip curling in irritation. "You don't want to know about my life." My arms find the piles of clothes I've amassed this week and begin shoving them into my luggage; I can't stay here any longer. I'll tear at the seams, spill my disastrous energy everywhere, a human oil spill that'll contaminate everything it touches.

"Sweetie, yes—I do. I—"

"What, so you can fix me? I don't need fixin', Evie. I am who I am. When will you get that?"

"I love who you are," she says defiantly, and I scoff, the hard sound of it causing her to wince.

"Sure. And pigs can fly." I zip my luggage shut.

"Don't go, Sloane," she pleads, and I deflate, knowing Clemmie's house won't be the reprieve I need and deciding to stay.

"Just—" she says suddenly, moving closer. "You'll tell me? If you really need me?" Concern, deep and rageful, wells in her eyes, and I resent myself for not being who she wants me to be. Someone who would never have put herself in this position in the first place.

"Sure," I lie, knowing I'd never force her to look at the mess I've made.

21

Andy

Pancakes. That's our Thanksgiving food of choice. Not turkey or pumpkin pie but pancakes and perfectly crisp bacon that you can smell two floors down from the apartment. Carm doesn't remember how the tradition started, how after Luis died we could barely afford to keep the lights on much less a turkey, but I remember. How we drove over an hour the night before to pick up food from the not so local food pantry. How the pepper haired woman hugged my mom, her eyes so weathered, so sad after having to turn not just our family but several tired moms with their gaggle of kids away.

Mom had pulled three doubles that week, working single shifts in between, just enough to buy the beater we'd been saving for for months. A wood paneled station wagon, the left side mirror hanging on by a mangle of wires. It was our first car since the van got repossessed and we were so excited that the long rides on the bus were now in the rearview. But that night, Mom looked gray, a woman defeated, beaten down by the world. The ride back to our place was long, silent. Even Carmen, didn't make a single sound. We finally pulled into the duplex we shared with an older woman, Lola, and Mom silently pulled a five year old Carm out of the car, went inside and went straight to bed. I remembered being so worried, about all of us, wondering if things would ever get better, if mom would ever get to feel content. In that moment Luis' death felt like more than just a loss, it felt like a curse.

The next morning, I woke up to the same smell filling my nostrils now, the sound of bacon sizzling on the stove as Carm helped Mom make different shapes on the skillet with the pancake batter. The crate of old Christmas decorations Mom kept when we moved strewn across the small living room.

"Andy put those up while we make our Thanksgiving feast!" she'd called, booping Carmen's nose with the pancake batter now running down her finger. It all felt too warm, too good, like a trick after the night before, too many emotions running through my body for me to pull them back in, to stop the quiet sob before it came. Mom's own expression seemed to melt, seemed to recognize all the tension. The pent up anxiety roiling through her was also affecting me. She flicked the stove off, set Carmen down and tugged me into her, a forceful but soft embrace.

"I know Andy, I know," she'd said her voice a quiet melody as she stroked my head waiting for the tears to stop. *"Things will get better. They will get easier. They always do."*

She hugged me once more, hard, like her body was begging me to understand, to know she was doing what she could, and I did.

"Wanna make a molehill out of this mountain?" Her smile was still tired but warm, like it had always been, and from that moment on that's what I've been doing. Trying to help her make these giant immovable things more manageable.

"Andy, that looks like shit." My sister's blunt tone has my

mom stifling a laugh, pulls me away from the past and into the now. "Call Sloane to help you," she croons, and my jaw tenses.

"Carmen! Language!" She smiles, flipping the bacon with metal tongs and Carm smiles primly at her, unaware that even if I called Sloane, she wouldn't answer. That she's avoiding me.

"Sorry. Andy, that looks absolutely dreadful." Carmen resumes her chastisement in a faux posh British accent that has Mom giggling and me rolling my eyes, swallowing back my self-pity. She's referring to the red and green paper rings I helped her glue together while watching Les Miserables last night. I'm trying to hang them from the ceiling but all I have at my disposal is a roll of silver duct tape and arguably, she's right...it does look like shit.

"Grab some cash from my purse and run down to the corner to get hooks or something. Marcus said they'd be open until noon."

I shrug on my coat, disregarding my mom's purse entirely as I leave.

Boston's different on this side of town. It's not all tree lined streets and cobblestone roads, but that doesn't take away from its charm. Moving here took some getting used to, no doubt, but the three of us have found a home here, a community. I see Nancy—an older woman who lives in the building across from ours and who's been trying to set me up with her daughter Maria for the past couple of years—holding a tin pan, thick black smoke fuming from it, a series of expletives escaping her. I lift a hand up, hoping I don't get roped into whatever is going on over there.

"Andrew!" Her thick Bostonian accent coats the vowels.

"Hey Nance." I smile, moving to continue my walk down the block to Marcus' shop, hoping she sees just how not in the mood I am to shoot the shit.

"Help me with this, will ya? This god damn stuffing is ruined and I can't get the damned thing to stop smokin'."

Rolling my neck and pushing Sloane to the back of my mind, I laugh, because that's all you really can do when you see Nance, hair in rollers, oven mitts on, and a cigarette dangling from her mouth, cussing in the street.

"Here let me—" I say, now by her side. I grab the pan, which is charred beyond measure and stick it under the hoseless spout, running the water until it's flooded the pan, the smoke thicker initially until it completely dwindles away.

"Prince Charming!" She elbows me and I fight my grimace, because nothing could be further from the truth. "You know Maria will be home this afternoon, I can—"

"Thank you, Nancy but I'm..." I trail off realizing I'm not anything but hopelessly fucking enamored with someone I can't have. Some who can't even admit they might want me.

"Oh shit, the turkey!" She runs in before I have a chance to finish and that's probably for the best.

I count the sidewalk cracks as I walk toward the corner store, trying and failing to keep from thinking about that kiss. That glassy eyed look she had when she pulled away, like she was shot, like the kiss itself was some kind of betrayal. I keep telling myself it was just a kiss, keep trying to convince myself it didn't matter, but the lie chokes me before I can swallow it.

There's a wrongness in trying to pretend she was nothing, in denying the way she felt against me. The way her sunshine and citrus scent unfurled into something too familiar, like a memory that didn't belong to me but fit anyway, one that might have replaced the lost summers spent growing up too fast after Luis died. Melted popsicles by the pool, salt clinging to sun warmed skin, soft exhaustion after leaving the beach. I could practically taste the sea on my lips when she pulled away and I wanted more, more of that life that felt so far away but somehow with her it felt like mine, like if I just held her tight enough it would materialize.

So I tried—let my lips feel every curve of her mouth, fingertips brush the soft skin of her cheeks, palm rest on the base of her neck as I pulled her into me and let myself dive into her. But she left.

She left and took that false memory, that dream, with her.

Bells jingle as I push open the store's door, the open sign blinking a harsh greenish blue light.

"Hey man," Marcus says, barely peering up from his newspaper. I nod a hello, spotting the aisle holding the office supplies and beeline to the scotch tape. I choose the generic, seeing it's three dollars less than the Scotch brand, and make my way to the register.

"How's Rebecca?" he asks, ringing up the tape and putting it in a plastic bag, the words thank you scrawled in red font.

"She's doing good," I nod, pulling out a few dollar bills. "No Thanksgiving plans?"

"Nah, keeping the doors open. We need the extra cash this year. Things have been pretty slow."

I nod because it's the same story I've been hearing from all Mom's neighbors. Everyone's been grasping from the same pile only to realize they're at the bottom of the barrel. It's fucked.

"You here for the rest of the day? I'll bring you over a plate."

He hands over the few pennies of change I have and I toss them in the little hospital donation box he has next to the register.

"It's cool, man. Nance already said she'd bring me something." He pulls the too-long-for-just-tape receipt from the register and I chuckle.

"Yeah, I think you'll want me to bring you a plate."

"Thanks man. Oh shit—wait." He pulls out a LOL

surprise doll from a box under the register's counter. "Promised Carm I'd save her one." Of course she swindled Marcus into ordering a box of these for the store. I pull out a ten dollar bill but he holds out his hand. "Just throw in another slice of your mom's pumpkin pie." He winks and I roll my eyes but laugh.

"Consider it done." I drop the ball into the shopping bag and push through the door, the crisp autumn air feeling icier by the minute. I regret not throwing on a jacket, solely relying on the gray sweater Mom gave me a few years ago. Once back on the sidewalk I pull out my phone, fighting the urge to look at the last message from Sloane for the hundredth time since I received it. I glance at it anyway, telling myself I need to open my message log to text Will back.

SLOANE

It's not that deep.

I wish my jaw didn't twitch, that the words didn't pinch. I asked her if she was okay, shortly after she bolted out my arms, and she had the audacity to tell me it's not that deep. As if I *wanted* this anymore than she did. I force myself to click back open my thread with Will because it's easier to focus on his life blowing up than my own.

I tap through the past few texts he's sent me, most of it regaling just how boring his grandfather's townhouse has been over the past week, some of it touching on the conversation he had with Olivia, but for the past few days it's been radio silence, much to my dad's dismay.

He's been relentless in trying to gain information on Will's disappearance and on who leaked the information that Ian used for the 'hit piece,' as he's called it. It won't take him much longer to realize he's just at his Pop's, to realize that a secret as big as the one Will was keeping could only be kept under-ground for so long.

But I can't help but wonder if, without Ian's scheming, it ever would've come to light. If Will or Ben or Gen would've had the courage to deal the devastating blow unless the house of cards was already beginning to crumble. And if this is just the start, how does this end?

I turn the key and hear the Charlie Brown Christmas vinyl playing through the thin walls. I'm shocked by the lack of noise complaints from our neighbors.

"Finally…" Carmen sighs when I walk in and I hand her the tape along with the LOL Surprise Doll that Marcus snagged for her. She lets out a loud squeal and Mom jumps out of her skin.

"Christ Carm, don't do that." The spatula she's holding is covered in a gooey pie mixture.

"I told Marcus you'd save him a plate." I nod to the counter now crowded with casserole dishes of various sizes. I can see the flush of pride in Mom's face, the one that reminds me just how far she's come and I know she's excited that she can provide for us, that she no longer feels like we are scraping by. I wonder how quickly that would dissolve if she knew just how much we were being helped, that without my father a lot of this wouldn't have been possible.

I sit on the barstool near where she's pouring a thick batter into pie crusts. I immediately dig into the fat stack of pancakes she left out for me but, unable to help myself, I reach over to swipe a finger through the mixture she's stirring. I let the pumpkin cinnamon flavor settle on my tongue as she swats me away, rolling her eyes playfully while moving to preheat the oven.

"So.." she says, in that tone she uses when she's being

mischievous. "Your sister's informed me that a very striking young woman has dropped her off after rehearsal more than once." I watch her eyes dart over and quickly find their way back to the oven. My silence condemns me as I slide back into my seat and shoot daggers at Carmen who smiles conspiratorially.

"Andy *definitely* has a crush on her." She over exaggerates just to annoy me and I reach over, pinching her arm. "OW!" She rubs the small red mark I left before slapping me hard on the arm. "*Jerk*! Don't even lie. Mom knows it's true. It's so obvious."

"It is pretty obvious." Mom nods, sliding on her oven mitts before opening the oven.

"How can you say that? You haven't even met her," I scoff and I know I sound like I'm twelve, but these women know the exact right buttons to push and are relentless.

"The constant checking of your phone....the lost stare you keep doing...shall I go on?" She slides the pies in then crosses her arms, sly perception in her eyes as she meets my gaze. Understanding sits just beneath, a softness Carmen can't pick up on because it's meant for me, and I flex my jaw, rolling my lips as my mom cocks her head.

"He's embarrassed!" Carmen teases using both fingers to pinch me.

"That's it!" I stand up throwing her over my shoulder and she giggles, using her small fists to punch my back harder than you'd expect from a girl her size. I toss her on the couch and raise my arms like I'm about to grab her again as she squeals loud enough that Todd from next door bangs on the wall behind the TV.

"Knock it off," Mom says sternly before loudly calling out, "Sorry Todd!"

We freeze, stifling our laughs. I pull her up and we both

move back to the counter, where Mom instructs us to help roll out a few more pie crusts.

"How many pies are you even making?" I ask, noting she currently has three in the oven.

"Can I meet her?" Her insistence is quiet and stern, the kind I can't side step despite the years of teenage rebellion I spent trying.

"Ask Carmen. She knows her better than I do." I sniff, shifting my weight down and into the rolling pin.

Mom gives me a sour look, chastising me, and rolls her eyes.

"Just admit it Andy, you're in *love*," Carmen sing-songs, still oblivious to the subtext. I huff a laugh I'm hoping pushes us past this conversation.

"We're friends. That's it," I say definitively, like saying it out loud will erase the feelings.

Those damn feelings.

"Friends who kiss!" Carmen practically screams and my head snaps to her.

"How'd you—"

"I was going to grab a drink of water and saw. She would've told me, though. We're close like that." She shrugs, standing to grab a pie tin from the stack.

"Kissed?" Mom asks, raising her eyebrows, concern welling in her eyes. "In this house?" she adds, for levity or for Carmen, and crosses her arms with a look of faux sternness on her face.

"It *really* doesn't matter." I focus on rolling out my own pie dough, not meeting her eyes, but I feel that tender expression she wears whenever she pities me. Whenever she knows I probably did mess a good thing up but doesn't want to rub it in. She moves her mixing bowl to the counter right in front of me and I feel her trying to force me to meet her gaze.

"Andy..."

I glance up to find her whisk mid air, staring at me knowingly and it bothers me because she doesn't know anything. She has no clue why I want Sloane. Why I can't have her. She must see something in my face because a small frown flickers at the corner of her mouth.

"What's wrong, honey?" She sets the whisk back in her bowl.

"I...kissed her." I pause, remembering. "And she ran from it. I haven't really heard from her since." I clear my throat, not mentioning that it was probably for the best. I carefully place my pie crust in the dish to my left, being careful not to tear it. I feel Mom's eyes narrow on me, her posture shifting.

"Well...did you chase her?"

I look up, surprised even though I shouldn't be. My mom will always find a way to take a woman's side.

"Chase her?" I scoff.

"Women love to be chased, Andrew. It's romantic." She picks up her whisk and slowly begins stirring again.

"I don't think she's the type who wants to be chased," I sigh.

"Oh please," she huffs. "Every girl wants to be fought for. They want to feel worth it. You need to decide if she's worth it." Mom shrugs, grabbing my pie dish to finish folding the crust over. "My god, the turkey will be done before you finish this crust." I fall back again in my bar stool, tilting my head toward the ceiling.

"You're being a baby," Carmen points out, her eyes glued to her pie tin like they were the whole time she eavesdropped.

"And you *are* a baby," I mimic her tone and she punches me in the arm so hard I wince.

"Carm..." Mom warns. "She's right, though. You're being a baby." She shrugs, opening the oven and Carmen snorts a laugh. "Now I know you don't want to listen to an old woman, but if you like this girl you need to show her that, honey. I know everything feels dire at this age, but things have a funny way of figuring themselves out. And you *deserve* to fight for what you want. Even if it ends up not turning out the way you hoped it would." She sets the timer on the oven, wiping her hands on the back of her pants. "If there's a will there's a way. And if it isn't meant to be, you'll know you tried." She kisses me on the head and goes to the pantry to find one of the ingredients needed for the stuffing she's set on making.

Deserve.

It's such a funny idea, deserving something. On one hand I think she's right, think that maybe I do deserve to be happy, to find someone who really sees me, thinks that I'm a good person despite it all. In reality though I know it's the opposite—that I don't *deserve* any of it, that I've been betraying the people who mean the most to me for years, and for what?

I look at the pies on the counter, reminded that I do this for them. That all of this is for them. And yet, what if she's right? That I deserve to just...try.

The conversation I had with Ian plays in my mind, and I let myself imagine it: wanting Sloane out loud like I did at that bar, unafraid to hold back, and with none of the guilt that's polluted my good will for years, if it worked. If he could really undercut him, free me.

"When do you think the turkey will be done?" I ask sitting up abruptly. Carmen glances over suspiciously but decides to ignore me going back to opening the tape I just purchased.

"A couple hours...why?" Mom asks, her eyes fixed on the hand written stuffing recipe in the notebook on the counter.

"I need to go grab a book I left on campus," I lie. "I'll be back." I grab my coat and slide out the door just as Carm opens her mouth to argue.

* * *

The city is quiet as I let my feet carry me up the steps of the MBTA. The train is fifteen minutes late which means I'm shorter on time than I want to be when I reach Cumberland Park, just on the outskirts of campus. The cobblestone streets are uneven as I weave past the closed store fronts my peers frequent but have always been astronomically out of my price range. I always aspired to be here, to be able to afford one of these three story walk ups, the townhomes owned by almost every family at my school but being here on Thanksgiving, seeing how quiet it is, how empty, I find that I miss Nancy yelling at me on the street, the obnoxious blinking of Marcus' open sign that you can see clear down the road. My community, or at least a community. Here, you can tell it really is just every man for himself.

The black doorway of my father's corner townhouse is ominous, the giant gold knocker something out of a horror movie. I know he isn't home, know he's out of town on business like he is most holidays, so it's a safe time to visit the person I'm really here to see. I lift the large gold bar letting it thud heavily against the wood door frame before raising it again and again until I hear a latch, the sound of a lock turning. The door creeps open and I notice inside the curtains are all closed, the home masked in shadow as Ian pokes his head out, his face uncertain until he realizes it's me, and he raises an eyebrow.

"You're alone?" I ask, peeking around him.

"Obviously." He rolls his eyes.

"But it's Thanksgiving..." I trail off realizing he's telling the truth.

"Just another day in the fabulous life of Ian Rivers. How can I help you Andrew?" He's annoyed and impatient—typical for him.

"You said you'd take care of my mom...my sister...if this all goes to shit."

Something like excitement flickers in his eyes. "I'm not a monster, Andy. Of course I would."

I nod, because I believe him. Because even though the past few years I've told myself the opposite, I do believe that he and I can be good, despite the man who made us.

"I'm in." I nod and I watch a cheshire like grin grow on his face.

"Come on in, brother." He opens the door wide for me to enter. "We've got work to do."

22

Sloane

"I need those."

Swiping the keys Grant was just eyeing off Evie's pristine marble counter, I brush past him and cut toward the sink to rinse the apple in my hand. The window kitchen curtains flutter in the icy breeze that pulls in, shaking the roses Evie just snipped from the bush in the back this morning.

I spin to find Grant glaring, not even bothering to hide the twitch in his jaw, lifting his gaze past me as he pulls in a breath. "Take Clem's car."

Something about Atlanta amplifies the tit for tat we've engaged in since probably the womb. Avoiding him in Boston was simple enough, what with my long days at the conservatory in the lead up to the Nutcracker and his long nights at practice. But here, back home with nothing to do but shoot him daggers anytime he even starts to mention that I'm not in California, we can't help but run into each other like this.

"I like that one." In all fairness, we both love Beau's 1969 Mach 1 Cobra Jet, probably because it's the car he'd use when he'd take us out one on one. But *I* love it more.

217

I cock my head to the side, flaring my eyes as I cross my arms only for him to scoff and grab the keys to the Mercedes instead. An eruption of deeply held emotion regarding the woman he's probably left on read all week, would've been welcome. More than that, I'd hoped he'd asked about our mom by now, would have wondered why I've been seeing her in the first place.

Instead, silent irritation comes off him in waves as he passes through the heavy front doors, letting them fall shut with an aggressive thud. Sinking my teeth into the ruby red apple I'm clutching, I tell myself I have time to convince him to see Connie. That before things really take a turn, I'll get him to her, give her a chance to tell him she's sick, to make amends. Maybe tomorrow I can convince him, or whenever one of us ends up folding with a hollow apology.

Footsteps sound on the staircase, and my frustration slowly fades away.

"Okay—is this better?" Clementine huffs a sigh, letting her plaid trench slip just far enough off her shoulders to expose the denim mini dress I forced her to try over her burgundy turtleneck. The trousers—that I'm sure the sales associate told her were multifunctional—were not going to cut it for dinner in Buckhead.

"Yes," I tell her, pleased that we're the same size shoe, admiring the way my black thigh highs wrap around her long legs. She really doesn't know how lethal she can look when she plays to her strengths. "Does your program dress code say *pretend this is a nunnery?*"

Her laughter sounds behind me as we head towards the car, sliding into the cool leather with the relief of two teen girls who just escaped Beau Fielder's interrogation before a night of near debauchery.

"The goal isn't really to woo patients. It's to therapize

them," she says as her laughter dissipates, her brows lifting when she notices Grant sitting in the G-wagon. "What is he doing?"

I squint across the long, circular driveway, trying to make out his facial expression and realize he's tortured. "Reapin' what he sows," I quip, turning the engine and gripping the clutch before pulling us out into the road.

"He looks miserable," Clemmie mutters, pulling out a compact to line her lips a dark maroon, the gloss she slides on after accentuating the fullness of them in a way I envy. "Here," she hands me the tube, like she can read my mind, and I quickly swipe it across my lips.

"He is miserable, because he's too much of a purist to understand that his girlfriend going to see her ex-best friend is not the same as your girlfriend *cheating* on you. Like, what was Gen supposed to do? Let him off himself because Grant's a pussy?" I battle the apple for a clean bite, then chuck it out the window before rolling it back up.

Clem coughs on a laugh. "The Will guy, right? Wasn't she, like, in love with him?" She shoots me a skeptical glance and I roll my eyes, pulling a stray strand of hair out of the sticky mess of gloss on my lips.

"Yeah. *Was.* Like forever ago. The point *is*," I tell her emphatically, annoyed that she's even temporarily on his side, "that she immediately went to find my brother after and he told her to leave. He's so insecure and...mean."

"Traumatized," she says under her breath, clearing her throat.

"We're all fucking traumatized." The car falls silent, just the tapping of Clem's fingers against her phone screen and the hum of the road buzzing beneath us.

"Whatever happened with that Andy guy?" she asks, and I hate that I didn't see it coming. She's so sly, so strategic, that I can barely hide the way my fingers clench the wheel when she says his name. "I *knew* it."

"Nothin' happened," I shake my head emphatically, my shoulders coming up high as I try to downplay the tidal wave of feeling rushing toward me.

That kiss never should have happened.

"You've always been a bad liar, Sloane Fielder. Tell me. *Please.*" Bottom lip jutting out, she pouts with big brown eyes.

"Fine." I press my lips together, remembering the way it felt to have his brush mine. "We...kissed."

"Okay. And then?" she asks expectantly, so certain there must be something more salacious because I'm me. Known for being risky and hot headed, famous for making crazy mistakes.

"And then nothing. I left." She turns her head slightly, like she knows there's more. "Okay, I *ran*," I mutter, flipping on my turn signal.

"Why'd you do that?" she whispers, implicitly understanding the way that kiss has burrowed under my skin, the way I want to keep it buried out of my heart's sight.

I breathe in, slowly exhaling into the truth only a friend like Clem could pull out of me. "I cried, Clemmie. He literally just kissed me and...it felt like he was crackin' me open."

"Oh," she blinks, letting my confession settle. "And how'd that make you feel?"

"Terrified," I say like it's obvious. "No one should crack anyone open. It should be illegal."

She nods to herself, her teeth digging into her bottom lip before turning back to me. "You know, not everyone's going to be like Elliot."

"It's not about Elliot," I say sharply and she flinches. I wish, not for the first time, that his name didn't exist so we wouldn't be able to reference him ever again.

"I mean, I could argue you'd never been more vulnerable than you were with him."

"It was a fling," I tell her and myself, knowing there was a point where I thought it was real. Until the end really—until he was late. Until he dropped me off with a packed bag.

"A fling wouldn't have left you waiting two hours after an operation that *clearly* benefitted him, too." Bitterness laces her tone, and I can't blame her.

"Well," I swallow, wanting to move on from the memory, "he's a piece of shit. *Clearly.*" I say it to please her, not because it rings true.

Some demented part of me still wants to excuse why he was late, why he didn't seem to care, why he was so flippant about us needing some time or space after shredding apart every ounce of independence I'd cultivated for myself before I walked into his stupid fucking seminar. It has to be that part of me that thought I loved him, that dove head first, blinded by talk of muses and passion and vision.

Thought being the operative word, though, because I really believed I loved Elliot. And yet, he'd never cracked me open with a kiss. Never.

"Elliot made you feel vulnerable, but he ended up being a piece of shit, and you're scared Andy will be the same," Clem says cautiously, like she's waiting for me to lash out.

"Andy's not a piece of shit. He's..." I try to think of the word, and my nosy friend urges me on by raising her brows. "Confusing. Hot and cold."

Addicting. I dream about that kiss and wake up hot, sweaty, frustrated by something out of reach that I know I'll never find.

"Well I say go for it!" She settles into her seat, a smug smile on her face.

"It's not that easy. I have...stuff." I shrug, turning off the busy street onto a smaller side street that leads to a higher end strip of bars and restaurants.

"Stuff?" She raises her eyebrows and I'm annoyed but appreciate how well she knows me.

"Yes, stuff..." I sigh. "I'm trying to paint and you know everything with Connie and—"

"Right, how is Connie then?" she interrupts, Clem's one and only flaw: her inability to let you finish a thought, which probably isn't the best quality in a therapist.

I bring the car to stop at the light, letting my head fall back against the headrest as I groan. "Can we not?"

"Sloane..." she murmurs. "We probably should. Are you even seein' anyone?"

"Why would I see a shrink when I have you?" I ask with mock sweetness, shifting into gear just before the light turns green. Turning onto Peachtree brings the start of Christmas to life, and it puts the street I grew up on to shame. Lit trees towers every few feet, line the streets with so much cheer that it renders this conversation totally out of place. "Oh my god, look at those nutcrackers!"

"Connie's dying," she says, flatly, the blunt end of it wedging between my ribs, making it hard to breathe. "That's just true, Sloane."

"Thanks for that," I say, pulling into a spot and jumping out of the car. The cold whips against my face as I pick up speed, desperate for a conversation that won't plunge me to depths of my despair, but I don't even know where we're eating. Clementine made the reservation. My hands ball into fists, gripping so tightly my nails bite into my skin, and I welcome the sting.

I need a cigarette. Or a drink.

If I was home, I could lay under my sheets and shut my eyes until the reality of it faded away.

I walk past her, over the curb, and stumble when my heel snags on a crack in the sidewalk.

"Jesus fucking Christ," I say to the random man leaning against a colossal pillar taking a call. He turns his nose up in disgust—a religious man, maybe. I gesture a small apology and keep walking, annoyed that Clementine's shouts only get closer and closer.

"Can you just," I hear Clem say behind me. "Sloane!" She grabs my shoulder and pulls me to stop, dragging me onto a bench. "I'm sorry. That was blunt but, I just meant that you should be talkin' to someone. You won't tell your brother what's going on, and I'm hundreds of miles away...you don't have any support. No one should shoulder that all alone. It's dangerous."

Skin itching for relief, I dig my nails deeper, my fists out of sight.

"I really am fine," I lie, my voice soft and earnest as I try to get her to drop it.

"Maybe tell Gen. Or Olivia, or Jean. I don't like that you're isolating yourself."

"Isolatin'?" I bark a laugh, rolling my eyes. "I told you, I'm fine. And you just said it yourself—I have friends."

A doorbell chimes in the melody of "Holly Jolly Christmas," and a mother and daughter stroll out hand in hand, a massive cosmetics shopper bag swinging from the girl's arm. An ache in my chest, I turn away so I can't see them.

"I know," Clem concedes, grabbing my hand. "I just love you. Want to make sure you're gonna be okay once...you know."

My smile pulls tight as I squeeze her hand and my stomach makes a sound that suggests it might cave in on itself. "I'll be fine once I eat something. Grant took the last bagel at breakfast."

Her face pinches in that way it does when she's worried about me and I know it's her own anxiety, her need for everyone around her to be doing fine because of her own situation, her own issues.

"Look Clem, I'm okay. I promise, and if I'm ever not you will be the first one I call." She nods, not fully believing me but her expression softening just enough that I know her fear is tamped down. "Now—please tell me where we are eating," I gesture to the line of restaurants and bars before us. "I'm starved."

She smiles, grabbing my hand and leading the way, just like she always does.

23

Andy

December

The smokey, jazzy alto of one of our regular acts coasts above the soft murmur of the club, and if it weren't for Ian Rivers taking up residence at the otherwise dead bar, I'd be at perfect ease. His glass sits empty as he flicks his eyes up, arching his brows in a silent request that has me scoffing.

"These aren't free," I tell him, polishing the same glass for the tenth time, my bicep sore from my early session in the weight room. Johnny shouts something to a small, over dressed man hunched over one of the tables before grabbing him the collar and dragging him out.

"No family deal?" he asks, a half-hearted smile tugging at his mouth. His usual vindictiveness hasn't shown itself all evening—and he's been here for two hours, tapping away at his laptop, peppering me with questions he doesn't bother explaining.

"We're hardly family," I remind him, rounding the bar to check on Johnny.

"You good?" I crane my neck around him to see the guy emptying his guts in a paper bag.

"What do people think this is? A dive bar?" Somehow, even his huff of laughter is accented as it turns into a throaty smoker's cough, and I smack his back. I don't tell him a comedy club that advertises a Jazz Night by using clip art burlesque dancers on the flier is only fractionally less grimy than a dive bar. He takes pride in his establishment. I do, too, but I've also seen kids, whose yearly tuition is triple most people's yearly salary, vomit into Ming dynasty era vases at department mixers. People without any respect for other people's shit will show that disrespect anywhere.

"Andy!" my half-brother shouts from the sticky bar top, shaking his empty glass at me like the entitled asshole he is. I stalk my way over, barely rinsing the glass out before filling it with soda water. "So that was actually rum and Coke, but whatever," he mutters into the glass, swirling his straw around.

"My shift's almost up." I shake my wrist out, checking the watch I only ever wear here. Lends credibility, I read; improves the likelihood that someone will tip me more than a dollar, I've learned. "You've got twenty minutes to make headway on your evil master plan, or whatever the hell you're doing over there."

"I..." he dips his head, scrolling until a smirk erupts on his face, "was trying to look for this." He spins the computer around to expose an outdated website, rows and columns full of names and date of births and...deaths.

"What the hell is this?"

"Death records. Step one to all of this is figuring out exactly what went on the record about Lily's death." He continues typing, pulling out a credit card before groaning. "Shit. I can't do it."

"Yeah, I would've assumed only family could do something

like that," I tell him, furrowing my brows. "Probably for the best. I mean, Lily had a brain aneurysm...it was random." I can distinctly recall the way Will's face hollowed out that semester. We all said he was going too hard at practice and he'd laugh it off, crack a joke about how the rest of us were gonna be left in the dust when the scouts started coming around.

I should've been paying more attention.

"You know what tipped me off?" Ian asks, leaning forward, his head resting on the bridge his hands form. "Wasn't Ben coming back. Wasn't Will acting weird."

"What, then?"

"That he tapped you to keep an eye on him. I thought, *why* would my father ask this kid from nowhere to buddy up with a Chapman? I mean, how did my father know *you* in the first place?"

I blink across the bar at him, my blood running cold as the front door chimes and a gaggle of women rush toward a table, just in time for the next act. "That is strange," I admit, feeling sick.

"Naturally, I started with you. Figured out you were my half-brother almost immediately because when I confronted him about it, he just slapped me." His gaze drops to the hard-top, his mouth pressing into a line. "I guess he told you shortly after so he could beat me to it."

"I'm sorry you had to—"

"Please. He hit me. You're poor. Maybe we're even," he says with a small shrug, and it has me pulling in a breath to compose myself. The middle aged crooner on stage breaks on a brittle belt, his voice the aural manifestation of whatever heartbreak he's on about, and the women go wild. "Anyway, it did get me to stop. Until Ben came back. Freaked him out—I could just tell."

My eyes narrow on him, like his inner thoughts suddenly glow on his forehead, obvious and hard to miss. "You put Liv on that story, just to poke the bear. Why?"

"Because I hate him, Andy. He's made my life hell for as long as I've had memory, and he made my mom's life worse when she was still here."

Fuck, I remember someone mentioning that she passed, and I hate that I just walked him to the lake of that probably horrifying memory. He found her, or so I heard.

"Don't feel bad for me. Pity is like...disgusting," he complains, his nose scrunching, and I can't help but laugh. His eyes crinkle at the edges, like making me laugh was some progress toward whatever congeniality we're meant to have as siblings.

"Fine. I don't feel bad for you. But I do need to know what the fuck I'm getting myself into, since you clearly know way more than me," I say on a sigh, wiping down the counter that barely got used tonight. I peek into my pocket, making sure the twenty-five dollars in tips from this four hour shift are still safely swimming around in there.

"I ask you questions, you keep answering them, *even* if you think you shouldn't." I wince, and he sighs in thinly veiled annoyance. "I know you think I'm fucking your friends over and—"

"I mean, you are," I remind him with a tight smile.

"In the short term. Do you know how twisted these people's lives are? They're built on secrets they don't even *know* they're being held prisoner to. What would it mean for Will to be free of his father? For you to be free of yours?" He pauses, waiting for me to answer. "Can you honestly tell me Liv would've been better off never knowing about Will and Lily?"

"No," I murmur, hating the truth. Accepting a lie would've

been so much easier, far less messier, but a lie, still. "So you want her death certificate."

"I *need* her death certificate. I'll figure it out. Just keep your eyes and ears peeled, okay? Especially about Will. He might remember something and just spill it." He slides his laptop off the bar, letting it drop into his messenger bag before hopping off his stool.

"Wait," I stop him, anxiety churning in my stomach like an endless frothy wave. "And if I have questions for you?"

He tilts his head in consideration. "What do you want to know?"

"What's he want with Sloane?"

Ian's eyes roll hard as he shakes his head, shifting his stance to cross his arm. "Honestly, it's small fish, but I guess he literally has no code of ethics." He checks over his shoulder, and I'm reminded that people in this town think Sloane, the grocery store heiress, is a novelty. "Something happened with a professor at her program. Guy's a legend, but apparently he does this *a lot*. Would wreck his reputation...could be illegal? I don't know."

"Oh," I say, nodding like he didn't just tell me Sloane did, in fact, run from something in California. "Right."

"Chin up, Spellman. Not everyone can live up to our dreams."

Agitation, hot and coarse, rushes down my neck. He turns to open the door but my hand flies to it before he can, holding it shut as I force my jaw to relax. "Insinuate something like that about her again," I tell him, quietly, "and I'll expose the fuck out of you."

He peers up at me, amusement playing at the corner of his mouth that I'd smack away if he hadn't just confided in me about our father. "Of course. My apologies."

* * *

Conference season is just around the corner, so I've been blackballed from any shifts later than ten p.m. The money's not nearly as good this early in the night, but I'm always grateful by the time we're running laps at six in the morning, the warm up before the insidious drills Ben has us doing. Will was insistent as captain, constantly pushing us to beat him, but Ben's somehow even worse—challenging us to best ourselves.

The dull ache in my shoulder, from where Grant nearly bulldozed me when he was playing offense, pulses at the thought of being up in six short hours, but the brisk wind, chafing across my face, distracts from it enough as I make my way out into the blistering Boston night. A horn honks, street-lights glint on frosted store windows, and the last of those horse lined carriages jingle in the distance.

I regret the denim jacket I opted for this morning, when the sun was out and the fluffy lining up to the collar seemed sufficient. Shoving my hands into my pockets, I trek down the sidewalk toward the lot I left my car in, only for a flash of blonde to steal my attention. Walking towards her isn't so much a choice as it is an instinct, and I'm in her orbit within seconds, like my body's forgotten the way she shrugged off our kiss.

She leans against the weathered brick of Boston General, head tipped back as she whooshes out a long, sustained breath of smoke. When she brings her head down to meet the lit cigarette, she goes momentarily still.

"Hi," she says, blinking before inhaling on the thin stick deftly held between her fingers.

"Can I?" I gesture to the cigarette, watching as she drops it to the ground and crushes it with her black leather boots.

"It's bad for you." She crosses her arms, her nose red tipped, her eyes bleary from the wind. I grant myself a quick up and down glance, craving that kiss just at the sight of her, and bite back a smile.

"But not for you?"

She rolls her eyes, scoffing as she glances away, a slow smirk tugging at the corner of her mouth.

I'm nervous, all of a sudden, as I try to ask her something meaningful. "I, uh, texted you back. Don't know if you got it."

There's no audible laughter, but it's in her eyes; they dance with amusement, softly scolding me. "I did...I guess I forgot," she says, absentmindedly, sort of bothered. "To be honest, haven't been thinkin' about you at all, Spellman."

I try to hide the hurt, try to school the harsh furrow of my brows, but she notices and sighs, like this is all so tedious for her.

"What are you doin' over here anyway? Don't you have like...practice in the morning, or whatever?"

Something about her brutality has me disinterested in perpetuating my lies, so I don't. She already knows about Carmen, about my mom, the apartment...most of it, anyway. "I just got off work."

"A job?" Disbelief creases between her brows. "How do you even have time for that?"

"I don't," I laugh, watching when she lets her eyes fall shut for the briefest second as she leans against the wall, throat bobbing.

"You doing okay?" I look at the hospital sign, and ask it, despite her distance, despite all the downplaying and her painful avoidance. I ask because I need to know. Her mouth twists anxiously as she tilts her gaze downward. "Is Connie—"

"She's fine. I'm fine," she cuts me off, tilting her head in defiance, the way she does. The way she did at the pool table, the warehouse, the party—always. *Always* so defiant, like any attempt at vulnerability is an attack.

So, I try again.

"And if you weren't fine...you could tell me. I'd listen, if you ever needed that."

She shoves off the wall, tired resignation in the dip of her shoulders.

"What about *it's not that deep* do you not understand?" Her teeth cut against each word as she tries, and fails, to be funny or flippant. Instead, I see the fragile sadness that floats in her gaze, and I want to take her inside. Hold her while she lets it all out, because I think I could take it. Think that, with all I've kept inside and managed, I could help her manage it, too. She needs someone, and I scoff at her utter refusal to acknowledge it.

"You know, I wasn't even gonna bring up the kiss, but sure, Sloane, let's talk about why you ra—" I push against the invisible shield she's straining to hold in place, only for her to snap.

Sloane's eyes harden, turn harsh. "Just forget about it. I have." It comes out on a puff of frosty air that lands like a punch, and I step back, frustrated.

"Right," I huff out, bitterness lacing my tone. "Next time I see you, I'll save you the trouble." The words fall heavy in my gut, dropping like a stone in a lake.

"Good," she whispers, sniffing against the icy near midnight wind. Her jaw works, side to side, as she eyes me, and I swear it's a million things left unsaid lodged in the back of her gaze.

Nodding, I walk past her, desperate for the right thing to say but coming up short. Like the years I've spent playing everything on the surface have created this deficit in me, and I'm incapable of reaching her because of it, incapable of dismantling this performance of herself she's so committed to. And she plays it so well, could trick almost anyone into believing that she's mastered carelessness, that she's a free spirit and not a broken one.

It feels wrong to see that and keep walking. But it's what she wants; it would take an act of fate to change her mind.

24

Sloane

"Less sad," Bob tells me as he passes by, his first critical input in weeks. "It's icy, whimsical holiday not...despair?"

I step back and see it: the frosty window panes, with the sheer silver gauzy curtains, give off a stormier vibe than I'd hoped. Rummaging through the boxes of curtains, I find pure white ones and hand them off to the tech's manning the stage cranes. When they've been affixed to the top of the backdrop, the hopefulness in their brightness is assaulting.

"This better?" I shout into the auditorium, only for Bob to muster a brief, distracted thumbs up. My neck, stiff as it is, cracks when I roll it, as I march down the center aisle and out into the lobby. The space teems with conservatory volunteers, rushing about with dustpans and jackets, tablets and ticket rolls, parking lot signage—all the things that should've been set up at least a day ago for tonight's opening performance.

The company did a final full run last night, has been sipping teas and meditating, but Gen more than the others. When she isn't dancing, she's lost in thought. When she is, I'm scared she's going to throw a limb out. The intensity she usually embodies has been sharpened since she fell out with my brother, like all that love's got no where to go, is just coursing through her like a rabid thing that might take aim at any moment.

I disappear down the corridor that leads to the restrooms, dimply lit with brass sconces, and notice, for the first time, the bulletin board tacked full of announcements. What draws my attention most is the art competition, slated for this coming spring.

Open to painters of all mediums.

Nothing, lately, has felt divine. Or cosmic. Everything's felt like sleet, pummeling me from the sky, indifferent to me standing here just *trying* to do the next best thing. I'm not even sure if I could paint something of substance in time, given my slow to return ability, but I rip the notice down anyway. Fold it up and tuck it into my back pocket, just as my phone rings with a call from the hospital. I pick it up, my heart suddenly balled high in my throat.

"Ms. Fielder? I'm sorry, but your mother's had a cardiac event. We're currently—"

"I'm on my way," I say in a jumble, my vision blurring as I run out of the hallway and through the theater to grab my keys.

Everything around me whirs, spins ferociously and I can't stop moving because of it, afraid of the force when I finally stop. I cut into traffic, ignoring the righteous blare of a horn, and taking deep breaths to staunch the bile threatening to spill. And then my breath turns jagged, the reality of what I might walk into at the hospital snowballing into a panic that seizes all rationality. I park in a fire lane, I speed past security, I take the elevator to oncology only for them to tell me she's been transferred to the PICU. And all the while, I wish, more than anything, that I wasn't doing this alone.

I can just hear Clementine, reminding me that I don't have to, as I pull my phone out and dial my brother. By the time he picks up, my voice has warbled into one continuous sob.

"Grant...Grant, I'm so sorry—" I choke on the tears, pressing the floor number over and over like it'll make this thing move faster. "Can you come to the hospital?"

The sound of tires burning against icy asphalt plays over the phone. "I'm on my way."

And then, even though I know how important this night is to her, I call Gen.

* * *

By the time I get to Connie's room, she's sitting up awake.

Alive, and smiling.

"Oh, you didn't need to come all this way just to—"

I cut her off with the wrapping of my limbs around her warm body, shutting my eyes so I can feel her existence right up against mine. I breathe her in, the sick and medicine and her powdery laundry detergent, and her vanilla body spray, and the clean stench of medical tubing attached to her crepey skin. All of it, I inhale so I can commit it to memory.

"Sweetheart," my mom says, her voice breaking, and when I look into her eyes she's crying.

"I thought you died." The muscles around my eyes strain from all the tears, but still they come, salty and hot, down my cheeks.

"Between you and I," she says, leaning even closer and

lowering her voice, "I could've swore I did. Turns out one of the nurses just looks like Jesus." She cackles, wheezing at her joke, and my watery laugh vibrates through me, helps the panic recede.

"Don't do that to me again."

"Have a heart attack? Well darlin', it wasn't the plan, but—"

"Ms. Tucker? We've gotta wheel you back for the angiogram."

"He's not the Jesus one," Mom whispers, eyes haggard but sparking with amusement.

The nurse gives me a sympathetic smile before wheeling my mom's bed through the door. "She'll be back soon enough. There's coffee by the nurses station."

In the silence of the room, I let myself shiver until the dread and horror leaves me. Until I'm still in my own body and it's safe to use my limbs again. When they are, I find that coffee at the nurses station and let the caffeinated bitterness cleanse the rest of the panic away.

Grant's broad shoulders are suddenly in the doorway of Connie's room and hastily drop my coffee, the brown liquid splashing over the edges, and wrap my arms around my brother, tears springing anew.

"Grant!"

"What happened?" he demands to know, studying my face with an eerie calm that tells me he knows this is about Connie. That he's pieced together more than I've told him.

"Grant, I wanted to tell you, I swear, I just, I don't know. I thought it would be better coming from her." I swipe at the tears collecting on the apples of my cheeks.

"What? What would've been better coming from her?"

My face crumbles, the words hardly piercing the veil I've

tried so hard to maintain. But this is one of those signs, isn't it? Connie's falling apart, and I've been in denial. "She's *dying*, Grant. Mom's dying."

Grant looks frozen in time, suspended, his gaze suddenly unfocused. "No...Sloane. No, she's not—" His words fail him, just drop off the imaginary edge as he finds the edge of the second hospital cot and sits.

"She is Grant. It's why I came here. Why I left California."

Without Connie's reemergence in my life, I might've found myself somewhere else after the abortion. After Elliot. Somewhere with a beach, a warm one. Somewhere no one would've known me. Instead, I came here, for her, to save her. I failed, though—am failing. My breath shudders with realization just as my brother's arms find me and pull me close, steadying me.

"I'm sorry I made you deal with this alone, I'm—I'm sorry for everything," he tells me, and I nod, let myself lean on him, the way I imagine maybe we did in the womb. The way we would on a long car ride to somewhere strange and new. The way we did before he boarded his flight to Boston, to his new life without me. The way we do.

The door sounds with the gentle tapping of Genevieve, and when she cracks open the door, replete in her pink tutu and crystal encrusted leotard, my only grin today cracks across my battered face.

"I wasn't sure you'd come," I admit, feeling the depth of her love for not just my brother but for me in the harshly lit hell of this hospital room.

"I'll always be here," she soothes, the balm neither my brother nor I were entirely sure we needed just a few months ago. "You know that."

I nod with fervor, turning to my brother who's fixated on Gen, whose attention is firmly stuck on the best thing he ever dared mess up. "Go, talk to her. She came this far." I nudge him by the shoulder, watching as he and Gen disappear.

It's only then, once all the angst feels well out of site, that I notice a puzzle peeking out of my mom's bag. It's got kittens on it, on a beach, and I take solace that on her worst day, it was a piece of me that she tucked tightly away, close to her.

25

Andy

The snowfall is going to be historic, according to the weather station Mom's had on all afternoon. The diner let her know she's off for the night because they anticipated closing early for the storm, to which my mom gasped, "What storm?" and promptly called Carmen to let her know she was on her way to pick her.

She insisted on staying for the Christmas Eve clean up—surprise, surprise—since most people had already gone home for the holiday. She'd catch a ride home before the storm kicked up. And for whatever reason, my mom let it slide. Decided she *didn't* need to drop everything and make sure her eleven year old daughter got home before the roads got blocked. From where I stand near the sliders that lead to the patio, the roads are more than halfway there.

"No—really I think—" I feel my heart rate in my wrist the moment I hear her.

"Absolutely not!" my mom squeals, cutting off the sweet smoke of Sloane's voice. "You have to stay. You can't even drive back in this. And to the airport?"

"You're so kind," she says, her voice rising, a little frantic. "But my flight's…" her voice dips out of my reach, and I know the last thing she wants is to be stranded here. With me.

"Oh, sweetie. You're not flying anywhere," Mom chuckles, just as Sloane nervously laughs.

I finally let myself move toward them and find her face illuminated by her phone screen, cold air funneling inside around her, Carmen clinging to her jean leg.

"A little late to make it for Christmas Eve," I say, clearing my throat. My mom's head snaps to me, Carmen's eyes sliding up to me in a glare, and neither of them move.

Sloane's gaze jumps to mine, panic flashing in her gaze before she slots behind something more practiced—nonchalance, carelessness.

"They're used to it."

"You didn't want to fly back with Grant?"

"Stayed for the theater clean up."

"Private jets fly all day," I counter, and shift my weight. I know how I sound, can tell how cold the words are coming off by the urgency in my mom's eyes, the silent plea to *knock it off*. I'd be lying if I said Sloane leaving didn't hurt me, that her rejection outside the hospital the other day didn't throw me for a loop, but what really gets me is that I can tell that it's fake. That she thinks I'd be so easily fooled by a performance I've given a thousand times over.

"I don't use the jet," she grits out, and I can see the way her jaw tenses.

"Just come inside. I'm freezing," Carmen complains, still clutching the outer seam of her pants while she trembles from the cold, refusing to let her go.

And that does it, Sloane averting her gaze so it won't collide with mine, striding into the space that feels smaller with all of us in it. Avoidance will be impossible, and I fight the urge to apologize. If she'd thought ahead and wasn't so reckless, she'd be in Atlanta by now instead of here, with me.

"This is...really generous of you, Rebecca." Sloane slips her heavy sherpa coat off and I take it on instinct, dropping it over the side of the couch as her orange blossom floats across my senses. Her eyes flit across the room, noticing the paper chain, the straw angels—all the DIY decorations we've come to associate with this time of year—and they soften. My molars press together, vulnerability turning my skin into this raw, easily perceptible thing. It's not lost on me that she's seen more of me than anyone in the three years I've been here. More than Will, even.

She saw my front, plowed past it, and then ran away.

"Please, call me Becs," my mom tells her, beaming. She actually beams at her and it shouldn't matter to me, but it does. Whatever tear exists inside me mends just barely, stitches itself back up only an inch, and the strain slightly lifts. I want to warn her not to care about her, but I think I'm just trying to warn myself, and that maybe, it's too late.

Fuck.

She's oblivious to what is happening inside me, oblivious as she starts to turn back to the door, only for Carmen to tug on her. "I just need to get my luggage," she laughs, relaxing for the first time since I heard her in the doorway.

"I got it." I lightly pull the keys from her hands and rush out into the blinding snowy haze, grateful for the sharp chill. The warmth in there was starting to suffocate me, so I take longer than I need to, standing outside the doorway with her yellow luggage while the cold solidifies the feelings just seeing her dislodged.

They're all at the table when I come back in, the same mugs she and Carmen were painting just a few weeks ago between their hands. A heap of whipped cream threatens to overflow from Carmen's mug, and small dollops seem to float in Sloane's and Mom's.

"You forgot these," I say, slipping candy canes from the tree into each of their mugs.

Sloane's gaze lifts to meet mine, mouth lifting into a hesitant, white flag of a smile. "How could we forget?" Cordial as it is, I decide to try and focus on the fact that whatever twisted friendship we had before that kiss might be salvageable.

"You do this, too?" Carmen says with wide eyes, leaning into the table like it'll bring her closer to Sloane.

"Of course. Who doesn't?" Sloane tells her in fake outrage.

"Heathens," Mom agrees, sipping her hot cocoa behind a heavily restrained smile before glancing at me. "Go on. Make yourself a cup."

Sloane peers up at me through her lashes, the corners of her lips tugging up like they can't help themselves, her eyes glittering the way they were on the roof.

"What's so funny?" I take the bait, knowing better. I always know better.

"That all the women in your life can't help but boss you around." Her smile falters for a moment, just as mine really springs to life. "Carmen and your mom. Obviously," she says with an eye roll that reminds me of the way she blew me off that first night at the bar, one hip pressed against the pool table.

"Obviously."

I imagine that she's blushing, the soft pink hue of it creeping along the same path as her freckles, but I wouldn't know. I stir my drink at the counter, back turned to her, until the mix is dissolved in the hot milk and I spray a mountain of whipped cream that could rival Carmen's, stealing the seat right next to Sloane. She eyes my mug, not bothering to hide her judgement.

"Cheers," Carmen giggles, clinking her mug into mine.

"You don't think that's too much?" Sloane says, her thick brows playfully scrunched together as she cocks her head at me, and Carmen starts to push back. "For an adult man," she clarifies, and I take a size gulp of both the toppings and the chocolatey drink.

"Should *too much* be in an adult man's vocabulary?" I ask, mentally betting on the way it'll fan the flames under her skin.

Like fucking clock work. Her eyes narrow on me as her blush deepens before she glances away. I shouldn't care that I can make her feel anything at all, but I do. I do, and that she ended up here, snowed in on Christmas, feels like some fucked up cosmic punishment.

Something hard slams into my shin, and I look across the table to see my mom's brows trying to tell me something through gestures. She slightly tilts her head toward Carmen, who's lost in the peppermint swirl happening in her mug.

"I'm sorry you have to miss out on your family's traditions this year," Mom tells Sloane, cutting me out of the conversation all together as punishment for my not safe for the little ears joke.

"Oh, it's fine. They probably won't even miss me," she shrugs, flipping her hair over her shoulder. She really believes that, I realize, when nothing in her gaze shifts even a little.

Christmas was always this monumental thing in our house. Luis would make us carol; Mom would make these cookie tins that we'd be forced to pass out, door to door; we spent the entire first week of December decorating together each night after school. We'd pick out our tree together, watch holiday movies every weekend, get matching pajamas. It isn't like that anymore, not since Luis passed, but I'd never be able to say my family wouldn't miss me. Of course, they would.

Mom's eyes sadden just before something sparks in them.

"Well. We're happy to have you. Carmen won't stop

talking about you," she grins, rubbing Carmen's back as she cuts her an outraged look.

"That's not actually true," Carmen says cooly, like she didn't drag Sloane into our house.

"I can't really stop talkin' about you, so I guess we're even," she tells her, and Carm lights up and smiles into her mug.

"Actually," Mom pops up, wiping her hands on an imaginary apron, "I could use some help with the cookies. If you don't mind helping me, Sloane?"

"The cookies?" Carmen chirps, just as I say, "*The* cookies?"

"Yes," my mom shrugs. "It's Christmas, isn't it?"

Sloane's gaze bounces between us as she tries to interpret the moment before joining her. "My brother is a master baker, which means I've become a master assistant. I'd love to help you."

"Me too!" Carm practically leaps out of her chair, heading to the pantry.

"You can figure out the movie." Mom points to the television, giving me a knowing glance that tells me she can sense the unease between Sloane and I. The cookies haven't been a part of our Christmases since Luis passed. We still watch a movie, but the cheer our traditions used to hold bled out years ago, was washed away by the river of everything that came after him.

"Mommy, can we play Christmas music?"

Sloane gasps, pulling her phone out, and moments later, *Christmas Wrapping* is blaring through the little counter speaker we mostly use for timers. Mom turns into a statue for a second, but I watch her breathe through it. Watch her hear one of Luis's favorite Christmas songs and smile at the sound. Sloane offers her a toothy smile, and my mom can't help but give one back.

"Put me to work, Chef," she says, lifting her hands with a pop of her shoulder.

Once I've found *Serendipity*, I sneak away to the back storage closet and set Luis's Christmas Village on the long built-in banister along the living room wall.

* * *

Predictably, Carmen only makes it halfway through. Mom, on the other hand, stays awake the entire time but is too mesmerized by the Christmas Village to really pay attention.

"I'm going to head to bed. Santa likes to come *early*," she says as the closing credits roll on screen, side eyeing Carmen and the drool stuck to her cheek. "There's a blow up in the hall closet and a bottle of wine in the fridge," she adds as a throw away as I lift Carmen up from the couch.

Sloane sighs, shooting my mom a sleepy grin. "A woman after my own heart."

Mom's laughter carries through the hallway as she yawns and cracks Carm's door open, pulling her sheets back so I can lay her down. Glasses clink in the distance as we tuck her in, and I reemerge to find Sloane sitting on the floor, back against the sofa, about to pour.

She lifts it in the air. "A drink, among friends?"

I know this is her calling a truce; her stepping over the elephant in the room and telling me it's water under the bridge, and I wish I could let it go like that. Wish the kiss and her words outside the hospital weren't still haunting me.

"Friends," I say, reaching for the glass, candlelight dancing across the small grin on her face as I try to let that be enough.

I settle in on the floor beside her as she sighs looking at the lit tree, memories I'm not privy to playing in her eyes. Something whimsical passes through her gaze as her lips part, her eyes settling on the top, where an angel stands watch.

Just looking at her is overwhelming. But wanting her isn't

new—it's the craving that's different. There's something fatalistic about it, a recklessness that I know I should run away from. Wanting her for a moment in time suddenly feels like a sick joke. This feeling, if fed, would turn insatiable.

I need to—I have to—compartmentalize the kiss, the way I guess she has, the way I do everything else, and just get through the night. Make this all bearable, because it's Christmas.

"You up for the roof?"

The idea isn't a coherent one—it's 4 degrees outside, the fire pit is probably packed with snow—but I say it anyway because I know she'll like it. The narrow slant of her gaze is laced with mischief.

"It's snowin'," she says, looking up at me through thick lashes.

"Seems like it slowed down. Maybe I can start a fire," I shrug, relaxing into the kind of cool I'm usually so practiced in, but fuck if I don't feel unsteady.

Her lips curve into a hesitant smirk as she rakes her teeth over them, glancing out the window before standing up. "I guess there's nothin' else to do."

We pull our coats on and I grab a few blankets, expecting the roof to either be covered in snow or damp from where it's started to thaw, and head up, bottle in hand. The terrace lights are still on, softly twinkling over the mostly snow dusted furniture and fire pit. Regardless, I attempt to start a blaze with the starter logs one of the neighbors keeps in the cabinet out here. Once the snow's been emptied, the log takes, warmth erupting into the dense chill around us, and Sloane hums her approval, stealing the blankets from my hold to spread them on the wet ground.

"Chairs?" I quirk my brows, waving toward the splintering Adirondacks that haven't been replaced in ages.

"Easier to see the sky from down here," she says, already on her back, blonde hair spilling across the dark comforter I found in the back of the closet.

I join her, knowing better than to try to convince her of anything, surprised that the ground isn't nearly as icy as I thought. Taking the wine bottle I unplug the cork and offer it to her, hating that I notice the way she doesn't avoid brushing her fingers against mine as she sits up to take it.

26

Sloane

A harsh winter swell rasps across the roof deck, and suddenly, we're in a snow globe. Andrew's laughter floats from somewhere unreachable, flits across my skin just like the snow, and melts right into me.

"Maybe we should—"

"No," I insist, crossing my arms, hands tucked under. "I love it up here."

From here, I can see that someone's window is still lit with lights, can still sense the sporadic brave soul daring to drive through a street that's piled high with snow. I'm a small, unimportant voyeur to the stars and the moon and the breeze, a witness to the ones still unable to let their mind rest for the night—like me.

"So. Rank them," Andy says, clearing his throat as he finally drops down next to me after starting the fire, unbothered by me or my holiday intrusion. "Rooftops."

"One: my roof in Atlanta."

"Okay, fair. Nostalgia or whatever." Tightlipped, careful smirk tugging at the corner of his mouth—all charm. And from the moment I decided to be normal about all this, about being snowed in here with him and Carmen and their sweet as pie mother, he's been nothing *but* charming. Like my transgressions over the past month are that easy to forgive. I smile into myself, slowly breathing out.

"Or whatever," I chuckle, pulling my coat tighter like it'll stop his contentment from bleeding into me. "The one from the party. And yours."

"Really?" he asks, chuffed, his cheeks already rosy from the blistering cold, and I roll my eyes. "That's it?"

Cocking head, I run my tongue along the tip of my teeth, curious. "I wonder what you really think about me. That I've been on a million roof tops with just anyone?"

His cheeks turn rosy as he takes a quick swig from the bottle. "Maybe? You're like...an heiress."

It dawns on me that he has, most definitely, looked me up, typed my name online and seen the overexposed snapshots of me leaving a bar when I was far too young to be served, seen the up-skirt ones that you simply can't pay anyone enough to take down. Seen the photos of me clinging to some guy's arm as we slipped out of a night club, the way I would before I took Elliot's seminar, because that all stopped when I met him. It had to. It wasn't the kind of thing a girl like me, so talented, with so much potential, should be doing...he'd said.

I take a cleansing breath. "The tabloids aren't real life, Andy," I tell him. "I mean, I go out. But I think they run the same photos every few weeks." I flick my gaze over to him. "So no. No other roofs."

"Why do you like them?" he pivots, eyes sparking with a curiosity that should feel invasive but instead feels like the warmest invitation. And when I suck in a breath, taking his curiosity and trying my best to serve it, it's because I, for some inane reason, want him to be satisfied. Because I can't help myself from seeing his eyes light up when I give him a little bit of me.

"I just...could always think better lookin' at the sky. Feels like my thoughts have room to exist, like nothin' can box them in." I pause, remembering the suffocation that peppered my youth. I can still remember trying to outrun it. "And I love being around people, obviously, but sometimes I just need a minute."

"It's an escape." And it's the way he says it—like he *knows*, in the marrow of his bones, what it feels like to crave it. Like he knows me.

"Yeah," I breathe out. "It's exhausting...pretendin', all the time. You know?" I ask, testing the waters, waiting for the invariable scoff or chuckle or silence.

A snow flake slowly falls between us, disappearing into the blanket.

"I do," he confesses, solemn and far too earnest for someone I'm trying to not want. "Maybe we should have a word."

"A word?"

"Yeah. If it's ever too much, you know if we're ever in the same place," he explains, briefly glancing away, "just say the word. We'll escape."

"Find a roof," I muse, wondering when it turned into this: him being someone who knows the right things to say to me.

"Find a roof," he repeats, his eyes falling to my mouth before he self corrects. "The word could be...pineapple."

"Why the fuck would I ever say that word?"

He chuckles, amusement manifesting in the fine lines near his eyes when he smiles. "Fair. Okay, how about..." he pauses, his gaze roaming over my face as I wait, my skin alive with a thousand small pricks. "Cassiopeia?"

Oh.

There's an unsettling swell within me, and my swallow only barely pushes it back.

"The constellation? Like, in *Serendipity*?" I nod, flustered. "That's a good one."

"What can I say?" he jokes, like the allusion is anything but romantic, and I clutch the edge of the plaid quilt, tugging it close and bringing the wine to my lips.

They tremble when the glass presses against my mouth, but it eases when the blood red liquid washes down my throat. It's not courage that it gives me, but clarity.

This thing between us, that has somehow only ever managed to fall on one side, mine or his, at any given time, only works because we've been nothing to each other. We've been friends—we *are* friends. Andrew can't know that I'm unreliable and turbulent, that I have a tendency to be disappointing. That I'm hanging on by the thinnest of threads. He can't understand that I have no desire to be someone's anything after thinking I was Elliot's all. He cannot truly, ever understand what it's like to lose all sense of self because of a man and his mistake, and the silence that comes after.

If he understood, he wouldn't look at me like I was something he could hold or keep. Really, he wouldn't look at me at all.

"I need to apologize."

He stills. "For?"

"For what I said to you outside of the hospital," I tell him, trying so hard not to be the girl that runs from her problems like Grant said. "I was just havin' a hard night, and my mom's doctor wasn't bein' positive about things...and I took it out on you."

"You don't need to—"

"And I need to apologize for the kiss," I add in a flurry,

letting the words and that moment fall into the space between us.

He scoffs, shaking his head like I'm foolish for wanting to rewind our clock at all. "Sloane—"

"I shouldn't have let that happen. I put us in an...unfortunate situation. It confused things." I focus on the edge of the blanket, pressing the knitted corners into the pads of my fingers.

"I wasn't confused. I wanted to kiss you. I *liked* kissing you," he says, matter of factly, like I already know this—because I do. Of course, I do.

"No, I know," I shrug, unable to cope with the things he's shoving my way. Maybe if I was less fucked up, less of a mess, I'd just gingerly take them from him. Cherish the words, the sentiments, return them.

"Did you not want to kiss me?" he pushes, trying to catch my gaze as I continue to avert it. "Because—"

"Of course I wanted to," I whisper because my nerves feel like a tiny, overloaded boat, careening toward the edge of a waterfall, and because I'm hoping reigning in everything else about myself will pull him back, too. "But I shouldn't have."

"Why not?"

"Because," I stutter, unable to tell him the truth. "Because we're friends and because—"

"Because it freaked you out," he says, unapologetically. "You felt—"

"I didn't *feel* anything," I tell him, gaze narrowed as I remember the overwhelming bliss that was his lips against mine.

His tongue slowly rakes over his bottom lip as he lets my words sink in, and where I expect them to be the death knell, he only reaffirms his gaze on me.

"Would that be so bad? To feel something?"

The urge to be honest, to tell him I'm tired of feelings that just sharpen into disappointment, sits right at the tip of my tongue, but it would be harder than the lie. Than pretending.

"I feel a rainbow of things, Spellman. Just nothin', specifically, for you." My lips roll, shielding each other from the cold.

"Because we're...just friends?" Disbelief hangs heavy in his gaze and he is relentless. It makes my blood run hot, my jaw clench, my molars grind, my skin flush.

"Exactly," I tell him through gritted teeth, watching the slyness of his gaze build, all of his reticence suddenly gone.

"And friends, who don't feel anything for each other, typically run away like that after a kiss?" The dark gold locks of his hair dusted with snow, the arrogant cut of jaw, the bitter lift of the corner of his mouth—they turn the cool expansive night into an oppressive taunt I can't help but wriggle under.

"Oh my god," I groan, moving to just leave but Andrew's hand nimbly wraps around my wrist, tugs me toward him, and it's electric, his callused fingers against me like that.

"No, really. If it was *just a kiss*," he says, not even pretending not to be wounded, "why'd you run off like that?"

"I had places to be, Andrew," I shout, stealing the wine bottle and knocking it back against my lips. "Aren't you the king of the casual hook up? Sometimes, people just like to kiss each other, and it *doesn't mean anything*."

Exasperation must line my face, has to be right there for him to recognize, but he skates the back of his hand against my cheek anyway, tangling his fingers in my hair. My breath turns ragged. My eyes water, my nose burns, my heart races.

"So if I casually wanted to kiss you, right now...that wouldn't mean anything to you?"

Every word he's ever said plays like a siren song in my memory as I try my hardest not to look at his lips. But it's more than this with him. He knows that, and he doesn't care. The way this isn't just about wanting each other, anymore, doesn't seem to scare him the way it scares me.

His question lands featherlight on my conscience, whispers across it, quietly daring me to forget all the ways I used to hurt after feeling just like this.

"Andrew, come on," I shake my head. "Why do you have to—"

"Because I haven't stopped thinking about that kiss since you ran out that door," he admits, easily, as I blink furiously through the snow flurry. "And I don't think you have either." He makes no attempt to hide his intentions, those eyes boldly dipping to my lips before locking with mine. "Doesn't have to mean anything. Unless...you have feelings for me?" he taunts, his fingers finding new purchase in my hair as he shows me just how much of a hold he has on me.

"I don't," I lie, schooling my expression into one of ambivalence and lifting my brows. All the while, my heart slams against my ribcage.

"Great. So kiss me, Sloane."

And at the sound of those words, falling from his lips, all the air on this roof, in the world, isn't enough—I have to take it from him. That's how hard the feeling washes over me, how intense the urge to fall into him and let him sustain me is. Because he's called my bluff, seen around the curtain, is holding up the mirror. Because he knows I'm stubborn and I hate to be wrong.

So I lean into him, but only an inch. And I let my anger and the tension spiral into something seductive, gazing up at him through my lashes. I lean in and sink my lips into his, bracing myself against the shock of it.

And just this—his lips against mine—heats me like a furnace, has me forgetting the snow still falling in uneven flurries. It's everything our last kiss wasn't, a kiss on my terms. A match to the box, gasoline on the fire. The battle between our lips, the reckless tangle of tongues, as I slide my hands over his shoulder and pull myself close to him, has him groaning, has him incapable of coherence and in the sea of pleasure that is his skin against mine, I can feel the fear receding.

This is what I wanted, I think as we tip over and into each other, hungry and unrestrained as our breaths coalesce, our touches deepening into something desperate. I taste him, the wine, the peppermint, our tongues twining around each other in slow torture and when I slip my hands under his sweater, his shirt, driving him crazy with the brush of my finger tips against his warm skin, he shudders. Face buried in my neck, he lays bruising kisses that I can't help but arch into, that pull the softest whimper from me.

Our coats come off in a haze of lust before I find the band of his jeans, desire coiling around my core. He looks at me with this heavy gaze, heated and hazy, like he can't think straight, and it only spurs me on more. I push him down to the blanket, run my teeth along the hard edge of his jaw, suck and taste and inhale the cologne on his neck, the sharpness piercing the last of my self control. The way I want this, with brutal intensity, with hot, all consuming recklessness, claws its way to the surface when I make my way down his chest. His heart beats so loud I can hear it, feel it against my hand as it rakes down the fabric of his sweater.

I look up at him, one hand pressing against his jeans, sinking my teeth into my bottom lip as I stifle my smugness and hide just how much I want—

"Sloane," he says, his voice hoarse like it literally had to grind to a halt.

I raise my brows and lift the edge of his sweater, trailing my lips along the warm, dark blonde hair dusted skin I find there, never taking my eyes off him. The moment he shifts out of carnal desire—I catch it, silently cursing everything.

"You're rushing this."

My breath runs ahead of me, and I fight to calm the anticipation still coursing through my veins. "Am I?" I grin, eyes narrowing, desperate to lose myself in those whims again. To stop talking and lose myself in pleasure.

"You know you are." He reaches toward me, brushes my hair back, looks at me in that gently enough that I bristle. "What are you so afraid of?"

"Nothing." I shake my head, my grin slowly falling the longer he peers into my eyes, the longer he only looks at that part of me when so much more is on offer.

"You sure?"

Beneath his cashmere sweater his chest rises and falls, his restraint evident in the bob of his throat. I seize on it, climbing up him until we're face to face, my hand on the cold ground around his head, our noses almost brushing.

"Maybe *you're* afraid. What if you're a disappointment?"

"I'm not worried about it," he murmurs, drawing me in with the overwhelming press of his hand on my low back and brushing his lips against mine. And when I hungrily dive into the kiss, he inches back, a subtle smile playing on his lips.

"If we do this, Sloane, we're not pretending," he tells me while every part of him is pressed against every part of me.

"Why would I? I've got nothin' to hide." I smirk, dipping to press my lips against his when he flips us and grins down at me from above.

"Keep telling yourself that, sweetheart."

My breath hitches as he drags his lips across my skin, softly kissing up my neck, my jaw. He presses another kiss at the base of my neck, his breath fanning across me until goosebumps erupt, dragging my pleasure through me like a hot scythe.

"Look at you, Sloane. I'm barely touching you."

I moan as he grips my hip with one strong hand, holding himself up with the other, running his thumb over top of my jeans, over my hip, squeezing. I clamp down around *nothing*, feeling out of control as he finally dips down, parting my lips with his and sliding his tongue along mine.

I'm boneless, limp, putty in his hands. His gentle caress could undo me, I think—nothing else required. His fingers make slow, tantalizing circles on my waist, as he kisses me with just as much tenderness, like he did at his door. When he grinds himself against, I *want* him to hear my whimpers, want him to know he can touch me everywhere. Like he can read my mind, he slides his hands up, palming my breasts before torturing me with a brush and a tug and a pinch and—my voice isn't even mine at this point. It's a mess of moans and almost cries, a long desperate plea that is new and not at all what I'm used to. It runs away from me, like a barrel rolling down a hill.

"I can't believe I've gone this long with really touching you," he mutters, his mouth just inches from mine as the need for him overwhelms me.

"I need—" I start to say before his hand snakes down to where I'm lifting her hips, desperate for friction. He pulls back, locking eyes with me when his touch ghosts past buttons and zippers, and he sinks two fingers in.

"I know what you need," he has the audacity to say, a cocky smile tugging at the corners of his mouth. "Just like I knew you'd be soaked."

"Tends to happen when anyone's touchin' you like this," I grit out as I tense around him, frustrated and flustered, because this would happen with anyone. He's practiced, and I almost tell him that in less than pleasant terms when he pulls out, circling my clit.

"Anyone?" he asks as I gasp. He drags in and out of me,

drives me to a euphoric wall of nothing because he's holding back. I shut my eyes against the strain, grinding my teeth before forcing them back open.

"Yup."

"Why don't I believe you?"

It's done something, my denial, my complete avoidance of the elephant on this roof—that every touch feels different. He moves down my body, still driving his fingers into me with impossible attention to every detail he's already mapped to memory.

"Because you're arrogant," I try to tell him, but it's swallowed by the cry I choke on when I feel his mouth on me, hot and wet, working in tandem with his fingers to push me over the edge. And I do, shatter around him and into him, tugging his hair, clawing at his head, pressing my hips up, surrendering against him, as he wrings the last of it from me.

"Fuck," he breathes, his jaw going slack as he looks up at me, like that wasn't his plan either. And even though I just came apart, I need it again—I need more. I push up, everything urgent all of a sudden, and he does the same, seeking me out. We collide, and that's really how it is. Catastrophic. Seismic. Torrential, a fucking typhoon of lust and longing that we couldn't side step any longer if we tried.

I can feel the way he can't have enough of me. His fingers digging into my skin, his lips rough against my skin, and I feel the hunger slam into me like a ton of bricks. He slides his hands under me, and it only urges me on, sinking my fingers into his scalp, raking my nails against it as he hoists me into his lap with no effort at all. His hands frame my face, hold me as he angles our kiss so it's deeper, one wrapping itself in my hair, before he suddenly breaks away to let his heavy-lidded gaze roam over every kiss swollen part of me.

It's too long. He looks at me too long, with too much

goodness for someone who I *know* doesn't usually find anything holy in this.

"Are we doin' this or what, Spellman?" I whisper, wetting my lips, trying to look past it.

Heart in my throat, he sets me down, laying me back on the blanket before hooking his fingers over the waistband of my jeans and tugging them off me. He turns to toss them on our coats, reaches in his wallet for a condom, and I pull my knit sweater over my head, the cold immediately biting into my sensitive skin. He turns, sees me, our gazes locking when he realizes my intention. I brush my hands across the blue lace of my bra before reaching behind me, before letting it fall to the ground. Slip my fingers beneath my underwear and shove them away.

"You could've—" he stutters, blinking past the reverence lodged in his gaze. "You're gonna freeze."

"So come warm me. What are you scared of?" I tease, leaning back on my forearms. His eyes roam over me as his lips part, his breath uneven, and it does something. To see him so unsettled by the sight of me.

"Honestly? That this will be over before it's started," he admits, dragging a hand down his face. My stomach pitches, like a tilt a whirl, dizzying me, because he can't mean it. It's a thing he says when he's with women, a line he barely realized he uttered.

I watch as he grabs the collar of his sweater and pulls it over his head, and the flex of his chest, the subtle power in his forearms, the cut of those muscles from a life on the court, from years spent doing and being everything for everyone he cares about—they have my chest buzzing with want.

He kneels on the ground, then braces himself above me. My whole body flushes, pulse throttling in my throat.

"You do this all the time," I remind him as his teeth graze past my collar bone.

"I think," he murmurs against the center of my chest, dragging his lips back up the column of my neck. "I think you might ruin me for anyone else," he whispers, and my hum vibrates against his lips as I consider the impossibility of it. I tell myself this is just more canned responses. More of his usual and not words that took root in him solely for me.

"I think you're stallin', my friend," I tell him, and he huffs a laugh, nipping at my skin. "What's so funny?" I run my hands down his back, feeling the dip and shift of his traps as he moves.

"It's funny," he says, nudging my head the other way so he can taste me there, "that I'm being honest, but you still think I'm just your friend."

He reaches down, kicking off his pants. I hear the unmistakable roll of the condom, feel him pressed against me, and I swallow hard as I avoid looking in his eyes. Because I don't want what I find there: the gentle care, the concern. I want him to take what he wants from me, want him to let me give him this part of me of my own volition. I don't want this to be part of some emotional bargain because this could be so easy, if he let it.

"Wait—" I muster an amused lift of my lips. "You're not secretly a virgin who's gonna get all attached to me, are you?"

Emotion, unnamed and long reaching, gathers in his gaze as he slides his palm across my hips, worshipfully dragging his touch back up my body. His finger tips linger on the goosebumps, trail every small imperfection they find, before he answers me.

"Not a virgin," he says, low in my ear, but that's it. No other promises as he brings his mouth to mine and swallows the possibility of any reassurance with his kiss. I arch up into him, unable to unwind myself, despite our distance from that inevitable fall. He grinds against me in long, rolling drags that have me groaning, have me pleading.

"Please," I moan against his lips. So close—everything is so close and nothing matters but this.

He doesn't even break the kiss when he lines himself up, just slows the twirl of his tongue with mine as he thrusts into me, and the sound doesn't even make it out of my throat. I'm so shocked at the fullness, tensing around him as pleasure pools, coils around the base of my spine. His hand wraps around my ribcage, holding me in place, and I look up into his amber flecked eyes, lit more by the Christmas lights lacing the roof. His forehead tips against mine, breathes whispering as we lay so inextricably linked, coated in sweat, despite the ice and wind, oblivious to the world around us.

Most shocking is the way I think this has ruined me. I feel him, hold him inside me like this, and can't imagine that I've held anyone else this way. I know I have—it just simply doesn't matter.

"Is this okay?" he huffs, catching his breath before dragging out, teasing me at the entrance.

"I've had better," I say, eyes falling shut as I moan, trying to separate the heat burning in my core from every rational thought I ever had, but they're collapsing into each other. The past is rendered pointless and unimportant with every thrust, and it becomes harder and harder to hold the mental line.

"That so?" He shifts so he's deeper, and *fuck*—tears well in my eyes and I will them to fall away when I hastily turn my head from him.

I can't name what I want from this, other than to not know where I end and Andy begins. To feel the inner most part of him wrapped around the inner most part of me.

But what does one do with that? It's an impossible ask, not

something you can actually give anyone. It's tragic and ill fated to want someone like that, but it'd be a lie to say it isn't what the songs are about. All the best ones.

"Andy," I whimper, already lost to the wave slowly breaking on my shore. He slides his hands under me, dragging me toward me as he sits up, repositioning himself. He slots himself between my thighs and thrusts from a new angle. My mouth falls open, loses the ability to stay shut, and I feel the start of the fracture, the splintering from the inside out, and he watches, his breaths turning more and more ragged. He flushes across the bridge of his nose, and I know this is becoming unbearable for him, too.

"Tell me this doesn't feel different," he dares, driving deeper, burying himself the way I've been secretly praying he would.

On its own, my head digs back into the blanket, a throaty moan filtering out of me as I try to tell him it doesn't, as I try to hide but he's laid me bare, is thoroughly wrecking whatever resolve I thought I had. I'm pulled taut like the strings on an instrument, seconds from snapping.

"Normal," I say behind closed eyes, just as a tear trails down into my hairline.

"Fuck, Sloane. Don't lie to me." His hand shoots down to where we're joined and swirls around me. "Lie to everyone else, but not me."

The demand has me shattering, my pleasure violently rolling through me, undoing whatever was left of my composure, and he sinks back in, leaning down to bring us together, thrusting and working me through my climax as he kisses me like he could do it forever. When he barrels into his, I can't do anything but hold his gaze, lifting my hips and cradling his jaw before he falls to my side. Our breaths float in the air above us, cold frosty plumes of exhaustion, and we lay there silently. Lost in thought.

The ghost of his touch is still everywhere and I wish on a star for it to haunt me forever. For me to never forget what this was like with him. Then, I turn to face him, nervous about what I might find: insatiable longing, questions I can't answer, the realization that I wasn't all I was cracked up to be. I swallow them back, knowing they shouldn't matter.

"See. Friends." I try for an easy smile but press my lips together instead.

Andy's gaze softens as he pulls a blanket over us, scooting closer and running his thumb across my bottom lip. "Whatever helps you sleep at night," he tells, brushing my hair out of my face, his fingers catching a traitorous tear.

But he doesn't press, doesn't push. Doesn't make me promise or answer anything at all.

* * *

Cinnamon sugar lingers in my nose as I help Rebecca, or Becs, slather each sugary spiral with a generous coat of cream cheese frosting. It occurs to me I haven't had a Christmas like this maybe ever. The warmth of the antique Christmas lights that I was informed have been in Andy's family since his Grandma was a kid make the apartment feel like a Hallmark movie, so warm that it can't possibly be reality—but it is, and it's hard to push down the jealousy that sprouts from the realization that Andy grew up wrapped in all of this love. Something in the way he looks at his mom, looks at his sister, is currently looking at me makes it possible, though.

Carmen's eyes are glued to the presents lining the edge of the tree as she absentmindedly glides her knife over the cinnamon roll in front of her, the frosting forming a large clump in the center.

"Psst…" I nudge her, her focus snapping back to what she's doing. Before she has time to smooth the frosting out, Andy snags the roll she's working on, shoving the whole thing in his mouth. I fight my amused grin, watching too closely as his tongue flicks out to catch the frosting smeared across his mouth.

"Andy! That was mine!" she bemoans, her brother smiling through a mouth full of roll, and she shoves him. "You're gross!"

He swallows before directing his smile at me, winking, and I know that I'm beet red, can feel it all the way down to my toes. Because I like him. *I like him.* Not just want him in that passing way you could want anyone who looks like him. It feels like a tangle in my head, this feeling I have for him, in his too warm house, with his too nice family and after last night, that tangle feels like a knot too overwound to unravel anytime soon.

I just smile back, a real smile. And I know he knows it's real because something softens in his expression, no longer playful but like he's laying himself raw in front of me, letting me have him if I want him. When he looks at me like that, I find it hard for me to remember the reasons I don't.

"Can we *please* open something?" Carmen's eyes are giant orbs directed at Rebecca, who hasn't hidden the fact that she's thrilled at this obvious pull between Andy and I.

"Fine!" she relents, throwing up her hands. "But only if Sloane opens her gift first." She gives me this mischievous side eye that reminds me of Mom and I wonder what Rebecca was like when she was younger.

"Oh you didn't have to—" I stutter but she cuts me off.

"Sloane. It's Christmas, and in this house Christmas means you get a gift whether you like it or not. Besides, Carm and I worked very hard on it." She winks, that playful expression identical to Andy's and I just want to hug her. Something floods my stomach, this strange revelation that this family sees me and wants me here. It's foreign and feels like a gift in itself.

She takes my hand, pulling me toward the tree, Carm bouncing on the balls of her feet with excitement and I feel Andy's eyes on me, tracking my movements so closely like he's scared I might disappear, again. He couldn't know that I needed this; that since Thanksgiving I've felt so lonely, like I could just slip away and, sure, people might notice, but they'd assume it was some marked part of me, some pillar of my personality, and they'd never come looking. I think Andy's family would look, though. I think they'd want to find me.

I carefully untape the small red package Rebecca fished out from under the tree, giving way to a tiny white box. I open it gingerly and can practically feel the anticipation coming off of Carmen, like steam in a tea kettle about to whistle. Inside is a long thin bracelet, expertly woven with different shades of blue. I swallow a hard lump now forming in the base of my throat.

"It's a friendship bracelet!" Carmen practically squeals, but then seems to remember herself, twining her fingers together awkwardly. "If you don't like the blue though I can totally make you a different one. Mom and I really didn't work *that* hard," she shrugs, but her smile bleeds through any attempt to be unbothered.

"No, Carmen—" I sniff back the tears crowding my eyes because no one's really made me anything like this before and the idea of this girl and her mom braiding a silly bracelet for me feels like much more than I deserve. "It's—it's perfect. I love it. Can you help me put it on?"

Her grin is almost better than the bracelet itself and she all but jumps me to put the thing on. I laugh, letting a few tears spill over and I can see in my periphery Rebecca smile, watch

Andy wrap his arm around her and for a second, I have that urge to run. Because this feels like a lot, almost too much, but I let myself feel it. Let myself pretend I belong here.

"I actually made you all something, too. You'll have to share it, though."

I move to my bag and pull out the construction paper I dug out of a cabinet last night, after Andy and I slipped back into the decadently heated apartment, noses frozen over, skin singed with ice and heated kisses. We didn't blow up that mattress—it would've been too loud. Instead, we laid on the couch together, stealing kisses as the Christmas tree glowed, between the million and two questions triggered by the stories I spied in every knick knack I saw.

He answered them, mindlessly brushing my hair back as I lay against his chest, only stopping to bend his head down and kiss me. And eventually, long after he'd mined stories of Evie and Beau from my mind, and chaotic tales of Connie from my heart, I felt him fall deeply asleep. I carefully extracted myself from his hold and, finally, after months of trying, created something I loved.

I hand it to Carmen downward, making up for the lack of wrapping. She moves toward Rebecca and Andy before the grand reveal and I feel a cold sweat trickle down my spine. I don't know why I'm nervous. I'm sure even if they don't like it they'll at least pretend they do. Still this huge part of me really wants them to like it, really wants them to like me.

Carmen flips the paper over and a hush falls over the three of them so only the light sound of Silver Bells plays in the background.

"Sloane..." Rebecca lightly places a hand on her chest and I bite the inside of my cheek waiting. I see her lightly sniff, her eyes going glassy the way mine did when I opened the bracelet.

I cried because I was scared to be seen. I wonder if she is, too.

The portrait is simple, the three of them sitting by the tree, a still from the night before that I etched into memory while we were crowding the couch watching *Serendipity*, the glow of the screen and the small Christmas houses on the mantel that belonged to Andy's step dad warming the painting. It's really their faces that I focused on, the love so deeply etched into each of them that I could see it in every line, every curve of their face, the way Rebecca is combing back Carmen's hair, Andy, nestled in behind them.

If watching Rebecca's reaction surprised me, seeing Andy's has destroyed me. His hand firmly grasps his mom's shoulder and his face is filled with not surprise, not gratitude, but something softer...deeper. Like he's seeing something sacred and doesn't quite know how to hold it yet. His eyes flick up to mine and it's like I feel the world narrowing, feel it pressing on me from every direction, just by that glance.

He mouths "Thank you," and I roll my lips together trying to control the emotion I'm sure is written all over my face. It hits me then: I thought I painted them because I wanted to give them something beautiful or at least as beautiful as them welcoming me into their home on Christmas Eve, but what I really wanted was to belong in that picture, too. As Andy's smile breaks, so slow and certain, I realize that if I wanted to, if I just stuck around, maybe I could.

27

Andy

There was one year, on my birthday, where I had no clue what to ask for. Mom and Luis bothered me about it for weeks, convinced I just wasn't telling them to save them the cost or the disappointment of not being able to get it. But I really didn't know, had gladly accepted that I'd more than likely get new shoes for basketball like I did every year. Good shoes cost you an arm and a leg, and I needed them, always.

At breakfast, over waffles with whipped cream and sprinkles, I unwrapped my new sneakers, some shirts that weren't second hand, and what felt like a book, wrapped tight in dark green paper. It was *Waiting for Godot*, and the binding was fine, gold threaded, and I could tell it was an important gift, not a last minute one. Luis didn't study theater formally—he went to fire school, joined the department, and read in his bunk. We'd go to the community theater often, but always for the holiday shows. This gift was the first time he told me, without telling me, that it could be for me, too.

Holding it, I knew it would always matter to me, and I hadn't even read it. My copy is now dog-eared, marked up with pencil and pen, worn. I never asked him why he gave me this one in particular, but I know he loved it. I know I love reading these two men waiting around for nothing, and maybe it's been a weird sort of comfort to know that there's nothing really waiting for me. That the things I have—my mom, Carmen—are my purpose and everything else is just gravy. It's helped me rationalize things, and I wonder if it did that for him.

I didn't know I needed something like that, but once I held it in my hands, I knew it'd always been waiting for me. Which is ironic, I know.

I'm bending the spine of it now, while Sloane sleeps beside me, just stirring. I brush her hair from where it's fallen in her face as she slowly blinks awake, smiling.

"Good morning," she says, light splintering through the blinds, pouring across the freckles on the bridge of her nose. "What's that?"

I flick my gaze to the old thing in my hands. "A play."

"Looks...well loved," she smirks, sitting up. The blanket falls away and she's not wearing anything when she snatches the play from my hands. "Can I read it?" she flips through the pages, her eyes making some assessment as her smile softens. "I'm goin' to read it, if you don't mind."

I watch her take this thing I love and it's easier than I wish it was to let her, so I kiss her instead of confirming what she already knows: that she can take anything.

Her hands find purchase in my shoulders before sliding down my back, and suddenly she's wrapped around me the way she was last night, and the nights before, and the night on the roof. I press her into the sheets, strands of blonde now stuck to her face, dewy and flushed, and I dip down to taste her lips, just barely apart as she inhales. I reach for my nightstand before driving into her slowly, feeling her clench tightly around me. I have to glance away, have to harden my jaw to draw my own pleasure back, only for her to sit up and force me against the headboard, straddling me once again. Hair cascading past her bare waist, she settles around me as her head falls back on a moan. That almost ends me right there.

"I'm not gonna last," I manage to mutter behind gritted teeth as she circles her hips, guiding me to the edge. I feel her start to move out of rhythm, shuddering and unraveling just as I let my own release slam into me. Fingers digging into my shoulders, Sloane falls apart, all the hot tension melting into me, an aching softness I want to somehow memorize.

"What are you feedin' me this morning?" she says against my ear before sitting back, the light catching in her eyes thrown back at me with the warmth in her stare.

"Pancakes?" I look up at her, dreading that this is the end of our solitude.

A week can easily feel like forever when you let yourself exist out of time. Together, in the limbo between Christmas and New Year's, in my bed or hers, on a nondescript street in the city or on a deserted sidewalk on campus, it's felt like we've traveled through a looking glass. The rules that define our existence haven't existed here. I haven't heard from Jean or my father; Sloane has declined every call from her brother or parents. And Connie's had a friend visiting and told her daughter, in so many words, to take the week off from hovering.

The conservatory's been closed. Most of the team's gone somewhere for the holiday's. We've been alone, and it's been the sickest trick because it's not real life. Our friends, our teammates, start funneling back into this world today, start slowly warping the glass we've holed-up on the other side of. We'll be forced to see things as they are. I worry reality will warn her off of this—of us. That she won't trust me to handle it.

"That'll do," she grins, sliding off me before pulling on one of my large hoodies. Hand on the door knob, I jump out of bed and stop her.

"I have roommates still here, Sloane," I tell her, my eyes dipping to where the hem of the hoodie barely hides the perfect swell of her ass. She seems to realize the moment I do, and sucks her teeth as she scans the room.

"Right," she mutters, pulling on the flannel pants that hang over my desk chair. "My virtue safer for you, now?" She moves to open the door and I press behind her, my mouth low in her ear as I grasp her waist through the sweatshirt she's swimming in.

"Not you I'm worried about. Just don't want to do something I regret if any of these guys look at you the wrong way."

Her laughter rumbles against me, smoke and honey, as we make our way to the kitchen, where we in fact see no one. Without hesitating, she finds the mixing bowl and pancake mix, measuring out just enough water before I nudge her toward the table. She flips the book over in her hand.

"So the theater thing," she says, pulling her legs up on the chair.

"The theater thing," I repeat, leaning against the counter as I watch her, arms crossed like it'll keep my heart in rhythm.

"What's the story there? It's kind of...random?" she laughs, tossing her hair to the side. "Caffeine?"

I turn the pot on, finding our least nicked mug.

"It was Luis's thing. He passed it on to me, and then to Carmen, I guess."

"Did you do, like, family plays?"

"No," I chuckle. "Carmen's always been into musicals, so *I've* been into musicals by default. Luis was into straight plays, though. We just...appreciated theater together. In high school I took the theater survey class and the director convinced me to go out for the fall play."

"That's a cliche. You know that right?" She fights a grin as I slide her coffee on the table, rushing back to flip the pancake.

"Oh, yeah. It was very good for me. Girls love an athlete who can do *Hamlet*." Claudius, actually—the villain thing was a goddamn birdsong, and my teammates were pestering the director to play even a tree before the semester was through.

Her cheeks deepen into a rosy hue and she brings her mug to her lips, hiding the flush with a weathered radio station logo. "A real Troy Bolton. Did you have a Gabriella?"

"Yeah," I laugh. "For a couple years. She got married right after graduation." Bianca, whose sporadic posts about her toddlers are a bizarre reminder of how much life has happened in the same span of time that Luis has been gone.

Her eyes fly wide. "Oh my *god*, Andy. You're jokin'?" The mug sounds against the table and she rests her head against her hand.

"I wish I was," I admit, slightly embarrassed but relieved to be telling her about my life. No one knows much, I realize, other than Will.

The pancakes are perfect, and I drench them in butter and syrup without checking before setting it in front of her.

"How'd you go from *that*," she cocks her head as she cuts into the stack, "to...this?" Her eyes don't lift when she asks, just flutter shut as she savors the bite.

I flip the trio burning in the pan, silently cursing the unevenness of this stove as I turn down the heat. "This?"

"You know. You're like...a different woman every weekend kind of guy," she says, pursing her lips, and I can't tell if there's jealousy laced in her gaze or true curiosity.

Raking a hand through my hair I sigh, pouring my own cup of joe before plating my breakfast and sitting across from her. "I think..." I cut a piece of the stack until it's mush, and Sloane sits there in silence. "I think Luis dying changed the way

I see things. And college is the time for all that, I guess," I tell her, regretting that this will always be her first impression of me as I shove the bite in my mouth before sitting back.

Gazing into her coffee, she squints. "I get it. You don't really know yourself yet, you know?"

"I mean, do you ever?"

Her eyes float past me, latching onto something as she squints. "I should grab my stuff."

Turning, I notice it's already eleven, and that Connie's supposed to be discharged at noon. The hospital's half an hour away, and I'm out of time. Her half eaten pancakes sit on the table as we pad back down the hallway.

"Will I see you tomorrow?" I say instead of *please don't go.* A small smirk plays at the corner of her lips as I step close and draw circles on her smooth skin beneath the hoodie, my gaze dipping to her lips.

"I haven't seen my friends in forever. I need to...debrief them," she adds with a small shrug before disappearing to the bathroom.

When she comes back, I'm mentally fumbling over ways to get reassurance. It's fucked, how lost I am to this feeling. "And what are you going to tell them?" I ask her, dragging her toward me by the hips. I gaze up at her, wanting nothing more than to pull her back down to this bed and...not even touch her. Just talk. Listen to everything she usually leaves unspoken or carefully tiptoes around.

I watch her change out of my clothes and into her own. Handing her the jeans she wore here, a folded up piece of yellow printer paper falls out of them. I know it's an invasion of privacy, but my curiosity takes the better of me as I unfold it, quickly skimming the flyer in my hands before it's snatched out of them.

"Excuse me." A playful smile dances across her face as she

repockets what I now know is a flyer for an art competition sponsored by the conservatory and Boston Museum of Fine Art.

"You gonna do it?" I ask, even though it's hard to tell if I have the right to.

She sighs, putting her hair up with a rubber band and pulling the front pieces only to get frustrated and tuck them back behind her ears.

"I don't know...I haven't really been inspired lately." She bites her lip, shyly like this is a half truth and she isn't ready to give me all of it.

I move behind her, running my fingers up her arm and feel her shiver at the sensation. "I think you're scared," I breathe into her ear. She turns on me quick. Hands on her hips as she cocks her head, that fire I love so much burning behind her eyes.

"And what might I be scared of, Andrew?"

One eyebrow up, I wrap an arm around her waist pulling her into me, a small gasp escaping her.

"The inspiration."

We stand centimeters from each other, our mouths so close I can feel her breath hitch on the bow of my lips. For a second her eyes are an open and heated blue flame, until her phone pings with a text pulling us both out of it.

"Shit, I'm gonna be late pickin' up my mom." She lightly pulls from my hold grabbing her stuff.

"Let me go with—"

"No," she tells me, pressing her lips together. "That's sweet but...it's fine. Really."

I nod to myself, wondering if I overstepped with the art show thing, with calling her out on lowering her guard but I know it's true. She's scared to let me in, maybe more scared than I am to let her.

Cradling her face in my hands I tip her head back, surprising her with a kiss. "You know you just have to ask, right?"

Her breath hitches when I look at her, and I want it to mean something. Desperately. She rakes her teeth over her bottom lip, softly smiling. "I know. But it's not like we're..."

"What?" My heart feels heavy against my ribcage, but I already know what she's thinking. She fought this so hard; she was never giving in this easily.

"You know," she shrugs, her brows and nose pinching.

"What I *do* know is that you," I pull her toward me, "are the only woman I'm seeing."

Her eyes turn like a deer in headlights before her blush deepens, and she glances away instead of telling me how that makes her feel. "You don't seem like the exclusive type."

I huff a laugh as she levels her attention back to me. "Do you want me to see other people?" I joke, my amusement falling when her lips don't lift at all.

"Maybe," she says, her throat bobbing. "I mean, don't like...stop your life for *me*." A laugh finally leaves her when she says that.

Asking if this applies in reverse is sure to irritate me, so I don't do it. Just pass a hand through my hair to distract from the voice in my head telling me to pump the brakes, to stop investing in this outcome. To stop believing there *is* an outcome.

She kisses me, quickly, pulling away like you'd rip off a bandaid. "I'll see you later," she tells me as she walks away, and once I've watched her drive away, I notice she took the play.

28

Sloane

Connie's asleep in her bed, and it's a relief to see her free of I.V.'s and wires. She's tucked beneath the striped sheet set I ordered for her when we found this place back in September. It feels like a lifetime ago. I sometimes wonder if the end of summer marked a cosmic shift that jolted me off my axis. At the time it felt like my world was ending, like the tracks had been switched, abruptly, without warning.

I watch the blue and gray melt together against the grain of the sketchpad. It's obvious that the better I've gotten at working with oils the rustier my watercolor has become. I close my eyes, trying to see mom's veins, the way they seem to be the only thing keeping her bones from breaking through pale translucent skin. I breathe in my nose transfixed on the way the blue seems to swim to the surface, a shade I've used in almost every work always begging to be properly blended, mixed into something new. I dip my brush into the small cup of water beside me, dabbing it into the same shade I let Carmen use, when the brush hits the page and the mixture bubbles in different directions, the blue now muted and ruined.

"Darlin', that's how you get wrinkles," my mom says through her sleep-addled rasp, sitting up against the headboard with a wince, I push the frown off my face. "I'm fine. Just old bones," she insists when I reach forward on instinct. "What's got you scowlin'?"

"Nothin'," I tell her, forcing forward a sincere smile. Because I *am* happy. Happier than I've been in months.

Thinking about it too hard, how happy I've felt, worries me. I didn't even feel this happy with Elliot; with him there was this constant swing, a dangerously dark low that always had to compliment the highs we'd reach. He saw me, he used to tell me, but when I didn't conform to his vision, we'd just fall. I could be such a disappointment. All of a sudden, though, I wouldn't be, and God was that addicting. It felt purposeful, to have someone guiding me into my best self.

Once we met two of his old friends for drinks after dinner. We never did dinner—it was always drinks, after nine, in some obscure, insufferably artsy part of town. Maybe so we wouldn't run into people, but I was impressed by the way he knew everything there was to know about being in the art world. We sat there, Elliot and I, the painters, Cleo, who worked with charcoal, and Ulrich, who also painted but exclusively with oil, and drank clear cocktails that reminded me of the rubbing alcohol Evie would pour over our scrapes. I felt so big, especially when the conversation turned to me and my work, how Elliot and I were fusing our talents together.

The grip he'd had on my thigh was the guide that night; when I spoke too much, he'd tighten it, when he liked what I was saying, he'd relax or stroke the skin there and I'd have to fight to stay focused. Cleo asked me what my plans were after I finished the program, and I told her about spending time abroad with some friends, doing the whole Europe, starving artist thing. My thigh went cold, his hand gone entirely. Later, he told me wandering around Europe was immature, and that he knew I was better than that.

"Don't look like nothin'," Connie cuts into my thoughts, and I pull in a deep breath.

"You ever look at your life different after some time?"

"All the time," she scoffs, rolling her shoulders back. "Can't see nothin' clear up close. And not the first time 'round."

"Hmph," I hum to myself, offering her my hand as she slides off the bed into the slippers I placed there when I let myself in a few hours ago.

"You hear from Beau and Evie?" Connie wades into the small kitchen, its glossy black counters so unlike anything she'd pick out for herself and lifts her kettle.

I shake my head. "They know better than to call me. I won't answer."

"I wish you would," she says on a tsk, boiling water for the instant coffee she insists on making. A perfectly good, if not premium, coffee maker sits right there. "You missed that flight on purpose, didn't you?"

"Of course I didn't!" I lean my elbows against the bar, eyes wide with amusement as she cackles and pours heavy cream into her mug.

"So who was this friend you stayed with?" She turns around slowly, warming her hand with the side of her coffee, her eyes crinkling at the corners as she takes me in.

It's like looking in a mirror, she told me while we waited for her to finish infusion. She said that seeing me reminded her of all the things she could've been. It was the saddest thing I'd ever heard, even though she said it with a smile on her face. She has no regrets, she told me on a different occasion. Not the saddest thing I'd heard, but maybe the most painful.

Nerves flicker in my chest, because I haven't spoken about Christmas with anyone yet. My mother is the first to know, and that feels so right. "Andy, actually. I take his sister home from the conservatory most days. That's how I ended up there, when everything snowed in."

"So can I meet him?" she asks, like any regular old question, and I startle. Mischief skips in her gaze.

"For what?"

"For fun," she laughs, coughing on the tail end of her amusement and I rush to her side, opening a cabinet to find her inhaler. "Sloane, please," she says on a wheeze, swatting me away. "Unless you don't want him meetin' a sick old lady, which—"

"Well I can't say no now, can I?" I shake my head, stifling a smile as I watch her meddle in real time. A mirror. "He actually asked to meet you."

"I like him already." She takes a big gulp of coffee, her brows lifting expectantly.

"I just don't know if it's a good idea." Every time I imagine bringing Andy into this soft, scary bubble, I feel like I showed up to class naked. Overexposed and scared for anyone to look too close.

My mom's eyes flit across my face. "Can I give you some advice?"

People who think they're dying are full of advice for the living, I've realized. I don't want her advice for that reason alone; it suggests she won't be here to give it to me later. Somewhere there's an hourglass, each grain of sand falling through the cinched passageway like a sick taunt. She asks if she can give me advice and I hear the grain fall, and I can't say no even though I want to, even though I want to pretend like we're not nearing another permanent shift in the makeup of my universe.

"Sure." Glancing out the window, I notice it's started to snow again. A snowy New Year's Eve.

"Let people love you," she says, her smile turning fragile.

I scoff, my lips hesitantly curving. "I love *you*, I love Grant, I love Gen, I love Beau, I love—"

"Not what I said," she says, her smile pulling tight. "You're so good at lovin' on other people, but receivin'? I fear you got that from me. That's my only regret. I told you I have none, but I lied. I regret not lettin' people love me. Might've saved me a whole lotta heartache."

"I do let them love me, that's the problem," I mutter, walking over to the window to watch the snow flurries float to the ground. They disappear into the ground, changing form so quickly, and I envy the ease with which they shape shift. No friction or resistance, just easy, languid conformity. I was never good at that.

"I think you do when you're not worried the well will run too deep," she says, suddenly right beside me. "Clementine. Gen. It's easy for you to let them love you because they've got their own lives. But you've never done well up close. Even as a baby. You'd get so whiny if I held you too long."

"Maybe I don't like bein' smothered," I retort, furrowing my brows before sinking into her couch.

"Maybe," she laughs. "You get prickly when you feel someone's pourin' everythin' into you, same way I used to."

"So you wish you'd let people smother you more?" I let out a loud huff, pulling my legs up and tugging the throw across me.

"No, darlin'. I wish I hadn't self-sabotaged so much. But," she says, carefully nestling beside me, "I reckon that's somethin' you can't learn from advice."

My mind wanders back to the inception of this conversation, and I remember the way Andy's hands melded themselves to my skin, the drag of them against my hips like he was desperate to hold onto any part of me. I know what he wants:

he wants me to surrender, to concede the part of me that craves being kept. That's scared of being inspired.

No one's ever kept me, is the thing. I am not the kind of person someone keeps; I'm the kind of woman who wanders, who runs, who gets left. I tried to let someone do that—keep me—and he shoved me right back to myself. Literally, all my shit in a duffle.

Here you go, Sloane. You actually weren't worth the trouble. You could've been so much more, but now I realize you never will be.

"What happens if they leave you?" I ask her, cuddling into her frail body as I spread the blanket across the both of us.

"Mmm," she hums, nodding her head. "Well, Sloane. Everyone's gonna leave you. That's life."

"I hate that," I chuckle, holding her hand in mine. I flip it over, tracing the lines there to staunch the emotion welling in my eyes.

"Me too, baby." She presses her head against mine, and we sit there for a long moment. "You'll be okay. You've got people who love you, if you'll let them."

29

Sloane

Olivia jingles so loudly, I can hear her from outside the bathroom where she's waiting with Gen and Jean. A heavy knock sounds on the stall as I shimmy my vegan leather bootcut pants back on, hiking them up to my waist and holding my breath to snap them shut, slightly wobbling in my heels, before Jean boisterously yells that "someone's in here." When I reemerge into the smoky haze of the club, Gen's smile is mischievous while Liv emphatically shakes her head no.

"Eroding my nasal cavities? For what?"

"Live a little," Jean rolls his eyes. "Sloane?" He lifts his brows, expecting me to follow but I shrug apologetically.

"Gives me a headache. But go, have fun my little snowbirds!" Patting Jean on the butt, I press a kiss on Gen's forehead, giggling when she spins and her mirrorball dress floats around her. They disappear into the bathroom, leaving Liv and I to absorb the bass radiating from the dance floor a few yards away.

Head falling back, she closes her eyes, a dreamy smile flitting across her face. "Everything's so different," she says before

283

turning her head toward me. "You know, I didn't even kiss anyone at midnight last year."

"Not Will?"

"No," she exaggerates. "He disappeared. And I didn't have...friends," she laughs, but it's sadness and relief all in one.

"Well. Now you have Ben." I rub her arms brusquely, and the gold plates on her skirt make music again. "You can kiss him *under the stars* and make a wish and be...stupidly happy," I beam at her, only to find her crying. "No. No, no, no. If you don't get it together I'm shovin' you in that bathroom and—"

"I'm fine," she mumbles, wiping her nose with the back of her hand. She's the weepiest drunk I've ever met. "I just was thinking about how I love Ben, so much, but how I'm so grateful that I have you. And Gen. And I guess Jean," she laughs, and it's garbled as more tears run past the waterproof liner I forced her to use in case something like this happened.

My chest constricts as I pull her into my arms, forcing myself to breathe. It hurts when people tell you they need you, doesn't it? Fear grips me when they do, because I know I'll never be exactly what they need or enough of it, and it's only a matter of time before they realize it, too. That no matter how much I love them, they'll notice all the ways I don't quite measure up.

"You're goin' to have your best year yet, Olivia Beckett," I whisper into her hair.

"I think you are, too," she pronounces. "I think Andy's in love with you," she slurs on a whisper, like we're two girls at summer camp swapping secrets.

"Definitely not," I laugh, remembering the bottle girl who hasn't stopped making passes at him all night. "And I wouldn't have told you if I knew you were gonna make this a thing."

"*I'm* making this a thing?" She gasps as our friends burst out of the bathroom, their irises larger than when they went in.

"Do you think he'll notice?" Gen says rapidly, blinking one two many times.

"Grant will live," I tell her as we all link hands like a human chain before wading back into the crowd of Bostonians, natives and transplants, who've gathered to shout down the new year together. Grant *will*, in fact, be furious, but he'll also blame me and love Gen anyway.

"Look at him," Liv says to me, meaning Andy, and Gen mouths *who* to Jean, who knocks his head in the direction of the table the men have commandeered.

"No."

"Leave her alone," croons Jean, who is, for whatever reason, maybe the most emotionally intelligent member of this little group.

"Well he's watching you like he's a man in a desert who hasn't had water in forty years!" she shouted over the music, and I wonder if he knows we're talking about him. But I won't look. I might see that girl orbiting him again.

"Forty's so specific," Gen giggles. "You're so weird. I can't believe I hated you."

Liv's eyes swell again. "I can't believe *I* hated *you*," she wails, throwing her arms around Gen as they start to bob to the synth and bass coasting through the speakers.

Jean links his arm through mine, fortifying me as we stride over to the table. Concern shades my brother's features as he peeks over our shoulders, standing up to scour the crowd for Gen.

"You know, while I love the whole protector vibe," Jean says, sliding in next to my brother, "Gen could literally gut someone with just her eyes. Liv too, actually." He steals his drink away and downs it before Grant can protest, flashing him two rows of alarmingly straight teeth.

"He's right," Ben says, unbothered as he spots his girlfriend in the crowd, an easy smile settling on his face, and Jean's laugh comes out like more of a squeak.

"You're peppy," Grant says, suspicion in his eyes, and Jean and I exchange a glance, fighting the laughter threatening to bubble up. "What'd you do?" my brother asks, to *just* me, and I feel the sharp pain of whatever feeling or realization I buried during our fight a few weeks ago. Because even though things have been forgiven, they haven't been forgotten. I'm still as careless and wild as I ever was and Grant is still the golden boy with the stick up his ass. I suck in my cheek, rolling my eyes as I form a retort.

"Don't be a dick, Fielder," Andy says, finally speaking up from his seat between Ben and Grant, barely glancing his way as he casually sips his beer. Instead, his gaze finds mine and they lock in quiet conspiracy. Something warm spreads across the open wound Grant left, like a balm. Grant scoffs, and I practically see the way it chafes across Andy's skin, can see in real time his careless smirk slip into something harder. "It'd cost you nothing to just, I don't know, give her the benefit of the doubt."

Ben's mouth presses into a straight line as he stifles a laugh, looking away from the table as understanding dawns on my brother. I'd assumed Gen would've mentioned the whole me and Andy sleeping together thing, in passing anyway. It seems she left that little bomb to me.

"Great. Thank you, Sloane, for doing the *one* thing I asked you not to do." He tears the cut back open, deeper this time, I don't know when it got like this between us or if it will ever be completely fixed. I thought maybe after he found out Connie was sick that he'd stop trying to push me away. Scratch at me until my self image matched the one in his head. It takes more than I wish it did to hide the feelings from my face.

"I promised I wouldn't *flirt* with any of your teammates.

You have no proof I did any such thing," I tell him with a shrug, crossing my arms as I narrow my eyes at him, begging him to argue but I hope he catches the dip of my mouth, the silent plea to let this go. To forgive me.

"You know what? It's none of my business," he huffs out, motioning for Jean to move, just as Andy's jaw twitches. I brace myself.

"You're right, man. It's not. But if you have a problem with it, you should probably talk to me—not her." My stomach dips at the suggestion that he should speak for me at all, but I can't help the warmth that creeps across my skin, up the back of my neck—the blush that blooms over my cheeks. He's in this dark corduroy button up that's rolled up his forearms, so I can see the tension there as he flexes his hands in a fist on the table, can see the tendon in his neck that twitches with irritation, and it's overwhelming that he's this irritated for me.

Overwhelming but enthralling, if my rush of adrenaline is any indication.

Grant shakes his head, fucking off to wherever his angel of a girlfriend is dancing the night away, and I *hope* he realizes she did cocaine on a dirty bathroom counter, and I hope his head pops off because he can't control every little piece on his happy little checker board.

"Ian's here," Jean shouts just as a voice from my childhood sings "it goes on and on" and starts pumping through the speakers, and Andy bristles. I don't know what the deal is, why this bothers him, but I can tell he'd rather avoid him right now.

"I think the dart board's free," I say before turning to Ben. "And I don't think you're gettin' away without stepping foot on that dance floor so, shoo!" His head rolls, only remerging once a resigned grin is etched in his face.

"You read my mind. You think I can bribe the DJ into something slow?"

"On New Year's Eve?" I chuckle as Andy steps down, brushing his hand across my waist in subtle possession. We disappear to the back wall of the club, farthest away from the rooftop patio that overlooks Boston Harbor, and find the vacant target. Andy gathers the darts and hands me all the reds.

"You get any better?" he says, stepping behind me as I line up my first throw, and I'm thrown back to the first night we met. The pool table, the darts, the cheesy pick up lines.

"This is my *thing*, Andrew. If anything, you were just messin' me up." I step away from him, throwing the dart. It lands within the triple ring, and I mutter a string of curses under my breath. His dart flies and does marginally better, and I sneakily lift my brows, pleased by the way it pulls a smirk to his lips, and the urge to lean against the wall and let him crowd me grows with every dart we throw. With one left, he presses up behind me, leaving no room for me to evade him, and reaches to guide my hand. It's a relief I wish wasn't so visceral —having him near me, touching me, holding me. One hand on my throwing one, the other settled on my hip, slipping beneath the band of my jeans, skimming the skin there like he always does. Like I love.

"Let's just try," he says low in my ear. I feel my pulse beneath the center seam of these pants; either they're too tight or my body is straining against them. We pull back and he counts; on one I release a breath and we let the dart fly.

Of course, it's a fucking bullseye. I round on him, feeling antsy in my own skin, only to find his heavy lidded gaze on me, filled to the brim with amusement.

"That was luck," I insist, quickly spinning to collect the darts for a rematch. A feminine voice sounds behind me, and when I flick my gaze over my shoulder I see the bottle service girl an inch closer than would be professional, all things considered.

"One more minute," she says, like she's forcing herself to sound breathy, her lips pouting in a way that can't be natural while tinsel sparkles in her dark brown hair. "You really should see the fireworks from the deck." She gives him these sex eyes and if I was closer, I fear I'd trip her. Instead, I turn back to the dart board and let the feeling roll off me, because I *told* him to see other people. That I don't want to be a roadblock for him, just like he shouldn't think he's one for me. The thought doesn't sit well, though, and I swallow, facing the harbor as I pass him his set of darts.

"Let's go." He offers me his hand, and I realize the little table fairy has flown away.

"Where's your friend?" My voice doesn't really sound like my own; it's clinical, like the kind nurses use with you when they're just covering for someone else and don't want to get attached but want to be polite.

Andy searches my face. "The bottle service girl?" he corrects, eyes narrowing.

"Yeah. I think she's expectin' a New Year's Eve kiss," I tell him, like a wing woman and not a woman he's been sleeping with, passionately, to the point of tears for the past week.

"And why would I want to do that?" He steps toward me, his head tilted down so I can see the exasperation in the crease of his brow.

"She's hot," I say, forcing a smile. The song changes to *What Are You Doing New Years?* as the crowd starts to move onto the icy deck, willing to brave the cold breeze that floats off the harbor in hopes of a fresh start marked by an explosion that'll obliterate everything they'd rather forget.

"Didn't notice."

"Come on," I say, my breath stuttering as he lifts my chin with a gentle grasp.

"I told you you're the only woman I'm seeing. I meant

that. I don't see anyone else, Sloane." The words burn across my skin, and I think if I could just get to the deck, I'd be able to think straight. "If *you* want to kiss someone else tonight, tell me right now and I'll leave," he says. I tilt my head, alarm widening my eyes, and I'm sure he's being dramatic. "I mean it, Sloane. I want *you*."

"Well, you've had me," I force a chuckle. "Numerous times. Many venues." The joke doesn't crack anything in him; instead, his throat bobs, and vulnerability slashes across his face.

"I want more than that," he says, shaking his head.

"You don't mean it," I insist, hearing the loud shouts from the deck.

Thirty, twenty nine, twenty eight...

"I do. Sloane, I..." *twenty four, twenty two...* "I can't stop thinking about you. And I've tried. It's no use."

"You sound stupid," I mutter, biting back the small smile that curves without my permission. *Fifteen, fourteen, thirteen.*

"I feel stupid. And I don't really care. Just...tell me I'm not crazy for feeling like this." His hand skates to the back of my head, tilting back and toward him like he's done so often that now, I crave it. My feelings are lodged in my throat, struggling to make themselves lucid and decipherable, but I feel them nevertheless.

Ten, nine...

"I read that play." It tumbles out of me, unlocked from the safe I'd placed it in when I decided it was something he never needed to know. That I read it and liked it and understood why he'd underlined and starred and creased the pages. That I read it and saw myself reflected in all that waiting. That I read it and wondered if that's what he saw in it, too.

"Yeah? And?" he asks like the news is bigger than it is, his eyes softening with too much hope.

"I still don't think this is all pointless. But maybe we can talk about it. Some time."

Five, four, three...

His sigh of relief, the distance he closes between us, the slight grin that tugs at the corner of his all too perfect lips, send a wave of belonging through me.

"I'd love that," he tells me. *Two...one...* "Happy New Year, Sloane," he says as fire erupts in the sky in the distance, as bells clang and people cheer, as his lips brush against mine and I let him kiss me tenderly, letting the feeling seep into my bones.

30

Andy

January

Stacks of thick hardback books line every corner of Glenn's office, forming a gradient so dark, the space can only be described as looming. Ian's been sitting behind our dad's computer for the past twenty minutes, trying to crack the password of a man who seems to hold no sentimentalities, especially when it comes to cyber security.

"Mother fucker," Ian groans. A message pixelizes on the machine signaling we are locked out for ten minutes.

"Maybe we should look around. Maybe he wrote it down somewhere?" I try to be helpful but am met with that dead stare he's given me more than once the past few weeks, wordlessly telling me I'm a moron anytime I open my mouth. It was my idea to go through the office and yet, Ian seems to think he thought of it himself. I considered that maybe we should look through the stark stacks of paperwork splayed on the shelves but Ian insisted that what we were looking for would be locked away, thus—we're hacking Glenn's password.

"Why am I even here, Ian?" I huff out, raking my hand through my hair.

"Moral support?" he shrugs, absentmindedly playing with a Rubik's cube sitting near the computer.

"You ever solve one of those?" I nod toward the cube he's spinning in a direction that will get him no closer to completing it.

"No. I didn't realize that was something people *actually* do." He lets out that sardonic laugh of his and I snatch the cube from his hands.

"You know—" I smirk, sliding the squares into their correct place, "you might have more friends if you weren't so snobby."

"Who needs friends when I have such an amazing half brother?" He smirks sarcastically back and relaxes into the rolling chair just as the final square locks into place. The cube shifts in my grasp and I realize the completion of the puzzle unlocked some part of it. He sees the cube shift, too, the top of it opening just slightly to reveal that it isn't just a normal Rubik's cube, but a box. Both our eyes widen simultaneously. "Looks like you and dear old dad have more in common than we thought." He jumps to his feet. "Don't just stare, Andy. Open it."

I hold back a grimace, cracking the small box open, revealing a thumb drive and a small silver key that looks like it belongs to a—

"File cabinet," we say in unison before looking at the numerous ones lining the far wall of the office. Ian snags the key from the box and begins turning it into them with little luck.

"Dammit," he mutters after the key gets stuck in the fourth cabinet he's tried. I sit behind the desk in the seat still warm from Ian, staring at the thumb drive when my knee hits something hollow in the interior. I glance under the desk and find a drawer hidden in the side of the desk, a small keyhole barely visible.

"Ian..." A chill passes through me as I consider that maybe I don't want to know what our dad's been hiding. That freeing myself from the man that made me may come at the cost of understanding all the horrible things I helped him do. Nausea roils in my stomach as Ian slides the key across the desk.

"Open it," he instructs but his eyes have shifted into the same haunted expression I know I'm wearing. Like he too realizes that there's no going back from whatever we might learn.

"Ian...we can stop if—"

"Open the damn drawer, Andrew." His voice is hard, despite the hollowness in his gaze. I turn the key, hearing the soft click of the lock before pulling the drawer open. Three cream colored file folders are laid in the drawer, each labeled with a name.

William Chapman
Elliot Walker
Rebecca Spellman

A boulder falls to the bottom of my stomach as I see mom's name, her folder significantly thicker than the other two and my fingers tingle with the urge to open it. To see all the tabs Glenn's kept on mom over the years—on me. The knowledge is bittersweet. I think this is the most care, if you could call it that, my father is capable of.

Ian slides past me, grabbing the folders from the drawer and dropping them on to the desk. He opens Will's first and there has to be over a hundred papers inside, from school records to candid photos taken of him around town. My pulse is racing at the sheer mass of information sitting in front of us. At the realization that there is a bombshell in this folder just waiting to be uncovered. Ian begins flipping through the pages when we hear the gears of the garage door thrum to life.

"*Fuck*," Ian whispers as both our eyes snap to the door.

"I thought you said he was going to be out of town this week," I hiss, panic shooting up my spine.

"Do you really think he gives me that much information? I just assumed..." Ian quickly snaps photos of the pages in Will's folder as I fumble around, trying to shove everything back into place.

"Hurry up," I urge, my heart crashing into my rib cage.

We can't get caught. Not when we're just getting started, when we're finally on to *something*.

The hum of the garage door quiets just before we hear a door slam. "Ian!"

He slams the folder shut, moving to swipe the remaining folders off the desk but it's too swift. Elliot Walker's folder goes sprawling to the floor.

"Shit..." Ian stands still for a second as we hear the door leading from the garage creek open. I drop to the floor, quickly gathering the papers back into a neat stack. The similarities pull the words and photos on them into focus, and I realize it's profiles of women that are strewn across the floor, their faces just iterations of each other: blonde, tan, young, just different enough that I can tell they aren't all the same person. I grab the last two when my eyes catch on deep blue eyes, eyes that I haven't been able to get out of my head. Blue eyes like the ocean and the night sky all at once. Eyes that I've memorized laying in bed next to me.

Her packet has multiple staples, is thicker than the others and cold dread fills my throat. Her name's typed neatly at the top.

Sloane Fielder

I hear hard footsteps approaching and hurriedly shove the packet back into the folder before carefully shutting the drawer, bile sitting high in my throat. When I look up, Ian's in a doorway on the opposite side of the room, frantically gesturing to me. I crawl across the room, sliding in just before the main office door opens. He silently shuts the door and we both melt against the wall, our breath fast and hushed as we hear Glenn enter the office. The sound of the computer powering up has me wincing, and I close my eyes because I know we are fucked when I feel the soft vibration of my phone. My father's name flashes on the screen and if I didn't know better I'd think I was having a heart attack.

I show Ian who vigorously shakes his head no, so I ignore the call, sending Glenn straight to voicemail. I hear him let out a loud sigh on the other side of the door, and suddenly my phone's vibrating again. Ian's eyes widen, Glenn's name filling the screen once again. He points to the far edge of the ridiculously long bathroom, as far from the door as possible and mouths an answer. I crawl against the cold marble, wedging my body in the furthest possible corner.

"Hello..." my voice is a hushed mumble, my hand shaking as I press the speaker to my ear.

"Andrew. Where are you right now?" His voice is harsh, abrasive against the cool silence of the bathroom. Terror trickles down my back, and I wonder if he knows I'm here, if he's trying to catch me in a lie, if he'll drag me out of here and use everything in my mother's file to make their life a living hell.

I look at Ian, his hands waving around, trying to conduct me to a response.

"The library, big bio exam this week." I wince, not sure if

my tone is calm enough to be believable. I hear Glenn let out a breath and can almost see the roll of his eyes, his expression so similar to Ian's.

"Any news on the Fielder girl? I need to know if she's talking." A knot forms in my throat, rage sitting at the center of it as I remember that packet remember the name Elliot Walker scrawled at the top of the folder it belonged in.

"Who's Elliot Walker?" I ask before I can stop myself, even though I know. In my heart of hearts, I know it's *him*.

Steady anger fills my ears like a loud thrum as I wait for my dad's response.

"Did she say something about him?" His tone is hopeful, like this is what he's been waiting for and I almost regret asking.

"Not directly...I just need to know what I'm looking for here..." I shut my eyes trying to focus my anger, trying to concoct a believable enough excuse as to why I haven't found anything on Sloane except for the obvious one, that I simply haven't been looking.

"Next time she brings him up...press on it. I need to know what she's telling people about that particular name." Pain radiates through my jaw as my molars clamp shut.

"Fine." It's a harsh whisper but enough for my dad as I hear the phone line end. We hear him ruffling papers in the background and Ian gives me a wide eyed look that warns me to be quiet. I shut my eyes, letting my head rest against the clean lines of the wall, and wish, not for the first time, that I never found myself in this situation. That I went to an affordable state school, focused on getting an engineering degree or maybe even pre-med, something that would allow me to help my mom without all the back stabbing and secrets.

"Andy...Andy!" Ian's voice is a loud hiss as I realize the room's gotten eerily quiet. "I think he's gone. Let's go." I stand up and follow as he cracks the bathroom door enough just to look out. He nods before opening and moves back to the desk.

"Dude!" I shake my head, eyeing the entrance to the hallway. "Later," I mouth, dragging him out the door and through the back entrance of the house until we are in the alley between Glenn's townhouse and the one next door. I put my hands on my knees groaning as I bend over, trying to shake off the nervous energy. "Remind me not to make deals with you again."

"You're such a baby," he says but his attention stays on the photos he took on his phone. "Give me a couple days to digest these. I'll text you when I'm ready to meet." He barely looks up and I roll my eyes.

"You know if it weren't for me we would've never gotten that rubik's cube open..." I tilt my head, positioning my hands on my hips.

"Are you...whining, Andrew?" He meets my gaze amused.

"Just, a thank you would be nice every once in a while," I huff out.

"*Thank you.* Now run along. I have research waiting for me and based on that call from Dad, you have a certain Fielder girl who needs your attention." He winks before rounding back around the house to the entrance we just came out of, leaving me rattled and relieved because this...might actually work.

31

Sloane

Small strokes, tiny and precise, in a deep ochre capture the way the sun turned golden an afternoon last summer—they cramp my hand in a way I've been craving. The smattering of oil melting together the way watercolor never could. The photo I'm using as inspiration sat in a box of my things, untouched until Grant suggested I start to unpack.

The dresser, he said with a smirk on his face, *was a great place to keep my belongings.* I glance back at it, pushed against the wall behind me.

The urge to finally settle came in the middle of the night. I began rummaging through all the shit I deemed valuable enough to keep when I left San Francisco. That's when I found the photo—the one I took while Elliot's chin rested on my shoulder. He couldn't understand why I'd want to photograph a sun that looked like it might burst. I couldn't understand why he thought a sun that ablaze wasn't impressive. I can understand now, though. Elliot couldn't appreciate anything that might supersede him. He bathed in his superiority like the rest of us bathed in bath water. He reeked of it, but at the time it was cedar and musk to me—a smoke screen of attraction that covered up all the ways in which he lacked. This far back, I think maybe he was a narcissist.

I dip into the pot of ivory paint just as the clouds outside shift, and the light filters in, highlighting my work. Sitting back, I rest against the side of the bed and consider adding a bird. Or two. And then I sigh, so content in the magic that's worked its way back into my fingers that I laugh. No one's home—Gen and Grant are off being the kinds of people who move their bodies for fun—so my amusement echoes a little, and I quietly make plans to pepper every wall of Grant's space with artwork he never asked for.

Must be them, I think to myself when my phone jingles and I bring it to my ear.

"Thank you because I'm starvin' and there is *nothin'* in the fridge and you know how I feel—"

"Ms. Fielder?" a papery voice comes through the line, and I frown. "This is Hannah Cooper. From Arts and Culture at The Journal. I reached out to you a couple of months ago but got no response. I'm just touching base—"

"I'm sorry, I don't talk to the press. I don't even know how you got my number," I say sharply, unsettled by her persistence. The e-mail last fall was violation enough, but somehow less personal? A voice over the phone always feels like someone caressing your arm. Way too intimate for strangers.

"The internet." She's cool, her voice sterile and chilly like stainless steel, and I don't like it.

"Right," I mutter. "Well like I said, I don't talk to the press. That's why I didn't respond in the first place. So—"

"I'd really love a moment of your time," her voice slips into a congeniality she has no business using with me, but it stops me from hanging up on her before she says, "to discuss Elliot Walker."

Heart dropping, I force a small intake of breath. "What for?"

Hannah's silent for a moment, just the shuffling of papers sounding in the background. "You were a student of his, until...well, until you stopped attending classes in late August of last year. Were you not?"

My lips press hard into each other, frustration welling in the tendons of my face as my cheeks turn crimson.

"I'm sure however you got that is a violation of my privacy," I tell her, my voice grittier than usual from the emotion that's welled up without my permission. "What rules did you have to break for that, Hannah? And *why* are you snoopin' around in my business?"

"You are just one of—"

"Lose my number, or you'll be hearing from my attorney." I hang up, letting my phone drop with a clatter against the drop cloth, and force myself to breathe, the air shakily whooshing out of me.

You are just one of...what? The possibilities curdle in my stomach when someone knocks on the door and I jut up, eager for a distraction. Outside I find Andy, in his leather Astor bomber, his nose red from the brisk wind, arms full of Chinese take out.

"You're an angel," I say on an exhale, my anxiety settling low in the background of my consciousness as tenderness presses to the fore. *She won't call again*, I think. *Just ignore it, she'll go away, he'll go away.* "How'd you know I was minutes away from eatin' my own hand?"

"Because I know you, Sloane," he chuckles and it's not like they say in the movies. The world doesn't tilt. I don't feel the butterflies I did when I first arrived in Boston—no. It's worse. It's that quiet static that seems to hum between us, the way his eyes meet mine and I'm excited to see the small creased lines that form at the corners, the ones I've memorized, that I know are coming because they always come when he sees me. It's not a whirlwind, it's not a storm; it's softer, steadier, scarier.

I step aside, shutting the door as he drops the cartons on the counter, and when I turn around I'm in his arms, so warm, despite the cold he just emerged from. A hand low on my back, he pulls me into him, his other skating around my neck as he consumes me with his kiss.

Falling into it is easy; it always is. But what I want is to dive into him, desperately, to forget every problem that tethers me to the person who will eventually fuck this all up.

He rears slightly back, studying me with the kind of concern that I'm still not used to seeing. "What's going on?"

He asks and it's like he's knuckle deep inside of me, ripping me open, but it isn't violent at all. His warm eyes constantly check if I'm okay and the desire to scrub the memory of myself from my own skin overwhelms me. To become something softer or quieter, the vulnerable thing they always end up wanting me to be no matter how many times they claim to like that edge that refuses to dull, because let's face it—they all want to be the one who finally smooths it out.

It terrifies me that if I let him in, that moment will come where he asks me to be less. But even scarier is that desperate, exhausting realization that I would try. For him I would try and all I can do is hope that unlike the others, unlike Elliot, Andy won't ask.

"I just got a call from a reporter," I finally say, and his brows furrow as his hold on me tightens. "About my old professor. Who I..." *You have to tell him eventually, Sloane.* "Who I dated. I dated my professor before I came here and it ended kind of badly," I say in a rush, wincing, my smile small and fragile as I wait for him to release me.

Something about my relationship with Elliot always felt

rebellious but we'd convinced ourselves it was the world that was the problem. We couldn't be seen laughing at a joke together while in seminar because *the world* was prudish and would judge me. Wouldn't take *me* seriously. It was never about him. As if he was immune to the judgement I was laden to.

Something about saying this out loud now, to Andy, feels different. Like my brain has finally come to terms with the thing that my heart still can't. The sensical part of me can so easily blame Elliot. He was older, he should have *known* better, he took advantage in the way only a girl can be taken advantage of when she's young and believes she is what everyone claims her to be.

I can see this truth for what it is—a girl manipulated and broken by a man. But in my heart I blame myself, could always feel the judgmental eyes of my peers when Elliot spent too long complimenting the brush work on one of my watercolors. Always heard my roommates quietly whisper when he'd drop me off at my apartment, blouse haphazardly buttoned because his wife was home and we had to use the back seat of his car. And the heart always beats the brain doesn't it? You can be so sure of something but that drowning feeling like a stone in your gut remains.

Andy's jaw twitches and I wonder if he blames me, too.

"You're mad," I say quietly. "You think I'm horrible, don't you?"

"What?" His concern swirls into a silent frustration, but still, he holds me. "Sloane, no. I…" he pauses, closing his eyes like he's carefully considering his words. "I don't think there are enough words in any language to fully explain how I feel about you, but mad could never be one of them." His breath skims the top of my head and I suck in a breath. "If I could reach back through time, if I could step in front of every moment and every person, that ever made you doubt yourself, I'd find them. If only to remind you, again and again, for as long as it took, exactly who you are." He shakes his head, making an attempt to soften his features. "I hate that you've ever believed you were anything but perfect." I watch as he packs away his frustration, neatly storing it for later.

The gentleness of his fingers against my skin is deliberate, and when I finally let myself relax it feels like falling, like letting go before knowing what's waiting at the bottom and searching for something solid, a foothold to stop the inevitable crash… and finding him, his fingers tracing circles on the freckles of my skin.

"This reporter though, if they keep bothering you…"

Something about the way he's holding me a little tighter, his mouth brushing the top of my head; I've never felt more protected. Never realized that I wanted to feel this way, actually, and my teeth tug at my lip nervously because it terrifies me. *All of it* terrifies me. I pull away, brushing invisible dirt on my pants, striding toward the lo-mein.

"I don't even know what she really wants. I hung up on her."

Andy quietly pads through the apartment, pulling plates and glasses from the cabinet, before joining me on the floor by the coffee table, a contemplative look etched into the strength of his brow. "And?"

"That's it."

"But it's bothering you," he challenges, sliding more than half the container of noodles on my plate, and I can't help but grin over at him. Two spring rolls get plopped there, too, plus a heaping portion of sesame chicken. All of which happen to be my favorite.

I lock eyes with him for a second, a warmth circling my heart and squeezing so tight, I worry I'll never feel this good again. *This good*, in the midst of all the other shit. That's the magic in being taken care of, being seen; that's the unexplainable that I worry will one day make perfect, deconstructable sense.

His brows lift, a reminder of the conversation he's trying to have.

"Yes, it's botherin' me. I closed that chapter of my life and I've got no desire to revisit it," I tell him, feeling confident and sure, my brain winning, if only for a moment and he nods. There isn't anything about that time that calls to me—not right now, anyway—and I watch as he lets me steer this ship. Lets me share what I want and leave alone what I don't. A privilege I've rarely been given.

Just past where Andy sits, I can see my bedroom door cracked open, can see my unfinished canvas and the late afternoon sun that fractures over the drop cloth. Like it's speaking to me, a silent petition to be finished.

His tongue grazes his bottom lip as an easy smile tugs there, and as hungry as I am, I'd rather feast on him instead. "Eat," he says, reading my mind or the heat in my gaze. "We have all the time in the world."

God, I want it to be true. More than anything. So I let myself lean into this thing I'm constantly scared will slip through my fingers.

"Was my brother nice to you today?" I ask him, spooling the noodles around my chopsticks. Andy's eyes roll as laughter chimes out of him and he leans back against the couch.

"I think he's only hard on me in front of you. Honestly, he's a peach," he says, shrugging his shoulders before popping a fried wonton in his mouth.

"A peach?" I feel my eyes go wide and my smile deepens. "Surely, not my brother."

"He just wants to intimidate me a little. I'd do the same for

Carmen." When he says his sister's name, it's full of endearment that causes my heart to swell. I wish my own brother would hold me in such high regard.

"I promise you, he's not that concerned about me," I tell him behind a mouthful of chicken, covering my mouth before taking a huge gulp of soda.

A doubtful look slots into his features. "You don't really think that, do you? He loves you, Sloane." I roll my eyes. "We haven't always seen eye to eye, you know...with Will being my best friend, but...he's sensitive. And he worries about you. He shouldn't be worried about *me*," he adds, smirking as he offers me a bite of his General Tso's that I gladly nip off the fork.

"No, I don't think he should be," I agree, fighting the happiness threatening to leave permanent dimples in my cheeks. "You can always tell how good a man is by how he treats the woman who raised him." He pulls his fork back, glancing down at his plate as he pushes some food around before deciding on a sliver of carrot.

"That so?"

"I think so. I mean you and Rebecca—prime example." I cock my head, thinking. "Grant's obviously not great with Connie, but he *worships* Evie. I don't know much about Ben's mother, but Liv's never said anything weird. Oh my god, but," I sit up, leaning across the table. "She did say Will and her like, barely speak. So," I shrug, taking a bite out of a spring roll.

"I don't know if that's really fair," Andy says quietly, like he's chewing on a thought.

"Defendin' him to me is futile, Andrew," I tell him. "He hurt *both* of my best friends. He's like...a sociopath."

"He's *not* a sociopath. He's just..."

"Do *not* say traumatized," I say right as he says it, and I scoff, amusement rolling through me. "You're just like Clementine."

"Empathetic?" he smirks, glancing up from his plate as he scoops up water chestnut.

"*Soft*," I giggle. "I'm empathetic. Some would say to a fault."

"No such thing. I told you—I think you're perfect."

"Mhm," I hum, taking another sip of my drink. "There he goes again." I brush the hair off the nape of my neck, warm from the blush he's constantly sending across me with just a glance, just a look. Right now, he's set down the fork he opted for instead of chopsticks, is blotting his mouth with a napkin, and is looking at me like I hung the moon.

I want to tell him to knock it off, to be serious, to look at me for who I am, but the feeling is intoxicating. And most of all, I want to believe him.

He moves to where I'm sitting, pulling me into him.

"Not so fast, pretty boy." I swat him away, taking another bite of my chicken before getting up. "I'm inspired, and I've got work to do. We have all the time in the world...remember?" I wink and make my way back to the sun soaked canvas.

32

Andy

The team's been off since Will left, like a kid learning to ride their bike, wobbly and unbalanced. I know Ben feels it, too, with the way his eyes slide around the court, looking for his brother before he finally settles on me. He gives me that smirk —his only tell. The ball comes at me like a bullet and I swipe it out of the air. The one advantage of Will not being here: I can play harder, move faster. Grant even slapped me on the back in the first half.

Maybe it isn't Will's absence that is upping my game, though. Maybe it's the tall blonde in the stands holding the hand of a tiny eleven year old, my number boldly plastered on both their jerseys.

They jump up as soon as the ball is in my vicinity. I can hear Carm's voice screaming, "C'mon sixteen!" and I let myself grin, let myself show the others that that little girl means something to me. Something I wouldn't have dared to do just a couple weeks ago.

In fact, I don't think she's even been to a game this season.

Normally, I'll get her and mom one ticket a season and hope that Mom's working. It's not that I'm embarrassed of them—I'm embarrassed of *me*. Who I become the moment I set foot on campus. The unserious play boy without a care in the world, the complete opposite of how I was raised.

I sink a basket, turning toward where they're seated in the stands and let that warm feeling flow through me as I watch the two jump and scream, both of them throwing the pom poms I'm sure Sloane bought at concessions in the air.

I'm glad they're here. It's not something I'm used to if, I'm being honest, having two people who care about me cheer me on. I sort of get it now—why Ben and Grant are always excited to see their girls front and center, the sappy gestures they make toward them mid game. I find myself wanting to do it, too.

The buzzer sounds, signaling the end of the fourth quarter. I was too swept up in the sight of my girls to notice I just landed the final basket of the night, the winning basket. I feel Grant's giant chest pummel me in a congratulatory hug as Ben swings his arm around me, ruffling my hair. The rest of the guys are celebrating our win, too, our ticket to playoffs and still I'm in this daze. The stands are abuzz, the excitement vibrating through them as stomping fills the bleacher lined court, but all I see is her.

She's still in the sea of movement, her dark ocean eyes locked with mine and for a second things feel perfect, a moment frozen in time. Just the upward tick of the corner of her mouth, the way her bubblegum pink tongue licks her bottom lip, letting me know she's mine.

With a blink it's over. The tidal wave of sound crashes into me as I feel dozens of guys slap me on the back, hollering congratulations, and when I look back she's gone.

I shower and change as quickly as possible, doing my best

to avoid Scott. It annoys him, I know, but now that Will's gone I don't really see the point in pretending to have any sort of a friendship with him.

"Spellman," his waxy voice calls out as I throw the hoodie on that Mom snagged from her church swap last weekend.

"Sup," I nod, quickly running my hands through my hair, eager to get out of here. Sloane texted me that her and Carm were waiting in the lot behind the locker room, the one for athletes and their loved ones. Something about Sloane parking there felt good. Better than good, it felt right.

"When the fuck are we going out dude? I heard Will's downtown."

My eyes narrow in Scott's direction, because I know he's bluffing. There's no way in hell Will texted, much less gave his location, to this douche bag.

"I haven't heard that. I haven't heard from him at all, actually." I slide my duffle over my shoulder slamming my locker shut.

"Just what I heard." Scott shrugs, but his irritation is palpable.

"What are you nerds talking about?" Josiah slides in between us, opening his locker.

"Trying to convince Spellman to go out with us tonight." Scott's eyes are clouded with suspicion as he looks me over and Josiah seems confused by the newfound tension between us.

"Sorry boys. Can't tonight." I clasp a hand on Josiah's shoulder and start moving toward the door.

"You hangin' out with Ian again?" I hear Scott call out from behind me and I freeze. Turning around slowly I meet his eyes, and normally when I look at Scott I can feel my brain cells begin to waste away, but tonight, something's different.

He knows something.

"I don't know what you're talking about." It comes out like a growl.

"I think you do, Andy. I think you know exactly what I'm talking about." His features form a sinister grin as he bumps me with his shoulder and strolls to the showers.

"That dude is a freak," Josiah mutters, shutting his own locker and I let a small breath move through my nose.

"Definitely," I nod, anxiety roiling in my stomach because somehow Scott knows I've been sneaking around with Ian. Whether or not he knows *why* remains to be seen.

It feels like the walk in freezer at the club when I open the door that leads outside and I wish I had something warmer than a hand me down hoodie as I approach the various cars sprawled throughout the lot. I hear Carmen before I see her, loudly belting the words to some song from High School Musical. I mistakenly allowed Sloane to show her; she hasn't stopped singing it since.

Sloane leans against Delilah's hood, her jeans hugging every curve as her head bobs along to the timber of Carmen's voice. She reaches her hands out, grabbing my sister and twirling her, and I can see that spark of happiness in Carmen that I feel in myself. Like this—Sloane—was the piece that's been missing for so long.

"Andy!" Carmen practically screeches when they finally see me and Sloane lets out that soft throaty laugh that makes my stomach dip.

"If it ain't the Lion's most valuable player!" Her toothy smile has my stomach somersaulting.

"Ah, I don't know about that," I breathe out as Carmen slams her tiny body into me for a full blown bear hug.

"Sloane said we could get pizza," she squeaks out.

"Oh did she?" I laugh and look at Sloane, her sheepish smile and the way her thick lashes brush her high cheekbones pulling a warmth up my neck that I wish my sweatshirt did a better job of hiding.

"I may have said somethin' like that." She kicks the toe of her red cowboy boots against the pavement.

"Then I think," I ruffle Carmen's hair, "that can be arranged."

* * *

"There. I took a bite," Carm whines, mozzarella cheese making a bridge between her and the slice of pizza she just bit into. I sigh, rolling my eyes and Sloane giggles, handing her at least ten dollars of quarters she just broke at the bar. Carmen's eyes widen like Sloane just handed her a small fortune and I guess to Carm, she kinda did.

"Have fun," Sloane winks and I watch as Carmen skips over to the large arcade connected to the pizza restaurant.

Dozens of other kids surround the pinball and claw machines and the more I look, the more I feel that tug of youth slipping away, the ambient glow of the machines reminding me of the summers Luis would take me to play ski ball. *'Boy's night'* he'd call it.

I watch Sloane watching those same kids slot quarters into the arcade games, an almost haunted expression on her face.

"Hey—you good?" I use the spatula to push another large slice onto Sloane's plate and she snaps out of it. She grabs the canister of red pepper flakes shaking until her pizza is almost drowning in them before smiling down at it, satisfied. "Sloane?" She looks up, her eyes glassy, face slightly flushed. "Oh shit. What happened?"

"Nothing, nothing. I'm fine." Her smile is sad as she inhales a sharp breath, picking up her slice of pizza and taking a large bite. I watch her, trying to see any sign in her face of what

312

she might be feeling. She must feel me watching because she wipes her eyes and then rolls them playfully, carefully chewing her pizza before taking a sip of her beer. "Wish this place had something stronger," she chuckles almost to herself before looking at me. "Has anyone ever told you it's rude to look at someone so hard?" The glassiness is gone but that twinge of sadness is still there.

"You can talk to me, you know." I nod toward the games, at the sheer joy painted across every child's face, trying to communicate that something about it makes me sad, too. She nods, chewing on another bite of pizza seeming to think something over.

"I think I'm just jealous," she says, pressing her lips together in a shy smile.

"Of them?"

"Of you." She bites her inner cheek and she must see my utter shock because she chuckles, that laugh I wish I could drown in.

"Why would you be jealous of me?" I pull my head back trying to see in her what she sees in me. Like maybe her expression will lead me to the thoughts in her head.

"You're just...loved, Andy." She looks at my sister, giggling with a boy about her age as they both clutch the wheels of the Nascar style game they're seated at. "Your family is warm. Is perfect." She takes another long sip of her beer staring down into it, refusing to meet my eyes.

"It hasn't always been like this Sloane...this easy." I take a bite of the crust that I notice she hasn't touched on her plate. "Most days, Carm and I would kill for what you have."

She huffs out a laugh. "That's crazy."

Frustration creases my brow as I observe a girl who's so starved for connection that she can't even see how good she has it. "Half of my wardrobe is from a donation bin." I pour the pitcher of beer into my own glass until a pale white foam hits its edge. "I've never been abroad, hadn't tried sushi until I got to Astor..." I laugh. "I ate reduced lunch at school, and was on every government assistance plan you could think of. Carm and I are close because I raised her when my parents worked overtime to make ends meet." I basically sold my soul to get us to Boston I want to say, but instead I watch her, the way she's picking at her sleeve, guilt washing over her features. "We're close because all we have is each other." I watch Carmen, feeling that glassy haze fall over my own vision.

"She'll know, Andy." I look over and Sloane's careful gaze focuses on me. "That you did what you could. That she might not have had everything but she had enough. She had you." She swallows hard and I consider her mom, the things she's told me about her adoption, that photo of her in that file.

"Did you have enough?" There's a steady burn between us, the heat of two people who aren't saying anything but also saying everything. She doesn't answer but I watch her eyes find my sister, full of sorrow, jealousy and hope and I know she feels the way I do. Like if she couldn't have this, at least Carm can.

"When I first met Luis he'd take me to an arcade in California, pretty similar to this one." I suck in a breath, feeling an urgent need to tell her the truth—a souvenir from my childhood that my dad can't strip away. I clear my throat, trying to disguise an emotion I'm sure is so clearly written across my face and keep my voice low, as if the memory will crack in half if I speak an octave higher. "It was just for bad days. I'd lose a basketball game, fail a test, be stuck on why my dad left...why he never came back." I see understanding flood her expression and wish she didn't carry this exact same wound. The way it worms itself inside every inch of you, every thought, every action, infesting every memory until all you are is an amalgamation of the ways you couldn't make them stay.

"He'd always remind me that even when someone leaves you behind it isn't some omen for the rest of your life." Her breath hitches at the words and I let my hand graze hers, let the tips of our fingers touch across the table. "I was so young. I just wanted to run from every connection at that point." I let out a sad laugh. "Luis helped me realize I was running because I was scared, that if I ran long enough I'd forget how to stay. How to let someone find me." The room feels heady, like we are both holding our breath and her hand urgently grasps mine in a plea to stay here—stay with her.

"How did you stop? Running?" Trembled air escapes her as she breathes the words. The question hangs between us, the heaviness of it muting the laughter around us, until we are just a we and the rest of the world has faded away. I let my eyes meet hers and I see it, all of what we could be together, both of our memories, the pain and the love rippling in the dark blue flecks of her gaze.

"Someone found me." My voice is a ghost of all the things I still want for myself, the things I can see that she wants too. We sit there, the moment quiet and winding around us.

"Sloane! Look!" Carmen's giddy voice pulls Sloane's focus as she moves her attention to my sister who's proudly pulling a large stuffed dog from a claw machine.

"Hell yeah, sister!" Sloane's smile moves into that too perfect mask, but I see it there, raw hot pain, pain I wish I could wipe away, wish I could consume.

"Ski ball?" She juts her chin out, her voice too chirpy as she chugs the rest of her beer, but it's there in her eyes—recognition that the moment we just had happened, that it existed and she can't just wipe it away no matter how much she wants to.

I nod, registering that this is her shield, her performance, the one her parents, the tabloids, hell, even her brother believe. But I've seen what's underneath and I know she's just afraid.

Scared I'll name that thing out loud. Something real, something breakable, a connection that terrifies her. So I let the pause stretch, hold her gaze just long enough to remind her I'm still here, still seeing her. Then I grin, letting my own mask fall into place.

"Yeah. Ski ball."

33

Sloane

February

Admittedly, I'd never spent a winter in the northeast. All I'd ever heard was that it was beyond dreary, that the landscape was like a corpse, and that it was frigid and barren. Since Grant moved up here for school and basketball, I only really forced myself to visit when all I'd need is a light jacket. Here I am now, though, bundled up in this long, crimson shearling coat we found in one of those high end consignment stores. One of Jean and Olivia's favorites, and now mine; Gen tolerated it, appeasingly playing dress up before bolting toward that gym her and Grant use in the city.

They're a little obsessed, those two. I forgive it, my brother and my—fingers crossed—future sister in law being so up each other's asses, because they're less weird about it than Olivia and Ben. They remind me of those teenagers you see at the mall, always in quiet, intense, telepathic cahoots about something the rest of us will never understand, like a book.

"Oh, thank you," Olivia sings up at the server, rubbing her

hands together before she clasps her steaming cappuccino. The streets twinkle, even without the holiday decor that was hastily packed up after the New Year came and went, as I peer out the window of the cafe we've found ourselves in, just Olivia, Jean, and I, our bags full of our spoils. A fire roars in the corner, and I consider taking the coat off when I catch myself in the glass and decide against it.

"So what do you think Gen will think?" Olivia's smile flattens as she looks between Jean and I with a stern expression. "Should I tell her? Or should I let Ben mention it? Like what is appropriate here?"

I roll my neck, hearing the bones crack as I sigh. "That boy irritates me to no end," I say of Will Chapman, who apparently can't leave us alone. "I vote not to bother her *or* my brother with his bullshit."

"It's not *his* bullshit," Jean clarifies, and I roll my eyes. "His dad's making him come back, right? That's what Ben said." Making him come back to finish the season and then join the draft, a year earlier than he was supposed to. *Whoop dee fuckin' doo.*

"He's an adult. Pretty sure he could just say, *no, fuck off.*"

Olivia shifts uncomfortably in her seat. "He seems...better. I know you hate him—"

"*Olivia,*" I moan, accepting my americano from the server with a quiet smile.

"He's just going to be in our lives, Sloane. Better get used to it," she reminds me, taking a snarky sip of her coffee.

"Andy hasn't said anything to you?" Jean's eyes narrow. "Aren't they besties?"

My lips purse as the door chimes and a group of girls comes rushing in, giggling as wristlet wallets full of charms jingle on their arms, the smallest of them catching my eye.

"Sloane!" Carmen squeals before tamping it down in front

of her friends. She shivers as she moves toward me, and I notice that beneath her coat is just a normal t-shirt, one I'm *sure* Rebecca would've demanded she replace if she'd been available.

"What's this?" I ask, clasping the hem between my fingers. "You want your brother to find you frozen in an alley way?" I rummage through my bags, trying to find the sweater that'll definitely be too big but will keep her warm nevertheless.

"I'm fine," she mumbles, blushing as she glances back at her friends that stare over at our table in awe. I pull an easy smile, waving as I hand Carmen the magenta cashmere pullover I just got, and she tilts her head. "Thank you," she mutters, shrugging off her jacket to pull it on. It's almost dress length on her, but it works with her coat. "I gotta go."

"No, of course," I wave her off, fighting a smile as I notice Olivia and Jean ignoring the girls ogling them. "Go be cool," I say, waggling my brows as Carmen flees back to her cohort. We can hear their whispering from here, and I try my best not to laugh too obviously.

"I feel a little famous," Jean says, popping his shoulder beneath his navy corduroy coat. The sun, almost set, reflects off the high points on his face, glints on the glossy panes of Olivia's hair, and I wonder at their lack of self-awareness.

"You are to those girls. They all go to the conservatory," I remind him, settling into the suede covered seat. "Anyway, they all follow the Astor Hill Gazette—know *all* about us, I'm sure."

"Ugh," Liv intones, her nose scrunching. "I can't read the Gazette."

"But you work for it...?"

"Exactly. I already know what is going to be printed. But reading the finished spins? Nauseating. They're never right, always horrendously slanted. Naturally, because of you–know–

who." She shoots a look at Jean who shrinks back before standing up a little taller.

"Well I do read the papers—all of them. How can you not? It's the world."

"It's not *the* world. It's like, one view of it." Croissants, freshly warmed up, are placed in the center of the table, and I greedily claim the biggest one. Jean cocks his head and is moments from challenging me to a duel, before he just takes the next one.

Olivia barely eats anyway.

"I eat!" she says in shock, and I wonder how many of my thoughts are not actually internal.

"Yeah but, you probably didn't want a big one. Right?" Jean says with false timidity, and my laughter rolls out of me, the warmth that builds there like my own little furnace.

"Whatever, gossip heathen," Olivia jokes, and Jean takes it in stride.

"Speaking of...this reporter from The Journal is like, harassin' me," I say, bringing my latte to my lips.

Jean freezes. "The Journal?"

I nod.

"And?"

"And nothing. I ignored her. She wanted to talk about Elliot." I make a look of disgust.

"Yeah, I bet. They're writing a whole *me too* series on him. Well, him but it's like a whole group of them."

I almost do a spit take. "I'm sorry?"

"I can forward it—" he starts to say before Liv's hand flies up.

"Pause. She's contacting you because what he did to you is apparently part of a very *me too-esque* pattern, and you're just ignoring her?"

"He didn't *do* anything to me," I chuckle, taking a bite of croissant.

"Really?" Jean asks me, suddenly irritated. "So the art show's not a problem then?" At the mention, my mind's eye fills with the dozen canvases lining the walls of my too small bedroom. The girls, Carmen in tow, wiggle their fingers at us as they file out of the cafe, caffeinated drinks they don't need in hand.

"Why would it be?" I haven't felt this inspired since the end of last summer, but they don't know that, don't know *everything* that happened. The only person who knows the whole truth is Clementine. And I think that's okay. Not every truth needs to be substantial. It can just be. Jean blinks over at me, his mouth doing this weird, confusing movement that has me shaking my head. "What?"

"Have you looked at the judges list?" he presses.

Dread sinks to the bottom of my stomach. "No," I say, sniffing as I rip off a piece of croissant and stuff it in my mouth. Liv's eyes skate between the two of us, and I see the moment she makes the same assumption I'm making. That Elliot, the man I very briefly told her and Gen about last fall when I forced the two of them together over female rage films, is going to be here. In Boston. At *my* show. "Shit," I whisper, my mouth full of croissant as fear rears its ugly head, the thought of seeing him again making me want to bolt.

"Yeah. I don't know if that's nothing, Sloane," Jean murmurs, his molars grinding, and I can't help but gnaw on my lip because he's right.

"Hey..." Liv soothes, her hand reaching out to hold mine. "What better way to show him what an idiot he is than to kick his ass at this show?"

"We'll all be there," Jean insists. "Literally, if he even *looks* at you, I'll be like—go fuck yourself, you creep." His eyes burn with intention, and I know he means it.

But I also know that Elliot can only get under my skin, and can only make me feel like his opinion matters, if I let him. That I am not the same girl he picked up from the clinic. And honestly, I *hope* I disappoint him, because the pieces I've painted in the month since my drive came back to me—the one I thought he siphoned away—are better than anything we ever created together.

"Yeah. No, I'll be fine. He has...no power over me, anymore," I say, trying to mean it, but my hand's only not shaking because Olivia is holding it.

"Good," she tells me, her warm brown eyes staring deeper into my soul than I thought possible for her. Usually I'm the one mothering them. "And in the meantime, consider talking to that reporter."

"I don't talk to the—"

"Anonymously. Sometimes, all you need is a little closure."

My phone vibrates in my pocket, and I take the distraction gladly. Relief washes over me when I see that it's Andy, sending me a pin to wherever the hell he is.

Johnny's Comedy Club

Eyes crinkling, I click my screen off. It's like a warm blanket, the feeling just the thought of Andy gives me, and I'm grateful I wound up stranded on Christmas. Grateful that fate pushed me into his arms on that snowy roof.

"It's that good?" Jean moans. "Like *oh I'm worried about seeing my creepy ex-situationship* but boom your current one texts you and it just washes away? The envy," he fake wails, and I can't help but let my smile crack wide across my face.

"Maybe," I shrug with a tight laced smirk, lifting my brows as the wave of anxiety recedes. "I should get going."

"Your prince awaits," Jean grins, and Olivia scoffs.

"That would make Sloane a princess," she laughs, knocking back the rest of her cappuccino. "You're more like a....mage. A witch. No—an elfin witch."

"What the hell?" Jean's brow creases.

"Mm," I nod, eyes narrowing as I push back in my chair. "No, I like that."

"Wait," Jean says, worried, "what am I?"

Olivia's chest rumbles with laughter as she refuses to answer, and I wave a silent goodbye, following my phone to the only place I've ever felt like I needed to be.

34

Andy

We file off the bus, our collective energy buzzing from our win against UConn as we step onto the slippery sludge, the late winter air having warmed just enough to melt away the snowy blanket we've all been hiding under. The dark mornings, the freezing evenings—they're usually enough to plunge me into a darkness of my own. But it was different this year. I know it was different because the addictive unease of longing that I've been convincing myself can't be love has been there every morning when I open my eyes, taunting me with its impermanence. Every morning, I have to shove it away.

Sloane offered to drive up, just for the game, but I knew to tell her not to. Between the new sets for the conservatory's spring show and the piece she's been working on for her art competition, she would've been giving something up. And I don't want her giving up anything for me. For anyone.

A smack on my shoulder jolts me back to the icy road I'm on the edge of, and I blink up to see Grant smirking at me. "Who knew you'd make another winning shot?"

"Me. I knew!" Ben says, knocking his head toward us as he

walks towards the athletics center that looms large in the darkness.

Grant shakes his head, chuckling. "Seriously, man. Nice to see what you can do without Chapman." Another smack before he saunters off toward his car, where I spy Gen leaning against the door, a grin on her face, having just arrived after following us back from Connecticut. Liv passes by and smiles at me, just as I notice a figure in the shadows, clad in a black suit propped against a town car.

My dad. His silent nod is a tug on the leash, and I'm overcome with resentment. Fear. Regret. There isn't any part of me stupid enough to think the other shoe isn't going to finally drop, and I walk over, jaw tight, steeling myself.

"You can run," he starts to say as I approach, his smile waxy and pliable, "but you can't hide." The way his features slot in and out of malice is disturbing, and I can't help but wonder if I used to do that. If I oscillated between performances to get what I needed in such an obvious way.

I shove my hands into the pockets of my letterman. "Was I running, or just at a game?" I tilt my head, trying to remain unaffected, but his amusement flattens into something sinister. My stomach drops.

"Cut the shit, Andrew." He pauses, scanning my face, and I wait, internally frozen. "That was you in my office." A statement, but I attempt to refute it anyway.

"I don't know what you're talking about. Is there something you need or—"

"Something I need," he mutters, and he's agitated. My mind spins, and I think he knows I haven't been playing my part. "This is about what you need. Always has been. But I think you forgot you need *my* help a lot more than I need yours," he spits, and I hate that I flinch.

A false memory of him slapping Ian plays across my

memory, and my skin crawls. All the money in the world can't erase his violence, and maybe I should've known that but I didn't. Overeagerness will do that to you—make you naive.

I glance over my shoulder, sensing someone's attention, and catch the red glow of brake lights as Grant's truck speeds out into the black night.

"I asked you about Elliot. I told you I need more information."

"You haven't told me shit." The heat of his voice turns into frost as he steps toward me, and the height difference is exaggerated. I lift my chin and look down on him, and watch his nostrils flare at the insult.

"Can't make up information, Glenn. Maybe Scott could give it a try for you," I tell him, walking a thin line. It's worth it, I think, to rile him up, at least a little. But when he huffs, the laughter is sick, sends a chill through my spine, and if I could press my heel into him like an insect, I probably would.

"You're not half as stupid as I thought." He walks back to his car, and I'm sure he's going to leave. Victorious relief starts to wash over me, just as he turns back around.

He lights a cigarette. Leans back against the car door. Smiles, slowly. Then, my phone rings.

Molars grinding, I check the ID.

"Mom?" My voice wants to shake, but I ground myself for her sake. "What's up?"

"Uhm," her voice is muffled, and I can imagine her sitting at the table, head in her hands. "Do you think you can talk to someone at your school about those conservatory scholarships? For Carm?" Her voice breaks when she says my sister's name, and I look up to find Glenn's vindictiveness bleeding into the otherwise innocent night. "They, uh...they pulled it. I can probably pay a quarter of it. Maybe if—"

"Of course. I'll figure it out. I promise." She sniffs, and I know she's nodding. "Seriously. Don't worry about this, okay? I'll handle it."

"Yeah, okay," she says, her voice gritty from tears that I know she's trying hard to rein in. "You get in okay? Jesus— how was the game?" It comes out so quietly. Painfully.

"We can talk about it tomorrow," I tell her, wishing I could fix everything now. Hating that I did this to begin with.

"But you won, right?" I hear her throat bob on the other end of the line.

"'Course we won. Get some sleep." I hang up before she can say anything else.

I hold Glenn's gaze, watch him blow a plume of smoke in my face as I step forward. "Was that really necessary?"

"You tell me. Did you really have to go behind my back? Team up with my son?" His eyes crinkle with feigned sincerity, and I almost laugh.

"You mean my brother? Am I not your son, too?" It's the oddest feeling, but there's this bone-deep sadness when I ask him, and it wraps itself around my disgust. It cracks itself against my soul, wondering if deep inside me I'll find what I'm seeing in him.

His lips twitch. "A waste, isn't it? To have two perfectly useless sons?" The words are leaden in my gut. There is, I think, some small part of me that will never stop wanting his approval, no matter how much he hurts me. The disappoint- ment must flash across my features because he stands up taller and slots into a new expression. "You can still prove yourself. To me. The chairman of the conservatory's board is just a phone call away."

I almost want to ask him how many people he's got, how many people he's a phone call away from black mailing, but I don't actually want to know. I want to be done with all of this.

Want to be clean of whatever the fuck he's doing. It hasn't been until now that I've considered I may never be.

"What do you need?" *Deceive, deceive, deceive.*

"It's your lucky day. You get to pick," he whispers. "Chapman's being difficult about coming back to Astor. Get him here, and consider yourself back in my good graces. *Or* you let me know what the Fielder girl is saying to that reporter. If you want to sweeten the deal, get me a recording of—"

"Absolutely not." Adrenaline threatens to rip the bones of my chest apart and I feel horrible. Fragile. "Nothing on Sloane. She's off limits."

He sucks his teeth, glancing at the ground before shooting his narrowed gaze back up to me. "You don't know this girl, Andrew. Swearing allegiance..." he shakes his head, turning around to pop his door open before facing back to me with an overstuffed file in his hands. "Here."

It looks just like the manilla folders we rifled through that day in his office, but this one's crisper and has Sloane's name drawn across it in thick sharpie. Freshly compiled, I think. My jaw flexes of its own accord and my father's lips spread a grin before he tosses me the file, leaving me to catch it.

"Look at it. Decide for yourself if you should waste your time with her."

I chuck the file back at him and he doesn't even try. Her photo slides into a small puddle as he laughs.

"I could give two fucks what's in the folder," I tell him, trying to not to look down.

"Suit yourself," he says, scanning my face. "Let's hope William's in the mood to listen to you, then." Pulling the door open, he drops into the seat of the town car. No driver in sight, because this must've been unexpected. My defiance surprised him.

"Wait—" I stop the door from slamming with the palm of

my hand. "I'll convince him. But you need to fix Carmen's scholarship."

His tsk grates against my skin, and I drag a breath through my nostrils as he shakes his head. "You deliver Chapman. I'll fix that girl's scholarship."

"*Carmen.*"

"Whatever." He shrugs, and I bite my tongue. "Better get going, *son.*" He peels out of the spot, icy water spraying up the sides of his wheels and all over the now soggy manila folder.

I grab it, clutching it by the open ended side, like I can stop her secrets from spilling out.

* * *

The noise of someone travels through the door after only a few knocks. Will opens it, dipping his head at me like I've broken some unspoken rule. Like I've popped his bubble.

"Spellman," he says, eye crinkling as he squints and smiles. "You missed me. Of course you did. Come in." He nods, inviting me into the fiery warmth of his grandfather's town-home, and I glance around looking for the old man. "He's at the farm in Penn. Annual shareholder's meeting, with my parents."

"Dan's a shareholder?" The Cabot's dairy is an empire. They *are* dairy, actually; their role in the milk lobby was mentioned in my freshman year marketing seminar. Being family owned and operated, boasting about their puritanical lines of succession, is part of the brand.

"My dad?" he scoffs as I trail him toward the back of the town home where he asks a woman in an apron to make two cappuccinos. I begin to lift my hand, tell her I can do it myself, but gravity has me dropping it. "No. I mean, he is through my mom. He only gets his shares once I come of age, or whatever."

He settles into an oversized chair, upholstered in deep emerald velvet, and I take the identical one next to it, across from a roaring fireplace. I'm relieved when the woman brings us the coffee and disappears, because middle aged servers always make me think of my mom.

"We pay her *very* well," Will laughs, taking a sip of the frothy drink. "And Georgia makes the best coffee. Literally poached her from a coffee shop. Well, Pops did. He's picky about his caffeine."

I swallow past the discomfort, but believe him. A wage is a wage. "You've been okay?"

"Me?" he asks like the question's out of left field, and my eyes flare in confusion before he laughs. "Yeah. I'm fine," he shrugs, taking another sip before focusing on the fire.

"Will?" His brows raise as he flicks his gaze towards me. "It's just me. You can tell me if you've been..."

"If I've been what?" he says, irritated. "I don't really know what everyone expects of me right now. Just plaster a smile on my face and move the fuck on?"

"Woah." I throw my hands up, readjusting my focus on him. The fire plays in his grey green gaze. "I'd be concerned if that's what you were doing. But if you said 'hey Andy, I actually feel like someone ran over my guts twenty times,' I'd say that makes sense." Will didn't know me when Luis died, so he doesn't know that I did hold it together. That I moved on because Carmen needed to heal more than I did.

I know there are fracture wounds, though; that because I didn't do it the right way, I'm constantly afraid of what will happen if I lose anyone else. There's this naivety you have before loss that convinces you you'd survive it if it happened—I don't know if I would now. I didn't do it right the first time and now look at me.

Will didn't do it at all, which feels like a work around. He's only really diving into the wreck of Lily's loss for the first time.

"Well, that's how I feel," he says, his jaw twitching as he pulls in a deep breath. "I feel okay sometimes. Like Gen's show. I almost went." His voice dips when he says her name, like it's trying to skip across the open wound. "I thought I was okay to go. But I wasn't. And that wouldn't have been fair to her, you know? She's happy, and shit. Isn't she?" He looks up at me, and all I can bear to do is nod. "Of course she is. Good," he says, jaw twitching.

He loved Gen. Loves her, probably. God, he is an emotional ravine, and here I am, knowing what I know now about my dad and Dan and...Lily. Fuck.

"And Lily?" I have to ask, because Ian's suspicion has made everything about her death feel that much heavier. Because I know he *really* loved her, and I can't imagine Sloane not existing at all.

But I can't *actually* have Sloane, I realize, throat bobbing as I wait for Will to tell me something, anything to distract from reality outside of this brownstone. Lying to her, after *everything*, at this point—I can't. It's so fucking heavy, and there's this small voice that is telling me I should've known I couldn't have her.

She will exist, though. Just not with me. I don't even want to think about the alternative, but Will's had to live with that feeling everyday, so I concentrate on him. "Tell me you've been talking to someone about that because I can't imagine it, Will. I don't know how you were okay after that."

"Well I wasn't, was I?" he shrugs, his jaw working as he gazes back into the fire. "I have a therapist that Pops insisted I see."

"Not your parents?" I think about what Sloane said about his mother, a subject we've skirted around since I've known him. Will's gaze slides to mine, a cynical smirk curving on his face.

"You've never met my mom, have you?" His laugh is bitter. "I'm incredibly inconvenient to her. And Dan thinks I just need to get back to playing ball."

The fire crackles as we let the silence stretch.

There are times when I think the universe is conspiring for me, but it's never in the way I want. I want things to work in the light, to land like a feather perfectly in place. Not like this, with a thud and creak, falling in front of me with a slap. Meeting Sloane felt like the former. Meeting my father was, in hindsight, the latter.

"And you think that's a...bad idea?" I probe, gently, like I'm a fucking surgeon.

"Go back to Astor where he can pull my strings and control me even more? I'm in this pile of shit to begin with because I trusted him." He leans back against the arm chair, knocking his head back and I watch him. His jaw works before he takes a breath and sits up. "He encouraged me to move on. Downplayed everything. And I was so desperate not to feel like..."

"Like you feel now?"

He looks at me, grimacing. "Yeah," he laughs. "My therapist says you can't outrun the pain. Drinking stops working when you stop doing it. And then it's just you and all your shit."

The notion is haunting, but somewhere, in my marrow, I know it's true. That energy is neither created nor destroyed; that these things we do and say and keep can only be transformed into something new. Outrunning them isn't an option, as much as we might try.

But Will is running. Staying away from Astor *is* running. It's a coping mechanism he's employing out of fear, not strength, and *maybe* coming back could be good for him. The realization is a relief, but then it's sour milk in my fucking throat because I'm someone who does this. Twists things for my benefit.

"Then come back," I tell him, beyond the sick sliding down my neck. But really: he either runs or he doesn't. I either run or I don't. These are the beds we've made, whether he realizes it or not. "Don't let Dan manipulate you into not doing what you love. Screw Dan Chapman. Screw feeling ashamed—"

"You don't get it," he huffs out. "They all hate me. And they should. I'm self-destructive. I need to...fix myself. Rehabilitate myself, if that's even possible."

"And that's what you're doing here? In this townhome designed for a geriatric patient?" I eye wheelchair lift. He probably spends his days peacefully dictating his grandfather's daily diary and going for serene walks, and I'm asking him to watch Grant and Gen go at each other at Vida's.

"The home is *accessible*," Will corrects me, and I can't help but roll my eyes, feeling grateful for his humor.

"Seriously, man. How much more healing can you do being so isolated?"

He swallows, his hands gripping each other. "You know, I'm not drinking. Or any of that."

"Oh. Shit." I blink, taking him in again. The sallowness has all but disappeared. The bags under his eyes are gone. There hasn't been a single weekend since we met where I didn't see him with a hangover. But that's not uncommon in and of itself. Still, I regret not noticing. I should've noticed. "Shit that's...big, Will. I'm sorry—"

He shakes his head, smiling genuinely. "Stop. I'm not drinking, for now. I feel better. It kind of fucking sucks being in pain all the time," he briefly chuckles. "But at Astor...I just, I don't know."

"That's fair. But we can do other things," I reassure him, just as the heavy front door opens, a bell jingling.

"We?" Will's brow lifts in doubt, a grin growing on his face as he stands. "Look what the cat dragged in," he laughs, and I stand to see Ben all bundled up in his winter coat. "Gonna convince me to come back, too?"

"Me?" Ben's voice booms, shocked amusement filling the room. "No way. I don't want you back. Do you know how much easier my life is without sharing the captain spot?"

Will turns toward me, hope glittering in the back of his gaze. "Sold." He strides toward his brother, grinning as he knocks shoulders with him. "Don't tempt me with a good time, Benjamin."

"Wait—really? Are you sure that's—" Ben starts to say, caution settling between his brows.

"Smart? No," he sighs, sending me a genuine smile that I work hard to reciprocate despite the guilt settling in my stomach. "But I can't live the rest of my life in spite of Dan."

Something proud and a little smug crosses Ben's expression as his lips tug up in a smile. "Okay," he says, rough–housing my shoulder. "Okay."

35

Sloane

The art institute was bustling when I arrived, but people have begun to trickle out. Amber yellow splays through the window on the farthest end of the hall, a continuous reminder of the impending dusk. This side of town is foreign to me, and my stomach lining feels thin from the meager granola bar I found in the bottom of my bag, and it took forty minutes to get here in the first place, all the way from Astor.

A pang of regret drops through my gut, but I breathe through it. It's not the competition; it's not the place; it's not the hunger. It's him—and I realize Jean was right when he told me it wasn't *nothing*. He's still pacing the hall, his gaze slicing through the work that's been left here in preparation for the show in only a few days' time. Doesn't seem fair that a judge would get so much lead time before the others arrive, but then, he's never been concerned with what's right or fair.

My gaze falls down to where my phone rests, the screen dark. Lifting it isn't the magic I hope it will be: still no text from Andy. The last thing he'd said was that he'd be working tonight, the last shift he'll be able to get in before the big conference game next weekend. I scroll back to the message he sent me a couple nights ago, because it's now my favorite thing. He'd said:

ANDY

Just got back. Contemplating climbing through your bedroom window, but I know you're sleeping and that your brother might murder me.

And we have time. But I missed you.

Thought you should know.

So I keep telling myself that we have time, and it soothes the angst wrapping itself around my chest every time I wonder why he's been so busy. I adjust the lamp to the left of my piece again, highlighting the center that feels like an abyss to me. It's still not right. And it's been over an hour.

Elliot Walker's god damned footsteps sound behind me and it's a heavy effort not to ask him to leave. *A little petulant, don't you think?* I know he'd say that. The corner of his mouth tugging upwards, a glint in his eye that could make you forgive the condescension, believe that it's just an evolved sort of endearment.

"Maybe try—" Elliot reaches around me and tilts the lamp. His voice is just the same: soft, perceptive, laced with quiet humor, like he knows something you don't. Makes you want to ask him or stay close enough to find out. "There. See?"

The light now falls across the fine glitter layered into the silhouette of the cliff so that it glints. An obvious choice. Not very thoughtful at all. Laughter climbs up my throat, breaks through in a surprising scoff that has him snapping his head away from the painting and toward me.

"Sorry," I apologize, because he's a judge. Not because I am. I look at him like he's new, but really it's the familiarity that allows me to notice all the ways he's actually so small. Towering over me, handsomely aged—barely gray at his temple, creases at his eyes. Stubble across his jaw. Full mouth, strong hands, but: insecurity, lodged in the back of his gaze. At that age, I almost laugh again, but remember. I want to win this. "I do love the way it makes the cliff shift into focus."

Some level of surety returns to his eyes when I appease him. And did I always do that, without a second thought? Probably. Definitely. It's uncertain ground for him. There's a level of authority he's taken for granted, that he's assumed bleeds into every domain of his narrow little life, and I just fell into it. Swam in it like I couldn't drown.

He smiles at me, and I press my lips together because they start to shake. "Hello, Sloane."

Pressure builds behind my eyes as I force a polite smile of my own. A flash of him handing me my shit plays across my vision before zapping away, and I realize the room's empty.

I remember that the room was often empty.

"Mr. Walker," I say, fighting the urge to fidget under his attention.

"Oh," he says, his brows furrowing as he smirks. "Is that where we are now?" He searches my face, amused as he shifts so that we're shoulder to shoulder. "*Last names?*"

"Probably should've always been last names. Don't ya think?" I feel him look at me as I look ahead, can sense his chest rising and falling in irritation.

"I always thought you were more mature than this," he chides, cocking his head back toward my piece.

Fuck him.

I want to rip it off the wall, but instead I pay him the attention he's desperate to steal. "Your mistake," I tell him, gazing up at him with none of the admiration that once came so easy, so hot, so fast.

Something shifts in him, in the room. When he walks away, and the urge to follow, to get a reaction, claws at me—so I do, because that can't be it. I want to exact a judgment against him the way he has on me, in a million small ways, even in his absence.

I want to tell him I don't even know what's good anymore because of him. I need to see him be a shell and then rip something dear from his corpse, because it would be the catharsis I think I need.

Elliot stops at a portrait of a woman looking in the mirror, done with oils just like mine. It looms, larger than the both of us, her doe–like features overwhelming this close up.

"What do you think of this?" he asks me, but his mind's already made up.

"The envy feels heavy handed—the green, I mean." He hums, nodding. "And whoever did this was impatient. The colors muddle here, and I don't think it's intentional."

"I told her the same thing." His hand finds my lower back and I step away instantly. Gaze narrowed, he assesses me, jaw clenched. "My student's piece. She's enormously talented, more than she knows what to do with." He inspects the piece again but it's half-assed because he's paying attention to me. Waiting for jealousy to leap on me like a cat.

I'm not jealous, at all. Concern is the thing I feel—concern and unease. The manipulation feels so overt, I start to question if I've ever seen things clearly a day in my life. Even now, I don't know if my estimation of matters is rational. Did Elliot take advantage of me, or does stupidity just wear the same mask? Is the sick feeling roiling in my gut my own making or his?

I walk away, back to my piece, and gather my stuff. He watches me, like a hawk, and his quickened steps echo in the deserted hall, the heel of his loafers sharp against the wooden floor.

"Let's grab a drink. I'm sure you know all the best spots around town," he starts to laugh before I look up at him from where I'm crouched.

"Why would I know that?" Instinct has my skin prickling with alarm, and his blinking is a sad attempt at soothing me as I stand up.

"You're young," he chuckles, stuffing his hands in his pockets. "If you're staying around here we could sit at the hotel bar. Or mine," he shrugs, and I'm spun. Desperate to leave.

"I can't. I'm meetin' my boyfriend," I tell him, swallowing hard as I pull my phone out and dial Andy. Who doesn't answer. Again.

Dread sheathes itself between my breastbone, right next to the worry. I'll go to the comedy club, because maybe his phone is dead, and then I'll feel like I own my mind again, because Andy makes everything make sense.

"Boyfriend?" Elliot's unhappiness is evident as I wipe dust from my hands on the front of my jeans. There was once a time where his happiness was paramount to me, where he'd conned me into being concerned about his contentment. I'd crunch my bones together to make space for him and his feelings, and I'm still shaking myself out from that, I realize as I let his disdain fall off the cliff of me. "Just feels quick. And not quite your thing," he sort of laughs, and I flick my gaze to the ground before staring him right in the eyes.

"Maybe you just didn't know me like you thought you did." I start to move toward the door, only for him to roughly catch my wrist.

"You know that's a lie. I remember you telling me that you loved how well I knew everything about you," he says, sly and overconfident. I shake him off.

"No one tells you *no*, do they?" I look at him in disbelief, pulling in a breath. "You don't even know what it's like to not have your way." Deep in the recesses of his gaze, I think I'll find whatever humanity of his used to appeal to me. But it's all rotten insecurity, shallow control as he scoffs and steps back.

"I should've known you'd talk to that reporter. Especially after the abortion." Annoyance—that's what I see in his eyes when he mentions it, and I feel sick. "It made you so irrational."

"What a horrible thing to say," I whisper, willing the hot, angry tears to stay hidden. "I didn't talk to that reporter. But maybe *I should*." Confusion flares across me, an unwanted heat, and I just need to see Andy. Tell him everything that's happened so he can help me piece it back together.

"Sloane," Elliot shouts from behind the threshold, and I stop, wincing. "You know I didn't mean that. You know what you do to me."

They're the kinds of words he'd always used with me because he knew I'd drink them in. And even now, the lack of apology feels irrelevant in the face of his weak, manipulative praise.

* * *

Coat pulled tight around me, I wade into the packed bar while a woman holds her own hair back, miming vomiting in the toilet to the sound of raucous laughter. My eyes fly to the billboard, where a WOMEN HAVE THE LAST LAUGH poster is plastered with today's date.

Andy's broad back flexes behind the counter with the way his arms must be crossed in front of him, a towel over his shoulder as they shake with quiet amusement. He's resting against the bar, unaware that I'm here, so I just watch him. The warmth already washes over me, just at the sight of him, and every dark feeling that Elliot pulled to the surface recedes.

Finally, I lean against the deserted bar counter and clear my throat.

He turns, slowly, before startling with shock. "Sloane," he says, sort of breathlessly, and a nervous scoff leaves me.

"Sorry. I didn't mean to scare you," I say, raking my teeth over my lip as I fight the urge to launch myself into his arms. He doesn't move, though; instead, he looks tense, like energy held too tightly, to the point of pain. "What's wrong?"

He blinks, his throat bobbing before his posture loosens. "Nothing. I just...wasn't expecting you, is all." He wears a tired smile and it's just that—worn, like he's practicing putting it on.

"I called. Did your phone stop workin'?" I smirk, hoping it disarms him, because this is weird. This is not a figment of my imagination.

He glances around the bar, accounting for the lack of customers, and rounds it, throwing the towel down, gently grasping my arms before tugging me to the back corridor of the club. Only steps away are the stage wings, but here, we're washed in barely lit darkness. A few feet away is the bathroom door I once found by feeling my way down the wall while Andy fended off a group of out of towners during happy hour.

"Andy. What the hell is happenin' to you?" I chuckle, still nervous but relieved by the closeness. Wrapping my arms around his neck, I pull him close, desperate to have him through all my senses. He'll ground me—I know he will. "Why are we hidin'?" I smile against his lips before I feel him press me against the wall, steal the breath from me with his kiss.

With one hand on the nape of my neck, his thumb bracing against my jaw, he holds me in place, the familiar slide of his tongue and feel of his lips cracking me open the way they always do. And then, suddenly, he stops, his forehead falling against mine as we catch our breath.

"I'm sorry I've been so busy." The words feel heavier than they should, said on an outtake of breath as they are, and I lock the night I had away, the dread from earlier slowly filtering away the longer Andy's hands are on me.

"That's okay," I tell him, shaking my head as I run a hand down the side of his beautiful face. And he really is beautiful—a story of a person, one you could never tire of, whose eyes I could float in forever. Whose being is quite literally the place I go to return to myself, like I am right now.

Does he know that? That he's where I go to be okay?

"I understand. I'm not mad," I huff a laugh. "I just missed you. Wanted to see your face."

His amber gaze falls from mine before he manages to lift it, the self-chastisement hard to watch. It's a look I'd sometimes spy when I didn't know him yet. When he thought no one was watching. Like he'd done something so awful, and he was turning the rot of it over and over in his mind. That feels so long ago, but I remember.

I start to ask him what's on his mind, just as he takes my hands in his, holding them in the small space between us.

"I'm glad I got to see you," his voice rumbles, low and promising, and I fight a smile.

"I'll come over. After you finish up."

"I'll let you know, okay?" I can see the tick of his jaw, even back here, and my head tilts in disappointment. "Give me a few days to get caught up on things. I haven't cracked open a book in weeks," he laughs, and the sound softens me. Reminds me to breathe. "How was setting up?" Alarm strikes in his eyes, like he can't believe he almost forgot, and I'd be lying if I said it didn't satisfy something in me, even if it reminds me of seeing Elliot.

"Fine," I lie. I won't tell him now, won't ruin the little bubble of relief I've blown for myself with him, in the dark of the club. Later. When he feels better and I'm not reeling from the shit Elliot said to me.

"Good. Good," he says, the words disappearing as he nods, something unspoken in the back of his gaze.

"Okay, well. *Text me*," I say, rolling my lips together as I walk away. His hand lingers on mine, his fingers brushing across the back of my palm as the distance grows and he says nothing in return, until finally, he's not touching me at all.

36

Andy

Ben finally blows his whistle, the blare so loud half of us roll our eyes and the other half practically jump out of their skin. I fall somewhere in between. Annoyed and on edge, the way I've felt most of this past week.

I've kept to myself, only meeting Will a few times to assuage my father but also me and my conscience. It wouldn't feel so heavy if I could see Sloane without feeling like a fucking fraud. All of it—the tabs I've kept on Will, Glenn's threat, Sloane—are so, so heavy. But there's something grounding about spending time with my old friend, something that makes the distance I've put between Sloane and I, until I can figure out how to fix this, more bearable.

Ben has us running shooting drills because Josiah missed every lay up in our last game. The team still pulled a win out of our ass but Ben, ever the perfectionist, insisted we played like shit. We find a good rhythm, bouncing, passing, and shooting amongst each other and I find myself getting lost in the steady beat of the ball hitting the court's maple flooring, until Scott's niggling little voice brings me back to my dreaded reality.

"I see Will isn't back yet…" his nasally voice filters into my trance and I feel anger reverberate through my jaw. I know my dad probably has something on Scott, something to make him this god damn annoying, but still—my empathy seems to run out whenever he's in my vicinity. I ignore him, moving to the other side of the court to shoot. Missing, I hear Scott sidle up behind me again. "You should know, I'll have to tell Glenn."

I sneer, turning toward him. "Fuck off, Scott."

He shrugs innocently as I swipe his ball, dribbling it between my legs before taking a shot.

"Nice!" Grant yells. He's taken court as Ben's second in command and honestly, he's given me more pointers about my game over the past few weeks than he has the past few years with Will here. It's made me notice just how talented the majority of this team is, like maybe we were all playing under water, drowning in the presence of our former captain. I nod back appreciatively before jogging over to grab my ball. I move to the layup line and again can hear Scott's heavy breathing behind me.

"Look man—it isn't personal, but—"

"Can you just fuck off?" I feel the eyes on us before I have time to process how loud that came out. A slimy grin spreads across Scott's face and I shove him, a little too hard considering he splays himself dramatically against the hard wood flooring, cradling his elbow. I roll my eyes, storming past him and slamming open one of the double doors, in desperate need of some air. February wind slaps me, its icy tinge burning the sweat from my cheeks.

I'm squinting into the bright mid morning sun when I hear, "Thank god. It's freezing out here!"

Just a few feet diagonal from me is Ian in a plaid overcoat and comically long scarf. He leans against one of the colosseum-like pillars that surround the basketball arena. "I take it you weren't expecting me."

"What makes you say that?" I know I'm more irritated than he deserves, but I know there will be questions about what just happened with Scott and my mouth is already turning sour from the lies I know I'll have to tell the team.

Ian's face pinches at the retort and I push my hand through my hair, trying to regain my bearings. I'm definitely on the verge of imploding, after all that's happened this semester. I feel like I'm back at square one, back to the person I was at the beginning of the year, just counting the days until I can escape this place, escape my dad, armed with a college degree that'll maybe help me never look back. After what happened with Carmen though, it feels like the thumb he has on me is immovable. An impenetrable thing that will slowly suffocate me until I'm just gone. Every bit of good in me squeezed from my being. The idea that this will stop after leaving Astor is laughable now because I doubt my father will ever let me go. Regardless of what I do next, there will always be what I did before, for him. It's a stain he knew, when he asked, I'd never be able to wash away.

"What's got you all shaken up, brother?" He's joking, I know, but the familiarity in that last word has me sucking in air, because it's real. It's true—it's factually what we are to each other.

I think of Will and Ben, how even with all that's happened this year the connection between them is so strong you can feel it the moment they're in the same room. Only in the past few months have I started feeling it with my own brother, this unspoken bond, the one I feel with Carmen every day. Like no matter what we do to each other, what we say to each other, at the end of the day we will be on each other's side. That's why it's going to hurt so much more when I say what I'm about to say.

I swallow past my nerves, my jaw grinding as I face him.

"I can't do this with you anymore." It comes out quiet and icy like the air around us. Ian stands there for a minute looking every bit like the way I used to see him. His face is too inquisitive, like he's hunting for a secret he can splash on his newspaper and if he looks at you just hard enough he'll find it. It softens quickly though, into the expression I've only recently got to know—kind, empathetic, misunderstood—and I feel sick. Sick over the fact that he's my brother, my family, and I can't do the one thing he's asking me to do. That I can't be the good guy to him or to anyone else.

"What happened?"

"Your dad—"

"Our dad." He raises an eyebrow and I shake my head because Glen *isn't* my dad in any way that counts. He made that very clear over the course of my life. "Look Andy...we can do this. We just need to—"

"I can't!" My palm slams into the pillar before I have time to stop it and my shout echoes between the aluminum landing above our heads and the cement of the sidewalk. I watch as Ian flinches away and think again of what he told me, immediately regretting falling apart even for a moment. I want to apologize but Ian's already shaking his head backing away.

"You know, I knew you were shallow Andy but I didn't know you were stupid." He turns his back, the wind whipping his scarf after him.

"Ian, I—"

He faces me again, now yards away. "Just chill. I have a plan, but clearly you're not in a position to be trusted with the inner workings of it..." he trails off, any unease he had from my outburst long gone as he scratches his head, considering something and it's hard not to admire his ability to bounce back. "Just do what he asks for now. You'll know when things are going down." He turns, walking toward the car lot.

"But how—" I begin to call after but I'm cut off.

"What the fuck..." a deep voice mumbles from behind me and I see Grant's face awestruck, his brows knit together, trying to make sense of what he's just seen. I feel stupid for not assuming one of them would run out after me, try to rectify what just happened with Scott.

"It's not what you think."

He squeezes his eyes shut on an inhale, rubbing his mammoth sized hand against his temples.

"What the *fuck* could it possibly be then?" His growl is violent, and panic flares in my chest because no matter which direction I look I can't see a way out of this. "You know what —" he holds a hand up to stop me from responding, "actually, just save it. You and my sister are just the fucking same." Disgust laces his tone and I feel my fists clench responsively at the way he's talking about Sloane.

"What is that supposed to mean?" I grit out, taking a few intimidating steps toward him. Pain courses through my jaw with how hard I'm clenching it, the anger at not just him but at my dad, at myself, threatening to erupt quicker than I can control it. At this point, I can't tell if I want to smooth things over with Grant or bash his face in for the comment.

"Ha!" He mocks me and the blood rises in my ears, seething anger spilling out in the glare I know is plastered to my face. "C'mon Spellman, go for it." He holds his hands out like an invitation jutting out his jaw, begging me to hit him.

But I don't want to hit him. Never did. No—I want to hit my dad, want to hit all of the ways I've completely fucked up my life by letting myself fall on his payroll, want to beat the knowledge out of myself that keeps me aware that all of the lies

I tell, all the people I hurt, keep Carmen in school, keep things afloat for my mom. Any shred of rapport, of dignity that I'd gained with Grant over the past few months evaporates, all of it meaningless now. I can see it in the disappointed crease of his brow.

"Jesus—you and Sloane. It's all id with you guys, all impulse, all the time. Do you ever stop and think?" he asks, exasperated like he's at the end of a marathon. Like this is the cherry on top.

Tears brim the corner of my eyes because he's right. Sloane and I are like lightning striking in the same place twice. Electric, magical, *dangerous*. If we weren't, I would've put an end to us already. That danger, the magic—it's why I'm letting myself believe Ian. Because if he can't fix this, I'll have to tell her everything. And then who the fuck knows if she'll stay.

"So what's the story Andy? What excuse could you possibly have for talking to Ian after everything he's done?" Grant crosses his arms. His face is so much like Sloane's now, trying to read me, trying to edge under the surface and see what's really going on.

I consider letting him, telling him everything if only to have one person who sees me for who I am, bad or not because the weight of all of these masks I'm wearing is suffocating. But I know if I have to choose one person, one person in this entire world to protect, it's not him. It's not Ian or myself. Hell—it's not even Sloane and that feels like a betrayal in and of itself, like someone is physically stabbing my vital organs.

But there's one person in this world more important than her, and it's Carmen. My baby sister deserves to not endure all this pain, to not have to sacrifice her morality every day just to make ends meet, to not see Mom crumble in front of her again and again. I'm doing this for Carm and remembering that sparks something in me. The resilience that burns anew reminds me just how good I can pretend, just how well I can put on show. But it's bitter poison, realizing what will get Grant to leave this alone, to not dig into what I've been doing. It could ruin things just as much as Sloane knowing the truth, but it's a risk I'll have to take.

The voice that comes out isn't my own but one I've grown eerily familiar with. "You need to chill, Grant. Your sister and I are just hooking up. It's not like we're dating."

It's like a flash, the feeling of Grant's knuckles sinking into my abdomen before I gasp in air, the breath completely struck from my lungs. I feel the cement against my palms now bracing the concrete trying to find air.

"*Fuck*," I hiss and Grant spits on the sidewalk beside me, and if he kicked me next it wouldn't be enough. It's the culmination of years of the worst karma. *This* is what I deserve.

"You're trash, Spellman. Stay the fuck away from my sister." He wipes his palms, and I expect his face to look angry or murderous, but instead I find him looking at me with so much pity, so much sadness, and that's somehow worse.

37

Sloane

March

My denim clad leg sinks into a pile of gray sludge as I step off the curb leading toward the hospital. I don't have the energy to even let out a sigh as the cold wet sleet soaks through the hem of my pants. And still my head throbs, like it has every morning, every afternoon, for the past few days.

Jean and I get trashed; we avoid our issues; we soothe whatever we refuse to talk about with the slow and steady burn of whiskey for me and gin and soda for him. We've gotten good at not talking about anything, letting our bodies dance, drink, laugh through the pain—all of it's hollow, though. Jean's gaze was empty when I left this morning, and I know it's probably what he sees in mine. I wish I could say it was just alcohol that we've been abusing, but that'd be a lie. Not a crucial one. No one really cares what we do, I've found. My phone's been eerily quiet, the rest of my tiny little world too busy for me. The big world, though—it's still there, waiting for me every night, so worried about what I wear or who I'm with even though it's always Jean.

I feel myself slipping back into my old ways. I've even been posing when I see a camera flash, trying to give them what they're looking for because why not? What reputation do I really have to uphold? Elliot reminded me of that, that this facade of an unserious, notorious, slutty party girl isn't really a facade at all. We are what we are. Elliot tried to mold me into something better but that was a complete and utter failure. I mean, I got *pregnant*. Forget that it was his fault—everyone always does—but I had to carry the sin of it. Would've been a physical reminder of a mistake he made. The mistake I made.

What is my fault, actually, was thinking I could be anything but who I've always been. It seems Andy's realized that. One away game and *poof*, the mirage fell. Call after call has gone unreturned and when I've seen him it's the same distance I've grown accustomed to, the one that's plagued me with everyone in my life for as long as I can remember. I start to become too much, start to feel too much, and they shrink away.

I feel my phone buzz in my pocket and see Clementine's name flash on the screen. I ignore it because I know she'll know. She'll hear it in my voice just like Grant could, that I'm back in my fortress. 'Not doing well.'

I wonder if she heard about Elliot being here.

I know she keeps tabs on me, that she worries. The idea of that makes me want to cry because I wish she didn't. Wish she could see that I don't deserve it.

I pull the heavy metallic handle leading toward the cancer treatment center, guilt already settling in my stomach from the lack of communication I've had with my mom over the past week and a half. For the thousandth time I wonder what the *fuck* is wrong with me.

My mom is dying, literally dwindling away in front of my

very eyes and instead of spending as much time with her as humanly possible I've been so absorbed in my own shit. Anyone else, I tell myself, would take that thought as some kind of wake up call, a moment that snaps them into being present, into paying attention to the people who actually matter. But me? All I feel is that familiar itch under my skin, the need to escape, run away from everything and everyone if only to escape the blame I know I deserve. Avoid the disappointment in their faces when they realize that I'm exactly who they thought I was.

"Constance Tucker," I say to the front desk woman, her hair pulled so tightly back that my own temples begin to throb, although that could just be the hangover. I watch as she types her eyes, carefully scanning the screen, a crease forming in between her brows.

"It appears she hasn't come in yet. Actually, do you know how late she's going to be? We may need to bump her to the next session." I blink, taking more than a second to process that Mom isn't here.

"She must have the times mixed up, let me just call her really quick." The woman nods and I hit **Mom** in my recent call log, shakily holding the phone up to my ear.

It isn't that uncommon. I got the late gene from mom, after all. She's almost always ten to fifteen minutes late...but thirty? Her appointments are always on Wednesday at one pm, so the idea that she got the times mixed up seems unlikely. The phone takes a second before sending me directly to voicemail, and now I feel it.

That prickliness against my skin, the way it feels like my lungs are slowly deflating.

My body welcomes the anxiety like an old friend, picks it up like it's always been there, waiting. I glance at the nurse whose face is too neutral. It reminds me of Grant.

You always jump the gun, Sloane.

I suck in a breath. "Phone must be dead." I smile weakly. "Go ahead and bump us to this afternoon. I'll go by her place and get her."

The woman nods, clicking into her computer looking for a new time.

"Four thirty work?" she asks and I appreciate her lack of annoyance. I nod before turning back into the gray sleet covered city, my mind flashing to all the moments my mom was exactly who Grant says she is. Us with trash bags ripping at the seams, Grant sharing the last can of spam while Mom was passed out on the couch, the lumps in every mattress that wasn't my own.

The stairs to her building haven't been salted in what looks like over a week and I feel my mouth tug downward because why didn't she call me. Why didn't I know her stairs were so slippery? The stale alcohol I consumed last night churns in my stomach, only making my guilt grow tenfold.

I should have been here, should have been helping her with all this. The inside of my cheek feels raw and blistered, the way it used to when I was a kid, nervously biting the inside waiting for the other shoe to drop. I hit her buzzer and nothing. Again, I hear the static blare and am met with no response. I see Leonard the super through the foggy glass pane of the window and wave him over with a mittened hand. He pokes his head out, coatless and unprepared for the blistering cold. He squints, confused.

"Hey there, I don't know if you remember me—"

"I do," he nods gruffly but there's a tenderness to him, like he's someone's dad or grandfather, like he knows how to talk to a girl on the edge.

"I need to pick up my mom for—"

He cuts me off again, his brow crease sending a ripple of confusion and panic up my spine.

"You just missed her. Weird...I figured she'd called you."

I let out a breath, tension I didn't know I was holding deflating instantly and I feel the weight on my chest lessen, allowing me to breathe again.

"Gotcha, thanks." I begin to turn and I feel his fingers catch my sleeve.

"Wait. I, uh...she left a few papers upstairs, you may wanna grab em?"

A myriad of forms and charts flash through my mind as I try to piece together what she may need for her appointment today.

"Yeah, of course. Thanks." There's a new levity to my voice as I step into the building shuffling down the long corridor leading to Mom's first floor apartment.

He slots a small gold key with the number 16 written in black sharpie in the lock, turning it into the knob until there's a definitive click. "Let me know if ya need me."

He gestures back to the door that leads to the super's office and I nod, confused.

It's dark inside but I can immediately sense the room's hollowness. Maybe it was the way the door swung open or the way a home smells when it's empty. Like if I just inhale deep enough I'll get that hint of strawberry buried in the smoky smell of Mom's Marlboro reds. Maybe if I don't flip the switch, reality won't set in. The thought crosses my mind as my fingers clench the small white knob. I feel my jaw shaking, vomit rising and I run to the sink letting the contents of night before, of every night before, come out.

A table. That's all that's left.

My lips quiver, as my mind begins the same barrage of excuses so permanently etched in my memory. *Maybe there was an emergency, maybe she found a place closer to Grant's, maybe she's surprising me, maybe—*

My mind begins to play out the various reactions I'll have to said surprise, the one I know isn't coming. I'll hug her, grasp her now frail body so tightly against mine, kiss her on top of her blonde head the exact same shade as mine. Promise her I'll be good, promise her the world, anything to make her stay. I feel my body slide down the wood paneled cabinets of her kitchen, feel my knees retract into my sternum, wrapping my arms around them, and I feel her again. That lost little girl, who just wanted to please, who put on a show, playing her part until she couldn't anymore.

Why couldn't I just be better, why couldn't I just ask for less, be less...maybe if I was less...

My thumbs find Andy's name in my phone. I hear the ring, this ominous endless thing, the tone so similar to how it was calling Elliot that day in the hospital. Andy isn't late, though. He owes me nothing, and still my thumb hits his name again. And I hate him but I hate myself more. I hate that I let this happen, hate that it keeps happening to me. That I need him, that I've ever let myself need anyone.

The tone sounds again.

"Just answer!" I scream into the emptiness. It echoes against the walls and I let my head sink into my hand. This isn't the first time I've felt like this and it won't be the last, because I'm the girl people leave. The only common denominator here is me.

I squeeze my eyes shut, screaming into my hand, muffling the sound. I get up and there's a hollow creak under the floor board my foot landed on, it's loose. Grant was right—he's always right. People don't change. I pull it up, the same way I did as a child, pulling out a half empty bottle of Jim Beam, a sticky note with familiar scrawl attached to the front the way she always had it.

drink me if your dyin

A scream like laugh bubbles out of me because she's always been dying, or wanting to anyway. Killing herself over time because it was easier and for once I relate to her. I use my thumb to unscrew the lid, letting the warm brown liquid hit my throat.

38

Andy

Rain clouds hang heavy in the sky, just barely breaking so that the day's last rays of sunshine can filter through. I scan the side street by my mom's apartment, crossing my fingers that Delilah isn't there. And I know it's cowardly, but lying to Sloane somehow feels worse. Distance, I've decided, saves her from the knowledge that would wreck her.

But she must already be at the hospital for her mom's treatment, or maybe she's still at the conservatory. She wouldn't, I imagine, want to see me anyway after what I said to Grant yesterday. I'm grateful when I round the corner and miss any sight of the red convertible on the small street, though it's immediately followed by guilt at the relief, then resentment that those emotions exist on a continuous pendulum for me.

It's why I'm here—I need to get off the ride. All this guilt... I don't know what to do with it. Don't know how to move forward. But here, with my mom, with Carm, I'm away from all of that. Even if it's temporary.

A laundry basket sits on the floor when I walk in, my mom on her tip toes as she piles sheets on the top rack of the hall closet. I do it for her, gently hip-checking her before putting the rest away. But when I'm done, and look down at her, her eyes are wet. Her arms are crossed, and she walks away from me, shoulders squared.

"What's, uh...what's going on?" I ask her, and just the look of disappointment she gives me is like a knee to my ever present bruise.

She glances down the hallway to Carmen's room, where *Hamilton* roars from her speakers. "You tell me."

My gaze falls for a fraction of a second before I see the mulish slant of her jaw harden. "I'm lost," I chuckle, taking her hand so we can sit on the couch. She yanks it away from me and I just *know*.

She starts to speak, only for her teeth to clatter against each other. She has to press her lips together to still them, and it takes every ounce of my will not to run from this feeling as she finally manages to look me in the eye. "When did you meet him?"

The words fall from her lips like the heaviest thing we've ever carried, and die on the carpet of the living room floor. My stomach feels hollow, and I wouldn't be shocked if the roof caved in. This has always been my worst case scenario. My one real nightmare, come true. I blink and I blink and I blink but my eyes wont stop watcring.

"Senior year." My teeth dig into my lip, and it's not nearly hard enough. I breathe in shallow takes because it staunches the tears I haven't shed since Luis died.

Her small gasp is unsteady as she covers her mouth with her hand. "What are you doing for him, Andrew?" she asks, and there's a sea of knowledge there that I, pettily, wish she would've told me years ago.

"Nothing," I lie, like maybe I can protect her from it. "It's... nothing." Pure disbelief floods her gaze when she looks at me. She's never looked at me like that. Like I'm someone she doesn't know.

"Then why did *he* fix her scholarship? Is it because he's the reason she has one?" Fresh tears well in her eyes, the ones that mine mimic in every way, and she looks to make sure we're still alone. "I never wanted you to know him. He's poisonous and—"

"I know," I cut her off, looking down at my hands as they cradle each other. "I know that now." I look up at the ceiling, exhaling as I scrunch my nose. "Fuck."

"Language," my mom mutters behind her tears. "You need to tell me everything, Andrew."

"There's no point," I tell her, and the hopelessness of it rocks me. "It's done. He...he paid for Astor. He got me on the team."

Her head knocks to the side, horror laced in her gaze as tears stream down her cheeks. "Why? Why does he help you?"

I breathe, sniffing back the tears. "I tell him things...about people," I shrug.

"About your friends," she says, matter of factly, something hard gathering in her gaze. "Will."

I knock my head to the side, looking past her, teeth grinding, head nodding.

"Who else?" she whispers, reaching for my hand in a move that sends a small wave of belonging over me.

"Don't worry about—"

"I'll worry about whatever I want, because I'm your *mother*. It is my job to worry about you, not the other way around. When—" her breath stutters as she swallows, flicking her gaze to the ground. "Luis would never have wanted you to put the world on your shoulders. To put *us* on your shoulders."

I wet my lips, stifling the sob that gets caught in my throat. "It wasn't fair. None of it was fair."

She nods, eyes red rimmed and glassy, and I wait for the invisible balm she'd always lather over my wounds when I'd come to her as a child, weeping, disappointed, fractured...but it doesn't come. Her lips tug into a sorrowful curve, wobbles as she stays composed, and says, "No. No it wasn't."

The shift in her gaze now reminds me that I haven't been that child in a long time. My small bones, my soft heart, grew and hardened into something I didn't even let her bear witness to; I slid into a darkness I thought wouldn't swallow me whole if I just moved into her light, Carmen's light, sometimes, but it did.

I look at her, the filter of childhood innocence gone for the first time I think ever, and don't only see exhaustion, and she looks at me like she sees a man and not her boy.

I exhale. "Any one he'd ask," I admit, keeping my gaze steady on hers as I force myself to be honest. "He wanted me to watch Sloane."

It's ripped out of me, her name is; it's been embedded in the bloody, jagged mess of my mistakes, haphazardly hung in the midst of it, always on the edge of skittering to the ground. But I say it, I say the truth even though the force of it is a wound in itself.

"And did you?" Mom asks, wringing her hands so weathered from years of using them to hold this small house together. I can't help but notice how deftly she always has, how the gentle firmness of her guidance right now is something I took from her when I decided to lock her out of my struggles, when I decided to struggle for her.

I shake my head, my breath still shaky in my chest. "No. I couldn't. I, uh..." I swallow hard, flicking my gaze up to hers from where my head hangs. "Ian helped me. A lot. He's my... brother," I tell her, voice cracking on the word, and her eyes lit up, fresh tears welling in her eyes.

"Oh," she croons, squeezing my hand in her hers. "Andrew, I should've told you. You deserved to know everything and I didn't tell you because I didn't want things to change even more. Especially after Luis." She rolls her lips together, shaking her head. "How is he?" she asks of Ian, and the familiarity of the question sends warmth, rather than sadness, through me.

"Funny. Really...fucking kind," I chuckle, sniffing back tears.

"Language," she smiles, and I hear the soft patter of rain as it begins to fall in the early spring sky. Dusk begins to spread, a golden glow cracking across the landscape through the mist of the shower, and I'm reminded of Christmas. Of the snow, of the roof—of Sloane.

"I messed up with her." I don't need to say who; my mother turns towards me, head knocking to the side as assesses me with soft intensity. "I pulled away. My...Glenn threatened you. And Carm. And I didn't want to but I pulled away because I couldn't stand to lie to her."

"So don't," she says, like it's the obvious thing. The easiest thing in the world. "Honey...you can't mold everything in this world with your own two hands. It's not up to you to save Sloane from a feeling. Or me, or Carm for that matter. You be honest, you show up, and what's meant to be will be."

"I can't..." I grimace, molars grinding. "She has so much going on. She doesn't need...all of this." What I don't say is that the thought of Sloane seeing me, who I really am beneath all the lies, scares the shit out of me. That ripping back the curtain and giving her a front row seat to all the ways I've fucked everyone over wouldn't just ruin us—that's the likely conclusion to all of this anyway. No, what I don't want is to shatter whatever illusion Sloane still has about this life. The magic and the whimsy, the way she swears there's a point to all of this? I want that for her. I always want that for her.

Like she can hear the turmoil in my mind, my mom shifts in her seat. "She doesn't need you to be perfect. None of us do."

"Mommy," Carm's voice comes from down the hallway, timid and uncertain. "Is...is everything okay?"

When I turn, there's that tell tale panic laced in her gaze, and I hate that we've scared her like this. Thrown her back into the hazy memories she has from after her dad died.

"Yes, sweetie. Your brother's just...figuring out what to do about Sloane," she says, reducing all of this to the only part that really matters. Carm drops all sense of immediate panic, her eyes shifting into pure anticipation.

"I knew something was wrong! What did you do, you ding-dong?" She leaps over to us, crashing into the small wedge of space between us on the couch. She narrows her eyes, concerned. "Are you *crying*?"

My laughter grates out of me, my chest rumbling with emotional exhaustion as I ruffle her hair. "Yeah, actually. I am. You should try it sometime." It's not something either of us really do.

"So what happened?" she demands to know as my mom loops an arm around her and tugs her close. "She's grumpy, and you're crying, and—why aren't you at her show?" Carm's eyes go wide as she shoves herself off the couch, exasperated.

"Shit," I still, before checking the time. "No, it starts...fuck. In thirty minutes."

"*Language!*" they both bemoan, but Carm's is cut off by her giggle. Mom brushes her hand down my arm in silent solidarity, and I don't need to say a thing.

I just get up, and go.

39

Andy

It's just far enough that in the downpour, I'm late. I hear the rain splatter with each hurried step I take, only for a flapping banner, hung in the entry, to stop me cold in my tracks. A name and a face—that's all it takes for every word I mulled over on the ride here to turn to dust. In the screen printed line up of judges is one of a man, maybe in his forties, maybe older, with eyes that laugh at you through the invisible lens, and his name is Elliot Walker.

Mouth open, I only faintly register the rain that falls on my lips as my mind is wrenched back to every time Sloane mentioned this guy, scouring the memory for a hint of... anything. Dread drips in my veins, gathers in my chest at the idea that she maybe wanted him here, that maybe she pushed against the idea of us because she was still attached to the idea of him—this man who hired the worst of the worst to watch her. To make sure she didn't step out of whatever arbitrary line he'd drawn around her.

But the thought doesn't sit right, feels...flimsy and routed in the impulse I still have to run. And I don't want to do that —don't want to make choices out of fear. Not anymore.

I push against the door and it drags open, the sound behind it rushing over me as I struggle to find Sloane in the sea of attendees. Delicately illustrated canvases engulf the walls, only leaving small gaps for pale moonlight to bleed through. Spot lights rest above each of them, so that the room feels pocketed with small scenes of life unfolding under the blanket of night.

The familiar breadth of Grant's shoulders registers from well across the hall, along with Will's intensely furrowed brows. He drops his gaze to the ground before picking it back up, shaking his head as Gen emerges from a joining hallway, clasping Grant's forearm, trying to tug him away. Will opens his mouth to speak, but suddenly wires it shut, his nose flaring and I fight the urge to move toward him, to stop whatever turmoil is about to unravel, because I'm not here for any of that.

Angst pulses beneath my skin as I scan the room for her again, my gaze snagging on Jean standing near a high top, his face strained, eyes dark as he furiously speaks to a man in the shadows, who stands just outside of a portrait's halo. When Jean steps toward him, out of the darkness, a curse flies from my mouth, my neck turning hot, and the rooms begins to suffocate me, is like a—

"About fucking time," Olivia says, appearing beside me, her cold hands on my wrist grounding me. I pull in a breath, push a measured breath out. "Where have you been?"

She searches my face like she'll find an answer, but instead finds something wholly indigestible. I know, because she scoffs, glancing away, the perceptiveness that's made her a good journalist reading me in under a second.

"Forget it. She's at the bar," she says, face drawn tight, an odd placed helplessness on her symmetrical face as she nods toward the dimly lit center. A makeshift bar is flooded with guests sipping their drinks while they lazily assess the art surrounding them.

And there, at the darkest edge, is Sloane. Golden hair falling around one shoulder, she tips her head to side, a dreamy, half-aware smile stretching across her mouth. She clasps the stem of her cocktail between her fingers and tips it back, teeth tapping against the glass before throatily laughing at something the woman next her says. She reaches a tanned arm across the bar, pointing at the turbulent oil painting beautifully bathed in warm lighting, only for the curve of her lips to dip into sadness. Fear grips me again as I take a step forward, desperate to set it all right, terrified of what it will mean if I don't.

I'm a yard from her, with in arms reach of pulling her into me and losing myself in her orange blossom, when a hand that isn't mine brushes against her lower back and a head that isn't mine dips low and close to her ear. It's universal intelligence, or a gut instinct, that tells me it's Elliot fucking Walker. And instead of running, instead of feeling scared, anger overwhelms me when I catch the way Sloane, despite the drunken heaviness in her limbs, shrinks away.

I can hear him telling her to slow down, can hear the foreign, out of place possessiveness that has her whirling on him, knocking his drink out of his other hand. The glass clatters to the ground, the crash lost in the raucous sea of Bostonians making the most of the organized chaos. Elliot's jaw hardens, shifts as he swallows, reassessing Sloane with a vengeful glint in his stare and I step forward, one second away from intervening even though I know it's exactly what she wouldn't want but—I don't care. Before I can do it, her midnight gaze catches on me, the corner of her mouth tugging up into a tired grin.

"You're here," she slurs, scoffing as she rests a hand on the back of a chair, bracing herself against it. She's in this orange, beaded dress that gives ways to those impossibly long legs, whose thin straps aren't enough in this weather. Her eyes are smudged, and it would almost look intentional if I didn't know her. If I didn't know the bloodshot strain in her gaze wasn't just from a few drinks but from the force of something greater that *I should know about.*

I should, but I don't, because I haven't been here, and the disappointment in her gaze is far less than I deserve.

"Sloane," I start to say, only for Walker to clear his throat like he owns the floor we stand on and my blood boils.

"Who is this?" he asks, pinning Sloane with a decisive glare that grates against my skin.

"Her boyfriend," I say just as Sloane insists that I'm, "No one."

She shrugs, shaking her head at me as tears well in her eyes and a stone lands in my gut.

"Can we talk?" I ask her, knowing I don't have a right to, keeping my gaze patient and level on just her. Her chest rises and falls, mouth painfully twisting around a thought.

Elliot smirks, some silent joke bouncing off us. "Sloane," he sneers, the grays at his temples glinting in the shine of a portrait light. "I knew you weren't taking yourself seriously but this? I mean—"

I hardly have a moment to notice that I've edged toward him, that my fist has pulled into itself, that the hard flat of it has cracked against his jaw. He laughs, blood sputtering out from his mouth as he grins with red stained teeth, my hand wrapped around his collar.

"She's whore. Just look at her," he seethes, eyes hard as steel as they slide towards her, and I don't look. I shove him into the bar cart, chest heaving. I watch his hand splinter as it smashes into a delicate wine glass, my own satisfaction growing when I notice his grin faltering. Ben pulls me away from the embarrassing man cowering against the wooden mantle, cradling his hand as his shocked outrage tries to find something kindred in Sloane's eyes but he finds nothing. Because her gaze is fixed firmly on me, is a storm of despair as she makes no move toward me.

No, instead, she runs.

I follow her through the crowd, wrenching myself away from Ben and through the doors that lead to the back. The lot there is decrepit, hasn't been kept up with like the front facing part of the building. Faded white parking lines appear in no sensible pattern, cracks in the pavement merging into each other until they end in craters that swim with sediment thanks to the rain.

"Sloane!" I shout, thunder cracking like a whip in the cold, wet air, and she stops just as the door behind me swings shut. "Let me—let me explain."

"Explain what?" she shrugs, arms reaching high as her hair begins to stick to her face, her neck, her shoulders, before her arms swing back down with the force of total resignation. "You're free, Spellman. We're not dating," she huffs, bitter sadness in her gaze as she parrots back the lie I told her brother. "You're not bound to me. No one is." She chokes on a sob, her breath catching her throat as she lets her head fall back, and I can't tell where her tears begin and where it's the storm we've caught ourselves in.

I'm with her in two strides, have my hands braced on either side of her face, my thumbs laid atop those freckles I love so much. "Baby—"

"I'm not," she spits, searing me with her undivided attention, swallowing hard. "I'm not anyone's anything. Never was." Jaw flexing, she pulls away from me, walking toward the end of the lot that merges with the side street the cars are parked on.

"Sloane...Sloane just—" I race after her. "You can't drive like this."

"Drove here just fine." She marches across the lot, stepping into a deep crater that has her falling forward. My arms fly out to catch her, pulling her in to me, and her face scrunches up in frustration, exhaustion painted on the delicate lines of her face as she frees herself from my embrace. "Why are you doin' this? I am givin' you an out, I'm—"

"I don't want an out, Sloane! I want in. I want all of it. I don't want to lie to you, I don't want to hide from you...that's why I'm here. To be honest. To try. I—" I pause, struggling to confront this final thing. "I'm here because I love you, Sloane, and—"

"Don't!" she shouts, falling to her knees, the word a tear in our sky that feels irreparable. That feels definite, a hard line she's thrown out in a desperate attempt to protect herself. "I don't want it. I can't—"

"Why not?" I drop her ground, blinking away the rain drop blurring my vision, and cradle her face in my hands again. "Sloane, I will make myself new for you. I will go anywhere. I will *do* anything you ask of me." She shakes her head, lips trembling before giving way to heart wrenching sobs that have me questioning everything. Her eyes find mine, horrified, but I press on. "I love you, Sloane. And if you don't want me because I'm not enough for you, because I disappoint you, because I'm a horrible fucking person—"

"You're not," she cries, watery and garbled.

"I am, Sloane. Push me away for all those reasons. God knows they're good ones. But not because you're scared. Please."

Her jaw quakes as she regards me, throat bobbing as the

rain washes the last of her mascara away so it's just those dark blue eyes, that scape of dreamy freckles that trail across the high points on her face, those full, rosy lips.

"Connie's gone. She left," she tells me, and the silent sob that rips through her fractures something deep within me. It spreads between my ribs, wraps me in the bone deep sadness is holding the woman I love so far under.

"I'm so sorry." I just hold her, brace her against me as the torrent of her loss tries its best to wash away with the rain. I brush back the wet strands stuck to her skin, stroking her head as she buries it into my chest.

"I'll lose my shine, Andrew, and you'll leave me, too. Everybody does. My own mother—"

"I'm not them, Sloane. I want every worst thing you *think* you've ever done so I can hold it up to the light and show you why I love you more because of it." Her lips press into a grim line, head shaking as she drops her gaze. "None of us are perfect, okay? And..." Telling her about Glenn and Ian feels wrong in this moment, but I know I have to. Know that I can only be what she needs if I'm not hiding who I really am.

The door to the lot bursts open, interrupting the rainfall's dull murmur and the start of my absolution, as Grant's voice rumbles across the haze.

"*How long?*"

"I can't deal with him right now," Sloane says to the ground, shoulders glistening as she slumps beside a shallow puddle.

I rise, turning to face him, only to see that he's not alone.

40

Sloane

I wriggle from Andy's grip when I hear Grant's voice the moment he's distracted, my heel catching on a small rock as I try to stand and I fall forward again on to my knees. Feels like I've been down here my whole life, begging for someone to say those words to me. I look up from the asphalt laden puddle.

I love you.

I feel the shape of the phrase in the way my heart is slamming into my chest, in the small pebbles of gravel lodged into my palms forming ravines of blood in the lines.

I love you.

Has there ever been a more painful phrase? Its impermanence, how many conditions it comes with? An idea we've turned holy, a wish that never comes true? It's Santa or the Easter bunny. It's the window I'd look out of, waiting to see my mom's beat up old Volvo, the tread on the tires screeching around every bend as she made her way back to us. It's the hope that someone would stay, just because you asked them to, just because you wanted them there. That someone could see you and want you and make you something they care enough about not to leave.

I feel slender arms on my shoulders, a second pair pulling me into a warm but slippery body.

"*Sloane*," they whisper and I wonder if this is all the love I'll ever deserve. Love from people who care but only in the periphery of their own lives, whose hearts are so full of someone else they can only give you the sharp edges of what's left until all you are is a series of those edges. You try to make them whole, pushing them together to make them mean more than they do.

Where did these people leave me though, these relationships I've poured so much of myself into? With bloody palms, knees raw from where I knelt, waiting to matter.

I pull out of Gen and Olivia's embrace, using my bloody hands to push the hair out of my face. "Stop. Just stop." I wonder if anyone can hear me over the downpour. I can see their mouths moving. See Grant holding Andy by the collar, pushing him back. Away from me.

"*He's been working with Ian the whole time.*" "*He's been lying to you.*" "*Look at the blast! He was hired to watch us.*" "*He's a liar!*"

A steady pulse of conflict thrums between me and all of them and I feel it now—the distance, the one that seems to follow me. And for the longest time I thought other people created it but maybe it's just another way I've protected all of them.

I step backward, feeling rain or tears or both fanning my cheeks. Grant said this would happen. He said I'd come here and mess things up. He's always right.

"Sloane, *please*! *Please*!" Andy's shout breaks the night air, heated and desperate. That false promise lives somewhere inside it, but he was never mine—I know that now.

Grant shoves him back. Ben grabs his arms, keeping him from me and even though I want to look away, I can't. The agony in his eyes tells a different story than the mouths around me, than this throbbing ache between us. Will it hurt more if I step forward or back?

"Hey. Hey—" Pale hands are on my face, shifting my focus. "We need to go, Sloane." Jean takes his jacket off wrapping me in its dry interior. "We have to go." His body is a shield between me, my brother, the world of Astor... and Andy.

Andy.

I see the door to the art show open, Elliot standing there, his victory carved into the sharp lines of his smile, celebrating the knowledge that I am exactly who he said I was. Exactly who they've all said I was. I look back at Andy one last time, let my eyes linger on the expression I've worn so many times. The one you wear when you realize someone's leaving. When they've left.

* * *

Fingers in my hair stir me from my sleep and I'm not sure if it's twilight or dawn as gray light peaks between the blinds of the unfamiliar space. It takes a second to remember that Jean put me up in a hotel. We didn't talk much, but he agreed to not tell anyone where I was as I turned the location off on my phone. It's a formula I've followed a few times now—to disappear.

Somehow she always finds me.

Evie's fingers untangle my blonde strands the way I'd sometimes let her do late at night, when she thought I was sleeping. When I needed her as much as she needed me, but I'd never tell her that.

I roll over, see her lined face, dark circles framing her eyes, a crease between her brows, a woman who's been worried for years. "I think...I really need you." I don't know if I meant to say it out loud, but there it is out in the open. I roll my lips together, pursing them to the side, as if the movement will hold back the tears that are already falling.

"Oh honey." She pulls me into her and even though her embrace was never a place I wanted to be, the comfortable familiarity of her arms is the kind that can only be achieved when someone's wrapped you in them a thousand times over. Where Connie's arms always felt like they were slipping away, Evie's were a constant looming thing, silently begging me to fall into them. I let myself inhale her powdery lemon scent, the poison edge of the Aqua-net missing, her hair in a low unwashed bun.

"I want to tell you...about California." I don't know why this feels like the insurmountable thing I need to cross before I can divulge anything else, why this feels like a betrayal.

My breath stutters as I bury my head into the comforter, her palm rubbing small circles across my back.

"Just please, don't leave. You can hate me, just please. Don't leave." My body folds in on itself, sobs breaking me open until I can't tell where this grief ends. I'm unraveling. I'm small again. I'm being ripped from front porches by unfamiliar hands, the wood still warm beneath my feet, the air ripping out of my lungs as I twist my head back over my shoulder, searching. Always searching. Years of my mother's face circle my memory in flashes. Eyes, mouth, the way she'd hold herself still so I wouldn't be afraid, because I never knew if this would be it. The last time I'd see her. Because leaving has always come without warning, love always something that disappears while I'm still reaching for it.

And then there's Evie. Fingers in my hair, like if she can untangle the strands she can untangle my knotted heart and find herself at the center of it.

"Sloane." Her voice is a careful caress trained by all the times I've pushed her away, kept her at arms length. "Sloane, honey. Look at me."

My swollen eyes find her face and I see a version of myself reflected back, the pieces I've broken off and tried to abandon so many times before. Tears form at the corners of her own eyes, her delicate jaw still, like if she moves too quickly I'll run away and I wonder how many times I have left. How many times she's memorized my face and wondered if it was the last time she'd see it.

"I had...I had—" My voice tumbles over itself, my chest a wicked trembling thing as I try to find the words. Her hands brush back my tears, our faces so close as we lay on the queen sized hotel bed.

"I know. I know you did." She nods, her tears breaking the surface as she tries to sniff them away.

"How—"

"Clem called." She gives me a sad smile, and guilt folds up my stomach until it reaches my throat and I feel like I can't breathe. She sucks in a small breath until her face morphs, the mask she's worn all the years I've known her slipping away until she's small too. A girl who just wanted to be loved. "I'm so sorry baby. I—" Evie inhales sharply, trying to stifle what is already out. "I wish that things were different, I wish I wasn't so—" she sniffs, wiping her tears away quickly, as if she's to blame for their presence. "I just wish I was someone you could've told. I wish I could have been there."

My face crumples as I realize she's not disappointed in me but herself. "I thought you'd hate me. I was giving up something you wanted so badly, something you prayed for."

"Hate you? Sloane, you are mine." There's a fierceness in her voice followed by another sob and I don't know if it's hers or mine. "I could never hate you. All those years of praying, hoping I'd have a little girl one day." She shakes her head, her eyes desperate for me to understand. "You are the answer to every one of those prayers. You and your brother. You are all I ever wanted. All I want." She takes my fingers, rubs warmth back into them with her hands like she's been waiting to do this forever. "You are my perfect, wild thing, Sloane. There is not one hair on your head I would change."

Her mouth tightens, words gathering behind it. "I just wish..." she swallows. "I wish you'd let me in. I wish you didn't have to brace yourself every time I reach for you. Wish you knew that nothing about you, not your fire, not your grief, not the way you feel everything fully, has ever been too much for me. I wish I would've pushed harder, broken the part that kept you silent when you so badly needed to be held. You were just a little girl, Sloane. You were *my* little girl and I gave you too much space, let you think that you were anything but the miracle that I prayed myself hoarse for."

She presses her forehead to mine, a steady stream of our trembling breath and tears between us as she sniffs back a smile. "Honey, I would go to the ends of this earth searchin' for you, would rip it apart with my bare hands if I had to. You're mine, Sloane. You always have been. And I will always find you."

"Connie left again." The sentence is choked and broken when I let it out and I watch her bite the inside of her own cheek. She nods this sad grave nod, the permanence of it signaling she knows more than I do.

"That's why I'm here." Her eyes squint with tears, like if she looks at me hard enough I might see what's behind them. "She called me." My eyebrows scrunch in confusion. "To be transparent, she's called me quite a bit over the years. Just to see how you and your brother were. I'd always give her your number. Update her on where you two were. She said you might need me...I didn't realize it meant she was leaving." She shakes her head, her sorrow so deep, so palpable that it feels like my own and I wonder if it is. I wonder if this is how it feels to let someone carry some of your pain.

"Being a mom is hard, Sloane. Harder than anyone ever tells you." She lets out a sad laugh and I sniff, realizing the pain I felt just hours ago has dulled, isn't fresh and hot, ready to erupt. "There is always something to feel guilty about," she continues softly. "Connie...she has her own battles, but she loves you enough to know you deserve more. Leaving has never meant she's stopped loving you. The world can be *so* cruel, especially to us moms and even more so to the moms who aren't ready. All the pain that comes from having a child, all that guilt? It can eat at you and there's rarely anyone there to make it stop. Most of the time they just push us to the side, make us feel worse for not knowing exactly how to be what our children need." She swallows. "I know that even when Connie's been stumbling through her own storms she's carried her love for you kids with her. Her love has always been yours Sloane, always, just as mine has." She uses her thumbs to wipe the last of my tears away, my eyes falling shut as she brushes my hair with her hands, and we lay in a comfortable silence.

I think about what Andy said, that night at the pizza restaurant, think about how I was so scared that I'd been running too long, that I'd never be found. But laying here, Evie's gentle breathing lulling me to sleep, I realize I was found a long time ago.

41

Andy

Luis's memory is an ever present thing but, sometimes, the urge to go to him will jacket me. Leave me unable to really do much besides turn my face against the pillow, like I did over and over again, all night and the night before, waiting for to feel steady again. Skipped conditioning; am still avoiding the texts from Coach about whether or not I'm getting on that plane tonight. The conference game is the last thing on my fucking mind. All that is, is Sloane. The broken way she stared after me as Jean pulled her away, despite my cries, despite my pleas. Sloane, a shell of herself. Sloane, all alone.

I pull myself up the pathway to Mom's apartment, wondering if this would feel half as horrible if Luis was on the other side of that door. He could make the worst of days better with just a look, a reassuring smile that would melt over me, soothe every anxiety I had. He was the first line; Mom was second. He took the brunt of everything for her, handed her the pieces he was too clumsy to reassemble, and together, they carried it all. Fixed everything.

In his absence, I assumed I could fix it all by myself. And

on the slow trek toward my mother's door, I realize that I haven't fixed anything. Just...brushed it under the rug, weighed it down with monied distractions. It's been pulled out from under me, though, and now—now I'm incapable of understanding how I'm supposed to be okay in the wake of Sloane.

I step into the apartment, the warm flow of the recessed kitchen lights drawing me closer to the dining room table where I can hear my mom's soft laughter, and let my keys clatter against the counter when I see my brother. My chest seizes up, my silent resentment for his thoughtlessness sticking to my skin even though I *know* it's not his fault. None of this really is.

If I'm being honest, his news blast that revealed my years of siphoning information from them for our dad, that linked me to the Rivers...it was past due. Should've happened years ago. The fallout from my choice was inevitable—my cowardice just delayed its spectacular crash landing.

"Sweetie," Mom smiles up at me, her eyes kinder than I've seen them in days. "Come sit."

I swallow against my discomfort, sitting as I avoid the uncharacteristic pity I find in Ian's gaze.

"Listen—" he starts to apologize, cheeks drawing upward as he grimaces.

"Save it."

"Andy," Mom chides, and I shake my head.

"No, what I mean is...you have nothing to be sorry about." I feel my jaw tick as I flick my gaze up to meet his. "I made my bed. I gotta lay in it."

Ian's eyes, wide as a deer's, don't move from mine. He seems stuck, like his usually quick paced rationality has nothing to hang its hat on, and has no clue what he should say next. So instead, he just says, "Why?" I furrow my brows, not understanding. "I blew up your life."

I scoff, the first smile in days twitching at the corner of my lips. "*I* blew my life up. You just wrote about it. You just told the truth."

He nods, his face softening as my mom reaches across the table and takes his hand.

"Ian's helping me figure out my options," she says, eyes crinkling with amusement.

"Options?" Gaze bouncing between them, it only takes a second for me to see the camaraderie already radiating there. And Ian, for all of his hardness, sits at my table like fucking putty every time my mom so much as looks at him. It's the love in her gaze that does it. I know, because it happens to me, too. That belonging I've always taken for granted? He's feeling it now, and it dawns on me that his life's probably been devoid of that for as at least as long as I've known him. It's a small silver lining to all this—that he's got someone in his corner.

"Well," Ian says, opening his laptop to show me the series of tabs open in his browser, "what my dad's been doing—withholding funds, canceling agreements, toying with Carmen's admission? It's harassment. I think your mom could sue," he explains excitedly, shoulder slightly hunched as he taps away at the keyboard. "I figured he would pull the plug on everything once I sent that blast, so I've been monitoring his inbox, the account he uses to pay you and—" he shifts the screen toward me and I rake my eyes over way more legalese than I'm equipped to interpret.

"Ian. I don't know what the fuck this."

"Language!" Carmen shouts from down the hallway, running to the table and perching right next to my half brother. "Did you know we have a brother?"

"*I* have a—" Mom and Ian both send me incredulous glares. "Yup. We do."

"Basically, I have more than enough evidence for a case. I'm not a lawyer, obviously, but we'll find one and take him for what he's worth." Ian slams his laptop shut, sitting back with a satisfying grin on his face.

There's joy at the notion that my mom has figured out a way to fill in the gaps of my recklessness, and there's relief, but neither do enough to alter the heaviness, the unsteadiness that hasn't dissipated—honestly, in weeks. I sit here, stagnant in the rushing water that is our life, and only feel the heavy weight of something pulling me under. I shut my eyes for a long second, almost wishing it would.

It's only Carmen who seems to notice, her attention warming my face from across the table as her throat bobs.

"I'm guessing you didn't fix things with Sloane?" she asks, her voice barely perceptible over the hum of the living room fan.

Ian looks at the table and Mom sighs, her jaw tensing with some unspoken thing I decide to ignore because I can't take more advice. Or more pep talks from people who think I deserve her. Losing Sloane is the price I didn't know I was paying when I sold my soul to my father.

I think maybe I want to feel the loss of her, want it to haunt me, as proof that once upon a time she was there and we were happy. I think maybe that's all I'm allowed to get.

"I'm gonna be late for the uh...my flight. For the conference game," I mutter, hastily pushing back from the table. Carmen looks up at Ian with alarm, who shrugs before giving me a brief wave goodbye, and if I wasn't so lost in my own sea of grief I'd laugh at the bond of theirs, already forming.

I swipe my keys off the counter, place a hand on the door, and try to leave just as my mom's exasperated exhale stops me.

"Wait—why'd you stop by, sweetie?" Her buoyancy hangs just behind the concern in her gaze as she checks one me with the tact of a mother, of someone who's known me forever—

with only a pinch of authority, because she knows I'll make my own mind up anyway.

I dip my head, my mouth pulling tight. "Thought I needed something but...it's not here."

Understanding crosses her gaze as she pulls me into a tight embrace, and I breathe in the familiar floral of my childhood. "I'm proud of you," she whispers before pulling away, eyes squeezing when she gives me a small smile as my brows pinch. "I know it hurts but...this is living," she nods, nudging me out the door, and I wonder if this is what they mean by 'worth it.'

If this is the other side of having loved, if this is the pain you never feel if you've never loved at all. I know, despite the cut I'm too numb to try to stop from bleeding, that I would've loved her a million times over, and I know I always will.

* * *

The last row—I never find myself here, but my usual spot near the front was cordoned off with back packs and duffels. A clear and deliberate message to not even bother. Grant's severe glare, that might as well have been an actual dagger, cut across any hope of reconciliation. Even Ben, usually level-headed and ready to smooth things over for the sake of the team, just gave me a pathetic smile, not even bothering.

It's damage that's done; the only person who couldn't care less is Coach. "All right. I know you shitheads are having marital issues—" Josiah snickers, only for Grant to smack the back of his head. "But in five minutes it's wheels up, and you're gonna get your shit together. This game is do or die. We lose this, we're not just out of the tournament—we risk losing our standing in the conference as a whole. Now, I don't have to tell you—"

A long whistle cuts Coach's speech off right before it was

about to veer into stats on the Wolves we're set to play tonight for a spot in the finals, and he lets his head fall back in irritation. Will's long arm settles along Coach's shoulder, a shit eating grin on his face.

"Oh come on, Coach," he says to the rows of teammates finally pulling their earbuds out. "You know you missed me."

"Take a seat," Coach groans, waving him off as he slaps hands on the slow walk down the aisle. "Alright, alright...let's hit the road."

Cheers, obnoxious and vulgar, sound from every seat except for Grant's, and I can see Ben's sympathetic nod toward his friend as he joins in. Clapping—because I'm happy to see him, and I'm pleased to see him looking so healthy and level headed and...not drunk—I nod along, pulling out my phone to find a playlist for the brief plane ride.

Suddenly, Will drops into the seat next to me, our oversized frames warring for space as my eyes narrow, eyeing the aisle seat he could've claimed before wondering why he's back here at all. I sit up, acutely aware that his fist or his knuckles could collide with me at any moment. He must see me tense because laughter cracks across his face, his green eyes churning with a joke I'm not privy to. The plane falls silent, and I can just feel the heads craning over head rests to see the aggression that's sure to erupt out of my old friend.

"Tough fucking crowd," he murmurs under his breath, still not moving over. The plane begins to press forward, gravity pulling us all back. "What'd you do?" he asks, a sly grin spreading across his face.

"Please, prepare for take off," a clipped voice comes over the intercom, and I shut my eyes, always hating this part. When I do, I can almost pretend Will isn't here, taunting me before possibly shattering my collarbone.

"Kind of ballsy of you to show up. Scott didn't. But, he's a pussy and...you're not." I see him shrug when I pop one eye open, my conception of his presence here getting hazier by the moment.

He knows about Scott and Glenn?

He sees the question in my eyes, reading my mind. "Figured him out a *while* ago. Why do you think I'm so mean but keep him close?"

I freeze, dread clawing up my throat as I slide my gaze to his. This must be the build up, the cat playing with the mouse before he rips me to shreds for the horrible, horrible thing I did to him. "Will, I'm—" I try to say, but his hand flies up.

"You know, when I found out, I *was* angry. Like, here's this guy I actually fucking trust, spying on me for my piece of shit dad...but then I realized I would've done the same thing in your shoes."

"That's not an excuse, though. What I did—"

"I mean, you didn't *really* do it, though, did you? You kinda sucked at it. That's why he had to get Scott." He cocks his head to the side, good will and mirth dancing in his eyes. "You know I would say shit just to see if it'd get back to Dan?"

My mouth forms an oh and stays stuck, the shock of Will's perceptiveness a reality I never considered. Just that—that I would underestimate him so much—has me feeling like the biggest idiot in the world.

"The thing is," he leans into me, dipping his head, "you never gave him the juicy stuff, did you? I mean, you didn't even tell him about finding me in the shower." His voice peters off, the cockiness he uses to mask his vulnerability cracking.

"Wasn't any of his business. You wouldn't have even been that...fucked up if it weren't for him," I tell him, throat bobbing as heat fans my cheeks.

Finally, he leans back, putting some distance between us. "Yeah," he huffs to himself, lost in thought for a long, protracted second. I turn toward the window, noting that we've leveled out, are already in the middle part of our journey to upstate New York. "Andy?"

I look back at him, my mouth in a grim line, ready for that final blow he keeps prolonging. "Yeah?"

"I forgave you a really long time ago," he says softly, his heavy brows furrowing. "I don't care. It's...water under the bridge. I've literally done worse."

"You should care," I grit out, desperate for his anger. "I spied on you, Will. You don't forgive me for that. You hit me. You...you never speak to me again."

Eyes narrowed, disgust wells in his expression. "Do you hear yourself? You sound pathetic." He shakes his head, scoffing as he pulls his hood up to block me out.

"You didn't deserve that." I search his face, watching as he rolls his eyes at me. "And you're allowed to hold a grudge. You don't have to...to just forgive all of us, all the time. Ben, Liv, Gen, *me*—we hurt you and you're allowed to feel that."

He cracks his neck, shifting his seat so he's facing me. "My therapist told me that, too."

"Yeah well...listen, for once." I tense my jaw, exhaling as I readjust in my seat. Silence stretches out between us, and I can feel Will dancing on the edges of small talk. His gaze flicks to mine, antsy and childish, like despite my insistence that he hold me accountable for violating his privacy he can't help but want to be my friend.

It's the same sort of innocence I clocked in him the second we met all those years ago.

The moment he lets his resolve break, I suck in a small breath. "So..." he says, knocking his head to the side. "Sloane coming up to the game?

I blink over at him, waiting for the punch line, or for his neutral expression to downshift into malice, or *something*—but nothing. He doesn't know. He's still so on the fringes that he has no idea.

"We're not—" I pause, the word like a stone lodged in my chest "—together."

He squints at me, ripping both ear buds out his ears. "Since fucking when?"

My eyes fall shut, head shaking as I swallow the bitterness. "Doesn't matter, Will, just—"

"Oh. It doesn't matter that the woman you're like…in love with is just, not in your life anymore? You're just fine with that?" Impatience lines the classic lines of his face. "What happened? That fucking blast?"

"It's complicated."

"*It's complicated*," he mocks, studying me with thinly veiled irritation. "Where is your decisiveness? You either love her or you don't. It's not complicated at all."

I can't stop the laughter that rumbles out of me, disbelief rising in my throat. "Not to rub salt in the wound but, what do you know about love?"

He pulls a face, a little shocked by my bluntness. "Uh," he sputters, "I know I wouldn't be on a plane to another *state* if the woman I loved and I were *complicated*. She's like…you're fucking puzzle piece. You're just gonna wallow in self-pity while your other half is out there, while your *life* is out there?" He gestures out the window, where city lights now start to bleed through the cloud.

"She doesn't want me, Will. It's not as simple as all that, it's—"

"Did she say that? Were those her exact words?"

"No, but—"

"Great. When you hear those, when she tells you she doesn't want you…" he swallows hard, a fleeting sadness passing in his gaze. "Then you'll know. Believe me."

The emptiness that aches within me, that tells me that something belongs in all that space, that that something is Sloane, glows, painfully sears against me because he's right. In the chaos, under that shattered sky, neither of us chose anything. We were torn apart by our circumstances, pushed into our own fractured pasts and away from each other.

"Prepare for the descent," that clipped voice comes again.

"I'll get you a plane," Will says, all smug as his phone lights up in his hand.

"What?"

"*I'll get you a plane*," he says again, slowly, shaking his head with a grin. "Fuck the conference. Go get your girl, Spellman."

42

Sloane

A voice rumbles in the hallway and, for a moment, I think it could be Andy. Blood rushes to my fingertips, floating flimsy hope to the top of my skin as I slowly roll to my side—until I realize it's Grant.

"You're sure?" he's asking Evie, and I don't hear her response, just her soft murmuring on the other side of the door. Eyes heavy, I drift in and out of sleep, only waking when something tricks me into thinking it could be him.

The winter I spent loving him is stretched wide when my eyes are closed like this, and I can almost forget that spring has thawed all of that away. In my dreams he's in my doorway, in my car, in a seat at the conservatory, watching me make sense out of oily pigments; watching me piece myself back together.

It's only when my back starts to radiate with pain from lying down for so long that I finally decide to move. Stretching my limbs in the cloud like sheets, I push up against the headboard and scrub my face as it throbs, the emotional weight of the past few days still pulsing against my bones.

I sightlessly reach for the freshly topped water on my nightstand, and of course it's there. Evie would've refilled it while I was sleeping, the way she would when I was a mangy teenager, sneaking in and out of her windows at all hours of the night. I'd escape back into the careful polish of the room she and Beau'd built me and not even bother to shrug off my jeans or wash the night off my face. Just slump against the quilt and wait for daylight to break across my cheek, wait to start all over again.

And when I did, there'd be a glass of water. Sometimes a note.

Swinging my legs off the bed, I find it with my hand.

Just grabbing coffee. xx mom

A smile pulls at the corners of my mouth, has slow tears pricking in my eyes before I sniff them away and brush my hand across my face. Hope still flits through my veins, but it's hesitant, scared that once I leave the sanctuary of this room, where I've let myself fall into Evie's security for the first time since she tried to hug me on her wrap-around porch, I'll fall back apart.

The door cracks open, effusive hotel light slicing through the darkness I'm still washed in before falling shut, Evie's footsteps quiet against the carpet. She sets the coffees on the little table and slowly drags the outermost curtain open so the gauzy layer still filters the abrasive—I check the time—*midday* sun.

My arms reach high above my tangled hair, a yawn rolling out of me. "I wish you hadn't let me sleep in so late," I tell her, reaching for the paper cup with *HC* scrawled on the side. "Thanks."

"Tried tellin' me they don't have heavy cream." She takes hers, *HC* and a plus sign with the number two on it, and smirks over at me, perching on the chair opposite me. There's a lightness in her gaze that I've rarely seen; there was always concern swirling in her eyes, like storm clouds, always this angst that I felt could leap out and smother me at a moment's notice. Right now, though, that almost feels like a fiction.

Evie looks at me and sees something she likes, and I consider that maybe it has nothing to do with how she's looking at me at all. That maybe, this was always there, and that it's *me* who's just now seeing it.

"I don't know how your brother does it up here," she laughs, those exaggerated expression lines reminding me that she's never shied away from feeling anything. Has always worn her heart right there on that sleeve.

I glance away from her, a knot in my throat forming anew the longer I remember the ways I denied myself her grace all these years. "What did he want earlier?"

"Just wanted to see him while I'm here," she says behind a sip of her coffee. "He's off to that conference game. Your daddy's goin', you know." The smile she serves me is so sated, I envy it; it's the kind of smile you give when love is working in everyone's favor, and I know seeing Beau respect Grant's choices, knowing he's finally supporting him the way she'd always hoped, fills her with more joy than it fills me.

And it does—I can't help that. I'll want the best for my brother regardless of his impatience for me. My heart warms knowing he'll see Gen and Beau in those stands tonight, just as it seizes on itself thinking of Andy on that court, looking up and seeing no one. Becs couldn't get the night off and Carm's not old enough to make that trek alone.

And I'm here. Every cell in my body yearns to find him, rejects whatever I'm supposed to feel about his deception. Hard as I try, I can't make that news blast hurt the way it ought to, and I think it's because I know his heart. Know that there isn't a single thing he's ever done that wasn't done out of love.

"Can I ask you somethin'?" Andy's absence weighs down on me as I watch her set her coffee down, see her give me her sweet attention.

That hair that's usually so stiff and immovable is soft for once, is a supple mass of pale blonde waves that brush just past her shoulders. "Of course, darlin'. What is it?"

Against the hazy afternoon light, she looks down right angelic. When I first met her, that's how she looked, too. Like she dropped right out of the sky on a mission, was just missing a trumpet. My knee jerk reaction was to tell myself she was too good to be true. That she was a temptation, a test of my allegiance to Connie.

My teeth tug at my bottom lip as I consider the question, the longing that won't let up wrapping itself around me the longer I keep it bottled up. "Did it ever scare you, how much you love Beau?"

I rake my fingers tips against my thighs, pulling in a breath as my molars scrape against each other. Worry holds me by the neck, and it's this silent fear that I'm not built for love. That the intensity of it will always threaten to swallow me whole; that it's not like this for everyone else.

Evie's lips twist in a wry smile as she moves to settle next to me. She hums, letting her head fall against mine. "Yes. That's how I knew. And I told him so. I said 'if you think you're leavin', think again.' Told him it was a done deal now that he had me lovin' him that much."

I stutter on my laughter, the nerves in my gut breaking into butterflies as my skin pricks with anticipation, that hope brushing right behind it. "I can just hear it. And what'd he say?"

"Well there wasn't much talkin'," she jeers, knocking an elbow into me as I stifle my giggle. "You're thinkin' about that boy, aren't you?" My brows pinch, wondering what she knows about Andy. "Jean stopped by. Told me all about that movie star lookin' boy of yours." She sighs, tilting her head. "Baby, I don't know if it's love or if it's forever. But what I do know, just lookin' at you, is that you're not done." She arches her brows at me, her lips tugging expectantly as tears gather at my waterline and I shake my head, sniffing.

"No," I say, voice thick with emotion. "I'm not done. But —" I pause, my heart swelling in my chest "—but I do know. That I love him."

I say it to Evie and, suddenly, it's all I want him to know. All I can do to keep my bones latched at the joints, keep my feet on the ground, keep myself from picking up the phone and just spoiling it, satisfying the urge.

"Mm. I had a feeling," she grins, standing up and offering me her hand. "Come on then. That flight's already in the air so *you've* got a plane to catch."

* * *

Those heavy jet wheels clunk against the runway, hurtling the Fielder Foods private plane through the early evening mist. When I check the clock it's only five, but my anxiety swears they must be warming up, are already at the venue, and are out of my reach for the foreseeable future. Anticipation churns in my stomach as I deplane, the pilot letting me know he won't leave the small airport reserved for private use until I call and tell him my plans.

And what is my plan, actually? I haven't a fucking clue. All that I know is that my mind hasn't settled since I left Andy in that parking lot, hair clinging to his forehead, agony marked on his beautiful face. It's the face I've seen when I've slept, the voice I've sworn I've heard when awake. I hate that I didn't stay, that I didn't fend them off me—hate that I wasn't stronger. But I was lost to myself that night, too, was so far gone, had been drinking without rest to near oblivion, and I know Jean was right. I needed to go, even if it meant leaving him alone with demons I wanted nothing more than to shield him from.

Something broke in his gaze when he pleaded with me across the splintered lot, like the perfection he'd fought so hard to mold was shattering in real time. The shouting. The yelling. The betrayal, thick in the damp air. And as I sobbed, I prayed for God to make it matter because *that* would've made it all easier, if he'd cut me so deep. If he'd irreparably sliced through the careful tapestry of this little world, but it just didn't—he didn't.

My boots clip against the tiled lobby, the red leather stark against the white squares, fear of the unknown lacing itself through the reckless hope I'm still clinging to. He could turn me away for all I know and I'd deserve it. Would have to accept it but—

"Sloane?"

My attention flies to him, standing at the front desk with his Astor duffle slung around his shoulder, decidedly not at the venue but here, at the airport. And I'm frozen in place, wholly unprepared for the way my longing would overwhelm me once I saw him again. I watch as his throat bobs, as the muscle in his jaw ticks, and I struggle to make sense of it.

"Oh," is all I manage to say. "What are the odds?" I ramble, nervously, wetting my lips as my teeth fidget with the plump bottom one. Adrenaline crashes against my sternum, his sudden appearance making it hard for me to get my bearings.

It's just that he's so handsome, standing there, eyes fixed on me like the rest of the room doesn't matter. So perfectly who he was that first night we met only it's more, because I know him now. Know how all of it is with him, just like he said I would. I feel the ghost of his arms around me from across the room, imagine the surety that always seems to wash over me when I rest my head against his chest, when I hear the steady thrum of his heart beneath me.

"What are you doing here?" His bag drops to the ground, an invasive thud in the otherwise quiet space.

"Private jets fly all day," I joke, before shaking my head, fixing my gaze squarely on him. I walk toward him, and his gaze drops to the ground before finding mine again. There's nothing timid or restrained—it's desperate and all consuming, and I swallow against it, trying not to jump the gun. "I came to tell you I'm sorry...for runnin'. For leaving you."

He shakes his head, stepping towards me. "You didn't do anything wrong, Sloane. I...I lied to you."

"You omitted the truth," I correct him, a small grin playing at the corners of my lips but he's not ready for it; guilt still slashes through his gaze, tortures him in real time, and I realize I have to let him do this. Have to let him bleed all of it dry before he'll let me bandage him up.

"I should've been honest. As soon as my father asked me to keep tabs on you, I should've let you know. And then when things changed...I had no excuse not to tell you other than I was scared. I thought I had it all under control, thought I was handling him."

I gnaw at my lip, the despair in his gaze like a knife between my ribs.

"I didn't even let myself *think* I could have you until it seemed safe." He closes the distance, taking my hands in his. "But then he threatened my mom, and Carm, and—"

I slide my hand along his jaw, lay it there to steady him. "I know. I know."

"I should've told you, but I was scared. Scared you'd run, but instead...fuck, I left *you* alone, Sloane. I hate myself for it."

Connie's empty living room sprawls in my memory and there's a small pinch of resentment that releases just as soon as it appears, and I let it go. It falls away like every other thing when he's holding me like this, when I'm this close to the only soul that's ever felt perfectly cut for mine.

"I'm sorry I wasn't there," he tells me, regret laced in his voice.

The wreckage of that night and the nights that followed, in the wake of Connie leaving, felt like an abyss I'd never find an end to. I think...if someone had held me through that, I might not have faced myself. Might not have hit rock bottom.

I take his regret, let it fall into the wound of that moment, and it ceases to exist. And I wonder if that's the power of all this, if love renders our worst moments nothing more than splinters that, over time, become nothing at all.

"In some twisted way...I think it all happened the way it was meant to."

"Fate?" he says, sort of breathless, his eyes searching mine for true absolution, and I nod.

"Oh, yeah," I laugh, watching as he forgives himself just a little. "I mean, what are the odds we'd both be in this random airport?"

"Actually," he murmurs as I stand before him, my eyes dipping to his lips as he does, "slim, because I was about to get on that plane." He nods his head at something behind me and when I look, a different private jet stands on the runway. I release a shaky breath, disbelief blurring my eyes.

"Where were you goin'?" I wait, heart lodged high in my throat, desperate to hear it. Hope hollows my chest out, leaves me unbearably nervous even though I know, deep in my soul, that he was coming to find me.

"You, Sloane. Always you," he breathes just as his hands grip me around the waist with life affirming force.

When he crashes his mouth into mine, every doubt that's ever lived between my bones falls away, is washed away with the adoration he pays to me with the hungry brush of his tongue against mine, with the unabashed way he holds me in his hands.

"Thank god," he tells me, his fingers tangling in my hair as he holds me to him, the wide breadth of his other hand pressing against my back as we weave a promise between us. I can feel the force of it with ever coming together, with every hallowed moan, with every sacred touch.

"Thought you didn't believe in all that." I smile against his lips, pulling slightly back so I can see the way his eyes shift at my tease. And they do, those amber flecks glittering right there in his gaze, just the way I love.

"I don't," he tells me, rolling his lips together as he shakes his head, his thick blonde waves falling across his brow. "I believe in you. More than I've believed in anything." His thumb brushes across my lips, fingers swiping at the tears trailing down the side of my face as concern flits across his gaze.

"I'm okay. I just..." I shake my head, righting myself as the words wash over me, demand to be breathed to life, and he loosens his hold. Stepping back, I sniff away the tears that won't stop running down my face, that always seem to fall when this man's kissing me within an inch of my life.

"I have spent my whole life running," I tell him with a helpless shrug, patting my cheeks like it'll make a difference at this point. Andrew's jaw flexes, his restraint on full display as he gives me the space to say this thing howling in my chest. "From everyone who loves me. And I'd always thought I was just...damaged goods. Like, I'd wrecked myself over the blunt edge of my chaos one too many times and everyone could see it." He starts to speak and I shake my head, smiling, my heart feeling lighter and lighter as the thoughts find purchase in the foundation we're tilling in real time. "But I couldn't run from you," I laugh, sputtering, and he smiles this soft, gentle smile that tells me he knows. That he couldn't escape us either. "You were...everywhere. And when you weren't, you were in my mind, all the damn time. So I thought maybe we could be friends. That I could avoid the inevitable loss that would be having you for real and losing you when you left. But you knew, long before I did, that it wouldn't work."

Andy's eyes are wet with unshed tears as he nods his head, his lips pressing together.

"We could never be just friends because I was always, *always* gonna love you. There is not a life I'm in where loving you doesn't happen—I know it in the marrow of my bones. That I love you."

Chest falling, he doesn't even try to hide the grin that cracks across his face, cupping mine in his hands. "I keep waiting for this to be a dream."

"It's not," I tell him, our noses brushing as he ghosts his lips atop mine. Those same ribs that only a day ago might've collapsed from the force of my tears are now at risk of bursting wide open; it's a contentment I didn't think was possible. "I mean all of it. And it's real. This is real."

"Good," he tells me, hoisting me up and I wrap my legs around him, looping my arms behind his neck. "Because I'm never waking up from this. I love you, too, Sloane. In this life, the next. All of them. You have them. They're yours."

And then he kisses me like I belong to him and he belongs to me, and nothing has ever felt truer.

Epilogue
Andy

April

I never opened that file. In fact, I shredded it with out a second thought, because whatever was in it wouldn't have mattered. The woman beside me, guiding us up this narrow road, could never be contained by anything or anyone, much less a manilla fucking folder.

Sloane grasps Delilah's large leather wheel, winding it around the mountain her family's summer cabin is nestled on. I squeeze her thigh and her smile shines brighter than the mid morning sun. Something settles in me. For once, I finally feel like I won. Like I'm in control and in charge of my own destiny.

As we make our way down the path the home sits on, I learn that *cabin* is an understatement. Sprawling green and wooden planks make up the home's exterior and I feel like I'm inside one of mom's Martha Stewart catalogues.

"Nervous?" There's a glimmer in Sloane's eyes when she asks and for a second this all feels like a dream. The happy ending I'd imagine as a child, a happy ending that felt so out of reach when Luis passed. Sitting here beside Sloane though, I realize this is real. She is real and sometimes happy endings aren't really endings at all.

I haven't seen anyone since the game other than her and Will. The thought honestly does terrify me. Sloane was so quick to forgive me, so quick to understand. I know the others won't be.

We need to rip off the bandaid. That's what Sloane kept saying as her and Evie discussed using the cabin for an impromptu trip over spring break.

Her eyes peek over at me as she pulls the car beside a large F150.

"Do you think your brother's going to hit me?"

She purses her mouth to the side like she always does when she's thinking. "Probably. But luckily we know you can take a punch," she winks, throwing open her door. I see a slender brunette on the expansive wraparound porch when I exit, her arms crossed, eyes narrowed.

"Livvie!" Sloane trills but Olivia's posture stays rigid. Sloane remains unfazed as I grab our luggage from her trunk and she approaches her. I can see the subtle shake of Olivia's head, the way she's glaring at me, her brown eyes growing darker just as Ben appears, plunking a large hand on her shoulder. Somehow, this alone softens her a bit. They turn back into the house and Sloane nods toward them, insinuating I should follow.

The kitchen is sparkling, a cheery butter yellow, one that my mom would probably throw a fit over, and I carefully set our bags on the ground.

"Pretty brave to show up here after everything." The grim line of Olivia's mouth tells me this is not actually a compliment, and I wince.

"Yeah, look—" I start and she raises a hand.

"Don't." I watch as Ben squeezes her arm and she lets loose a breath. "If Will can get over it, so can I, I guess...but I don't trust you, Spellman and if you so much as make her *frown* again—" she points at Sloane, her glare sharp enough to gut a more innocent man. "I will personally come to your house, chain you to your bed and set it on fire." She smiles this innocent smile that doesn't at all match the words that just came from her mouth.

"Okay killer, calm down," Ben says and Sloane chuckles.

"She's serious." Sloane pushes herself on the counter, lightly tapping me with the toe of her boot.

Just as I begin to nod at Olivia we all hear the screen door creak open. Large heavy footsteps followed by light almost cat-like ones sound in the hallway.

"I was easy. *They* won't be." That evil grin is back as Olivia struts into the hallway, probably to warn Gen and Grant before they come in.

Sloane tenses on the counter and I wonder if I should be bracing myself too, but honestly, I only care about what one person in this room thinks about me and somehow, she's on my side.

"What are *you* doing here?" If Olivia's glare was violent Grant's is murderous, his palms immediately forming fists at his side.

"I told him I'd owe him one." Sloane's tone is amused indifference which only makes her brother angrier. Again, that light tap of her toe against my side, as if to say *she's got this.*

"Jesus Christ." Grant's grumble is low and guttural as he rakes his hands through his hair and I wonder how much it's taking for him not to clobber me right now. Ben moves himself so he's standing between us, like he too is waiting for Grant to pummel me and Olivia's expression is almost excited.

"So what we are *not* going to do," Sloane slides off the counter, "is be rude." She sidles up to Grant, placing a hand on his shoulder and, I don't know if it is some sort of twin telepathy or what, but he seems to relax slightly. "I invited him." She says it just to him, her eyes telling a story that I think only he will understand.

I put my hands in my pockets hoping to look non threatening but maybe to also hide that my nerves are picking up. It's my girlfriend's brother after all—want him to like me. Eventually anyway.

"Hope I'm not imposing." I give a meek smile as all eyes snap to me, all filled with similar amounts of suspicion and anguish. Except for Sloane's. Hers are the reason I'm here, because she's looking at me like she's seeing the sun, like I'm better than I am. She looks at me like I'm already the person I want so badly to be. Something in Gen settles in that moment, like seeing the way Sloane's looking at me is enough for her, and she rubs Grant's arm.

"I know as much as you do," she tells him, and he melts under the movement. It's sort of hilarious to see how this tiny delicate little thing pulls all his strings. "But the more the merrier right?" She looks at me now, her smile bright and forgiving and a mixture of relief and sadness flood my chest, because I can see why Will loves her, and can also see why he doesn't deserve her.

A knock on the door interrupts the tight tension of the room.

"Open up, sluts. Your favorite friend is here!"

I watch as a huge smile blooms on Sloane's face. She jogs to the front door and, instead of the gushing I think we were all expecting to hear, its an eerie silence followed by hushed whispers.

"Are you sure this is the best time?" Her voice is rushed and panicked.

"It's important. You all need to hear it." The sharp tone is vaguely familiar and my stomach drops as I realize who it is.

Jean walks in first, a guilty smile on his face as he enters. "What? Not happy to see me?"

And then I watch as my brother enters the room. "I think it's me that they are unhappy to see," Ian tell them, that smirk on his face.

Grant and Gen both stiffen this time, anger pulsing between them and tightly wrapping around Ben now too ,which is concerning since he's usually the more level headed of the group.

"Are you fucking *kidding me*?" Grant all but booms and Ian doesn't even bother to flinch, just gives Grant a bored look.

"Listen, I can leave after I say what I came here to say. But you *all* need to hear it." He looks at Olivia and there's something there, a history none of us are privy to. They were pretty good friends up until her and Ben.

"How about you go fu—"

"Wait—" Olivia interrupts just as Grant begins moving toward Ian. "We should listen to what he has to say."

Ian nods a thanks, something unspoken being communicated between the two of them. We all file toward the kitchen, sitting at the long oak table that fits all of us comfortably, with Ian at the head.

"First," Ian begins, hands clasped in front of himself as he clears his throat. I don't think I've ever seen him nervous and something about it has me squirming in my chair. Sloane sets her hand on top of mine and I settle into the movement of her thumb on my skin. "I owe you all an apology." Grant scoffs and Jean shoots him a glare. "I know how it looks but every step I took over the past year, every secret I told, was all part of a larger plan."

"A plan to ruin our lives?" Ben throws out, eyebrows high. Ian rolls his lips together, guilt riddled across his expression. Jean squeezes his hand.

"I'd hardly say he ruined your lives." Jean's voice has a fierceness in it I haven't heard before. "Sure, he didn't make things *easy* but I think all of you are better for it. I think those blasts pushed us all together in ways we never imagined." Everyone gets quiet for a moment and Jean nods to Ian, signaling him to continue.

"My dad," he breathes in, "*our* dad..." Ian nods to me and I return it. "He's an awful person. He's spent years hiding and covering up things for men who are much worse. Men who've done *unimaginable* things." An eerie silence falls over us, each of us listening intently now. "I've had to unwind your secrets, get to the root of why things were the way they were to get to the bigger point. To find out the truth."

"And what truth was that Ian? What was so bad that you had to expose me?" Olivia spits out and we all see the betrayal between them, the pain he caused when he sacrificed his friend.

"I have proof that..."

I feel myself leaning in, unsure of what he could possibly have to say. What he's found he's kept tight to his chest, not even telling me.

He pulls in a breath and the room falls silent. "...proof that Lily Newhouse was murdered."

Acknowledgments

We've said this with each book but *this one* was certainly a labor of love. Sloane and Andy did not come to us quickly. It wasn't a spontaneous, simultaneous burst in our minds. Their story was a slow, gradual realization that bloomed over many cups of tea and more late night couch conversations than we can count.

Knowing we'd gained so many new readers, we knew we wanted to stay true to the ethos of our love stories which, we think, is rooted in female main characters who truly center themselves. College romances, both in real life and in fiction, are fraught with conflicting interests, bad decisions, and the impulse to please everyone. That last one—that instinct to put other's needs above your own—is something we really try to challenge when we write together.

This novel, that we wrote in the midst of a sea of reader feedback, really asked us to buck genre conventions and stay committed to the kinds of narratives that we, as readers and authors, love to lose ourselves in. It took the encouragement of each other, as well our little village, to do that—to stay the course.

That village is the usual suspects, and is still a small one: our spouses, who pretend not to wake up when we squeal over a realization at one a.m.; our cover illustrator, Bailey Sulcer, whose illustrations have single handedly pulled readers into this universe and whose support means the world to us; our readers and especially our street team of O.G. readers, who hype us up endlessly; and our children, who are little readers and storytellers in their own right.

We couldn't have written this book without any of you.

About the Author

Sydney Madison is a best-friend writing duo based in Orlando, Florida who write angsty yet heartwarming love stories with an edge. While they revel in the lighter side of life—like sushi dates and book chats—they dive deep into the complexities of love and relationships in their writing. Balancing heart and intrigue, they craft stories that explore the shadows of relationships not always acknowledged in the typical happily ever after.

When they're not conjuring up their next novel, you can find them plotting their literary escapades over spicy tuna rolls and plenty of caffeine!

Sign up for their newsletter on their website and follow their Instagram to stay up to date!

Also by Sydney Madison

Astor Hill

Second Position